Shades
of
Gray

Shades

of

Gray

Vicki Hinze

St. Martin's Paperbacks

SHADES OF GRAY

Copyright © 1998 by Vicki Hinze.

Excerpt from *Duplicity* Copyright © 1998 by Vicki Hinze.

ISBN: 0-312-96610-5

Printed in the United States of America

St. Martin's Paperbacks edition / July 1998

10 9 8 7 6 5 4 3 2 1

To Taylor Pickett

Author's Note

While Special Operations is real, I've fictionalized aspects of it, including its location. Clare Air Force Base, California, exists only within these pages. I've taken this artistic license to insulate the families of current Special Ops officers because, unfortunately, some, like the adversaries in *Shades of Gray*, have little respect for these families' privacy and/or their security.

It is fact that, as families, these loved ones endure enormous sacrifices so that their spouses, fathers, or mothers can perform vital, and often life-threatening, missions. Missions that serve and protect all Americans, and save the lives of many.

Please accept these differentiations, understanding that they're depicted as they are in *Shades of Gray* not out of ignorance, but out of concern and respect.

Blessings,

Vicki Hinze

Shades

of

Gray

One

The banging on the apartment door threatened to knock it off its hinges.

Laura Taylor sat straight up in bed, her heart in her throat. She tossed back the covers, bumping the novel she'd fallen asleep reading to the floor. Fear clawed at her stomach.

Bury it, Taylor. She recalled the drill by rote. *Bury it. Intruders seldom knock.*

But that didn't mean whoever was pounding on her door in the dead of night was friendly, and in her position assuming that it did could be lethal. Amateur intruders seldom knock, but at times professionals do. It could be a diversionary tactic.

Someone could already be inside.

Slinging on a robe, she grabbed the canister of pepper gas she kept in the drawer beside her bed, resenting that break-ins happened even in military communities like Fairhope, California. But they did happen. One *had* happened, to her.

She crossed her bedroom, her every nerve on alert. The hammering at the door mirrored the jackhammering of her heart, and her throat turned ash-dry. Hugging her back to the wall, she slid against its gritty surface, and inched down the narrow hallway, broadening her focus, scanning for any shift or movement in the darkness, seeking sensations of any cool August night air drafting in through broken glass, an open window or door.

She stumbled over her shoes. Banged her hip against the edge of the kitchen bar. Pain shot through her side, and she swallowed a curse because she always left her damn shoes there, and she knew it. Allowing herself to get careless, her skills to get rusty, was a good way to wake up dead.

Steadying herself, she moved on through, skirted around the wicker-and-glass dinette into the adjoining living room, then on to the front door. It was at times like this one, and during the break-in, when she felt most grateful she'd had survival school training during her active duty days as Captain Laura Taylor, Air Force Intelligence Officer and Communications Research Specialist. Despite the sweat trickling down between her breasts and the fine hairs on her nape standing on end, whoever tried coming in wouldn't find a docile woman waiting to become a victim. She had the Air Force to thank for that, even as she acknowledged her covert work for it could have prompted this midnight visit.

"Laura?" A man called out and rapped again against the wood. "Laura, it's me—Jake."

"Jake." Relief washed through Laura, and then evaporated.

She and Jake Logan had been friends for a decade, but the only time he ever had come over in the middle of the night had been when his ex-wife, Madeline, had done something god-awful—usually to their son, Timmy.

One kind of fear replaced another and squeezed at her chest. Laura twisted the cold dead bolt, heard it click, and then opened the door. "What's wrong?"

Bitterness seeping from his every pore, Jake slumped against the frame, looking like six-foot-two of defeated thirty-four-year-old man, his jet-black hair wind-tossed, his strong face all angles and planes, outraged and ravaged. "She's suing me for custody of Timmy."

Madeline. Again. Laura nearly cried. Jake had tried everything to make his marriage to Madeline work, but she'd opted to continue downing Scotch. He'd spent years trying to get her sober, but finally she'd committed the unpardonable sin: endangering their son, Timmy. And after that, the craziest in a long string of her crazy stunts, he'd issued her an ultimatum: dry out in a rehab center, or he'd sue for divorce. She'd opted to drink. Now she'd dried out—for the moment. Unfortunately, her dry spells never lasted long—and she was suing him for custody of Timmy.

The injustice stung. Deeply. It wasn't fair or right. Madeline had dragged Timmy through enough hell. More than enough. And God knew Jake had been tried by her fire twice as often as his son. When would their aggravation with this woman end?

Laura opened the door wider and motioned him inside. "Have you talked to your lawyer?" Gregory Radon was a great attorney. Surely he could put a quick stop to this insanity.

"I've talked to him. And then I tried to find Madeline." Jake came in. As tense as strung wire, he paced between the sofa and wicker dinette table, dragging his hand through the black hair at his temple. "No luck. She's pulled a disappearing act."

It was probably a good thing for them both that she had, and that he hadn't found her. Laura clicked on a lamp, set the canister of pepper gas on the coffee table, then relaxed back in a chair beside the sofa and waited for him to vent enough so that they could talk this through. She hated seeing him upset. Not only because she literally owed him her life and they'd been best friends for years, but because she loved Timmy as much as Jake loved his son.

"The upshot is that Lady Justice isn't just blind," he said, stopping at the edge of the light pooling on the mint-green carpet. "She needs a reality check."

A prick of irritation at that remark slithered up Laura's back. But she knew this wasn't Jake talking so much as his anger and frustration, and so she let the comments slide, and straightened a sprawled stack of magazines on the coffee table. *Modern Family* looked comfortable there, beside *Popular Science*.

"Because my job is risky and I'm away a lot, I provide a 'less than stable growth environment' for my son. In other words, it's a toss-up," he muttered, a warranted amount of anger riddling his tone. "My odds of retaining custody of Timmy are about equal to Madeline's odds of getting custody of him."

Shock, stark and deep, surged through Laura. "But she's a drunk," she said, too surprised to pause and state that bald truth diplomatically.

"Sad commentary, isn't it?" Jake looked down at her, letting her see his weariness of fighting Madeline in his eyes. "I'm a Special Operations officer in the United States Air Force and, because I risk my neck so often for my country, I've got the same odds as an alcoholic of keeping custody of my son."

It was a sad commentary. An infuriating one, too. "So what did Radon say you can do about it?" If Jake said "Nothing," she swore she'd spit nails.

He rapped the back of a chair in his pacing, then stopped in front of her. "According to the good attorney, I could 'greatly enhance' my odds of winning a custody battle by getting married."

"Oh, God." Anything but that. *Anything* but that.

"My feelings exactly." Jake nodded. "He says a wife would be there when I can't be, giving Timmy 'a higher probability' of having a more stable home life with me." Jake let out a grunt that clearly depicted his thoughts on that recommendation.

After the hellish years he had spent married to Madeline, that suggestion and comment had to sting. Sting? Hell, it had to scorch. They'd had any and everything but peace and stability.

Agitated, she shifted on her chair and swept her auburn hair back from her face. Her thoughts raced. Jake married again? And Madeline gaining custody of Timmy? Just the thought of either soured Laura's stomach.

She couldn't let this happen. Not to Jake or to Timmy. She knew how much pain it would cause them, especially Timmy. How could she not know? She had grown up as an only child in New Orleans without much of a family. Her parents had loved each other to distraction; so much so, they'd had little love left over for their daughter. Laura had never belonged. She had been alone, an outsider, and she had never forgotten how much that had hurt. She'd sworn to herself that one day, she would have children of her own and things would be different. But thanks to a ruptured ovarian cyst and a non-functioning ovary, she'd had to watch that dream die. Then Timmy had been born, and from the moment she had first seen him, just minutes after his birth, she had considered him her surrogate son.

No, she couldn't let this happen. Not to him. The anger and guilt of not preventing it from happening would eat her alive. Resolve hardened in her chest. She'd be damned before she would risk Timmy being raised by a neglectful alcoholic who loved Scotch more than her son. He would *not* feel like an outsider.

As a resolution occurred to Laura, she said it aloud, having no idea what kind of reaction to expect. "You could marry me."

Jake stared at her for a long moment, his soft gray eyes shining with gratitude, then hardening with determination. He plopped down on the sofa and buried his face in his hands. A minute elapsed, then two. Finally, he leaned forward and propped his elbows on his knees. "You've been the best friend a man could ask for, but you've done so much for us already. I can't ask you to marry me, too."

"You didn't ask." Laura shifted over to sit across from him in her favorite chair. The beige velour snagged her silk robe, exposing her thigh. She tugged it closed, then smoothed it over her kneecap. "I offered."

Thinking it over, he vacillated between the pros and cons, his expression shifting half a dozen times. "No." He sighed, as if he carried the weight of the world on his shoulders, rolled the copy of *Popular Science* into a tube, and then smacked it against his open palm. "No, you can't."

The more Laura considered it, the more sense it made. And the more reasonable it seemed. "Why not?"

"Why not?" His tone turned incredulous.

"Yes. Why not?" Laura narrowed her gaze in warning. "We know what kind of antics Madeline's capable of, Jake. We've got to do whatever it takes to protect him from her."

"*I* have to do whatever it takes," he corrected, dropping the magazine back onto the coffee table. It landed with a firm thunk. "Look, I'm grateful for everything you do for Timmy and me. Trying to figure out how to deal with him most of the time . . . well, I'd always be floundering without you, and I know it."

"Then doesn't it make sense that we do this?"

"No, it doesn't," he insisted, forking both hands through his hair. "It's exactly why we shouldn't." Jake leaned back and put on his most serious I-mean-it look. "When Madeline got pregnant and her father insisted she abort, you helped me to accept what I had to do for Timmy's sake. You helped me through that nightmare of a marriage, and the even worse divorce."

"Of course. Friends do that kind of thing for friends, Jake."

"You've done more, and we both know it. You've always helped me with Timmy. Hell, you've been more of a mother to him than Madeline ever thought about being. But I can't have you marrying me for him, Laura. I won't. Even for a best friend, that's just . . . too much."

"Do I have any choice in the matter?" It was her life. And it should damn well be her decision. The man would protect her to death, if she let him.

"Don't get your hackles up." Jake let his gaze roll toward the ceiling, then focused back on her. "I just think that you deserve a life with a man you know is going to be there for you when you need him. I work missions with survival odds between two and ten percent. That's not going to change."

She resisted a compelling urge to sigh and just announce that they were going to do this, and to tack on an "and that's final." But it was too soon. Jake had to vent and discuss this some more to see the big picture and draw the same conclusion she had seen and drawn. "I was in Special Ops. I know what goes on there."

"Then I shouldn't have to remind you that when one mission is over, there's another one waiting in the wings."

Did he think she had forgotten? How could she forget a job that had determined her whole lifestyle? A job drilled into her until she lived, breathed, and ate it? How could anyone? No one forgot it. Ever. "Listen, all of this is just smoke. And smoke doesn't change facts. You need a wife."

"The *last* thing I need is a wife." He grunted, slicing his hand down the thigh of his black slacks. "Even a damn divorce hasn't given me peace from the one I had."

How could Laura dispute that truth? "You need a mother for Timmy," she rephrased. "I can be that, *if* I'm your wife."

"And what do you get?" he asked, then answered himself. "Nothing."

"I get a son." Only she knew how much that would mean to her.

Jake's broad shoulders slumped, telling her he had more than an inkling of the importance of that to her, and his voice softened. "I can't be a husband again, Laura. I won't." He rubbed at his forehead, clearly irritated and unsure of what to do with all his frustration. "Don't you understand? We'd have no future."

"Of course, I understand." She stiffened, and persisted. "But to keep Timmy, you need a wife. I know there isn't anyone special in your life, so that leaves me."

"Why in hell would you marry a man with a son and no future? You, of all people, should have better sense." He laced his fingers atop his head and closed his eyes, as if silently cursing, or praying.

When he reopened them, he glared at her. "It's highly likely I'll never live to see thirty-five, and we both know it. Think about that. And think about yourself, not just Timmy. Are you forgetting who you are?"

"No. But I think you might be."

Agitated and obviously bent on reminding her anyway, from his perspective, Jake began pacing again, hanging in the shadows just beyond the lamplight. "Look, you went into the military to do high-tech communications research and you became an expert—a captain in Intel who could pick her pet projects and her terms, and you did it. Yet all of that still wasn't enough for you."

She'd loved her work in the Special Ops intelligence community, and she still loved her research. But it hadn't been enough, which was exactly why marrying him made sense. "I haven't forgotten, Jake." Nor had she forgotten Madeline's part in why she was no longer in the military. That, however, Laura had sworn to herself she'd never tell Jake.

He'd said the last thing he needed was a wife, but it wasn't. He didn't need more guilt, which is exactly what he'd feel if she told him how Madeline's antics had affected her and her career.

He stopped near the table and glared over the slope of his shoulder back at her. "Damn it, you know you hated the constant danger of working Intel. You hated not knowing where you'd be tomorrow or next week, never mind next year."

"Yes, I did. Enough to get out of the Air Force to get away from it."

"You hated having no idea what mission you'd be on, or where you'd be performing it, and you walked out—as much as anyone can walk out of Intel—to get yourself a personal life."

Was he going to laundry list her whole life here? "All of that is true, but—"

"Then why are you telling me you're willing to give up a personal life and put yourself right in the middle of all of the things you hated again?"

"Because I am willing." Laura looked him right in the eye. "And that's exactly what I'm telling you." She lifted a hand, palm upward. "I'm willing."

He dragged a hand through his hair, spiking it. "You're forgetting about Madeline. As much as I wish she would, she isn't going to go away." A grimace flattened his generous mouth to a tight slash. "If I've accepted nothing else in the two years since the divorce, I've accepted that she'll be a thorn in my side until the day I die. You can't be willing to accept that, too."

"Yes, I can," Laura said without hesitating, then leaned forward in her chair, a little amused by the disbelief in his tone. "Listen, you're right about all of this. But you're forgetting the one reason that makes all of it insignificant."

He lifted his hands, and the button on his left shirt-cuff winked in the lamplight. "What the hell could make all of this insignificant?"

"Timmy." Her throat sandpaper dry, Laura dredged up her courage and then spoke from the heart, something she had rarely let herself do with anyone, including Jake. "I'd do it for Timmy," she said. "I love him, Jake."

The skepticism in his expression wilted, and the hard lines in his face softened. "I know you love him, but we're talking marriage here. This isn't a day at the park in San Francisco, or a week in the Sierras playing in the snow. You'd be sacrificing your shot at a happy, normal life with a real marriage."

She bristled, and her tone went flat. "I'm aware of the difference."

"I didn't mean to insult you." His exasperation escaped on a sigh. "Ah, hell, Laura, you know what I mean."

"Yes, I do. I got out of the Air Force because I wanted to put down roots in a quiet and peaceful life. But, in case you haven't noticed, my friend, it's been four years since I took off my captain's bars, and my roots and the rest of me are still single.''

Unable to sit and speak this frankly, she stood up and moved behind the stuffed chair, then grasped the back of it in a knuckle-tingling grip, wondering why in heaven she smelled lemons. She despised them, and she knew for a fact there was nothing in her apartment that even resembled the scent. ''You know how much I wanted children. You also know my biological clock didn't get a shot at ticking before it shut down. I'll never have children myself, but I have had Timmy. In my heart, he's my son, Jake, and he always has been. And right now, my son needs me.''

Jake stared at her, a little surprised but even more awed. Laura had let him glimpse inside her on occasion, but never like this. And in her expression, determined and yet vulnerable, he realized the truth. Her suggestion to marry him truly had nothing to do with him. It had to do with what was best for Timmy.

Relieved by that, Jake moved out from the shadows on the floor into the lamplight and plucked at the nubby fabric on the back of the sofa. He considered her proposal from that perspective, and, in the end, he decided she made a lot of sense. But they had to be perfectly clear on the terms of this agreement. He didn't dare to not be crystal clear.

''You're right,'' he said. ''I do need a mother for Timmy. But I don't need a wife.'' His gray eyes turned steely. ''If we should do this, as egotistical as it sounds, I would have to know you'd never make the mistake of falling in love with me. Not ever.'' The skin between his brows furrowed. ''My mortality rating is bad at best. *We have no future.* You can never forget that, and you can never take the chance of loving me.''

They had been friends for over a decade. Did he think this was a news flash? ''I know.''

His frown deepened, and his voice grew even more stern. "I won't love you. And I won't forget it—not for a second. I can't forget it, and I can't handle any guilt or regret or the worry of wondering that you might. I won't worry, and I won't regret, Laura. And even five or ten years from now, I won't tolerate recriminations or reprisals being tossed into my face because of the way things are. I'm telling you now exactly how things will always be. I've got to know you understand that, and it's okay with you. Otherwise, I can't do what I have to do."

The job. *Duty first.* How well she remembered the drill. And as warnings went, this one wasn't so bad. She'd heard worse from him, and those had worked out amicably. "Quit ranting and listen to me, okay?" When he stopped at the other side of the coffee table and stuffed his fist into his pocket, she went on. "I don't love you, Jake. I'm not in love with you, and I can't fathom, even in my wildest imagination, ever being in love with you. So none of that is a problem."

That blunt disclosure had the logical man fighting the male ego in Jake, and he suspected Laura knew it. What looked suspiciously like a smile tugged at her lips. A muscle in his jaw twitched.

"You'll have your home and your life, and I'll have mine," she said in a tone so calm and reasonable it set his teeth on edge. "We'll just do what we've always done: work together for whatever is in Timmy's best interest. The only difference is we'll be married."

"So you accept that's all our relationship can ever be?" Jake asked, still unconvinced. How could she be satisfied, settling for so little for herself? He had to be missing something she hadn't considered. "I'm serious about all this. We'll never be emotionally close. We'll never be a real couple, or any more of a family than we are now."

"We certainly won't," she firmly insisted. "But we will be married, and that'll 'greatly enhance' your odds of keeping custody of Timmy. That's what matters most to me."

Jake stared at her in disbelief. "Why?"

Laura accepted it. He wasn't going to relent. Not until he felt satisfied, and to give him satisfaction, she had to bare even more truths. Ones she preferred not to think about, much less discuss. Still, this was for Timmy. She would do it, but she'd be damned if she could look Jake in the eye when she did. She focused on the placket of his gray corduroy shirt. "I was a vulnerable child." Saying that out loud, even after all these years, still rattled her. "I didn't like it. And I won't have a child I consider my son vulnerable. Not if I can stop it."

He dipped his chin and stayed silent a long moment. Obviously her disclosure about being vulnerable had taken him by surprise. Or maybe it hadn't, and he didn't want her to know that he had surmised that truth a long time ago.

He lifted his chin to look at her. "We'd be taking a shot, but it could be for nothing. Madeline could win the custody suit, anyway."

"Highly doubtful," Laura countered. "I'm clean, with strong credentials and no history that could hurt him. Dr. Laura Taylor, formerly Captain Laura Taylor, will round out your superiority nicely, I would say." Lord, how she wished she felt as confident about that as she had sounded.

Surprise flickered through his eyes. "You're even willing to flaunt your titles on this?"

Hating pretentious titles, she blanched. But for Timmy? Anything. Even that. "Yes."

Jake's lip curled, hinting at a crooked smile. "You really are sure about this."

Finally, he was coming around. How could she not be sure? "To keep Timmy away from Madeline, I'd marry the devil himself. You can be ruthless, friend, but you're far less daunting than the devil."

Laura *had* thought this through. And Jake supposed he could understand why she would find settling for him acceptable. Even without a future, she wanted to feel connected to someone outside herself—to Timmy. And from living through Jake's marriage to Madeline along with him, Laura knew the hell a traditional marriage involved. Not loving him and being Timmy's stepmother, when she already considered herself his mother, was emotionally safe. "Can you tell me straight out you know and accept that the only reason I'm marrying you is to keep Madeline away from Timmy?"

"I know and accept it," Laura said without reservation, then issued a warning of her own. "And I want to know you accept that Timmy is the only reason I would marry you."

"Of course." He shrugged. "Why else?"

The man had no idea of his appeal. Which is probably why they had been able to be friends and keep their relationship purely platonic.

It took a lot more discussion—actually, until dawn was breaking outside—but finally, Laura settled his fears and the worry cleared from Jake's face.

"Okay," he said, rubbing his lower lip between his forefinger and thumb. "Okay, let's do it."

"Okay." Laura stood up, feeling buoyant. It wasn't the traditional proposal or acceptance, and theirs wouldn't be anything like a traditional marriage. But it would serve the purpose and hopefully put a damper on Madeline's plan to bring more turmoil into Timmy's life. A sacrifice for both Laura and Jake, but one that— *please, God!*—would spare Timmy.

That possibility alone made any sacrifice worth the price they had to pay

Two weeks later, in a Lake Tahoe chapel, Laura Taylor put on an antique white lace dress, held a bouquet of pale yellow roses and baby's breath, and became Jake Logan's wife.

It never occurred to her or Jake to exchange wedding rings, and the justice of the peace had to remind Jake to kiss his bride.

Two weeks and three days after the wedding, Madeline went on another drinking binge, and dropped the custody suit.

That news came to Laura via Jake, who met her for lunch at the Golden Dragon, a tiny Chinese restaurant they frequented. He suggested they have their marriage annulled.

Awash in relief over the dropping of the suit, Laura considered the annulment for nearly two minutes before deciding against it. "No," she said, watching a brunette waitress who was as thin as a rail scurry from table to table, refilling glasses from a frosty pitcher of iced tea. "No annulment."

About to take a bite of spicy-smelling lo mein, Jake paused, his fork midair. "No?"

"No," Laura insisted, removing a smelly lemon wedge from the saucer of her hot tea and dumping it into an ashtray. "What if something should happen to you? Considering the job, we know it's a strong possibility."

He put his fork down. "Custody of Timmy would automatically revert to Madeline."

"Exactly." Laura leaned closer, across the red-clothed table, then dropped her voice to a whisper to avoid being overheard by the two women lunching at the next table. "I know that's eaten at you inside for a long time—worrying about that happening. It's worried me, too. And now we have the opportunity to do something about it. I think rather than get an annulment, we need to pursue a stepparent adoption.''

Jake opposed. Strongly. "No, you've sacrificed enough for us already.''

While other diners came, ate, and departed, he went on to reiterate every logical reason in the book why she shouldn't want to do this, informed her that Madeline would never give her consent, and then reiterated it all some more, in case Laura had missed anything the first time he'd said it.

When he paused for breath, Laura interjected, "But she's an alcoholic, Jake.''

"True, but she's one with substantial credentials. She spent years in the intelligence community as an assistant to Colonel James, and that will strengthen her custody odds.''

"Even if she was only there because of her father?'' Of course, Colonel James had hired her. Her father, Sean Drake, was a well-respected CIA legend and offending him was paramount to offending God. James was far too slick to offend God.

"It doesn't matter,'' Jake insisted. "She was there. That's what shows up on paper.''

Laura groused and fidgeted on her red vinyl seat. "But everyone knows she was an airhead and a drunk, Jake. Even her boss knew it.''

"She got Excellent ratings on every employee review.''

"Okay,'' Laura conceded. "So to stay in Sean Drake's good graces, Colonel James covered for her. But, over the years, she's pulled a respectable succession of crazy stunts. They can be verified and testified to, and that would have to strengthen our case.''

Jake mulled that over, and after Laura swallowed her

last bite of sesame chicken, she interrupted his ponderings to remind him of the bottom line. "We have to do everything possible to never leave Timmy vulnerable to her," Laura insisted. "We have to, Jake, because otherwise only God knows the damage she could do."

Timmy could *not* be an outsider.

Two

⌒

Two years later

Cheese dripped from the tines of Timmy's fork. "What if Judge Neal asks me why Mom's got an apartment and only lives with us some of the time?"

Swallowing a bite of hot lasagna, Laura waited for Jake's answer. After two near-misses at getting this adoption through, and two times of surviving Madeline sobering up and withdrawing her consent, they were all worried about the court hearing with Judge Neal tomorrow. And reassuring Timmy, when feeling unsure herself, wasn't the easiest thing in the world for Laura to do. *So much could go wrong.*

Jake put down his fork, then wiped at his mouth with his napkin. "The judge isn't going to ask you that, son."

"How do you know? He could."

"Because I know," Jake insisted. He set the napkin down on the light oak table and let his gaze wander over to the lacy white curtains on the back door's window.

Laura couldn't get upset about Jake's terse response.

They'd been at this "what if" business the entire time they'd cooked dinner and all during the eating of it. Everyone's nerves had worn thin.

Timmy stabbed a green bean with his fork. "What if Judge Neal asks me how come my mom and dad don't sleep in the same room? All my friends' moms and dads do. He *could* ask me that." Concern *and* curiosity burned in Timmy's eyes. "What am I supposed to tell him?"

"Tell him your father snores," Laura suggested, insinuating a mischievous lilt in her voice in an attempt to ease Timmy's concerns and to diminish his curiosity. She hated seeing him worried—no nine-year-old should be under this kind of pressure—and she hated even more him seeing himself as different from his friends. She remembered how awkward being different had made her feel. While she and Jake tried to minimize those things for Timmy, their situation *was* different, and that was the simple, unavoidable truth.

"Dad snores?" Timmy grinned.

"Loudly." She winked at him. "Now stop worrying, Tiger. Your dad and I will be there with you when you talk with Judge Neal. Everything will be just fine."

"But—"

"It'll be fine, Timmy." Laura too had wearied of the worry, and she still had to tell Jake that Intel had reactivated her as a communications consultant on Operation Shadowpoint. Lousy timing, with court tomorrow, and the news would surely go over with Jake about as well as a lead balloon.

What exactly the operation was, she had no idea, and she had no need to know. She rarely did know the mission on these consultations, which were growing less frequent because more trainees now had the required expertise. Still, times arose when an expert was needed, and during those times, Intel would temporarily activate her to do the consult. She was also subject to recall as an active duty military officer, though the odds of the Air Force recalling her were slim, unless the United States went to war. Most Intel consults took only a couple of hours to clear. Some, a few days. So far, none had kept her activated longer than that.

On Shadowpoint, she'd been asked to identify and eliminate the reason for a communications breakdown between Home Base and three operatives in the field. She had to admit that she enjoyed feeling the adrenaline rush again. It had been a while, thanks to Sean Drake. If not for Madeline's father's resentment of Laura's friendship with Jake, she would still be an active duty military officer working on her communications designs full-time and a full-time communications consultant for Intel. Drake had threatened to destroy her career, with an assist from her research funder, Colonel James. Deactivating in Intel and leaving the military was the only way Laura could stop them. So she had. Now, she was a civil service employee attached to the Publicity Office who did her communications research and development designs quietly—actually, covertly—on the side, and she assisted Intel when her expertise was needed. It wasn't a perfect situation, or what she'd wanted but, under the circumstances, it was the best she could do.

Squelching her resentment against Drake and James, she avoided looking at Jake and gazed across the table at Timmy, who was still hard at the *what-if* questions. The only good thing about her not being on active duty in the military or active full-time in Intel was that her absence removed her and her family from the dangers inherent to the job. Her consults did pose the potential for danger, but typically she was in and out of the operation quickly, and only those with the highest security clearances ever knew she had been involved.

Much safer for Timmy. There was solace in that.

Still, this Shadowpoint consult was serious enough that she had to tell Jake about it, and she would—just as soon as they got Timmy calmed down and into bed for the night. "Stop worrying, Tiger," she said to him. "Your dad and I will be there."

Outside, tires screeched.

Seconds later, the beams of bright headlights flooded in through the kitchen window. A car jumped the curb and headed straight for the kitchen. *Oh, God, was it going to hit the house?*

"It's not stopping." Jake jumped up.

Closest, Laura snagged Timmy, knocking a chair against the wall. She pulled him away from the outer wall, out of the kitchen, then shielded him behind her and watched Jake run toward the front door.

Through the arched opening between the entryway and the kitchen, she saw the car finally stop. Its still-running engine had the walls and window vibrating, and Laura's nerves shot. And Timmy was as white as a sheet. "It's okay, Tiger." She swept a shaky hand down his hair, praying she wasn't inadvertently lying to him. "Just stay put until your dad assesses the situation."

A car door slammed. "Where is she?" a woman shouted, her voice slurred. "Where is she?" A pause, then, "Don't you dare tell me to lower my voice, Jake Logan. I'm not married to you anymore. You can't tell me what to do. Where is the bitch?"

Madeline. And Timmy had to have heard her. For God's sake, why couldn't the woman think of him just once? *Just once?*

"Timmy." Laura cupped his trembling chin. From the pain haunting his eyes, she knew he'd recognized Madeline's voice. "Why don't you go take your shower now, okay?"

The fear and anger burning in his eyes seeped into his voice. "It's Madeline."

"Yes, it is," Laura admitted, more relieved that it was her than someone else. There were other possibilities. With Jake's job, terrorists or malcontents seeking revenge or intelligence information were a possibility and a potential threat.

Timmy's chin quivered, and he looked a blink from tears. "She's drunk again."

"I'm afraid so." Laura swallowed hard. How could the woman keep doing this? Why did she insist on continuously hurting Timmy this way? "Go on now, and don't forget to brush your teeth. Dad and I'll be in a little later to say good night."

Biting down on his lip, Timmy clenched his jaw. "She's gonna do it again, isn't she, Mom?"

Laura didn't have to ask what he meant. Twice Madeline had pulled her consent before Jake and Laura could see the adoption through to fruition, and this felt frighteningly like a prelude to a third withdrawal. "I hope not."

"Me, too." He walked through the entryway, then across the family room and down the hall toward his room.

"Damn it, let go of me, Jake! I want to talk to the bitch, and I'm not going anywhere until I do."

Fuming, Laura forced herself to stay in the entryway until Timmy stepped out of sight, then she went to the door. Madeline was yelling loud enough to wake the dead. No way could Timmy—or every neighbor in a three-block radius—not hear every word. Jake and Timmy deserved so much better than this. So much better than this.

Laura stepped outside, down onto the concrete landing, and saw Madeline sway on her feet. Her car had stopped closer to four feet than six from the kitchen window. The engine was still running, the lights were still on, and half the sod that had been the lawn now clung splattered on her car's back fenders. So much for all the work they'd put into grooming every blade for the past two weeks. Laura grimaced. "I'm right here. What do you want, Madeline?"

She jerked around, her black suit as crumpled as if she'd slept in it for a week. Her once beautiful face, puffy and bloated by alcohol, twisted with hatred that ran soul-deep. "You're not getting him. Timmy's mine." She thumped her thin chest with a wild, waving hand. "You got Jake, but you're not getting my son."

"I understand." Laura crossed her arms over her chest, hiding the hurt and holding it inside. "Is that it?"

"You coldhearted bitch. Timmy belongs to me. He's mine. M-I-N-E."

Laura ignored the woman and swiveled her gaze to Jake. "Should I call the police?" That had been their attorney's advice.

"No." Jake frowned. "Timmy's upset enough without having to see that, too."

Truthfully, Laura felt a little relieved. The neighbors were gawking. Discreetly peeking out from behind their drapes and through the slats of their mini-blinds, but gawking. That infuriated and embarrassed her. Hell, it humiliated her, and she knew it had the same effect on Jake. "She obviously can't drive." A diplomatic understatement; the woman could barely stand. It was a shame her overindulgence hadn't shut her mouth. "I'll go call her a cab. You get the car off the lawn."

"Don't talk about me like I'm not standing here." Madeline tried to sling off Jake's grasp on her upper arm.

He held fast with little effort. She was tiny, about

Laura's five-five height, and Jake towered over them both. "That's enough, Madeline."

"Nothing is black and white," she shouted at Laura. "I told you, there's always shades of gray. Damn it, I told you. . . ."

She had told Laura that. Repeatedly. But what exactly she had meant by it, only she, God, and the demons that drove her to drink knew. Laura turned to go inside.

"Don't walk away from me, bitch." Madeline fought Jake harder, spitting her words out from between her teeth. "I hate it when people walk away from me!"

Jake restrained her, kept Madeline from going after Laura. The woman was sick and they should have compassion, but a resentful part of her half-wished Jake would turn Madeline loose so Laura could legitimately belt her in self-defense. It would be wrong, but after so many years of these type altercations, her tolerance level had dipped low. At the moment, it had dipped to nearly nonexistent. Yet Laura understood the value of discipline, so she restrained herself and retraced her steps on the walkway to the covered landing at the front door. Only she would know she tasted blood from biting her tongue. There was solace in that.

Madeline screamed. "*Don't walk away from me!*"

Without looking back, Laura went inside, shoved the door shut, resisted an urge to kick it. She jerked up the phone, shaking in fury and fear that Madeline would stop the adoption again. Muttering intermittently against the aggravation, the frustration, and the indignity of putting up with stunts like this one, she first called a cab to come get Madeline and then phoned Bill at Green's Automotive to come and tow away her car.

In the morning, the woman wouldn't have a clue

where she'd left it, and Laura would rather pay the towing fee than risk Madeline returning here so soon. Laura's tolerance definitely had sunk too low to risk her having the patience to deal with that.

Hanging up the phone, soul-weary and worried half-sick about tomorrow, she glimpsed Timmy out of the corner of her eye. Hunkered against the hallway wall, he looked so lost, so alone and afraid, it broke her heart. The urge to physically force Madeline into a serious attitude adjustment hit Laura hard. Instead, she went to Timmy, stooped down, and then hugged him close, trying to absorb all the fears from him. "I'm so sorry, Tiger." The child was shaking like a leaf. "Are you okay?"

"She scares me, Mom."

"She's sick, honey." Laura rubbed little circles on his back, trying to soothe him. "Really sick."

A few minutes later, Jake came back inside.

Timmy was still shaking. "Is she gone, Dad?" he asked, his eyes wide.

"Yes, son." Looking as weary as Laura felt, Jake tried to reassure Timmy. "And Bill Green just left with her car. Everything's okay, except the front lawn. We'll need a truckload of dirt and a good bit of sod to get rid of the tire ruts." Jake heaved a sigh and rubbed at his neck. "Guess that settles the question of what we'll be doing next weekend."

"Guess so," Laura said. "But Sutter's Mill will still be there the weekend after for us to visit. We can handle this." That was true, if annoying. Repairing the lawn only required time, money, and hours of back-breaking work and sweat. The real worry was in wondering what Timmy would require to heal from this.

Jake scooped up Timmy and hugged him to him. Though Laura felt down to her core the regret and worry Madeline had put in Jake's eyes, she pretended not to see it.

Half an hour later, they had all calmed down considerably, and Timmy was back to the *what-if* questions Judge Neal might pose to him.

"Stop worrying." Jake ruffled Timmy's hair. "You'll turn gray before you're ten. Mom and I will be there, son. Didn't she tell you everything would be fine?"

"Yes."

"And doesn't she always tell the truth?"

"She always has," Timmy conceded, sliding a longing look at Laura that this time she was being honest with him, too.

"We'll be there," Laura repeated to reinforce it, hearing the phone ring.

Closest to the phone, Jake grabbed the receiver, then answered. "Logan."

His shoulders tensed, and he buried his expression under his professional mask. "Fine." He glanced at his watch. "I'll be there in twenty minutes."

Laura's heart wrenched in her chest. It was a business call. He was being sent out on a mission.

Tomorrow in court, Jake wouldn't be there.

Three

~

As a Special Assistant to General Bradley Connor, Jake expected to contend with interruptions of his personal life and with sensitive missions. But did they always have to come at the worst possible time?

Normally, to meet with the general, he would dress in Class-As rather than the regular uniform of navy blue slacks and pale blue shirt, but Jake opted for the regular. It was a Sunday night, and anything that had Connor summoning Jake then would render the issue of uniform moot.

He drove to headquarters, clipped his building access ID to his shirt pocket, and then nodded at the security guard just inside the front door, doing his damnedest to keep his grimace to himself. Most of the time Jake didn't resent the interference of his duties on his private life, but being called in and ordered to report directly to General Connor's office for briefing when Jake should be at home reassuring Laura that Madeline wouldn't dare pull the damn papers again, and reassuring Timmy that this time would be different and the adoption would go through, had Jake feeling nothing but resentment.

Oh, Laura had bailed him out with Timmy. She always had smoothed over challenges with an incredible ease Jake felt grateful for, and he envied. Being truthful about the odds of the adoption going through with Jake absent—*slim as a pencil, but they'd give it their best shot*—she'd cuddled Timmy and urged him to not lose faith. Things *would* work out. Then, ever so gently, she'd reminded him that Jake had no choice. He had to go to help others who couldn't help themselves just then and, as his family, she and Timmy had to understand the importance of that.

"Responsibility isn't a coat," Timmy had said, wise beyond his years.

"Right." Stroking his nape, Laura had given him one of her soft smiles. "You're either strong enough to wear it all the time, or you leave it in the closet and suffer when it's cold."

Timmy's anger had drained to resignation. He'd stiffened his thin shoulders, and his expression had turned solemn. Tilting his chin up, he'd looked into Jake's eyes, and then he'd asked, "Daddy, when are you going to have time for me?"

So simply put. Yet if Jake lived to be a thousand, he'd never forget the pain flashing through Timmy's eyes, or the determination in the set of his chin that meant he would patiently wait until Jake did have time for him. Remorse shafted straight into Jake's soul and, as it had then, guilt flooded him now. And not for the first time since Madeline had opted for Scotch and Jake had divorced her, ripples of doubt that he was a good parent crashed over him in confidence-eroding waves. *When would he have time for his son?*

So long as he was assigned to Special Ops, everyone and everything else in his life had to rank second. There were no other options.

The guard at headquarters' front desk gave Jake a snappy salute. With the familiarity of the long-performed, Jake returned it and then headed down the long tile walkway, bypassing the elevator for the stairs. At that moment, he had too much frustration roiling inside him to ride up to the third floor. Maybe a stint on the stairs would give him a breather—time to shift gears from "Daddy" to "Major." Laura would do her damnedest to see to the adoption; of that Jake had no doubt. Like she'd told Timmy; they had to have faith. All of them—including Jake.

What he'd ever done to deserve her, or what he'd ever do without her, he had no idea. And he prayed he'd never find out. Amazing, considering that living with her these past three weeks was slowly killing him.

Laura wasn't a quick-kill type of woman. She didn't send men spiraling into fantasyland with a quick glance or a glimpse, though she was just as lethal. Laura seeped inside a man, into his every pore, until one day it hit him like a sucker punch that he couldn't imagine his life without her.

In their thirteen-year friendship, she'd done a damn lot of seeping into Jake Logan. But nothing in comparison to what she'd done to him in the past three weeks.

What had happened? What was different? He'd actually started having fantasies of theirs being a real marriage.

After his stab at wedded bliss with Madeline, him having fantasies of a real marriage with Laura had to be the sickest twist his mind ever had taken. They'd been friends for years, for God's sake. Best friends. And it wasn't as if they had never awakened in the same house. Jake couldn't even claim unfamiliarity as the reason, or household intimacy. They had lived together platonically twice before now. True, it was only to convince the social workers theirs was a normal family, and as soon as Madeline had jerked the papers,

Laura had moved back to her apartment. But she hadn't affected him like this either of those times. Hell, during survival training, they had even slept in the same sleeping bag to share body warmth. Okay, so he'd had a few fantasies then, but who wouldn't? Laura was a beautiful woman. Inside and out.

Yet she had married him only for Timmy. Because she was his friend, and not because she wanted a husband. Jake couldn't afford to forget that. Neither of them needed the pain of dreaming about a future. He likely didn't have a future, and *they* had agreed no future. He couldn't afford to forget that, either.

Still, those fantasies were giving him hell.

What would it be like to have a woman really love you? To have Laura really love him?

That he never would know had him suffering a potent shot of pure envy. Anger at himself chased on its heels, and Jake chided himself for thinking of the forbidden and foolish. He didn't know what being loved would be like. He never would know. And he had accepted that a long time ago, when Madeline had deliberately gotten pregnant with Timmy. So why did something Jake had sworn off wanting now have his temper escalating into overdrive?

For Laura, he decided. She deserved better. She deserved more, and no way could Jake be indifferent to that, or to anything involving her, even if he was helpless to give her more.

Forcing thoughts of her and Timmy to empty from his mind, Jake opened the door to the third-floor hallway. The smell of pine cleaner hanging heavy in the air, he walked by the dark and empty offices lining both sides of the hall. Typical for a Sunday night. Only the Operations Center would be an active hub. Monitoring various operations worldwide, activity there never ceased or shut down.

After dumping his gear, Jake made his way to the general's office.

Connor's door stood open. Walking over the cool gray carpet toward it, Jake paused at the threshold. The general sat behind his desk, staring up thoughtfully at a painting of General Patton. Everyone in Ops knew of the general's admiration for Patton. He had fought with his men, not hugged safer perimeters, and Connor emulated him. He'd done well, too. He had been awarded the Purple Heart in two campaigns, one of which had been in the Gulf War. Jake respected the man. That helped a lot, considering some of the things Connor asked Jake and the rest of his team to do. It was hard to follow a man into a war zone if you lacked respect for him as an officer, or as a human being. With Connor, that wasn't an issue.

Jake also had worked for the man long enough to know what his staring at Patton's portrait meant: tough decisions were being weighed and made. Hell was coming to call.

"General?" Jake asked, surprised to find Connor alone. Where was the rest of the staff? And why were they meeting here and not in the briefing room?

Connor turned his gaze. "Jake. Come in."

Flirting with sixty, his dark hair graying at the temples and his bright blue eyes absorbing, wise, and assessing, Connor exuded quiet dignity, but he didn't smile. Whenever Jake thought of Connor, it was through a powerful memory that to Jake epitomized the man. Those who had been at last year's Air Force Special Operations Command—AFSOC—Christmas dinner understood this; many felt the same way. Eight weeks before that dinner, AFSOC had lost a WC-130 from Keesler Air Force Base in Mississippi. The crew of six Hurricane Hunters had penetrated the eye-wall of Hurricane Pearl and, on departing the eye of the storm, due to faulty equipment, the plane had crashed. All six crew members—the pilot, co-pilot, flight engineer, dropson officer, weather officer, and navigator—had died in the Class-A Mishap.

Performing a myriad of missions worldwide, AF-SOC had suffered four different Class-A Mishaps that year. All of the twenty-four crew members had families. Twenty-one had spouses; nineteen of them had children.

At the dinner, General Connor had paid tribute to those men and women and their families in an impassioned, emotional toast, commending their courage and loyalty and dedication to duty. He had mourned their personal sacrifices, and then he'd cracked his champagne glass against the edge of the podium.

The glass had shattered.

And in a room of three hundred military and civilian Special Ops personnel and their spouses, there hadn't been a dry eye or a heart not lodged in the throat, including Connor's own. For every officer and spouse present and personally untouched by the tragedy knew it easily could have been them lying among the dead, or mourning their dead, just as everyone present understood the symbolism of the broken glass. It had, in General Connor's eyes, held the greatest honor possible—a toast to heroes—and it could never again be filled to an equal honor.

Connor seldom ordered. He didn't have to; he'd earned devotion, earned respect as a leader, strategist, and warrior. His men would follow him to hell and back. And they often had.

Jake slid down on to the visitor's chair across the wide desk from the general. Whatever was coming was worse than bad; Connor's expression traversed miles beyond grim.

"We've got a problem down in the Florida Everglades, near Alligator Alley, Jake. ROFF isn't a religious organization.''

Religious Order for Freedom. Jake translated the acronym, then nodded. "What is it?"

"According to CIA preliminary reports, a terrorist group." Connor's jaw went tight, his back rigid. "One amassing a biological warfare arsenal."

Bad news was barreling down the pike to worse. Jake grimaced.

The general moved to a cabinet at the far wall of his office, then reached for the coffeepot. "Jurisdiction is messy. ROFF's headquarters is east of Sunniland. State land. But an agent on-site reports incidents occurring in Big Cypress National Preserve. There are also two separate Indian reservations in the immediate vicinity that could be affected. Needless to say, they're not happy at being dragged into this, or at being infringed upon."

Jurisdiction wasn't just messy. It was a nightmare. The state of Florida, the CIA, the FBI, two Indian tribes, and the governmental agencies assigned to protecting their rights were all involved. Americans pitted against Americans. The worst kind of nightmare. "So the mission's a coordinated effort between all the factions holding jurisdiction."

"Correct. Operation Shadowpoint." General Connor walked back to the desk with two cups filled with steaming hot coffee. He set them on his blotter, sat down, then leaned forward and laced his hands atop his desk. "Because of our experience with biological warfare, and the bird's eye reports of extensive special operations training being evident in the way ROFF does business, we've been assigned to spearhead the mission."

Jake's stomach curled. "The leader of ROFF is from Special Ops?"

"No," Connor said, flatly denying one of his men could be involved in an act of treason that threatened Americans. Then, as if he thought better of it, he re-stated himself, sounding torn between anger and de-spair. "He could be. That hasn't yet been determined. For his sake and ours, I hope to God he isn't one of us. But indications are it's a strong possibility."

Jake prayed the CIA agent had erred about this. Getting screwed by the enemy was one thing. Getting screwed by your own was another entirely. It was twice as insulting, and even more infuriating. No wonder Connor was briefing Jake alone rather than with the staff. He hadn't asked, of course. "Need to know" ranked paramount within headquarters' walls. But with the possibility of one of their own being involved, the general's rationale projected clearly. The circle of the informed on this mission would be damn tight.

Connor passed a cup of coffee to Jake. "Three months ago, the CIA infiltrated ROFF. Their agent's first report tagged ROFF's leader as a Special Ops pos-sible. The CIA informed me and the OSI."

Jake covered a wince by rubbing at his jaw. The Office of Special Investigations would have to be in-formed, of course, but that it had been only served to make the situation more galling to Jake. From that point on, everyone in Special Ops was considered sus-picious and placed under intense scrutiny, and they would remain so until they had been ruled out as sus-pects, or until Jake revealed the ROFF leader's identity by nailing the bastard's ass to the proverbial wall.

"You understand why we're going solo on this brief-ing?"

"Yes, sir." Under the circumstances, Connor had no choice. That the enemy could be a member of his own staff had to claw at his gut. It didn't do Jake's a world of good, either.

"Since that first report, intel coming in has been sporadic and sketchy. A month ago, the agent feared his cover had been compromised. CIA sent in two operative backups. Then, three days ago, orders came down from on high to abort the mission."

Abort? With a possible biological arsenal present? Jake would love to hear the rationale behind that decision. From Connor's frown and the thickening of his voice, he'd opposed. Vehemently.

"All three men were to rendezvous for pickup about twenty miles inside the Cypress reservation. Locations are pinpointed on the maps." Connor passed over part of a file, and his voice dropped a notch. "It was a no-show."

None of them had made the pickup? Jake's nerves tingled and stretched tight. That meant one of two things. They were being held captive, or they were dead.

"We want you to determine the operatives' dispositions and, if they've survived, to rescue them, Jake."

"Yes, sir."

Connor shoved his cup aside, then leaned forward over his desk, knowing personal considerations shouldn't come into command decisions, but acknowledging that they had to enter into the equation. For all their training and skills, his warriors were still men. And a good commander knew his men.

Connor knew Jake Logan. Knew he had been trapped into an unwanted marriage by Madeline Drake Logan, the daughter of CIA legend, Sean Drake. Knew she had a serious drinking problem, and for that reason, Jake had divorced her. He had married Laura to protect Timmy, and he was after the adoption for the same reason. Why Laura had agreed to the marriage only she and Jake knew, though if Connor had pegged her right, her reasons included her owing Jake for saving her life.

And because she loved the boy. A blind man could see how much she loved the boy.

"Jake, I know the situation with Timmy and Laura and Madeline, and that Timmy's up for adoption tomorrow with Judge Neal. The JAG will see to it that any special forms required are in the judge's hands before then."

Evidently, the Judge Advocate General had already been apprised, and the decision had been made to assign Jake. No surprise there. "Thank you, sir."

"The timing on this is unfortunate. But I am asking you to take on the mission because of your credentials. Simply put, you've already established credibility with the rest of the team and, considering the circumstances and the potential fallout, that makes you the best man for the job."

Public Safety major, Risk Management minor, Safety School, Air Command and Staff, Air War College, jungle and water survival training, pilot training; communications, combat, emergency medicine, and a personal defense expert. The team members were acquainted with his credentials, and that probably had assisted in easing the tension between the factions holding jurisdiction. That was important because for all their coordination, the factions still ranked fiercely competitive. And Jake was a known entity to some of them. When his F-15 had been shot down in a Middle Eastern border skirmish and he had eluded captivity, and then again when he'd successfully infiltrated Kuwait while it had been under Iraqi occupation, Jake had worked closely with the CIA. On both occasions, with the aid of brown contact lenses, he'd posed as an Arab and gathered useful intelligence.

Still, Jake felt torn. Bringing down one of their own. A corrupt one who dared to taint the reputations of the rest of them and to jeopardize their mission, but still one of their own. And right now Timmy and Laura needed Jake.

"The team supports the decision a hundred per-cent," Connor said. "No one in Special Ops has more extensive training, or better odds of surviving."

Pencil slim, but we'll give it our best shot. We have to have faith that everything will work out. Responsibility isn't a coat . . .

Nudged by Laura and Timmy's words, Jake mentally accepted responsibility, swallowed hot coffee that burned his throat, then set down his cup. It scraped against the corner of Connor's desk. "Yes, sir."

Connor nodded, his pupils narrowed to pinpoints, and a muscle twitched in his cheek, as if what he was about to say soured his mouth. "Personal affairs in order?"

Current powers of attorney for Laura, insurance ben-eficiaries up to date, Jake's Last Will and Testament executed and duly notarized. "Always, sir."

"Good." Scrawling his name onto a document, Con-nor closed the file, and then passed it over the desk to Jake. "Nothing routine on this one. You report only to me. Secure line."

"Yes, sir."

"Any questions?"

Millions of them. But none he could ask. The rest of what he needed to know would be in the file, which he'd read, commit to memory, and then lock in the vault. "No, sir."

"Fine." Connor let out a sigh. "Gear up and be on the flight line in an hour."

Jake stood up, skirted the chair, and then moved to-ward the door.

"Good luck, Jake."

The hairs on Jake's neck stood on end. Never before had Connor wished him luck on a mission. That he did now had alarms blaring in Jake's mind and a question burning the tip of his tongue. Though he feared the answer, had never asked this question on any other mission, he asked it now. "Sir?"

"Yes?"

"What are my odds of surviving this mission?"

"According to the bean counters . . ." Dread flashed through Connor's eyes and his jaw went tight. "Less than two percent."

Four

∽

"Mrs. Logan, where is your husband?"
Wishing she knew, Laura broke into a cold sweat. First, she'd had to deal with Madeline and her antics, then with Jake leaving, and now with a change in judges. Why in the name of God couldn't Judge Harrison Neal, who had a ninety-two percent stepparent adoption approval rating, have waited one more day to let his appendix get acute? Then she could be talking with him about her adoption of Timmy, rather than with Judge Victor Barton. "Bad Ass Bear" had a lousy sixty-seven percent approval rating, as well as a reputation on other cases for consistently rendering maximum sentences.

Jake gone, and all her research up in smoke over a damn appendix Judge Neal didn't need anyway. Didn't it just figure?

"Mrs. Logan, I don't have all day." Bear drummed his fingers on his desk. His shock of gray hair stood on end, proving he'd heard a lot of horrific cases in his forty-plus years on the bench in the State of California court system. "Could you answer my question, please? Due to Judge Neal's unexpected illness, I have a double caseload today."

Judge Neal's unexpected, poorly-timed, and ex-tremely-inconvenient-for-Bear-too, illness, gauging by the impatience in his voice. "I apologize, your honor." She glanced to Timmy, seated beside her, and the judge's question flew right out of her mind.

Timmy's eyes were saucer-wide and his cheeks were as pale as sand. He looked so much like Jake, with his midnight-black hair and dove-gray eyes. Her heart-strings suffered a familiar little tug, and she noted how tense Timmy had become. With all of her own misgiv-ings, reassuring him wouldn't be easy, but she dredged up enough confidence to give him a wink.

"Mrs. Logan?" Bear frowned down at her over the top of his black-frame glasses. "It's customary for the parent, as well as the prospective parent, to attend these proceedings. Where is your husband?"

Bear was thoroughly irritated now; his brows had flattened to slashes above his eyes, and a muscle in his jaw ticked as steady as a pulse. Facts were facts, and she might as well face them. He'd walked into his chamber angry, and her answer wasn't going to do a thing to sweeten his mood. "I don't know."

Surprise streaked through his eyes and made tracks of the deep groves that ran alongside his mouth, nose to chin. "You don't know?"

God help her, with him growling like that, she didn't stand a chance of getting him to approve this adoption. Not without compromising Jake. "No, sir, I don't. Not exactly."

"Is he even in the state of California?"

He could be anywhere in the world. "I'm not sure."

"When will he return?"

She stiffened. Bear would like this response even less. "I'm afraid I don't know that, either."

His frown deepened further, and he rubbed at his forehead as if it were pounding. "Mister Logan does know he's supposed to be here, doesn't he?''

"Major Logan." She corrected him, then nodded. "Yes, sir, he knows. Unfortunately, he was sent TDY last night." Good grief, this wasn't getting a bit better. Now Bear's face had gone red and he had no-way-am-I-agreeing-to-this-adoption scribbled through every outraged wrinkle.

"TDY?"

"Temporary Duty," she explained. "Jake is in the Air Force, your Honor." Maybe this disclosure would soften his attitude. "When duty calls, he has no choice but to answer. Even if this proceeding is a thousand times more important to him personally. You see, a military officer's first obligation is to his country. His family must come second, and—"

"I'm aware of the military officer's obligations, Mrs. Logan." Bear flipped their file closed.

His decision had been made.

Laura's heart sank, and then it thudded as hard as if she'd run a two-hour race, all uphill. This adoption had to go through; Timmy's safety demanded it, and she and Jake had sacrificed so much to make it happen. Bear couldn't just say no, not without hearing her out. She had to *do* something. *Fast.* "May I speak with you privately for a moment, your Honor?"

"I've been a judge a long time, Mrs. Logan, and never, not once, have I approved a stepparent adoption when the natural parent of the child, namely your husband, failed to appear in my chamber during proceedings."

Timmy gasped.

Laura laced their hands and then squeezed his tightly. More than a little irked at Bear for frightening her son, she met Bear's scowl with a frown. Holding it wasn't easy though, even if his callous attitude had pricked her temper. The man sounded as mean as he looked. "If it were possible, Jake would be here. It's not. And, while his absence might seem odd to you, to us it's just another routine challenge. We face them with monotonous regularity, your Honor. All military families do. We're accustomed to missed birthdays, first days of school, Christmas pageants, births, graduations, surgeries, and, yes, even adoptions. But before you find fault with us, you should pause long enough to recall that it's our willingness to endure those challenges which allows people like you to enjoy life without them."

Before he could interrupt, much less yell at her—he looked dangerously close—she tamped down her temper and turned to Timmy. "Honey, please go sit on the sofa in the waiting room for a minute. I want to talk with Judge Bear alone, okay?"

Timmy nodded, looking wary. "You're not gonna cry, are you?"

"Of course not." She plastered a smile on her lips, knowing it more closely resembled a snarl. Hopefully, he'd be so relieved she wasn't going to cry he wouldn't notice the difference.

He noticed. Tugging at his necktie, he gave the judge a sympathetic boy-are-you-in-for-it-now look, then walked out to the waiting room.

"Close the door, Tiger," Laura said, without looking back. "All the way."

Wondering if all mothers had invisible eyes in the back of their heads, Bear watched the boy. Good quality navy blue suit, classic white shirt, red and blue silk tie that he clearly hated wearing about as much as Bear himself hated neckties. But Timmy's shoulders weren't slumped, and his spine was straight; his self-esteem appeared intact. He was well mannered, too, and that sympathetic look he'd shot Bear had been downright amusing. Though not nearly so much so as Mrs. Logan's slip of tongue. A slip she obviously didn't realize she'd made. Judge *Bear*. He'd nearly given in to the urge for a knee-slapping laugh. He didn't, of course. He had an image to maintain. But he'd sure wanted to do it.

She was a beautiful woman. He'd give Jake Logan points for taste. About thirty-five, classic bones, auburn hair sheared to her chin, shiny and smooth and framing her face. Her eyes were a remarkable shade of blue, too. Like the sky in summer, when they weren't reprimanding him. Then they darkened to the sleety color of storm clouds. Striking, that. She feared him, but she hadn't cowered like most. Hell, the woman actually had stood up to him and had put him in his place about Jake's absence. Bear had to respect that. And she smelled like spring flowers just after a soft rain.

Beautiful and vulnerable, but the woman was holding out on Bear. And he, by God, meant to find out why. It was his responsibility to make sure Timmy's interests were protected. Having come from an abusive home himself, that was a duty Bear took to heart, which evidenced itself in his ratings. "My name is Barton," he told her, having no idea why.

"Excuse me?" She glanced up at him, her eyes not quite focused.

What was she fishing for in her purse? "Barton," he explained. "You told Timmy my name was Judge Bear. It's Barton."

"Oh, God." Her cheeks flamed red. So did her neck.

He'd lay odds the woman was praying for an earthquake to crack open the floor and suck her down. It was all Bear could do not to laugh in her face. He knew his reputation. Close friends had called him Bear all his life, but Laura Logan couldn't know that. However, Bad Ass Bear was a moniker he'd earned on the bench. One he liked and worked hard to retain because it reminded him that he was doing his job well, and that what he was doing affected lives. It mattered.

"I'm so sorry," she stammered.

He bet she was. She reminded him of his daughter, Crystal. Other than his wife, Crystal had been the only person to ever call him Bad Ass Bear to his face. He had no idea why, but he felt certain that if he and Laura Logan met outside his court, she'd have the guts to do it, too.

She held out two documents, and Bear took them. "What are these?"

"Powers of attorney Jake left with me." She swept her hair back from her cheek. "I'm afraid I left you with the wrong impression earlier. Jake is extremely responsible, and he loves us very much."

She didn't quite meet the judge's eyes during that admission, and he couldn't help but to wonder why.

"Jake never leaves home without a thought to his family, though we do sacrifice a lot because of his career. He sacrifices, too, and we understand that. Timmy and I consider it our patriotic duty. On that part, I think I was clear, and as truthful as I can be."

Had she lied on another part, then?

"My point is, while I don't know exactly where Jake is, I do have a number to call in case of an emergency. And those." She nodded to the documents. "In Jake's absence, I can transact whatever I must for him. If he didn't trust me implicitly, he'd hardly grant me his unlimited, indefinite powers of attorney."

Bear looked down at the documents. One was unlimited for a year, granting her blanket authority. The other was unlimited and open-ended, with an attachment that gave her full authority to make any and all decisions, specifically citing medical treatment and matters regarding Timmy.

Bear noted the date. He withheld a frown, but he

didn't like the looks of this. Not at all. Of course, it was common for parents to do all sorts of things right before court that they never had done before then. Yet, while Mrs. Logan looked determined and scared stiff, she also looked as if she was hiding something important from Bear. And he'd be damned if she'd leave his chamber with the boy before Bear figured out what.

He started digging. "Does your husband go TDY often?"

"It depends." She gave him a delicate shrug. "Long-term planning is a challenge. Truthfully, sometimes short-term planning isn't much easier."

"Why then didn't you have these powers of attorney before yesterday?"

A puzzled frown wrinkled her brow. "What?"

"They're dated yesterday." Bear lifted the documents, then scanned the file. "You've been married to Jake Logan for two years. What if prior to now Jake had been TDY and Timmy had needed medical treatment?"

"Oh," she said on a relieved little sigh. "We get new ones every time, er, from time to time. But I have permanent authorization filed with the hospital at Clare Air Force Base. That's where Timmy is treated."

"What if he were away from Clare?"

"The other hospital would call Clare, and they'd fax a copy over."

Bear persisted. "And if it were after hours?"

She gave him a solid frown he'd have to be dead to miss. "The records department at the base hospital never closes. But if there should be an earthquake, or a flood, or some other disastrous act of God, then I'd just flip out the card I carry with me." Clearly anticipating another comeback, she added, "And if someone had stolen my purse, then I'd just not mention that god-awful 'step' word. We don't use it, and they'd never know the difference. Bottom line is that Timmy *would* get treatment."

The woman surprised him. Bear had thought her docile. Holding out on him, but docile. And perhaps she was docile, but not when it came to Timmy. "So you'd lie for him," Bear said softly. "Is that what you're telling me, Mrs. Logan?"

Her expression went from tense to taut, but her gaze blazed hot with defiance. "Yes, that's exactly what I'm telling you. In an emergency situation, I'd do whatever I had to do to see my son protected. If you want to fault me for that, well, you go right ahead. And before you bother asking, I'll just tell you that this adoption won't do a thing to change that fact. Either way, I'll always do what I have to do for Timmy."

"For your husband?" Bear asked, not sure what to make of her impassioned speech.

"For Timmy," she countered, glaring at Bear as if he harbored a few loose screws. Then she tilted her head, and added, "And for Jake, too. He'd expect it, and so would I."

The shadows had left her eyes. They were friends as well as husband and wife, that much was clear. "Mrs. Logan, you know I'm not intimately familiar with your case. I'm aware your husband is an Air Force Major, but what exactly does he do?"

She met his eyes easily. "Whatever his superiors order him to do."

"Whatever, whenever, eh?"

"And wherever, your Honor."

The guarded expression returned to her face, and again her eyes looked haunted. She feared for her husband's safety. Bear supposed that natural, considering. "There's a note on the file that this adoption proceeding was started twice before and stopped prior to completion. Why is that? Did you change your mind?"

"Of course not!" Laura hissed in a gasp, and nearly died of embarrassment. *Had she really just shouted at Bad Ass Bear?* Good Lord, she must have lost her mind. She licked at her lips and warned herself not to foolishly lose her temper again. Without Jake being there, Bear needed little reason to kick her out of his office without the adoption papers, and Timmy's security required them. "Madeline withdrew her consent."

"Madeline?"

"Jake's ex-wife," Laura explained. By the look on the judge's face, she was in deep kimchee. She was going to have to spill out the whole sordid story, or he'd never sign on the dotted line. "Madeline is an alcoholic, your Honor. That's what caused the divorce, and it's one of the reasons this adoption is so important."

"I see."

He didn't. Not yet. "Madeline actually lost Timmy once. Lost him, for God's sake. He was only three years old at the time. Jake was positively frantic. We found Timmy in the park, unharmed, thank heaven, though it took a long time to calm him down. He was half-starved and positively filthy. It broke our hearts. Madeline had to have been on a long binge that time, though I'd talked to Timmy on the phone just the day before and he'd told me he was okay."

Laura still beat herself up about that lapse in her judgment. She should have gone over and seen Timmy for herself. "As I'm sure you can imagine, Jake was livid. He told Madeline he'd had it. She had to get help, or he'd get a divorce." Laura shook her head and stared at the ceiling. "He'd tried repeatedly to get her into a treatment program, of course. And she'd made a litany of promises to go, but she never followed through on them." Laura looked back at Bear. "After that incident, Jake had no choice. He made the right decision, your Honor, but it was by no means an easy one for him. It might sound a little old-fashioned, but marriage is sacred to Jake.''

Bear had heard that before about marriage. Beliefs were one thing. A man living by them too often proved to be another matter entirely. "You helped Jake search for Timmy, then?"

"Six hours worth." She nodded. "We were terrified. There'd been a boy kidnapped in the neighborhood not two weeks earlier, and I couldn't help but to fear he'd taken Timmy, too."

Bear dipped his chin, getting a fix on how Laura Logan's mind worked. "But you didn't tell Jake about that, did you?"

Her cheeks reddened and she wrung her hands in her lap. "Not until after we found Timmy, no. Jake was so worried already. I just . . . couldn't."

Bear hated to ask, but he had to know. "Mrs. Logan, were you and Jake having an affair during his marriage to Madeline?"

Her eyes widened and anger flooded them. "Absolutely not."

He believed her. "But you were friends."

"Yes. We met thirteen years ago at jungle survival school. I was in the military too then." A hint of a smile curled her lip. "I'd just started working on a fascinating new communication device—" She caught herself, hushed, and the guarded look returned to her eyes. Resigned to having to disclose the confrontation between her and Paul Hawkins, she continued. "During one of the exercises, an officer also there for training flipped out and tried to kill me. Jake saved my life. The officer lied about the attack, pulling the she's-a-woman bit."

"What bit is that?"

"I had become emotional and overreacted because I'm a woman, and women do that." A delicate snort conveyed her feelings on that theory and tactic. "It was too absurd. I could have shaken the man. I didn't over-react, of course, and Jake said so at the hearing." The hearing, where Hawkins had been dishonorably discharged from the Air Force, and Laura had learned what it felt like to have someone look at you with pure hatred. "If Jake hadn't stopped him, the man would have killed me." Remembering it still gave her the shivers. "Anyway, Jake and I have been friends ever since then."

"Until two years ago, when you married. Two years ago today, in fact." Another occasion important to Jake and Laura Logan that he'd miss due to duty. Bear looked up, and his voice went soft. "Happy anniversary, Mrs. Logan."

"Thank you." Laura swallowed hard. *Oh, please, please don't let him start putting dates together. Please!*

"I couldn't help but notice that you married a few weeks after the former Mrs. Logan filed suit against Major Logan seeking custody of Timmy."

Couldn't Laura get even one small break here? "That's correct, yes, sir."

"I presume the two events are connected."

If his gaze got any harder, he'd bore her right through the floor. She could lie, but some instinct warned her not to do it, and she trusted her instincts. As a former Special Operations officer like Jake, she'd often had to rely on those instincts to stay alive. Still, her voice dropped to just above a whisper. "We do all we can to protect Timmy."

"From what?"

She forced herself to meet his gaze. "From anything that might harm him."

"Would that include a drunken birth mother?"

Put like that, it sounded so cold and heartless, when it was anything but. Madeline was an adult who refused treatment. Timmy was a helpless child—and their responsibility. Not a bit less terrified than when Timmy had been missing, or when on a mission a year ago, Jake erroneously had been reported dead, Laura silently nodded.

Bear tapped his pen against the desk, then leaned forward and braced his face on his hand, his bent elbow propped right in the center of their file. "Do you love Timmy, Mrs. Logan?"

The fear left her face and she openly smiled. "With all my heart."

"I noticed he calls you 'Mom.' Did you or Jake ask him to do that?"

"No, sir. He asked if he could, and I told him he could call me whatever he wanted to, so long as he called me whenever he needed me."

"How'd Madeline react to that?"

Laura blinked, then shrugged. "I'm not sure she's noticed."

Bear nodded thoughtfully. Between Harrison Neal's notes and Laura Logan, Bear now had a firm grasp on the situation. Major Jake Logan was a Special Ops officer in the Air Force. His lovely wife, Laura, a former Special Ops officer and captain, was now a civil servant, a publicity officer in the Public Affairs Office at Clare Air Force Base. Jake had saved her life thirteen years ago and they'd been close friends, but no more, ever since. He'd divorced his wife for neglecting their son while he was away on duty, and because she was an alcoholic who cited stress as her reason for drinking and refused to get help. When she'd sued for custody of Timmy—an attack of conscience. That happened often—then Jake had panicked and had asked his friend,

Laura, to marry him in order to better his odds of keeping custody of Timmy. She'd agreed to protect the child.

Yet now, two years later, Jake and Laura Logan were still together.

Why?

Because Jake's job was dangerous and the former Mrs. Logan still posed a threat to the boy's safety? Could be.

Because Jake could be killed on or off duty, and Timmy would be left vulnerable? Maybe.

Bear had a hunch that with a quick look at CNN Headline News, he'd have a good fix on where Jake Logan had been sent TDY. Special Ops officers were deployed to hot spots around the world. Of course, even if specifically asked, Mrs. Logan would claim her husband was away on a routine training mission. But Bear knew that these officers acted as forerunners to those hot spots. They rendered search and rescue missions. But they also performed assignments they couldn't admit to, in places they had officially never been, interacting with individuals who didn't exist, on topics they could never discuss.

Such was the nature of many Special Operations.

And that would explain the fear that crept into Laura Logan's eyes whenever Bear treaded too closely to the topic of Jake's work or his whereabouts. Considering the importance of why she was here, she didn't want to lie to Bear. But she wouldn't compromise her husband's safety either. Bear understood her dilemma. Respected it. Hell, he even admired her handling of it and its challenges.

Yet the Logans could still be together for a number of other, unconnected reasons. Because friendship had grown to love. Familiarity. Trust. A hatred of being alone. Or they could be together solely for the boy.

What their true reason was, Bear couldn't know. Not without talking to Timmy.

What Bear had learned was important, and now he understood. Laura Logan wasn't being evasive because she didn't want to tell Bear about Jake's job. She *couldn't* tell him. She knew little herself—safer for her that way—but what she did know, if revealed, could jeopardize her husband's life, and that Laura Logan never would do.

Feeling better now that he had a grasp on this situation, Bear leaned back in his chair. "Is there anything else you want to say to me, Mrs. Logan?"

Her eyes stretched wide and she swallowed hard. "Only that my husband is a good father, and I'm a good mother to Timmy. We both love him very much." She lowered her gaze to her lap. "Jake's job is . . . sensitive." She snapped her gaze up to Bear's. "But that doesn't mean Timmy isn't the most important thing in the world to Jake. He is. Truly, your Honor."

The woman looked torn between ordering and begging him to sign the papers. Bear figured the ordering would cost her dignity less, but she'd willingly do either. That eased his mind a good deal on the matter. "I'll talk with Timmy now."

She looked stunned. "You'll decide today then? Without Jake?"

"Perhaps. We'll see what Timmy has to say," Bear told her, unwilling to commit. "Would you ask him to come in on your way out?"

"Yes. Of course." She gathered her purse, obviously forgetting it was open, and a tube of lipstick tumbled out along with a rabbit's foot, a four leaf clover laminated in plastic, and a rock. "Sorry."

Timmy's lucky charms, or hers? Bear withheld a smile by the skin of his teeth. Regardless of whom the good luck pieces belonged to, they had Bear breathing easier. He liked the way this case was shaping up.

Laura ushered Timmy back in, then stopped at the door.

"Mom?" The boy looked back at her, clearly unhappy she wasn't coming along.

Laura smiled brightly and nodded toward the chair, dropping her voice to a whisper. "Just talk to Judge Bear a few minutes," she said, lifting a white string of lint off his shoulder.

"But . . ." Panic edged the boy's voice and his wiry shoulders went board stiff.

By Bear's reckoning, it was an unreasonable fear. What wasn't right here? What was he missing? The interaction between them was fine; the boy undoubtedly depended on her for guidance and protection, and she certainly loved him. Even now, when she shook like a leaf, she smiled bravely to convince Timmy everything was all right.

"It'll be fine." She halted Timmy's protest. "Just tell the truth."

That stunned Timmy; his jaw had dropped open. And what exactly was Bear to make of that?

"It's not a test, Tiger. Just tell the truth." She eyed Timmy levelly, then pulled the door closed.

Seeing a crack of light along its edge, Bear frowned at the door. "All the way, Mrs. Logan."

When the door snapped shut, Timmy jumped. He looked scared to death but tried to hide it, just as Laura had. That too worried Bear, who recalled too many times during his youth when he'd been left alone with the demon bastard who'd fathered him. Lord, but he'd hated those times. And he'd resented them.

To put the boy at ease, Bear softened his voice and smiled. "Come sit down, and let's talk awhile."

Bear made small talk, deliberately trying to get

Timmy comfortable enough to lower his guard and speak freely. They talked baseball—Timmy was a big Cardinals fan, though his mom had refused to let him wear his cap to court.

After a few minutes, Timmy's pulse no longer throbbed at his throat and his Adam's apple stopped bobbing every ten seconds. Glad to see both, Bear asked, "Do you carry a wallet, Timmy?"

"Yes, sir." He pulled out a blue nylon wallet from his hip pocket. "I have to have my ID on me, in case I get sick or something."

"Would you mind if I took a look?"

"No, sir." He passed the wallet across the files on the desktop. "But I swear I ain't carrying."

"Carrying?" Bear opened the Velcro clasp.

Timmy's cheeks flushed red. "You know what I mean. Protection. For girls."

Condoms? Shock streaked up Bear's backbone. "I'd think not. You're only nine."

"I know. Most of the kids at school carry, though. I did too, so the guys wouldn't hassle me," he confessed as if it were a god-awful sin he was revealing. "But then Mom ran my wallet through the washer and—"

"She went through your wallet?" A woman should never go through a man's wallet. No more so than a man should go through a woman's purse.

"She and Mrs. Miller were just drying stuff out," Timmy said, defending her with offhanded ease. "That's when Mom found it."

Lord, Bear could just imagine the ruckus. "Who's Mrs. Miller?"

"She takes care of us, and we take care of her. Her husband died, and she's really old—thirty-nine and holding, she says—but she loves baseball."

More than a housekeeper, Bear surmised. Like one

of the family. "What happened—when they found the wallet?"

"Mom told Dad, and then *strongly* suggested he and I have a serious discussion."

"Oh, boy."

Timmy nodded enthusiastically. "I thought I was dead."

Bear's grimace turned real, and deep. "Really?"

"Naw. Dad was serious, though. And not too happy. He can look mean when he wants to," Timmy confided, then gave Bear a lopsided grin. "He said until I understood the meaning behind sex, I'd best only use the—you know—for a water balloon."

Bear laughed out loud. What a treat this child was; easy to see how he'd captured Laura's heart. And his father's, too.

Wishing he'd been a fly on the wall during that conversation, Bear flipped through the photos and then stopped at one of Laura, Jake, and Timmy. They were all wearing red clown noses and laughing, looking happy and acting silly at some kind of festival, judging from the Ferris wheel in the background. That scene settled on the favorable side in Bear's mind.

"Timmy, have you seen your mom lose her temper?" Though pushing sixty, the hurt boy in Bear had to know absolutely and unequivocally this adoption was best for Timmy. That he'd be treated well. Cherished. Loved unconditionally.

"Oh, yeah." Timmy slid closer, onto the edge of his chair, then propped his arm on the edge of Bear's desk and groused at the tight tie choking his neck. "When Mr. Flint said I cheated on a test, Mom got really . . . lost her temper."

Bear waved to the tie. "Take that thing off before it smothers you. We're just friends, having a little chat. No need to be formal."

"Thanks." Timmy couldn't wrangle out of the tie fast enough. When it hung loose, he gulped in air deeply.

Bear buried a smile behind his hand. "Better?"

"Lots." He grinned.

Something occurred to Bear. Timmy *never* referred to Laura as "Laura," always as "Mom." That came too natural to be anything other than the way the child thought, which meant that's how he felt down deep. Bear liked it. "So your mom got angry at you for cheating." Couldn't fault her for that.

"I didn't cheat," Timmy insisted.

Confused, Bear looked back from the photo to the boy. "But you said—"

"She was ticked off at Mr. Flint, not at me. For calling me a liar." Timmy looked righteously indignant. "I wasn't lying. Mom asked me, and I told her I hadn't cheated. That's when Mr. Flint called me a liar."

"And when your mom lost her temper."

"Boy, did she. She pounded her fist on his desk, and even yelled. Old Man Flint—" Timmy halted abruptly, and his face burned red. "Mr. Flint, I mean. She told Mr. Flint that if he didn't take it back, she'd go to the principal and complain. Just because I was eight, that didn't mean I didn't have integrity."

Eight. Last year. "Did Mr. Flint take it back?"

"You bet he did." Timmy looked pleased by that fact. "Mom's really nice, but you don't mess with her when she gets like that."

"I would think not."

"When Dad got home, I told him about it. He knew something was up because Mom had fixed double chocolate fudge brownies and chocolate ice cream for dessert. Those are Dad's favorites. He said Mom's a little protective of me.'' Timmy shrugged as if that mattered little.

But his action and the tremble in his voice proved very telling. It mattered a lot. The boy loved Laura Logan, and he trusted her completely. And if that wasn't the best reason for granting an adoption, then Bear didn't know what the hell was.

''You're close—you and your mom.''

''Well, sure.'' Timmy looked a little uncertain, then gave Bear a crooked grin. ''Dad says we're partners in crime.''

Bear couldn't help himself. He grinned back. ''Criminals, eh?''

''Yeah. But not really,'' Timmy quickly assured him, distinctly recalling who he was talking to, and why.

Then Bear asked a question he already could answer. ''Timmy, do you think your mom loves you?''

''Sure.''

No hesitation, nor any doubt. Bear liked that, too. ''Do you love her?''

''Yeah. But don't tell the guys at school.'' He grimaced. ''I'm taking enough heat for not carrying. They find out I love my mom too, and I'm history.''

''Everything said in here is confidential,'' Bear informed him. ''I won't say a word.''

Timmy looked enormously relieved.

Bear turned to the back of the photos, and saw one of another woman. She looked too much like Timmy not to be his birth mother. Odd, that he'd carry her photo in his wallet. She'd caused him a lot of pain. ''Who's this?''

''That's Madeline,'' he said easily. ''She had me.''

''I see.'' Now what should Bear make of that? Timmy obviously cared for the woman or he wouldn't have her photo in his wallet. Hearing him talking on,

Bear turned his attention. "I'm sorry, son. What did you say?"

"I said, I don't look at it much, but Mom says it's not right for any of us to be mad at Madeline. She's sick, and we have to have compassion."

"You do have compassion, but you're still mad at her, aren't you, Timmy?" Bear asked in a voice made soft by memory, empathy, and understanding.

"Yeah. She used to get drunk and forget me places. It was scary—when I was a little kid. Not now that I'm big, of course."

"Of course."

"I stay away from her now."

Hearing his own determination to stay away from his demon bastard father in Timmy's voice, Bear nodded, comprehending completely Timmy's state of mind regarding his birth mother. He didn't hate her. He just didn't want her to hurt him anymore.

"She came to our house last night, and almost drove her car into the kitchen. We were going up to see Sutter's Mill—they found gold there a long time ago—but now we have to fix the grass this weekend instead."

Bear held off commenting. "Was something wrong with her car?"

"No. She was drunk." Timmy sighed. "I tried not to let Mom see how mad I was, but she could tell."

"Moms are smart that way."

"Yeah." Timmy stared at Bear's desk. "One time I heard her tell Dad that Madeline pulled the adoption papers because she had an attack of conscience." Timmy pursed his lips. "She's done that two times, so far."

Timmy apparently wasn't supposed to hear that conversation, but he had an opinion, and he wanted to voice it. "What do you think?"

He shrugged, but his gaze was fiercely intense. "I think she got worried her dad would get mad at her for giving me away. She cared what he thought. I didn't like him much, and he didn't like me, either. He's dead now—but don't tell Mom."

Madeline didn't care what Timmy thought, and his resentment of that seeped through in his tone. "Your mom doesn't know Madeline's dad is dead?"

"Sure, she knows that. We went to his funeral and everything. Madeline didn't, though. Mom and Dad thought that was weird, but I was too worried about looking at him dead to care."

"Did your parents make you look at the body?"

"No. They told me I didn't have to, but the lid was shut anyway. I was glad about that."

"So what doesn't your mom know, then?" Bear asked, a little confused.

Timmy looked at him as if Bear were an inattentive child. "She doesn't know I don't like them. Either of them," he deliberately repeated.

"Why not? If you told her, would your mom get angry?"

"Worse." Timmy grimaced.

Bear didn't like the sound of that. Could he have misjudged Laura Logan? "How could she be worse than angry?"

"She'd cry."

He hadn't misjudged her, after all. "Ah, I see."

Timmy gave Bear that look universal to men reacting to a woman's tears. "Dad and I don't like to see Mom cry."

Dad and I. Interesting. Bear rubbed his lower lip between his forefinger and thumb. "Does she cry often?"

"Naw. Just at sappy movies, and when Madeline takes back the papers. She cries a lot then." His gaze drifted. "And sometimes when she looks at me or Dad and she thinks we don't see her. She gets this weird look on her face. Kind of like we zapped her with a stun gun, or something. Then she cries."

"Touched," Bear said almost absently, recalling times when he'd caught his dear wife, Annie, looking at him and their daughter that same way.

"Huh?"

"When she looks at you like that, it's because she's feeling tender," Bear explained. "You touched her heart."

"Touched." Timmy smiled. "Yeah, that's kind of what Dad said. Anyway, we don't like Mom's tears. She's got a gentle heart, and it's our job to protect her. It's kind of hard because Madeline is always doing stupid stuff like last night."

And Timmy had about a bellyful of resentment because she did. They loved Laura. And she loved them. Whatever she was withholding from Bear, it couldn't be anything that jeopardized Timmy's welfare. Bear's decision was made. He nodded. "And now you want her to be your legal mother as well as your mom."

"Yeah." Timmy scratched at his neck, then gave Bear a frank look he recognized from Laura's earlier one. "It feels right," he said, tapping a finger to his chest, as if too embarrassed to say the words aloud. "In here."

"Yeah, to me, too." Laura Logan could have told Bear about these incidents with Madeline and hadn't. They were no doubt damaging to Timmy, and yet she'd not mentioned them. Likely she hadn't wanted it to appear she was slurring the birth mother. Bear kind of liked that. And these incidents were likely all she'd been withholding. Bear eased his glasses back onto his nose. "Why don't you ask your mom to come back in now, and we'll get this wrapped up."

"Yes, sir." Timmy went to the door and then called his mother.

Laura sat on the sofa waiting, worrying, praying, and nearly wringing the skin right off her hands. They'd been in there forever. Five more minutes of this, and she'd have a complete nervous breakdown. Jake would just have to forgive her. She could take him fighting international terrorists, rescuing hostages, and infiltrating enemy territory in war zones. Hell, she could take fighting those things herself, which was a good thing, considering her Intel reactivation on Operation Shadowpoint: a fact she should and would have disclosed to Jake last night if Madeline hadn't pulled that stunt with the car and he hadn't been called out on a mission. He'd be upset that she hadn't told him, of course, but Laura could deal with that, too. Hell, she could deal with *anything* else. But she couldn't take five minutes more of this. God, not of this.

"Mom," Timmy called again.

She nearly jumped out of her skin. "What?"

"Come on. Judge Barton wants to talk to you again."

Timmy didn't look upset. That thought gave Laura the courage to demand her legs get enough substance in them to carry her back into Bad Ass Bear's chamber. "How did it go?" she whispered.

Timmy smiled at her. "I like him."

Whatever had happened, it couldn't have been that bad. Not if Timmy liked the man. No one liked the man. Maybe it had gone okay. Maybe Timmy hadn't had to tell the judge that although she and Jake had been married two years, they'd really only lived together as a family under the same roof, this time, for the past three weeks. Long enough for the social worker to come out and be convinced theirs was a normal, well-adjusted, happy family.

She slid down on to the chair she'd occupied earlier.

The judge's secretary, Emily, followed them into the chamber. She was short and round with frizzy gray hair and glasses that dangled from a gold chain around her neck. "Judge Barton?"

Bear adjusted his glasses and looked up.

"There's a Mrs. Madeline Drake Logan on the phone," Emily said, her tank of a voice booming off the walls. "She says it's vital that she speaks with you immediately—regarding this case."

Laura and Timmy's faces both blanched white, and they literally clung to each other.

"She's gonna do it again, Mom," Timmy cried out in anger and fear.

"Oh, God." Laura locked hands with Timmy. Her knuckles went as white as her face.

Laura Logan was doing her damnedest to soothe the boy and to not let him see her fear, but it emanated from her. She was terrified. And while Timmy was too upset himself to see it, to Bear it was crystal clear. Both Laura and Timmy leveled you-can't-let-her-hurt-us-again looks on Bear that would arouse and engage protective instincts in the devil himself.

None of them had any illusions on why Madeline Drake Logan was calling. She'd withdrawn her consent twice already. This time, she'd waited a little longer. So long, thank God, that the choice had become Bear's.

"You know my phone policy, Emily," he told his secretary, not feeling even a twinge of doubt that he might be making a mistake. "Take a number." He scribbled his signature on the documents. "Then stamp and formally file these. I'd like the Logans to have a copy before they leave my chamber."

Five

⌒

The lighted Pizza Hut sign reflected on Laura's Mustang's windshield. Distorted by darkness and fat raindrops, it looked eerie.

Inside the building, Laura slid into a red vinyl booth, sporting chills and goose bumps. "God, I'm soaked." Her empty stomach protested. "And I'm starving."

"Me, too." Timmy slumped down in his seat across from her, slinging water from his face off his fingertip. "We should eat dessert pizza first."

"Use a napkin, Tiger." The restaurant wasn't very busy. Laura was glad about that. She needed a little quiet time to absorb the good news and to just enjoy. The last two days had been hell on her nerves, but it had been worth it. Every bit of it. "So you want to eat dessert before you run out of room, eh?"

"Yeah." He swiped at his face, then wadded up the napkin and tossed it onto the table. "Saves a belly-ache."

"That's worth considering." Her skirt pinching her waist, Laura tissued the rain from her face, then put her keys into her purse. They snagged a package of Wrigley's spearmint gum, and it tumbled onto the floor. "Oops."

"I'll get it." Timmy reached down and grabbed the package, then dumped it into her purse. "How come you carry gum all the time? You never chew it."

Some training a person never loses. The inner wrappers made a crude but effective signal-blocking device. She raised her eyebrows at him. "If we run into a leaky dike or something, you can chew the gum and we'll use it as a plug."

"Yeah." He laughed. "We see busted dikes all the time."

"Hey, it only takes one."

Grunting, he rolled his gaze. "Whatever, Mom."

The waitress appeared with glasses of water and Laura placed their order. "We're too hungry for a menu," she said. "Just bring us a large pepperoni, a root beer float, and a sweet iced tea."

Timmy grinned. Laura winked at him, knowing she'd ordered his favorites. "It's a celebration."

"Yeah." He shoved the salt shaker aside, over near the pepper. "I wish Dad was here, too."

"So does he, sweetheart," Laura said. "I know. We'll celebrate again when he gets home."

"Root beer floats, twice?" Timmy asked.

"Why not?" Laura hiked a shoulder. "You only get adopted once."

"All right." Timmy laughed.

Laura did, too. So did the waitress, who was putting the pizza and drinks on the table. "Congratulations," she said, her eyes twinkling, as she walked away.

Sensing someone at her shoulder, Laura glanced over, and her joy turned bitter. Madeline. Her raincoat was unbuttoned, and beneath it, she still wore the same black suit she'd had on when she tried her best to drive her car through the kitchen.

"You bribed that damn judge, didn't you?"

Laura masked her expression and dropped her voice

in the hope that Madeline would, too. "This is a private party, Madeline."

"Yes, I'll bet it is." Anger flooded her face and she swiped a hand over the table, knocking everything on it onto the floor.

Dishes clanged, pizza flew, and the root beer float splattered foamy ice cream and soda on chairs three seats away.

"The party's over."

The disturbance gained the attention of the manager, a brawny man about thirty, and he started over to the table.

"If you leave now," Laura said from between her teeth, "I won't have you arrested."

"Is everything okay here?" the manager asked Laura.

Laura didn't answer, just held Madeline's stare, ready for anything to happen.

Madeline leaned closer and the smell of sour Scotch tortured Laura's nostrils.

She dropped her voice so only Laura could hear. "This isn't over. I'll get the adoption overturned," she said, her eyes glinting slivers of steel. "And I'll get you and that goddamn judge for this. You might have bribed him, but you can't bribe me."

"Miss?" the manager persisted. "Is everything okay?"

Madeline glared back at him, then pulled herself upright and stumbled to the door.

Timmy sat woodenly staring at Madeline's retreating back, following her with his gaze until she left the building and the door swung closed.

"Everything is fine," Laura told the manager, forcing herself to smile. "We just had a minor accident. Totally my fault."

"No problem," he said, clearly aware Madeline had

caused the disturbance. "We'll get you some fresh food and drinks right away."

Laura gave the man a genuine smile. "Thank you."

Shadows from the ceiling fan's twirling paddles flickering over his face, he nodded, then headed toward the kitchen.

Timmy's jaw dropped open. "We're staying?"

Bless his heart. Laura reached over the table and clasped his cool hand in hers. "Remember me telling you that we can't control other people's actions, only our reactions to the things they do?"

He nodded.

"Well, if we leave now, then we're letting Madeline control our actions. I don't think we should do that. We came here to celebrate—and I've waited a long time to legally be able to call you my son—so I vote we stay."

Timmy thought it over, then agreed. "Yeah, me, too. We control us. Not her."

"Right." Laura could have hugged him. And she would have, except Madeline still sat outside in her car, watching them.

The swamp smelled dank.

Even gliding along in the airboat, the air felt thick and heavy and wet. The humidity had to be a hundred percent.

Alert to the night sounds, Jake identified them. The Everglades teemed with wildlife; in it, there were sixty-eight species of threatened and endangered animals—which he'd been warned not to terminate—alligators, the nocturnal raccoon, and snakes. Tons of snakes. He had seen a few in the moonlight but so far none had threatened him. Still, he knew to be on guard. Among others, rattlers, copperheads, and cottonmouths thrived here. They had to thrive there to earn a mention in the geographical briefing.

In survival school, Jake had insisted Laura kill the snakes, saying she feared them more than he did, and she had to overcome it. If ever taken prisoner, that fear would be used against her. Jake smiled at the memory. He'd rather face a platoon of the enemy armed to the teeth than a single rattler. She had known the truth, of course. Just as she had known the truth when he'd called her last night. The woman understood him as well as she understood herself, and she had understood that this time things were different. This mission was different.

Laura had taken care of Timmy even before he had been born, insisting to Jake that his son have a father he knew loved him. She'd been right about that. Timmy was worth every ounce of hell Madeline had put Jake through, and then some. And Laura had stood fast and loyal, helping Jake through all of it. Yeah, Laura was nothing if not long on loyalty. A good friend. The greatest. But fantasies were fantasies, and she could never be more.

I won't love you. And I won't forget it—not for a second.

He'd said and meant it, and he hadn't forgotten it, yet those wifely fantasies still were giving him hell. Why, he had no clue. He dealt with life and death every day. They had no future. He and Laura couldn't have each other. Not now. Not ever. And he knew better than even to fantasize otherwise.

Jake goosed the engine. A rush of warm air breezed over his skin. Still, she was special. He recalled a C-130 crash during a readiness exercise last spring. Jake had been assigned to the Accident Investigation Board. He'd known and worked with three of the eight crew members who had died.

After the six-week investigative TDY, he'd returned home with raw nerves and bruised inside. He'd seen too many die.

"It's the nature of the beast," Laura had said. "You do your duty and, if you survive, then you do it again."

She had sat with him, silently offering her support just by being there.

Jake hadn't been able to tell her then how much that meant to him. Friends just don't talk about some things, and that was one of them. Not even married friends. Especially married friends.

Less than two percent.

He had no right to tell her anything. They'd made an agreement. Settled on terms. And it was best for both of them to stick to them. They had no future. She didn't love him. Wasn't in love with him, and even in her wildest imagination, she couldn't fathom ever loving him. That truth still stung his ego, but it was right. For them, it was right.

The heart plays hell with logic, and the heart always wins. Jake had learned that lesson. And he didn't need a refresher course to remind him of it.

Watching a swarm of fireflies, he slowed the boat. A lot of stumps protruded up from the murky water. Tall and thin, they looked like spindly, twisted sentries, and he couldn't risk hitting one hiding just below the water's surface and screwing up the prop.

He couldn't risk a refresher course, either. In fact, last night he shouldn't even have called home. But knowing his survival odds, he had to talk to Laura and Timmy . . . just once more. Just in case.

So he'd buried the nagging fantasies, blaming them on the mission's adrenaline rush, and phoned home. And knowing it could be the last time he'd talk to either of them, before he could say a word, he'd had to force his heart out of his throat and back into his chest where it belonged.

"I've got a few more minutes of pounding the ramp before the flight takes off," he'd told her. "Thought I'd call and wish you luck tomorrow."

He was flying out and letting her know it. Aware their phone could be tapped by Intelligence, friends or foes, she had known better than to ask any questions or act as if this trip was unexpected or abnormal. But in his mind's eye, Jake had seen her scrambling for the remote, tuning in to CNN and muting the sound, trying to get a fix on where he might be headed.

"Thanks," she'd said. "We need all the luck we can get."

His voice had dropped a notch, unsteady as hell. "I wanted to wish Timmy luck, too. Any chance he's still up?"

With that request, she'd also known Jake was worried about this mission. To awaken Timmy, who always went to bed at The Big Nine-O, Jake had to be damn worried. And that no doubt had terrified Laura.

But her voice had come out as smooth as silk. She knew the drills. No surprise. No regret. No awkward emotions. "I hear his CD player. He's up. Hold on a second."

Timmy had come on the line, sounding sleep-fogged, and Jake had pictured him curled up on his *Star Wars* sheets, holding his lucky rabbit's foot. He always slept with his lucky rabbit's foot and his stuffed tiger. And Jake had wondered: Would he ever again get to slip into the bedroom during the night and watch his son sleep?

"Hi, Daddy," he'd said.

Daddy. Not *Dad*. Jake veered left, avoided a thick clump of swamp grass. Timmy definitely just had

awakened. He considered himself too old for *Daddy*
anymore. Jake missed it.

They'd talked for a few minutes, then Jake had said,
"Good luck tomorrow. I'll be thinking good
thoughts."

"Yeah."

"Hold down the fort." Jake always said that to
Timmy before leaving. Always. "And take care of
Mom." That, too. Funny how many little traditions
they'd developed without him realizing they were de-
veloping them. "I love you, Tiger."

"I love you, too, Dad."

Jake's heart swelled, feeling too big for his chest.
That was the reason he did what he did, took the risks
he took, led the life he led. For Timmy.

When Laura had come back on the line, her voice
had cracked. "Hurry home safe."

Hurry home safe. Jake squeezed the boat's steering
wheel and adjusted the throttle. She'd known, all right.
In thirteen years of friendship, of crises and triumphs—
hers and his—not once had Laura Logan ever said anything like that to Jake.

This mission wasn't routine. Jake knew it, and with
that phone call home, Laura knew it, too. That was a
fringe benefit of marrying a former Special Ops officer.
Or a curse. Rather than being blissfully oblivious, she
had recognized the signs of trouble. And the signs of
fear.

Jake's life was always at stake. They both knew that
came with the job. But he wasn't always under immediate threat.

He was now.

And, God help him, he was fighting it hard but falling into a trap he had sworn to steer clear of forever:
Seeing Laura, a woman he could never have, not as his
friend, but as an attractive woman. As his wife.

The airboat's engine groaned.

Jake pulled back on the throttle, slowing the boat to a stop near two twisted oaks on what looked like a little island of solid ground in the marsh. He wished he could be at home with her and Timmy now instead of in this sweltering sweat box of a swamp, getting eaten alive by mosquitoes. He wished he knew whether or not the damn adoption had gone through.

With less than a two percent chance of survival, Jake really needed to know if the adoption had gone through. And, since he was wishing, he wished he knew if Laura even had remembered that today was their anniversary. Telling himself that he was merely curious, that it didn't make a damn bit of difference, he wished he knew if during their two-year marriage she ever had thought of herself as his wife.

Had she? Even once?

Six

When Laura and Timmy left Pizza Hut, Madeline was nowhere in sight.

Laura checked her watch. Madeline had pulled out of the parking lot a good fifteen minutes ago, but an uneasy feeling that she was close nagged at Laura and kept her on alert. Madeline had been in Intel, and even an airhead screw-up with a serious drinking problem could pick up a lot of potentially dangerous skills there, which is why Laura braved the rain to run a hasty check on the car. She hadn't lost sight of Madeline since she'd left the restaurant, but Laura hadn't seen the woman come in. She could have done something to the Mustang then.

Everything looked okay, so Laura told Timmy to get in, then cranked the engine. Jake had been on her back for at least three years to replace it, but she liked the old car. It fit her, and it felt comfortable.

She backed out of the slot, shifted the four-on-the-floor transmission into first gear, and then pulled out onto Manzanita Street into traffic. Street lights turned the wet pavement into shimmering amber gold, and the rain came down in thick sheets, pelting against the roof and hood. Passing the bowling alley, she flipped on the defroster, then turned the wipers up a notch.

Timmy adjusted the strap on his seat belt, then reinserted the end into the slot. It clicked it back into place. "Mom?"

"Mmm?" Why wouldn't the transmission shift into second gear? The damn thing seemed stuck. She checked the rearview mirror. It was blissfully empty of headlights. Slowing down, she again attempted to shift. Nothing moved.

"What's wrong with the car?"

"I don't know. It seems frozen in first gear." That couldn't be due to Madeline. So while it was a nuisance, it didn't inspire deep concerns.

"Can we make it home?" Timmy sounded worried.

"Sure." She flashed him a smile. "It's only a couple more blocks. We'll just have to go slowly."

Reassured, Timmy turned his gaze back to the windshield. From the set of his jaw though, something was on his mind. Something important. He'd hinted at it during their celebration dinner, but he hadn't yet come forth with whatever was troubling him. Maybe he needed a little encouragement. "What's eating at you, Tiger?"

"Nothing." He shrugged.

"Uh-oh."

He frowned at her. "What's that mean?"

"Every single time you say 'nothing' in that tone and you shrug, it's something." The windshield misted over. She flipped the wiper control up to High, then watched the blades sweep the glass, hearing their familiar *clack, clack, clack.* "Come on," she said, half-figuring he needed to vent about Madeline's stunt at Pizza Hut. "Out with it."

Timmy let out a sigh that could part hair on a woman's head or turn it gray. "I was just kind of wondering something."

Now he was shoving his tie deeper into his jacket pocket. Whatever this was, it meant a lot to him. Timmy never fidgeted or hesitated unless he was carrying a bomb of an inquiry. "About what?"

"You're really my mom now, right?"

"Right." Satisfaction warmed her chest. Finally, she had a son. An adorable, wonderful, eat-your-heart-out-the-rest-of-the-world son.

"Does that mean you'll live with me and Dad and Mrs. Miller forever and really be my mom now? Or are you going to move back to the apartment again?"

The longing in Timmy's voice had Laura curling her fingers around the wheel until she held it in a raised-knuckle grip. Her heart beat so hard she could feel its pounding in her temples and toes. She had to tread softly here; she knew that well. When she'd moved in with Timmy and Jake the first and second times, she and Jake had explained carefully that the reason was to get Timmy adopted. Their live-in housekeeper, Mrs. Betsy Miller, who'd once been Laura's newly widowed next-door neighbor, had helped them reinforce to Timmy that Laura living with them was a temporary thing.

But, as kids do, Timmy quickly had grown accustomed to having a mom and a dad around, and when Laura had moved back home, Timmy had been hurt and angry. He'd sulked for weeks, until Laura had nailed the core cause of his upset. Despite her and Jake's reassurances that she loved Timmy as much as always, he had gotten it into his head that she thought him too much trouble, so she'd left him, just as Madeline had left him. Timmy, bless his heart, had felt abandoned and unloved.

This time, before Laura had moved in, she and Jake had emphasized their living together as a temporary arrangement even more strongly, and they'd thoroughly explained the reasons necessitating it, trusting that Timmy was mature enough to understand the truth. He had understood. But, evidently, the little boy who yearned for a real mom still resided there inside him.

God help her to handle this right. For all of them.

The transmission whined. Laura eased off the accelerator, pushed in the clutch, and then again tried to shift. Still frozen and refusing to budge. Her voice went soft. "What do you want me to do, Timmy?"

"Having a mom would be kind of nice." He turned away from her and stared out through the side window. "If you wanted to stay with Dad and me, it'd be okay."

He wanted a mom around desperately. Tears swam up into Laura's throat. "You know I love you with all my heart, right?"

"Right."

"Either way. Living in the same house or not."

"Either way."

His idea held far more appeal than it should. "I'll talk it over with your dad." Whenever he got his buns home—which she hoped would be soon. She also hoped he'd return safe. "But no promises, okay?"

"Sure." Timmy shrugged.

Laura hated his shrugs. She really did. He only shrugged when something mattered too much—cut too close to the bone. She reached over and clasped his cool hand with hers. "On the same planet or not, much less in the same house or not, I'll love you forever. That's a promise, Tiger."

"And you never break your promises," he said, sounding gruff, but grinning. "Yeah, I know."

"And?" She hiked an eyebrow at him.

"And I love you, too." His grin widened, spreading cheek to cheek. He rubbed at his stomach, devilment dancing in his eyes. "Even if you do make me eat too much pizza before I can have the dessert kind."

Laura laughed, just as he'd intended. God, but he was so much like his father. Jake pulled that stunt regularly. Get too serious, too close, and he teased his way back to emotionally safer ground.

"Mom." Looking out the side mirror, Timmy gasped. His voice screeched, loud and tinny. "That car's coming up behind us too fast."

Laura darted a glance into the rearview mirror. The car was coming far too fast, and with only first gear, she couldn't speed up to get out of its way. It was going to hit them.

Laura reached over, pushed against the back of Timmy's head. "Keep your head down between your knees."

The car clipped their right rear fender.

Laura jerked. Timmy grunted. Glass broke; the taillight had shattered. The Mustang skidded on the wet pavement. Laura gripped the wheel hard, veered right, and glanced back into the mirror. Damn it, why couldn't she get a fix on the car? Was it Madeline?

The car hit them again.

Suffering the jarring jolt, Laura yelled, "Stay down, Timmy."

Passing under a street light, she kept her gaze glued to the car behind her. When the light crossed its hood, she recognized the car. Madeline's. Damn the woman. If she wanted Timmy so badly, then why in the name of God was she risking killing him?

Madeline backed off, and Laura's blood chilled to ice. She was setting up to come at them again; Laura sensed it. What could she do?

She scanned frantically, looking for some way out, some safe place. A residential neighborhood on the left. A Wal-Mart parking lot full of people and cars on the right. And at the foot of the lot—a dumpster.

A plan formed, and Laura whipped into the lot behind the dumpster, then slammed on her brakes and stopped. "Stay down, Timmy. Don't move." She watched the mirror in a cold sweat and saw Madeline pull in behind her and stop about fifty feet away.

Laura had one shot at this. One shot, and her timing had to be perfect, or she and Timmy would get creamed. She clenched the steering wheel in a white-knuckle grip. *Please, God. Please!*

The lights moved. Madeline was coming . . . fast.

"Mom." Timmy's voice rattled with fear. "She's gonna hit us again!"

"Stay down!" The temptation to move burned strong, then stronger. Laura fought it. She watched Madeline's car barrel down on them. Not . . . yet. Not . . . yet. Not . . . *now!*

Laura stomped the accelerator. The tires spun and churned up smoke, squealed, and then gained traction on the wet pavement. The car lunged forward. Fishtailing out of Madeline's path, Laura grappled for control and got it.

Madeline rammed into the dumpster.

Metal crunched. Glass broke. And her car came to an abrupt halt.

A safe distance away, Laura pulled to a stop and then dragged in three deep breaths, steadying herself. "You okay, Tiger?"

He sat up and stared over at Madeline's car. "Yeah."

"Good." Shaking head to toe, Laura patted his hand. "Stay here. I'll be right back."

Fury fueling her, Laura stepped out into the rain, slammed the car door shut, and then strode back toward Madeline's car. The front end had folded. It wasn't going anywhere, not without a tow truck.

Madeline climbed out of the car, unfortunately, screaming.

And Laura had maxed on listening to it. She stormed over to the woman. "You've annoyed me in the past, but this time you've gone too far."

"I've annoyed you?" Madeline huffed. "You bribed that judge, bitch. I know you did."

"You want Timmy, then you give it your best shot to get him legally. But don't you dare ever endanger his life with antics like this again. Jake might not have your ass jailed, but I will." Laura trembled with rage, spat out from between her teeth. "Stay away from us, Madeline. Stay away, or you'll wish to God you were safe in jail."

Madeline leaned a hip against the door of her car, looking for all the world as if she were out on a Sunday drive rather than standing in the rain being confronted by a woman she'd just attempted to run over.

"He wasn't in danger." She lifted a hand and twisted her lips into an infuriating smile. "My foot slipped and I slid on the wet pavement. That's all. I didn't hit you intentionally."

"Three times?" Laura grunted. "Right."

Madeline shrugged. "Accidents happen."

"Tell it to the authorities. Maybe they'll buy into that trash, but I'm not." Laura stiffened her spine, lifted a warning finger. "Stay away from us. And don't you ever, ever jeopardize Timmy again."

Madeline laughed and snorted. "Or what?"

Walking away from her, Laura turned back, stopped, and stared at the woman. At that moment, she hated Madeline through to her very soul. "Or I'll kill you."

Madeline's jaw went lax, and she gaped at Laura.

Shocked herself at that disclosure, and so outraged that she feared she might do it, Laura returned to her car and then quickly drove away.

Which upset her most, she couldn't honestly say. That Madeline had endangered Timmy's life, or that Laura had threatened to kill the woman, and she'd meant it. Never in her life had she lost control like that.

But never before had she been a real mother.

Motherly instincts. That's what it was. Had to be.

And how exactly was Jake going to react to knowing the adoptive mother of his son had threatened to commit murder?

When he found out, he would understand perfectly— or he'd hear a lecture that would make him wish to hell he had.

Jake would have to move in from here on foot.

He removed his night vision goggles and set them aside, slung the strap to his black carryall onto his shoulder, then left the airboat.

Moonlight slanted through the trees. Spotting a half-inch long, grayish beetle feeding on a meleucca tree, he skirted the trunk. Scientists had released that beetle as part of a program to restore the wetlands, which were becoming overwhelmed by the meleucca trees. Neither the beetles nor the trees were native to the area. Someone had dumped the seeds and started the trees. Now someone else had dumped the beetles to keep the trees from overtaking the wetlands. The logic in the situation reminded Jake of Madeline's father, Sean Drake.

He too had tried to insinuate himself and his attitudes into others. Jake hadn't liked the man. He'd respected Sean's accomplishments, which were legendary in CIA circles, but as a human being, Jake's former father-in-law had been a walking disaster area.

He'd never forgiven Madeline for not being a son, which went a long way toward explaining many of the challenges Madeline now faced. Rather than accepting her, Sean never approved of her, and Madeline had followed him like a puppy, trying to please him. Sadly, she never had. He had died, and she only had succeeded in destroying her self-esteem and then her spirit. A damn shame, that.

Sean Drake had had an equally warped perspective about his work, and Jake knew exactly what the lean and wiry spy would have to say about Operation Shadowpoint. *Finally, Jake, you see the truth. Spying on spies is as natural as breathing.*

Drake was wrong about that. Jake didn't like the idea of bringing down one of his own, though if it was necessary, then he'd do it. Duty and honor weren't just words, they were a code Special Ops men and women took into their hearts and lives. Yet Sean relished being critical and scrutinizing, whether or not it was just. He thought he knew best. And the only time Jake could recall seeing a gleam of excitement or enthusiasm in the man's eyes was when he'd dug up dirt that could destroy lives and breach trust.

But Shadowpoint was different. It wasn't spying on spies. It was a coordinated effort, a cooperative venture to save the lives of spies and of innocent Americans. So maybe Drake liked unearthing dirt, but Jake hated it. And he'd never swallowed Drake's claim that all the factions, including the hallowed Air Force, liked nothing better.

Disagreeing with Madeline's father wasn't conducive to Jake having a peaceful marriage. But what else could he expect from either of them? From a daughter who feared living her own life? Who had been devastated by her father's first heart attack? Anyone would have been devastated, but he had laid a guilt trip on her worthy of an Oscar. What could Jake expect from a man who, on learning his only child was pregnant with his grandchild, insisted she have an abortion, and insisted Jake encourage her to do that?

Jake had done the opposite and married her instead. It still amazed him that Madeline had gone against her father's wishes, though if Jake hadn't married her, he wondered if she would have held out. Whatever the reason Drake had been so opposed to Madeline becoming a mother, or why on that one front Madeline had had the courage to defy him, wasn't important anymore. Both of them, thank God, were out of Jake and Timmy and Laura's lives forever—provided the adoption had gone through.

Pausing to orient himself to his surroundings, Jake leaned against the trunk of a moss-laden oak. Moonlight trickled down through the dense trees and sparkled on the dew-damp ground. Beautiful, in its own way. Hot and muggy and bug-infested, but beautiful in its own way.

He hiked on, clearing his mind, listening to the soft call of an owl and opening his senses to any warning alerts. Letting his instincts guide him through the marsh, he tramped through wet grass and tall weeds that rustled in the sultry night breeze.

About ten miles from the rendezvous point, he came upon a small clearing. Seeing three dark lumps on the ground, he stopped, and then took cover on the northeastern rim behind a clump of pungent-smelling swamp grass. The lumps were bodies.

The operatives' bodies.

His stomach in knots, Jake scouted the area, looking and listening for signs of anyone, for movement or traps. He came upon three sets of tracks leaving the immediate area. Three men, judging by the size and depth of the prints in the marshy sand. His boots making soft sucking sounds in the mud, he followed the tracks half a mile to make sure the men hadn't doubled back. Convinced they hadn't, he returned to the clearing and then examined the operatives.

The mouths of the first two men had been sewn closed with a thick monofilament. Deep-sea fishing line. But there was no blood, not even at the needle's points of entry. Stitched shut after their deaths. Small mercy, that. And no signs of physical injury to any of them that would explain their causes of death. But they were covered with a thin, odorless film of dust.

ROFF isn't a religious organization. It's a terrorist group. One amassing a biological warfare arsenal.

Recalling General Connor's words, sweat beaded up on Jake's neck and rolled down his back. Strong anthrax? Botulism? Those were the two germs currently most favored by terrorists.

Moonlight caught and reflected on the edge of something white in the third man's hands. Jake squatted down, then pried open the man's fisted fingers. A photograph?

Jake blew off the dusty film covering it, then squinted, straining to see who or what was in the picture. Not daring to use his flashlight, he held the photo up to the moon, and studied the woman captured. Wearing jean shorts and a yellow shirt, her hair swinging down over her cheek, she rested on her knees, planting flowers near a gazebo. Jake's gazebo. A shiver slithered up his spine.

Laura.

Seven

$\mathcal{E}$ ager to get out of her wet clothes and shoes, Laura dumped her purse on the kitchen cabinet and greeted Betsy Miller. "We're home."

"High time, too." Short and round with soft white hair that clung in wisps to her cheeks, Betsy breezed into the kitchen, smiling at Timmy, her soft, powdery scent hovering pleasantly around her. "So tell me about your pizza party."

"Don't you want to know about me talking to Judge Barton?" Timmy frowned at the woman who had become his surrogate grandmother.

"Of course." She pulled up a chair and sat down at the heavy oak table. "I just thought first you'd want to complain about eating too much pizza before getting dessert, that's all."

Toeing off her shoes, Laura laughed. Betsy knew Timmy well. And she gave him no clue, Laura noticed, that she'd called home with the news that the adoption had gone through. Betsy, being the blessing she was to all of them, knew Timmy wanted to tell her himself. If he thought about it, he would know Laura had called home, of course. Betsy had sat here on pins and needles, just as Laura had sat on them outside Judge Barton's office. Nevertheless, in listening to Timmy's recap, the woman's kind eyes sparkled and her expressions shifted to depict her changing emotions, as if she'd not heard word one until now.

"Well, it's about time those—" Betsy glanced at Laura, who'd picked up the phone. "That message isn't fit for mixed company." She turned her gaze first to the answering machine, then to Timmy, and then back to Laura. "My Andrew would agree."

When Betsy said her dearly departed husband, Andrew, agreed with her on something, Laura paid attention. It didn't happen often, and the warnings always had proven accurate. She looked down at the blinking red light and nodded. "I'm calling the garage. The Mustang's transmission is acting up."

"It's frozen in first," Timmy said.

The mechanic answered on the second ring. "Green's Automotive."

Laura shifted her attention to the call. "Bill, this is Laura Logan."

"Uh-oh."

She frowned. Bill had sided with Jake about replacing the Mustang. More than once. "Don't start."

"What's wrong with the heap now?"

"Transmission," Laura said. "It's stuck in first." Now what were Timmy and Betsy whispering about? Timmy's eyes were twinkling. Must be something good.

"I'll send someone down to pick 'er up first thing in the morning."

"I can drive it in." Laura made herself a note and stuck it up on the fridge under a magnet that read, *Push here for Maid Service. If no one answers, do it yourself.* The pink dot to push, of course, lacked a depressible button.

"Naw, we'll tow 'er. I want 'er here early, not at noon. Just put the key under the mat."

"Under the mat. Got it. Thanks, Bill." Laura rubbed at her forehead and scrunched up the note. She hung up the phone, then turned around. Why did Betsy and Timmy suddenly seem solemn? She could almost smell their disappointment. "What's wrong?"

Timmy looked to Betsy. She fidgeted with the pearls Andrew had given her for their twentieth wedding anniversary; clearly dressed to go out. "Did I forget something?" Laura asked, feeling guilty. Other than on birthdays, Veterans Day and Memorial Day, and, of course, her and Andrew's anniversary, Betsy never dressed up or wore her pearls.

"No, no," Betsy assured.

"Well, what is it, then?"

"It's nothing, dear," Betsy said, shifting toward the table. "It's just that, since it's your anniversary, I'd planned to take Timmy to my sister Alice's with me for a visit. Until Saturday, we'd planned. I even got tickets to the ball game. But with the major being TDY, your car being broken down, and Madeline acting up, I'm thinking we'd best just stay put and keep you company."

"Timmy." Laura swiveled her gaze to her son. "Did you ask Mrs. Miller to get tickets to the game?"

"Yes, ma'am." He jutted out his jaw. "If you want something, Madeline says, you've gotta ask for it because people can't read your mind."

Laura reminded herself of her promise to herself to never speak against Madeline or her friends to Timmy, to do nothing to make him feel uncomfortable talking about her. Prying definitely broke that promise, so she bit her tongue. Still, standing alone, her advice wasn't a good lesson for Timmy. "I think she's right and wrong, Tiger."

"We've been saving for the tickets, Mom. Me and Mrs. Miller."

"That's right," Betsy confirmed. "For six weeks."

"Good," Laura said, then turned back to the matter at hand. This was an opportunity to drive her point home, and she wasn't going to let it slip by her. "Asking for things is fine, Tiger. But what if you know it isn't within someone's power to give you what you want? Is it right to ask them for it anyway knowing that having to refuse you will hurt them inside, and they'll feel guilty that they've disappointed you?"

Timmy grunted. His neck turned ruddy and he sent her a wise look. "You're talking about Dad, and me being mad at him because he had to go TDY last night."

"Yes, I am." Laura leaned back against the counter and rubbed her stockinged toes against her instep.

"I'm sorry, Mom." Timmy sighed. "I wasn't thinking."

"It's okay." She smiled, very pleased with him. "Now about this going to the game—"

"No, we'd better not," he said, his jaw drooping nearly to the floor.

"Don't you want to go?" She knew he did; that's what he'd been so excited about while she'd been on the phone and he and Betsy had been whispering. He loved visiting Alice's.

"Sure, I wanna go, but we better stay with you. Especially after Madeline ran into us—"

Betsy gasped. "She *what*!"

"It's okay," Laura said quickly. If Jake weren't so opposed, she would already have been on the phone to the police having the woman arrested. "Her car's messed up, but everyone is fine."

Timmy looked up at Betsy. "We got a broken tail-light."

Eager to change the subject—Betsy looked ready to call in the national guard—Laura reverted back to the ball game. "Tiger, don't you want to see the game?"

"I can go a different day," he said.

Touched, Laura's heart softened. "Absolutely not. I want you to go now and have fun."

Betsy frowned. "I don't think—"

"Really," Laura insisted, knowing Betsy loved ball games every bit as much as Timmy. "Jake's Jag is here. I'll be fine. Besides, you and Timmy need to celebrate the adoption, too. And we control us. Not Madeline." Laura looked at Timmy. "Better get your Cards jacket and your glove—and don't forget your toothbrush."

Timmy grinned, then ran down the hall to his bedroom.

Betsy yelled after him. "I've got your toothbrush, but don't forget your rabbit's foot. I'm not driving all the way back for it again, Timothy James Logan." She reached around the corner into the dining room and pulled out a little brown overnight bag and her purse.

She'd known Laura would insist, just as Laura knew full well that Betsy had come back home for the rabbit foot twice before, and probably would again a dozen times in the future.

Laura's skirt pinched at her waist. Wishing she'd been more disciplined and not eaten that second slice of chocolate dessert pizza, she shifted away from the counter and nodded toward the answering machine. "Who left the 'unfit for mixed company' message?"

"Madeline." Betsy grimaced, making her feelings on the matter clear to anyone with eyes. "She's in rare form tonight. Drunk and watching soaps. I heard the music and recognized it right off."

Laura frowned back at Betsy. They both knew what soaps and Scotch meant. Madeline was on a Class-A binge. Miserable and damn determined everyone else be miserable with her. As if Laura harbored any doubts.

"I'd wait until we're gone to listen to it," Betsy advised, her round face twisting with irritation. "It'll only upset the boy." She adjusted her purse strap on her forearm, not meeting Laura's eyes. "Actually, my Andrew would insist you wait to listen to it when the major gets home."

Half-tempted to do exactly that—it'd already been an emotional roller coaster of a day—Laura pasted on a smile. Betsy was truly worried to bring her dead husband up twice in one conversation. "Trust me, Betsy. There's nothing that woman can say to me now that she hasn't said at least once in the past thirteen years. It'll be fine. And I really appreciate you getting Timmy out of Madeline's line of fire. The adoption going through has her riled up. She'll calm down in a few days."

"I'm sure you know best, dear, but—" Betsy fell silent, then smiled at Timmy, who'd come back into the kitchen. "Ready, Tiger?"

Timmy grinned up at her from under the bill of his Cards cap. "Yes, ma'am."

"Then kiss your mother and let's go."

Your mother. Your mother. Laura really was his mother now. Her chest fluttering, she opened her arms, then squeezed him tightly. "Gosh, but I love you." Her throat thick, she smiled and let him go. "Got your rabbit's foot?"

"Right here." He patted at his jeans pocket, then held out his hand.

Laura wrinkled her brow, puzzled.

"The keys. Didn't Mr. Green say to put 'em under the mat?"

"He did." Laura fished her key chain out from her

purse then passed the ignition key to Timmy. "I'd forgotten already."

"That's okay." He gave her his sidelong, partners-in-crime grin. "I remembered."

"Yeah." Laura smoothed his hair, then watched him walk to the door where Betsy stood waiting. "Have a good time, and behave yourselves."

"We will," Betsy said. "See you Saturday night."

Timmy looked back at her. "Love you, Mom."

Tenderness welled in her chest and her eyes burned. "Me, too. Be safe."

When they'd gone, Laura unfastened the button on her skirt at her waist, swearing next time she *would* forgo the second piece of dessert pizza. Eager to call the deed done, she poured herself a glass of wine, took a fortifying swig, then tapped the flashing red light on the answering machine, wondering if the message had been left before or after the Pizza Hut fiasco.

"You bitch," Madeline screamed. "You bribed that judge. I know you did."

Obviously, before. And just as obvious, the woman didn't know spit about Judge Victor "Bad Ass Bear" Barton.

"You think you're so smart, don't you, Laura? First you steal my husband, and now you steal my son. Well, maybe you are smart. But maybe you're just being your typical, shortsighted, stupid self. What difference does it really make whose name's on that piece of paper? What have you gained?

"Down deep, in places you never talk about, you know you haven't gained a damn thing. Because under all the fluff is the truth. And the truth is neither of them will ever love you as much as they loved me. . . .

"So you lose, Laura. You live my life, and you forfeit your own."

The soap's theme song sounding in the background,

Madeline's outrage turned to laughter that bordered on hysteria, grating on Laura's raw nerves.

"Isn't that a hoot? You haven't gotten away with anything. You, or that bastard Barton. . . .

"Can't say I didn't warn you. I distinctly told you nothing is black and white. It's all shades of gray. You should have remembered that. . . .

"Barton should have, too. God knows he's old enough to have learned it on his own, but it appears you both need a reminder. So that's what you're going to get." Madeline let out a little grunt. "By the time I'm done, you'll both wish to hell you'd never met me."

"Safe bet," Laura told the machine. Having heard more than enough, and knowing Madeline would rant on until the tape cut off, she lifted her hand to erase the message. Some sixth sense warned her against it, so she saved it, and then shut off the machine, feeling more than a little tight-jawed herself.

The woman knew right where to aim her arrows; Laura had to give her that. She blew out a frustrated breath, then took a sip of the cold wine. "I just don't get it. I can design a communications device that can be implanted under a man's skin and track him via satellite anywhere in the world. I can do things with communications that ten years ago would have seemed like something right out of *Star Wars*. I can do all that, and yet I can't find a way to block solicitors' phone calls or hate messages on my own damn answering machine. *Why is that?*"

Realizing she'd been shouting, Laura pulled in three sharp breaths and then expelled them. No. No way was she going to take a stressful but beautiful and joyful day and let Madeline ruin it. No way. Laura would calm down, center herself, and nip this nonsense in the bud.

But as she calmed, fresh pain surged through her chest. For all Madeline's lies and refusals to acknowledge Laura's place in Jake's life, about one thing the woman was right.

Jake and Timmy would never love her as they'd loved Madeline.

And that hurt. Depressed, feeling vulnerable, alone, and adrift, Laura showered, wishing Jake were home. She toweled off, slipped on one of his T-shirts, and rubbed the soft cottony fabric against her stomach. If he knew she slept in his shirts whenever he was away, he'd either laugh at her or consider it a breach of their agreement and be ticked to the high heavens. But right now she didn't give a flying fig. She'd had a hellish couple of days and by God she needed comfort.

By the time she sat down on the den sofa, she was a heartbeat from tears. Drunk and watching soaps, it appeared a certainty Madeline would file suit and attempt to have the adoption set aside. It wasn't right or fair, not that either seemed to make any difference. So little in their lives was right or fair. She and Jake had waited two years for the adoption. And now when it's finally come, Jake isn't even here. Damn it, it was their anniversary, too.

Indulging in a moment of self-pity, Laura curled up, propping a soft teal throw-pillow against the sofa's arm, under her ribs. Had Jake remembered? Did their anniversary mean anything to him? In the past three weeks of living with her, had he even once wished there could be more between them? Had he even once seen her not as a friend, but as a woman? As his wife?

God, but she missed him. In ways she knew she shouldn't. And she knew he would be worrying himself sick about the adoption hearing, too. Like the other wives, she'd been trained not to bother him when he was TDY with personal matters he could do nothing about, so it hadn't occurred to her to call him—until now. She could leave a message for the Ops Center to pass along to him. That would be perfectly acceptable, since it'd ease his mind to know the adoption had gone through.

She stopped berating herself for letting her emotions slip over the friendship line. There was no harm done, provided Jake never knew it. And he'd certainly never hear it from her. She'd fight these feelings. Hard.

Promising herself that, she called the number she'd been given. If he should be able to check in, a message would let him know things had gone well in court today. The news that they might have to return to court could wait until he got home, as could the news of Laura's communications consultant reactivation. Right now, the last thing he needed was more worries.

A man answered on the third ring. "Special Operations. Captain Perry."

"Hi, this is Laura Logan."

"Yes, Mrs. Logan."

"May I leave a message for Jake?"

"Yes, ma'am. Is this an emergency?"

"No, it isn't. But it is important." What in the world was going on there? The Ops Center was always busy, but seldom frantic. Why all the background noise? Odd—unless something of major importance had just broken loose. "Just tell him the adoption went through."

"I'll get word to the major ASAP, Mrs. Logan, and congratulations on the adoption."

More noise. More elevated, urgent voices. Something serious was wrong; Laura felt it. Shivering, she hugged herself. "Thank you, Captain."

"Yes, ma'am." He broke the connection.

Seeing horrific visions of another Class-A mishap,

Laura hung up the phone, shaking and hoping to God Jake was okay.

Dizzy and sweat-soaked, Jake pulled the airboat into a small inlet—the predesignated rendezvous point—then cut the engine. Why the hell hadn't some genius designed a field test he could perform to check for biological contamination? He'd had no choice but to enter the swamp without protective gear. If he'd been intercepted, it'd have been impossible to explain being suited up. But even without a field test, which could have warned him early on exactly what he'd been exposed to and directed proper treatment, Jake knew he'd been exposed to something. With the dizziness, bouts of sweats, and nausea, how could he not know?

By necessity, he'd touched the photograph of Laura and carried the corpses to the airboat, having to make three trips from the clearing to it. A strong surge of thought-numbing fog washed through him. Shaking his head, fighting disorientation, imbalance, and an inability to focus, he reached into his black carryall, scraping his knuckles on the zipper. He dug around blindly, locating a blister pack of antibiotics, and then dry swallowed the two pills.

If ROFF operated like most terrorist groups and contaminated the operatives with strong anthrax, the antibiotics would handle it and Jake would be fine. If it was botulism, he was in trouble. He'd waited too long to self-medicate. But ROFF could be producing toxic germs that alter genetic structure. Those germs were less commonly used because of their long-term environmental contamination effects, yet with a fanatic group, who knew? It was entirely possible ROFF didn't give a damn if they destroyed the eco-balance of the Everglades along with Jake Logan and the three CIA operatives. If that proved to be the case, then the damage was done. There was no cure for gene-altering germ contamination. And that left Jake a walking dead man.

Water lapped at the hull of the boat. Jake could get into the water, wash off some of the germs, but then he'd contaminate the water and the damage would ripple out from there, carried by the wildlife. Tempted, but unwilling to do that, he slumped down, too dizzy to stand. Pain squeezed his stomach. He grunted and forced himself to think. He'd made it to the rendezvous point with the operatives. Soon their ride would arrive and, in a couple of hours a clean-up crew would be dispatched to the swamp to assess damages and do all that could be done to remove any residue. Then Jake would have his answers. Would know if he'd live or die.

He stared at the corpses and licked at his parched lips. Until then only the killers and the three dead men could answer the question of what had been used to kill them. And only they knew the significance of Laura's photo.

That condemned Jake to waiting for the autopsy reports. Condemned him to waiting to ask Laura why her photo had been in a dead CIA operative's hand.

Sweat on Jake's forearm gleamed in the moonlight and the brisk night breeze chilled him all over. His teeth chattering, sweat streaming down his face, he rolled his gaze west, trying to spot their ride. Nothing there. Not yet.

Bury it, Logan. Bury it. He had to stay conscious until they arrived, to warn them to suit up to avoid contamination before making physical contact. He had to tell them about Laura's photo.

She could be a target as a means of getting to Jake. His head swimming, his stomach lurching, he gritted his teeth, fought to think, to stay alert. Or Laura could still be an operative, as she had been when they'd met thirteen years ago.

No. He swept his clammy brow with the back of his arm. No, she was his wife now. If she were still an active operative, she'd have told him. Wouldn't she?

She would . . . *if she trusted him.*

Breathing erratically, his clothes sweat-soaked and clinging to him, Jake focused on steadying his breaths, just as he had when he'd taken a knife in the lung a few years ago. He'd needed surgery, but had refused it until an OSI officer could get to the civilian hospital and certify that while under anesthetic, Jake didn't disclose any classified information. Without the OSI officer, Jake had two choices. Surgery without anesthetic, which was highly opposed by both him and physicians, or no surgery. The order against self-medicating was concise and clear. Beyond an aspirin, you don't do it. And being professionally medicated without OSI present was considered a risk to national security. Knowingly or not, the officer could compromise a mission, could cost people their lives—and he could lose his security clearance, as Jake could now, having taken the antibiotics. He'd been issued them, but prior to self-administering, he needed authorization. To get that authorization he would have had to break communication silence with a simple "147298 requesting 4," then wait for the blissfully short "Tango" response. But, fearing transmission interception by ROFF, he hadn't dared risk it. Not until he got the bodies out and safely into Ops hands. Within them lay evidence and vital information.

Maybe for similar reasons, Laura hadn't told Jake she was still active in the intelligence community. It'd be just like her to decide he had no need to know, and that knowing would somehow endanger him. Still, the woman was his wife. She should have told him. He had clearance, so she certainly could have told him. It had to be a matter of trust.

Sean Drake flickered through Jake's mind. When the truth came down to brass tacks, did anyone trust anyone? Really?

But maybe ROFF was sending Jake a message with Laura's photo, telling him he'd better cooperate with them or ROFF would target Laura. Or maybe the CIA operative killed was telling Jake that Laura had been designated a ROFF target.

Or maybe the operative was warning Jake that Laura was the Special Ops trained head of ROFF.

An icy shiver raced up Jake's backbone. His stomach burned like fire. As impossible as that scenario seemed, Laura had the skills and training. She *could* head ROFF. The question was, *would she*?

His instincts said no. His heart said the idea was crazy and insulting to her. But both his instincts and heart had been wrong before, and this matter ranked too important to rely on them alone. Guilty until proven innocent; that was the military position in situations such as this, and for everyone's safety, that had to be the official stance. To consider her innocent, Jake needed proof. Concrete evidence against someone. Indisputable, concrete evidence against someone.

Laura was either an innocent, or guilty of treason against the United States Jake had sworn to protect. A victim—or the enemy.

She was his best friend, his wife, and, God help him, Jake had to prove which.

Eight

Tuesday night, the phone rang.

Laura dragged herself from the fog of sleep and squinted through the dark at the clock. Who'd be calling just before eleven? She grabbed the receiver, and bumped it against her chin. Suffering the sting, she grumbled, "Hello."

"Mrs. Logan?"

She didn't recognize the man's voice. "Yes?"

"General Connor here."

Oh, God. What had happened to Jake? Laura squeezed her eyes shut. He couldn't be dead. No, he couldn't be. If he were dead, the chaplain would come to the house. No, not dead. But maybe Jake was hurt, or being held hostage. "Yes?"

"Could you come out to the base, to headquarters? I realize it's late, but I need to talk with you."

To talk with her? Maybe this wasn't about Jake. Maybe it was an Intel consultation call. But if that were the case, then why did she have this feeling of dread ripping like clawing talons through her chest? No. No, it was about Jake. Her intuition screamed it. "I'll, um, be there in twenty minutes."

She tossed back the covers and scrambled out of bed. Where were her damn shoes?

The kitchen. She'd left them in the kitchen, under the bar. She always left them in the kitchen under the bar.

"Thank you, Mrs. Logan."

Heading down the hallway, the thick carpet cushioning her rushing feet, she sensed he was about to hang up and quickly stalled him. "General, is Jake all right?" Why had she asked? Connor couldn't tell her. Not on an unsecured phone line.

"Of course," he said smoothly. "Just get here as soon as you can, Mrs. Logan."

Mrs. Logan. He'd lied. Oh, yes. This was about Jake. Her heart shattering, she tossed down the phone, finished jerking on her jeans, grabbed her shoes and purse, then headed out the door.

Halfway to the Mustang, she remembered it had broken down.

From the kitchen, she called a cab, impatiently explained to the dispatcher she couldn't wait fifteen minutes for a ride, and then hung up. Mrs. Miller had her car. The only choice left was to take Jake's Jag. It was his pride and joy and he'd be mad as hell at her or anyone else for driving it—even he rarely drove it—but this was an emergency. She snagged the keys off the peg by the back door, then ran out to the garage.

The engine purred as soft as a kitten. Laura forced herself not to speed, not to stomp the gas pedal and fly to the base. Her thoughts ran wild. Fear caught her in a death grip. And beneath it all, the truth pounded through her as forcefully as a heart beats during an adrenaline rush. Her feelings for Jake had changed. They'd grown far deeper than friendship.

When it had happened, she didn't know, not exactly. And she resented it with every atom in her body because she'd made an agreement and she'd broken it. It didn't matter that only she knew it. Honor was honor, disclosed or not. How could she be so stupid? So foolish? How could she let herself fall in love with him? *They had no future.*

Still, she prayed. Please. *Please, don't make me lose him, too. Please!*

At the traffic light, she waited for the signal to turn green. On proceeding through the intersection, she turned off her headlights, approached the base entrance, and then waited for the armed guard to salute the officer's sticker on the car window and wave her through the gate.

Regret washed through her, and a hot tear rolled down her cheek. It dripped off her chin onto her beige silk blouse, leaving a wet spot. Good grief, why couldn't she ever get this love business right? Just one time in her life, she should be able to get it right. But she hadn't. Not with the men she'd dated, and certainly not with Jake.

She loved her husband as a wife should love her husband. But he could never know it because she'd sworn never to take the chance of loving him. Sworn it to herself, and to him. And now this.

Now . . . this.

Inside headquarters, an armed escort led Laura upstairs, and then to the third in a long row of gray doors. A blue sign with white lettering on the wall read, *Briefing Room.*

She nodded her thanks, trembling, fearing once she entered this room, her life would never again be the same. The urge to run away slammed through her. She fought it. There was no place to run, not from the truth. *Nothing stays hidden. Sooner or later, the truth always finds the light.*

Hadn't her father told her that a million times? Hadn't she seen it proven true time and again?

Summoning the courage and strength to face whatever came, she cracked open the door. The smell of lemon oil poured out. Though she hated the tart and bitter scent—had hated anything resembling lemon since, as a child, her mother had made her suck a dozen of them for cursing—Laura stepped inside.

Her knees went weak. At the end of the long conference table, to Connor's right, sat Jake. He looked tired and drained, and he pounded out negative vibes powerful enough to screw up any signal on any frequency, but he was alive and in one piece. *Thank you. Thank you so much. Thank you so much. . . .*

Connor cleared his throat. "Come in, Mrs. Logan."

She walked over to the table. "Jake?"

He didn't look at her. Why wouldn't he look at her? Maybe he wasn't okay.

The little hairs on her neck stood up.

"Please, Mrs. Logan." General Connor smiled, but there was no warmth in it, only tons of suspicion. "Sit down."

Following the general's hand signal, Laura stumbled on to a chair across the table from Jake. He lifted his gaze to her, and she wished he hadn't. Dooubt clouded his eyes. Doubt such as she'd never seen in him before. She hated it. "What's wrong?" He was peaked. His hair was damp, and she smelled soap. He'd just showered. "Jake, you're scaring me. Are you all right?"

He frowned at her. "It depends, Laura."

Odd answer. "On what?"

"On what you know about ROFF."

ROFF? She frowned her puzzlement. "Excuse me?" Why were both men looking at her as if she'd done something terribly wrong?

"Speak openly," Connor told her, then rocked back

in his chair. It creaked softly. "We all have clearance here."

Confused and unable to shoulder the censure in Jake's eyes—it hurt more than she thought she could hurt—Laura frowned at Connor. "If I understood what you're asking, I would speak openly. But I don't."

Jake rounded on her, his words stiff and sharp. "I'm asking what you know about ROFF. What part of that don't you understand?" His scowl deepened; the muscle under his right eye ticked. "Just answer the damn question, Laura."

Jake was livid and not bothering to hide it. He rarely got this upset, and that he was now rattled her. Fortunately, her own temper threatened to rear its ugly head. Ordinarily, she would object, but right now she'd take strength wherever she could find it—even in anger.

"Answer the major, Captain," Connor instructed. "What do you know about ROFF?"

Captain? The major? She was a civilian now, not active duty Air Force, and he was her husband, for God's sake. What in the name of heaven was going on here? "It's a religious organization headquartered down in the Florida Everglades. Three CIA operatives infiltrated and were having communications trouble." This disclosure would hurl Jake from livid to outraged, though there was no getting around it. *Nothing stays hidden.* "The design isn't one of mine, but I was consulted."

"You were consulted, *Captain.*" Jake clenched his right hand in a fist. His knuckles raised up like knobs. "Is that it?"

Oh, how she wished she could deny it. His reaction removed any doubt about his feelings on the matter. The admission would cost her dearly. "Not as an Ops Officer, no. I haven't been recalled to active duty. But as a communications consultant to Intel, yes, I was consulted. So, please, don't call me captain.'' He knew how much she hated titles. Was he deliberately baiting her? ''And what I've told you is all I know about ROFF, except that the mission was tagged Operation Shadowpoint and it was aborted.''

''Anything else, Laura?''

The accusation in Jake's tone hung in the air between them, and the truth hit her hard. He thought she was withholding information from him. ''No, not really.'' Okay, so she hadn't told him about the Intel consultation, and he had clearance, so she could have—and she would have, if Madeline hadn't interrupted, pulling that stunt with the car. But Jake had no way of knowing that, and her not telling him had stung his pride. Still, he knew her, damn it. Of all people, he shouldn't question her integrity. Yet he was, and that battered her pride. And it infuriated her.

She frowned at him, determined to keep her temper controlled, though his doubt had turned her anger from an asset into a challenge. ''I intended telling you, Jake. But . . . things happened.''

A snap decision—not her favorite kind of decision to make—but she would not disclose Madeline's antics in front of the general and further humiliate Jake. He might have no qualms about shaming her, but she wouldn't shame him. ''Look, I've been patient here. Now I want to know what this is all about. I'm not active duty military any more, I'm a civilian—just a temporarily-activated communications consultant for Intel. That's all. I don't have to put up with this.''

''Yes, I'm afraid you do.'' Jake's eyes flashed black anger. ''And we'll ask the questions. You just answer them.''

General Connor cleared his throat. ''The major is right,'' he said to Laura, looking uneasy and as if this disclosure to her about her professional status wasn't unfolding as he'd planned. "As soon as Jake reported the photograph, you were recalled to military active duty and permanently reactivated in Intel as an expert communications operative. You'll remain active in both until further notice, and you're assigned to me."

Laura sat there, too stunned to do more than clench her hands in her lap. What photograph had Jake reported? Why would Connor personally reactivate her? Recall her to active duty? Place her under his direct command?

The answer hit her like a ton of bricks. So if she proved to be involved with ROFF, he could try her in a military court—court-martial her—and keep the civilian sector out of it.

On the surface, being manipulated like this infuriated her. A slick move, to be sure, but would it prove to be a curse or a blessing to her? That, she didn't know. Couldn't know. Not yet. So she kept her objections to herself, and held her silence.

"Are you ready to answer the questions now, Captain?" Jake asked, a muscle in his jaw twitching.

If he got any madder, odds favored it'd kill him. The veins in his neck stood out like thumbs and his throat and face were blood red. What had happened? He didn't lose control like this. Not even when Madeline had lost Timmy, or when Laura had been told erroneously Jake was dead, had he lost control like this. And he seemed bent on deliberately pushing her hot buttons. Jake never had done that. "Fire away, Major," she replied, her tone biting.

"Me first, if you don't mind." The general tapped a gold pen against a yellow legal pad, then let it fall against the table. When the noise stilled and the room grew quiet, he leveled on her his uncompromising gaze. "Captain Logan, have you committed any act to compromise the security of the United States?"

Nine

~

"What?" Outraged, Laura jumped to her feet.

"Sit down, Laura." Jake stared up at her, his eyes as cold and distant as his voice. He looked at her as if he wasn't sure he even knew her. "And answer the general."

At a total loss, aching and furious that she'd worried herself sick over his safety and yet Jake treated her like this, she glared at him, deliberately letting him see her devastation and anger. Compromise security—*her*? "I have not."

The general eyed her every bit as warily as Jake, and with equal suspicion. "The three CIA operatives who infiltrated ROFF have been killed."

"I'm sorry." She paused, and let that information sink in and disseminate. Was that it, then? Was Jake upset about the deaths? He'd worked before with the CIA. Perhaps he'd known the operatives. "But what do they have to do with me?"

Jake looked at the general, who nodded, then pivoted his gaze back to Laura. "One of the operatives had a photograph in his hand."

"Yes?" What the hell did that mean?

"A photograph of you, Laura."

"Of me?" Surprise streaked up her spine, set the roof of her mouth to tingling, and the lemon smell overwhelmed her, made her nauseous. "Whatever for?"

"That's what we're attempting to determine." Jake calmed down visibly, softened his voice, and his color returned more to normal. "From the outside looking in, we've deduced a couple of theories. We're working them all, which is why we're talking with you about this."

Interrogating her was more like it. She folded her arms over her chest. "And what have you deduced, Jake?"

"That we're being sent a message."

"What kind of message?"

"That's where it gets blurry."

She grunted. "This is absurd." But the rationale for questioning her loyalty suddenly became clear. She hated it, took serious offense to it professionally and even more so personally, but she couldn't lie to herself and say she didn't understand it. Or that, if the situation were reversed, she wouldn't have felt angry and asked the same questions of Jake, because she knew damn well she would have. The implications still hit her hard, like rocks slammed against the back of her skull: totally unexpected and very painful. "Oh, Lord. You think I had something to do with the operatives being terminated!"

Jake's gaze slid back down to the table and his hand again curled into a fist, proving the accuracy of her suspicions.

He doubted her. Sincerely and deeply doubted her. Knowing it hurt her every bit as much as Madeline's saying Jake would never love her as he'd loved his ex-wife. Laura screamed silently. *My damn blouse is still wet with tears I cried for you, and you doubt me?* She masked her hurt under a husky rasp. "Am I being accused of a crime?"

"Have you committed one?" Jake asked.

She glared at him. "Not yet."

General Connor blew out a sigh that rippled the loose pages on the yellow pad in front of him. "Let's calm down," he said, turning a warning look on Jake, then rounding his gaze back to her. "No, you aren't being accused of a crime. At least, not at this time."

So she could be accused later? Her stomach fell, clenched into knots. *Of treason?* God help her, that's what they were talking about here. *Treason.*

Connor leaned forward and propped his elbow on the table. "At this point, we're merely trying to determine intent. Clearly we were meant to find the photo, and we need to know why."

"Intent," she repeated him, her bitterness seeping into her tone. "And what have you decided, General?"

"I haven't." He hiked a shoulder. "It depends on who put the picture in the dead man's hand. If ROFF, then I'd surmise that their organization has identified you as a target and they want us to know it. Which raises another question. Why? Are you targeted because you're Jake's wife, or because you've been a communications consultant on Shadowpoint?" His gaze hardened and bored into her. "Any hypotheses?"

"No." Speaking more sharply than she intended, she softened her voice. "How could I know why? Only ROFF can answer that question."

"Or," the general went on in a calm tone, as if she hadn't cut loose with an outburst, "perhaps the CIA operative was warning us that ROFF's marked you as a target."

Not knowing what to say to that, Laura held her silence.

Jake lifted his gaze to stare at her. "Or the operative

could have been warning us that you're the head of ROFF.''

Her jaw fell open. "Don't be ridiculous. I live in California, for God's sake. Why would I head a religious organization based in Florida?''

He held her pinned with his gaze. "Obviously, that's another of the things we're attempting to determine.''

Palms flat on the table, she leaned forward, nose to nose with Jake. "Well, then. Let me give you all the help I can. I don't have the first damn clue. I don't know why the photo was there, who put it there, or what it means. I'm afraid that's all the answer I can give you, because that's all the answer I have. I don't know, Jake.''

He dropped his voice to just above a whisper—a signal between them that she'd raised her voice. "Maybe you can help us figure this out.'' Sounding deceptively calm—so calm it raised chills on Laura's skin—he leaned toward her. "Why would a publicity officer be in the need-to-know loop on Operation Shadowpoint?''

He knew she'd deceived him, and the costs would be even higher than she'd imagined. Laura slumped down in her chair and let her gaze drop to her hands, folded in her lap. "I've already admitted I was consulted on the mission's communications.''

"Why?'' He shrugged. "It's not your design. You said it wasn't your design. Didn't you say it wasn't your design?''

She cast a frantic glance at General Connor. His brow had furrowed. Now, he too knew she'd deceived Jake. She swallowed hard, knowing she should have told him. She could have told him, but initially she hadn't wanted to increase the risk to him. Since her consultations were a rare thing, she'd thought only to spare him. And when she'd decided the consults warranted telling him, Madeline had preempted her by nearly ramming her car through their house, and then they'd been comforting Timmy, and while that was still going on, Jake had been called out on a mission. But Laura really didn't want to disclose all that in front of the general. Madeline was an embarrassment. She had caused them all enough humiliation already, and this kind of nonsense could negatively impact his career.

"Yes, I did say it wasn't my design, but I was consulted." Laura forced herself to look at him. "To be certain, you'd have to ask those in charge why they selected me, but I suspect their reasons were simple ones. I'm a communications expert. I know the system, and I was on-site."

"You are an expert." Jake stared at her as if seeing her for the first time in his life. "The question I'm asking myself is, *at what*?"

Embarrassed, hurt, and so bitter she thought she might die choking on it, Laura stared at him—and said nothing.

Sometimes there just weren't words to adequately express or justify your rationale and reasons, much less your feelings. Unfortunately for her, this was one of them. Regardless of what she said, she'd only make the matter worse.

"Until today, Laura Logan," General Connor said softly, "has officially been a civilian publicity officer, Jake. But she also has had other, additional duties."

Jake swung his focus back to her and narrowed his eyes. His tone chilled, cold and unwavering. "You're still in Intel."

No one ever retired from Intel, and he knew it. They might go inactive, as she had, but they didn't retire. That she'd been temporarily reactivated by Intel as a consultant and hadn't told Jake hurt him. And now he was striking out, rebelling by hurting her. "I'm an expert," she said, staring at a framed sketch of a Stealth bomber on the wall behind Jake's head. "On the rare occasion, my expertise is needed. Like you, when called, I serve as best I'm able."

She swiveled her gaze, lifting it from his chest to his face. *Betrayed* might as well have been stamped in black ink across his forehead. He radiated it like a broadcasting tower beams signals. Her insides twisted. Her mouth went dry, and she licked at her lips. "Jake, I can explain—"

"No," he interrupted, lifting a hand to stop her. "No, you can't explain this."

"But—"

"No, Laura." He slammed a hand down on the tabletop. "I have Top Secret security clearance. There's no reason in the world you couldn't have told me. You *chose* not to do it. And there's only one reason you made that choice." Disappointment joined the anger burning in his eyes, and the edge in his voice grew sharper still. "We're friends—married, for God's sake—but you still don't trust me." He swallowed hard. "No, you can't explain."

Clearly surprised, and valiantly trying to hide it, the general cleared his throat.

Though she'd preferred not to air this publicly, Jake had left her no choice. "Look," Laura said, ignoring the general and his discomfort. "I would've told you, but Madeline pulled that stunt with the car—and there have been several other stunts since then, by the way, which I've handled—and then you got called to report. There was no time to tell you, Jake. I know the drill. When you're being sent on a mission, my job as your wife is to relieve you of all personal pressures. Well, I did that, and now you're condemning me for it."

A sliver of hurt that he had condemned her crept into her voice. She buried it, then went on. "I haven't done anything wrong. Whether we're talking about my career or my duty as an Ops officer's wife—as your wife—I do my job for the same reasons you do your job. I don't know why the hell my photo showed up in the hands of a dead CIA agent. I don't know why ROFF would be interested in me. I have nothing whatsoever to do with that organization, Jake, and on that I swear my life."

"What about Timmy's? Would you swear his life on it?"

Oh, but he read her like a book; knew her too well. "It's a moot point." She clenched her jaw. "Since I'm innocent, he'd never be at risk."

Jake glanced at Connor, whose answering nod was so slight that if Laura hadn't been specifically looking for it, she'd have missed it.

"We've obviously upset you," Connor said to her. "As regrettable as that is, I trust you understand why we must investigate."

She wished she didn't. Wished she could cut loose with a ton or two of righteous indignation and dump it on their heads. But she did understand. Still, she was too upset to admit it without getting her own pound of flesh. "Do whatever you have to do, General. You can't prove what isn't true. I swear to you right here and right now that I've never done anything professionally or personally that should have you—" She slid a frosty glare toward Jake—"or anyone else questioning my loyalty." She stood up. "Now you either give me some proof of wrongdoing on my part or you back off, because, reactivated and recalled or not, I've had enough of this."

"Laura," Jake said, his expression softening and filling with regret.

She glared him silent.

General Connor raked a hand through his hair and

leveled his gaze on her. "You're right. We don't know that you've done anything to give us reason to question your loyalty, or to suspect you of any wrongdoing. But this photo raises questions which must be asked and answered."

"And now you've asked them, and I've answered them as best I'm able." Laura lifted her chin, her insides quivering. "That's going to have to be good enough, General. There just isn't any more I can give you."

He stared at her a long moment, then finally blinked. "Jake, why don't you step out into the hall and stretch your legs?"

Looking torn, Jake stayed put. "My legs are fine, sir."

Connor slid Jake a level look. "That's an order, Major."

Surprise flickered through Jake's eyes. "Yes, sir." Jake walked to the door, his shoulders stiff.

When behind him the door clicked closed, Laura sat back down. Connor looked uncomfortable, as well he should. Treason. *Her?* Good grief, what a sick joke.

Only it wasn't a joke. It was sick and god-awful, but real and no joke.

He leaned forward, elbows and forearms flat against the table, then made a tent of his fingers. "I'm afraid that we have a little dilemma here."

By her reckoning, they had several. Not sure which one he referred to, she held her silence and waited for him to explain.

"The way I see it, you're either a very loyal ally, or the enemy. Frankly, I've yet to fully determine which."

Her heart chugged in her chest. Something specific grated at the man; she could see it in his eyes. "What do you want to know?"

"I've read your records. I know about Dr. Laura

Taylor Logan, the communications expert. But I don't know enough about Laura Logan, the woman, and how she thinks,'' he said. A puzzled frown creased the skin on his forehead. "I'm having trouble grasping a . . . situation.''

"What is it?'' she asked, knowing it was expected. "Maybe I can enlighten you.''

"I'd appreciate that,'' he said, sliding forward on his chair. "A captain with a stellar career in front of her leaves active duty in the military and goes inactive in Intel. And though she's reputedly one of the most respected experts in the communications field, she takes a job as a publicity officer and plays at working on her communication designs as an additional duty rather than devoting herself to them as her primary duty. Why would a captain do that?''

Laura's face went hot. She was the hard-to-grasp situation. "Don't you mean, why would I do that?''

"Yes, that's exactly what I mean.''

Laura resisted the urge to squirm. *Nothing stays hidden.* She could tell him the truth about Madeline's father. About the threats he'd levied on her for Madeline's benefit back then. Through the friendship with Jake, Laura had been making Sean Drake's daughter miserable and when she was miserable, Madeline doubled her alcohol intake. Sean couldn't have that. So Laura had a choice. She could either stay away from Jake and Timmy, or Sean would have a chat with his good friend Colonel James, and Laura would fail to get funding to buy so much as a pencil. She could kiss her communication device design research good-bye.

Sean Drake had the clout to make that happen. Colonel James held the purse strings on all of Laura's research. He could poison her projects and plague every other one she touched with funding challenges. Laura had been quick enough on the uptake to know that regardless of what she did regarding her friendship with Jake, Sean Drake would screw up her career. That had been hell to swallow, but since he'd ruined her joy in working solely on her designs with his threats— Colonel James would certainly scrutinize to death her every move, anyway—she'd opted to end her career before Drake and James could do it.

That had been the one move Sean Drake never expected she would have the courage to make. There was solace in that.

Yet disclosing such an altercation with the now-deceased CIA legend would only arouse more suspicion in General Connor, and he already had enough to be on the verge of having her arrested for treason. Yet without making that disclosure, her walking out of here to go anywhere except the brig would take a miracle.

Take a long shot. Opt for another truth.

She followed her line of thought. "Stability, fewer TDYs, and no PCS-ing," she said, referring to the permanent change of stations that sent military families hop-scotching around the world to different bases every two or three years. Just about the time everyone in the family settled in, orders came to move again. "Timmy needed me more than the communications field."

"Timmy." Connor pinned her with his gaze. "But you weren't yet married to Jake then."

"No. But Madeline was already drinking, and Jake had an assignment with a lot of TDYs. The year before I made the career move, he was gone over two-hundred days. Someone had to keep watch over Timmy. Jake couldn't, Madeline wouldn't, and so I elected me."

"At Jake's request?" Connor speculated.

She gave him a negative nod. "Jake would never ask that of me."

"So, because Jake saved your life in survival school,

you took on this responsibility and decided to do this yourself.''

Gray area. She had to be careful, to give Connor the truth, and yet not disclose all of it. *Nothing stays hidden.* ''I made the decision alone, yes.''

''I see.'' Connor shuffled some papers near his right forearm. They crackled. When they stopped, he looked back at her. ''Is that why you married Jake? Because you owed him?''

Thank God. In this, she could be totally open and honest. ''Not exactly,'' she said, then went on to explain. ''Back in survival school, when Paul Hawkins tried to kill me, Jake knew his testimony against the man wouldn't be popular, or win him any friends. But he didn't bend. By his actions, he said, 'I saw what happened, Laura. I trust your perception. And I'm not going to let anyone whitewash the truth and bury this.' ''

''So you did marry him because you owed him.''

''I owed him, but no, that's not why. You missed my point.'' Laura drew in a breath, stared at the general, then expressed aloud feelings that before now she'd kept hidden in her heart. ''I married Jake to help him keep custody of Timmy. But even more so, I married him because Jake takes a stand. He lives his convictions and he sacrifices for something more important than any one man, or any one family. Even when it isn't convenient, or when it costs him more than a man should have to pay, he does what he feels is right.''

She let her gaze drift down to the table and lose focus in its sheen. Her voice dropped a notch. ''When he's away, I go to sleep at night thinking it's okay to rest easy. We can all sleep safe, because he and others like him are out there doing what needs to be done, and they're not going to let anyone hurt us. They're going to stop them. Even if to do it, they have to die.''

She blinked, then looked back at the general. "That's why I married Jake Logan."

Connor sat perfectly still for a long minute. Then another. And then another.

Finally, he stood up, walked to the door, and ducked out into the hall. "Jake," he called.

Jake came back into the conference room and slid down on to his chair. Not once did he look at Laura. That hurt so much she thought she just might hate him for it.

The general returned to his seat and slid his yellow pad over to the side. "For now, we'll operate from two perspectives. One, that the photo is a ROFF message to Jake that his wife is being targeted as a means of getting to him. And, two, that you, Mrs. Logan, are a target due to the communications consultation. My gut reaction is to follow up as if ROFF expects Jake's co-operation, or they'll harm you."

Jake frowned. "General, Laura being threatened—"

He lifted a hand. "I understand, Jake. It's a risk we all take when we marry, and again when we have children. Countermeasures will be taken."

"Countermeasures?" Laura asked. Them talking about her as if she weren't in the room irked her. But at least Jake looked repentant for doubting her. It'd take a long time for her to recover from that, if ever she did. "What kind of countermeasures?"

The general looked her straight in the eye. "That's classified information, Mrs. Logan."

The bottom dropped out of Laura's stomach. She resisted the urge to cover it with her hand to calm it down. She *had* clearance.

But he'd called her *Mrs. Logan*. At least mentally, he had reassigned her from being a captain to being Jake's wife. Either way, she still had clearance. So

Connor didn't believe her, or else he was being prudent.

She studied his face and still couldn't read beneath his masked expression. But whether he was disbelieving or prudent, she didn't give a tinker's damn for the feelings either aroused.

"We'd all better hope this stems from you being Jake's wife, and that it's only a threat." The general put down his pen. "If your Intel position hasn't retained integrity, we've got serious trouble."

Laura hiked a shoulder. "I'm not following. This is a religious organization, not some group of fanatic rebels bent on overthrowing the govern—" The truth virtually smacked her right between the eyes. Of course it was a fanatic group. Of course it was. "Jake?"

He didn't elaborate, just turned back to the subject. "If ROFF knows you're active in Intel in any capacity on this operation, then the danger increases tenfold. To you and to me. Maybe even to Timmy."

"Oh, God." The blood drained from her face, and her body chilled, stone-cold. "Jake, I never thought—I mean, until I walked into this room, I was just an occasional consultant. I don't get . . . involved anymore. I haven't in a long time. And I never dreamed Timmy would be in any danger whatsoever."

"He probably isn't." General Connor stood up. "Why don't you go on home now, Mrs. Logan, and give us a chance to sort this out."

Home. No charges. At least not yet. Laura fumbled for her purse, stood up, and looked at Jake. Sensing his confusion and despair, she felt her throat constrict and her chest tighten. Even now, knowing he doubted her, knowing he would never love her, not even for a second, she still loved him. "The adoption went through."

Staring at the far wall, he closed his eyes.

"I thought you'd want to know." Tears choked her, and she couldn't say any more.

He nodded, but he didn't look at her.

Initially, she had kept her secret about the consultations to protect him, and now she would pay the price for having done so. He thought she didn't trust him, and that had hurt him deeply. God, but she regretted it.

Feeling like a slug, she walked to the door, then paused and glanced back at him. He hadn't moved. How could he think she didn't trust him? She owed him her life. He was her best friend. Her damned husband. Even if he had lapsed and doubted her, she'd explained now. He should be over it. Yet he still refused to cut her any slack, to grant her even a micron of understanding. And not sure whether she lashed out at him in anger for that, or in her own despair, she tightened her voice. "I'm late, but happy anniversary, Jake."

He didn't answer.

When it became obvious he wasn't going to answer her, she berated herself for trying to get to him with something she knew meant so little to him. He really wasn't her husband, so how could that barb incite a twinge, much less sting? It couldn't.

Her shoulders sinking into a slump right along with her spirit, she tugged at the doorknob.

"Stop by my office and pick up a Glock," Jake said softly. "If ROFF's targeted you, you need to be prepared."

She waited for Connor to object to her being armed, or for Jake to say anything more, but neither spoke. Wordlessly, she walked out into the hallway, her stomach churning resentment. Resentment and remorse.

Jake had given her good advice, even if she did wish she could ignore it. But playing ostrich and burying her head in the sand carried the same risks as making blind assumptions. She might not be a real wife, but she was a real woman and—at least for the moment—a real mother. She wasn't eager to wake up dead. She'd carry the gun.

As she snapped the door closed, she heard General Connor let out a gruesome sigh. "Just what the hell kind of marriage have you got, son?"

Too bruised and wounded to risk hearing Jake's response, Laura walked away, wishing she herself could know.

They had a piece of paper legally binding them together. A second piece of paper declaring they shared a son. But they had no kind of marriage.

Just as they'd agreed.

And because they had, Laura suffered what she'd sworn she would never suffer in their relationship.

Regret.

Ten

In a short time, a lot had changed. And none of it was for the better.

Just as on any other night, Laura had gone to bed with visions of not waking up until the morning. But this night, she had suffered the attacker dream, which had led inevitably to the reenactment nightmare of Paul Hawkins's survival school attempt on her life. Stress always spurred those damn nightmares; it was as predictable as a personal, handwritten invitation. Then she had been awakened in the dead of night and summoned to headquarters. She realized she had come to love Jake and feared he was hurt, but instead, she had found him with her boss. They promptly had notified her she had been fully reactivated—a slick, jurisdictional move she still wasn't convinced was in her best interests—and then doubted her integrity by asking her if she had committed treason.

Had the whole world gone crazy?

Back at Jake's, she pegged the keys to his Jag on the rack just inside the back door, then dumped her purse and the bag from Baskin-Robbins on the kitchen counter.

A chill crept over her skin, and she looked around.

A couple of cups, rinsed and placed in the sink, awaited their turn in the dishwasher. The latest in the *New Dawn* series of novels rested open-faced on the bar next to the telephone, right where she had left it. A rubber band lay in the bottom of the fruit bowl, along with a penny and a twist tie from a bread loaf's wrapper. Nothing looked touched, or amiss. She toed off her shoes and shoved them with the flat of her foot under the ledge of the bar. So why did she have this uneasy feeling? Something had pricked her comfort zone and alerted her instincts.

Certainly, a lot had happened, but most of it had occurred away from Jake's house. She shrugged off her light jacket, tossed it over the back of a chair at the table, then smoothed a hand over the hip of her slacks. Funny, until now she'd always loved Jake's home. It was quiet and comfortable, a typical single-story brick suburban house filled with a lot of opaque colors and plump cushions to soften the oversize leather furnishings. But right now the house felt too big and empty, and she felt small and insignificant in it.

Even without Timmy's exuberant presence and Betsy Miller's warmth, Laura wasn't deluded enough to convince herself it was really the house sparking those feelings. It was Jake. Never, not in thirteen years, had he acted so cold toward her and made her feel so isolated from him. Never had he doubted her. Not even when half the damn class at survival school had sided with Paul Hawkins had Jake expressed a moment's doubt in her. But he did now. Then she had loved him for being steadfast. Now, looking back, before that fiasco had ended, she had come to love him for more reasons. And over the years, her list of reasons why she loved him had lengthened considerably. But only in the last three weeks, since moving in this last time, had she fallen in love with him. Something . . . different had happened between her and Jake. Chemistry. And something more she couldn't peg and saw little reason to, considering their circumstances.

She loved him, but tonight she thought she just might hate him, too. And if riding both sides of that well-documented fine line between love and hate wasn't enough to send her running for raspberries then nothing was.

What she needed was a thorough drowning of her sorrows, she thought, digging into the white paper bag and then lifting out its contents. Tossing the half gallon of chocolate fudge ice cream into the freezer, she re-called the clerk's goofy look when she'd asked him if it came in fifty-gallon drums. Hell, it'd probably take at least that much and a couple dozen batches of brownies to sweeten Jake's sour mood over this.

And though she had serious doubts, a quart of rasp-berry yogurt might get her through her own stint at wallowing on the dark side. She tore open the top of the carton, grabbed a spoon from the drawer, then dug in for a bite. Today she had become a mother. Had realized a lifelong dream. She should be elated, not depressed to the gills. And she wouldn't be—well, not nearly so much—if Jake just hadn't doubted her. Even the raspberry yogurt couldn't get her through that.

She stabbed the spoon into the carton. Maybe men were all intrusive jerks. Maybe they all dissected every action and deed constantly, looking for hidden agendas. Maybe they were all suspicious asses who couldn't step across a mud puddle without a permit or proof it wasn't a sinkhole.

Men were notorious for having to climb a mountain of proof to gather evidence that something exists before believing it, while women—far more reasonable hu-man beings—felt quite comfortable operating on faith.

They just leapt to the top of the mountain, trusting it strong enough to sustain them.

She was suspected of treason.

Treason!

Her heart wrenched. She had been so devoted to the military all of her adult life, and this was the thanks she got? She took another bite, then two, then three. She could lose Jake and Timmy. Her job. Everything.

Her head throbbing, she spiked the spoon into the yogurt again, warning herself to drown her sorrows a little slower. Without Jake and Timmy or her work, what would be left of her life?

Nothing. Nothing at all.

Laura shut out the chilling thoughts, closing her eyes. She didn't know what would be left, not really. And she feared she didn't want to know. To the world, it appeared she had it all: a gorgeous husband who was sexy from the bone out—principled, dedicated, loyal— everything a woman looks for in a man. She had a son who would capture even the most jaded heart. A terrific career, where she had been compensated fairly and offered opportunities for advancement that were limited only by her imagination. All around—everything a woman could want. And it would be, if any of it was real.

But it wasn't.

The back of her nose burned and her eyes stung. Refusing to cry—she had gotten herself into this situation with her eyes wide open and had no one to blame but herself—she swallowed another bite of yogurt, and let the cold sliding down her throat soothe her. *Nothing stays hidden.*

It was time to take a cold, hard look at the truth. Now. Just in case she ended up arrested. Potential catastrophes aside, having her integrity questioned tonight had given her a whale of a wake-up call. It was time for a major change in her life. One that would net her a life that encompassed more than Jake and Timmy, her work, and her dedication to it and to them.

In the case of Laura Taylor Logan, the facts were these: Jake loved her as a friend, and would never love her as a man loves his wife. Or he had loved her as a friend until the photo surfaced. Now he doubted her. That happened, of course, right on the heels of her realizing she'd fallen in love with the man, despite her promise to herself not to let that happen. After so many years of thinking about him as just a friend. It still amazed her that it really had happened.

Timmy loved her as a surrogate mother—only because Laura had poured so much into loving him—but he didn't and never would love her as a mother. Not unconditionally, nor irrevocably. Hadn't she learned that after she'd moved back to the apartment and he'd distanced himself from her? If she hadn't pushed, he'd still be distant.

That concluded her foray into family, as otherwise she had none.

And on the career front, the facts didn't look any less bleak. Shortly after Sean had issued his threats to ruin her career because of her friendship with Jake, Laura had been sent TDY to the Pentagon and she'd run into Colonel James in the hallway. She hadn't known Jake and Madeline's former boss well, even though he managed the funding on her research. Tall and oddly handsome in a slightly rumpled way, he'd asked her about Jake and Timmy. Then he had dropped his voice a notch, low and intimate, almost seductive, and asked, "How's your implant device coming along?"

She'd gone ice cold inside. Not at him asking about the device, but at him linking Jake and Timmy to it. She'd known then that she was standing on a foundation of sand and that it would shift and her career would tumble. Sean Drake had gone to Colonel James, just as he'd threatened to do. Outwardly, she had shrugged at James, deliberately evasive. "Oh, still working on it."

That had been the truth, so far as she'd gone. At that stage, the satellite-tracking device had been no sweat; its design was down pat. Getting the implant to emit bicolor signals—red to signify "alive and tracking," and blue to signify "dead and tracking"—had been the part stumping her.

She licked the creamy yogurt from her spoon. Now she'd nailed that, too. It had been simple really, once she'd considered the change of body temperature. Just months ago, she had introduced a more complex, tricolor design, though she hadn't yet field tested it.

"I'm sure you'll figure it out," Colonel James had told her, saluting a junior officer who'd walked by.

His smile had seemed sincere, but even in memory, it curdled her stomach. He'd irked her in ways she hadn't consciously grasped, but understood at gut level. There, brilliant red signals had flashed: *Warning! Warning! Warning!*

And all the briefing drills she ever had received on counterintelligence had replayed in her mind.

Unsure if she'd sensed the truth, or if paranoia had set in because Sean had intimidated her, she had kept her doubts about Colonel James to herself. She hadn't even mentioned her uneasiness to Jake—especially not to Jake. He would have gone toe to toe with Sean Drake over the threats. He had gone toe to toe with the man on several occasions before then, so it hadn't been difficult to justify keeping silent. When push came to shove, she had no actual proof of Colonel James doing anything wrong, only a gut feeling. If those gut feelings had been discussed with Jake, then they would have had to acknowledge the possibility of wrongdoing. Jake would have been put in the position of having to decide whether to keep quiet about it, or to report it and investigate his father-in-law. Sean would have ruined two careers: hers and Jake's. Besides, just her suspecting Sean Drake and Colonel James were corrupt was rough enough, and she'd already paid in spades. To get away from Drake and James, she'd had to deactivate in Intel, forfeit active duty, and give up communication design research and development as her primary duty. Without hard evidence, she shouldn't have to pay any more.

That whole sordid situation, at least so far, had stayed hidden—a blessing she was grateful for. She only hoped it stayed hidden forever.

Now General Connor, her boss due to the reactivation and, in deactivated times, her boss's boss, suspected her of treason.

"Except for having her husband's lunatic of an ex-wife to contend with, these are the facts of the life of Laura Taylor Logan," she whispered, stepping into the entryway and heading toward the living room. "And, boy, are they grim."

Something crunched under her stockinged feet.

Laura looked down. Shiny slivers of glass caught the light from the kitchen and threw off a glare. The slender window beside the door had been broken.

Someone had been—or was—inside the house.

Memories of the man who had attempted to break into her apartment before she and Jake married flashed through her mind. Memories of him slashing at her with a knife, her wresting it from him, and cutting his face through his ski mask.

She still smelled him. Still saw the blade and the blood. And his scent still evoked memories of another attacker. One who'd nearly killed her. Paul Hawkins. The knife-wielding intruder had been skilled in hand-to-hand combat; no novice or amateur. He'd eluded Fairhope and Sacramento police, and the California Highway Patrol. Even with his DNA, he'd never been caught. He was a pro.

Had he come back in real life, as he so often did in her dreams?

The hairs on her neck lifted. Her instincts slipped into High Alert, and her muscles coiled, preparing for the unexpected. She backed into the kitchen, set down the yogurt on the edge of the bar, then retrieved the Glock from her purse. Grateful now Jake had suggested it, she began a systematic search of the house.

Betsy's room, laundry, kitchen, and the bath off it— all clear. Nothing appeared disturbed. No odd scents or sounds. Living room: only the ticking of the old wall clock and a pillow out of place on the sofa, as if someone had rested against it. Odd. Laura lifted the pillow, and caught a whiff of perfume. It wasn't her Ritz, though the scent did tug at something familiar to her. From where, she couldn't recall. It was sweet, subtle. . . .

She put the pillow back down, then inched her way down the hallway, through her room, and then through Jake's. Everything appeared fine. So why did she still feel . . . invaded?

She looked into Timmy's room, and the reason became glaringly apparent. "Oh, God." Her heart slid up into her throat. She started to shake and broke out in a cold sweat.

It was empty.

The whole room had been stripped bare, ceiling to carpeted floor. Even the picture hangers had been removed from the walls.

What looked like a glass lay on the floor in the center of the room. Her flesh crawling, Laura entered cautiously to get a closer look at it.

It wasn't a glass. It was a bottle. Anger rode hard on the heels of fear, and her knees gave out. Laura crumpled onto the carpet, reached for it, but then recalled the possibility of fingerprints, and jerked her hand back.

It was a half-full bottle.

Of Scotch.

Eleven

He's safe. He's safe. Betsy says Timmy is safe.

Laura sat on the floor in Timmy's room, clasping her knees and rocking back and forth, letting the litany replay through her mind. Staring at the cordless phone, the Glock, and the bottle of Scotch, she prayed she'd soon believe it enough to stop shaking. She'd talked with him herself. So why couldn't she get past feeling he was in danger?

The obvious conclusion about this was that Madeline had broken in and stolen all of Timmy's things. But Laura couldn't look only to the obvious, not with the ROFF possibility. Should she call the police, or military security?

The bedroom door creaked.

Laura snatched up the Glock, rolled over onto her stomach, and took aim.

"Whoa!" Jake held up his hands.

Laura let out a sigh of relief, not caring if he heard it, and lowered the gun back to the carpet, her heart still threatening to rocket out of her chest.

"What the hell happened here?" Jake walked over.

"Timmy's fine." Laura pointed to the bottle of

Scotch. "It appears Madeline thought it was time for him to move."

"Damn her." Jake reached down for the phone.

Laura topped his hand on the receiver with hers, stopping him. "She's pulled a few felonies in your absence."

His brows shot up. "Felonies?"

She filled him in, starting with Madeline's call to Judge Barton, which necessitated telling him the reason Judge Neal hadn't heard the case, then related the Pizza Hut fiasco and the ramming of the Mustang incident—omitting her threatening Madeline for fear the shock would lay Jake out. He looked awfully pale. Then she finished up with arriving home and finding the window broken and Timmy's room bare.

"Where's Timmy?"

"They left before this. He doesn't know."

Jake frowned. "They who? Where'd he go?"

"To a ball game and then to Alice's with Betsy. They'll be back Saturday night."

Betsy had remembered their anniversary. So had Laura. He recalled her acidic, "I'm late, but happy anniversary, Jake," on departing from headquarters. Her tone had gotten to him, but he couldn't complain. He'd doubted her, and she'd known it. He'd hurt her too, he thought, spotting the yogurt carton. Driven her to eating raspberries, for God's sake. "Did you call the police about any of this?"

"No. I know you're opposed, and she's upset Timmy an enormous amount in the last few days."

"I see." Jake rubbed at the back of his neck. His muscles had knotted. "Well, she's gone too far. We need to report it, Laura. All of it."

"Do we?" She glanced up at him. "What if it wasn't her? What if it was ROFF setting her up? The Scotch is rather obvious."

"Madeline's about as subtle as mud. Why would she suddenly become less than obvious?"

"I've got a feeling, Jake."

"Okay. Okay." Grimacing, he reached for the cordless phone. His fingertips brushed against Laura's knee.

She jerked as if he'd burned her.

"Sorry." He dialed Connor's secure line and informed him of the situation. When he hung up, he told Laura, "We're to sit tight. A security crew will be over in a few minutes."

She didn't acknowledge hearing him.

He shrugged out of his jacket and hung it on the doorknob. It was time to get all this tension between them resolved. He hadn't thought she'd be here, but when she hadn't been at her apartment, he'd dared to hope she'd come home. "I appreciate your staying."

"Do you?" Sparks of uncertainty glinted in her eyes.

He nodded, then deliberately steered the conversation away from the photo and far, far away from Laura's consultations. His feelings on that were too raw. He needed time to let them settle, to recoup. The past few days had been pure hell. "If Madeline should attempt to overturn the adoption and you're not here, that could complicate things."

"More than you realize." Laura stared at him, her eyes flat and serious, her voice dread-laced. "She's drunk and watching soaps, Jake."

He closed his eyes and let out a sigh that could power a sub station for a year. How much more did they all have to take from her? "We don't need another one of her major dramas. Not now." Not with Shadowpoint, and Laura involved.

Laura lowered her gaze to the floor. "It doesn't seem as if we're going to have a choice." As if by sheer will, she returned her gaze to him. "I didn't mean to hurt you."

He stared at her long and hard. Her eyes were dark and stormy, and tension riddled her face. "We've been best friends a long time."

"Yes, we have." Bitterness etched her tone.

She felt betrayed. Understanding that, but unable to sincerely apologize for doubting her, he frowned. "Laura, I want to ask you something. Whatever you tell me, I'll believe you. The photo—well, it was a shock."

"I suppose it was." She tilted back her head and sent him a look that warned him she saw far beneath the surface of this and didn't like what she was seeing. "But tell me, Jake. What shocked you most? You hoping I wasn't in danger because I'm your wife, or you hoping I'd committed treason?"

Jake's face burned hot. That she might be hurt because of him—that was the worst. A hundred times worse than her committing treason. Shameful but true, and he wouldn't lie about it, not even to himself. Yet dwelling on it wouldn't resolve a thing. "Can we get past the anger and down to the base of the matter?"

"The base of the matter is that there is no base." She grunted. "Even with a thirteen-year friendship, not to mention a marriage, between us, you suspect me."

"You're a viable suspect, Laura." He walked over to the window and leaned an elbow against its ledge. "Do I *think* you're involved with ROFF? No, I don't. But I don't get to operate based on what I think. I protect the interests of the United States and, in its eyes, there's valid reason for suspicion against you."

He blew out a sigh and paced a short path along the far end of the room. "Personally, you're my best friend, and my wife. But my personal feelings don't come into this, and they don't give me a choice. I made an oath and I have to keep it. You made that same oath. Can you look me in the eye and tell me that if our situations were reversed you'd ignore your oath?''

She glared up at him but, as the words penetrated her anger, the starch left her shoulders and her jaw went slack. ''No, I can't. I'd like to, damn it,'' she confessed on a sigh. ''But I can't.''

Honest. Thank God. Jake thought. ''Then don't condemn me for doing what you'd do yourself.''

She rubbed at her temple. ''I'm not.''

Could he believe her? Unsure, he watched her closely. She lifted her chin, then quickly tucked it back to her chest, as if she wanted to look him in the eye but couldn't make herself do it.

''I'm hurt, Jake,'' she said, just above a whisper. ''But I'm not condemning you.''

That he understood. He'd be hurt too, down to the core. Anyone in Ops would be. ''Is there anything else you haven't told me—aside from your sporadic reactivation in Intel, which is now a full reactivation?''

She did look at him then, and the sadness in her eyes could melt cartilage in a man's knees. ''Only that the transmission's gone out in the Mustang,'' she said. ''Bill Green got backed up with work, so he's postponed towing it to his shop until first thing in the morning.''

Glib. She was rallying, and Jake was glad to see it. He could handle Laura's anger, but her being hurt got to him. Especially when he'd had a strong hand in causing it. ''Did the transmission fizzle on the way back from headquarters?''

''No.'' Shame flooded her face. ''Earlier Monday night. I, um, took your Jag to headquarters.''

''My Jag?''

She glared up at him. ''Don't get testy, Jake. When Connor called, I thought you were in trouble, and I couldn't get a cab. It was an emergency."

"Fine." A knock at the front door kept him from saying any more. "I think the security crew's arrived."

It was nearly two A.M. before the security personnel finished up and left the house. And Jake was worried about Laura.

With only the light above the stove turned on, she stood in the kitchen, wearing her teal silk robe, and eating raspberry yogurt, God help him, straight from the carton. She'd been through hell the last couple of days, and the strain showed. "You okay?"

She looked at him as if he'd lost his mind. "Now why wouldn't I be okay?"

"Don't bite. I was just checking." He held off a frown by the skin of his teeth. "Do we really need sarcasm?"

"What would you suggest?" Her eyes hazed, as if she realized she was facing two hundred pounds of wounded male ego. "Tears? Raging?" She grunted, then dropped her gaze. "I could accommodate you on either, but I won't."

He hated that, hated it that he'd caused so much of her distress. Feeling guilty as hell, he poured himself a glass of milk at the fridge. Toeing aside her shoes from beneath the bar stool, he sat down across from her, and downed half the milk. "I'm sorry about all this trouble."

"She's responsible, Jake. Not you."

"Still, if it weren't for me—"

"Don't you dare say it. Not to me."

Loyal to a fault, and gracious. Light from the stove spilled over her hair, turning it golden, and the urge to kiss the anger and weariness out of her tempted him. He squelched it, uneasy that he'd felt it at all. "Wanna talk about what's bugging you?"

"It depends." A frown creased the skin between her brows. "Have you calmed down?"

"Substantially." Until he found out if Madeline had destroyed Timmy's room, anyway. His stomach growled, reminding him he hadn't eaten in twenty-four hours. He snagged a banana from the fruit bowl and peeled back its skin.

"I left out a minor detail earlier," Laura said. "About one of the altercations with Madeline."

Eating the banana only made him hungrier. Sliding back his chair, he cringed at the scrape of its legs against the tile floor and walked over to the pantry. Canvassing the cereals and finding more dignity in eating Cheerios than in the kid's stuff, he grabbed the box from the shelf, then gathered the milk carton, two bowls—he'd long since gotten Laura's number on this—and a couple spoons.

"Which altercation?" There was quite a list for such a short time. The adoption had driven the airhead over the edge, he supposed.

Dumping the stuff on the table, he poured cereal into a bowl and then splashed in some milk. "Can I have a waiver on your shirts-will-be-worn-at-the-table rule?"

"Yeah." She sat down beside him. "I'm feeling magnanimous." Swiping up a spill with her bare hand, she snatched his bowl, a spoon, and then scooped up a bite and munched down.

He had Laura's number, all right. "Which altercation?"

"The one where she tried to run over Timmy and me." Laura dipped her spoon back into the bowl, her gaze intent on the cereal. "I threatened to kill her, Jake."

Surprise rippled up his back. Laura? Kill Madeline? After years of her pushing Laura's buttons every time she could? "What pushed *you* over the edge?"

Laura lifted her gaze to his. "Timmy was in the car. She could have killed him."

That disclosure spurred the temptation to kiss her. It doubled and hit Jake stronger, harder, and deeper—an eclectic mix of regret and elation. Nearly buckling to the temptation, he mentally wrenched himself away and buried those inclinations. With their agreement and less than two percent survival odds hanging over his head, he'd be the worst kind of bastard to encourage Laura to fall in love with him. The worst kind.

Having lost his appetite, Jake shoved his bowl off the placemat, then laced his hands together atop the table.

"Well?" Laura moved the cereal box aside so she could see his face. "Aren't you going to say anything?"

"I understand."

"You do?" Her eyes went wide.

He'd stunned her. "Don't you think I've felt that way about Madeline a thousand times? At least a thousand times?"

"If you hadn't, you wouldn't be human."

"I'm human," he said, watching her gather a knife and a peach from the fruit bowl. When she returned to the table, she sliced some of the fruit into both of their cereal bowls. "Back during the assignment at Eglin, down in Florida, she got to me big-time. I'd hoped the move there would get her back on track, but I was TDY a lot. She drank even more." He debated a second, then decided what the hell. "I got called on the carpet for it."

Stunned, Laura's jaw gaped. "You're joking."

"Nope. Straight off the plane from a three-week stint in Saudi, I got summoned to the colonel's office. He wasn't a happy commander. Madeline had gotten lit at the club and had made a spectacle of herself. The colonel's wife was 'appalled at the poor example Madeline was setting for the other wives,' and the colonel was ticked to the gills.''

Laura winced. ''Ripped you a new one, eh?''

''Oh, yeah.'' Jake grunted. ''The worst part was I couldn't do a damn thing but sit there and take it.''

Sympathy and a fair share of pity flickered through Laura's eyes. ''Embarrassed you to death, I'm sure.''

Jake cocked a brow at her. ''Wouldn't it you?''

''Yes, it would.'' Laura tucked her foot up under her on the chair. ''Is that why you never told me about it?''

''I guess so.'' He knew so. Even now the humiliation of the incident stung. ''The colonel issued me a direct order to get my wife under control before she undermined morale.'' Jake snorted. ''Who can control another adult?''

''No one.'' Laura patted his forearm, conveying her understanding of his sense of helplessness and resentment. She handed him his spoon, silently encouraging him to eat. ''How'd Madeline react?''

''With the usual promises.'' He dragged the bowl back over. ''She was ticked off, though. Within two days, she got three traffic tickets on base. I had to go to Traffic Safety School.''

Laura muttered under her breath. ''Sounds as if she knew you'd be held responsible for her actions on base.''

''Oh, yeah. She knew. She got the tickets deliberately. Flagrant violations that had the MPs shaking their heads.''

''Hell hath no fury.'' Laura saluted him with her spoon. It glinted light from the stove hood.

Not caring for the amused lilt in her voice, Jake

frowned at her. "You could pretend a little sympathy. It was a degrading experience, Laura."

"I'm sure it was, and I'd be sympathetic, but it's outrageous. Madeline drinks, and you get reamed. Madeline baits the military police into giving her tickets, and you sent to Traffic Safety School." Laura let out a delicate grunt. "There's a logic gap the size of Texas in this picture, Jake."

"It's logical. The Air Force only has jurisdiction over active duty members. I was the active duty member of the family, therefore, I was held responsible."

"Powerful weapon for vengeful wives bent on punishing their husbands."

"Only if it's abused." Jake wagged a warning finger at her. "Don't get any ideas. The next stint I'm forced to pull in Traffic Safety, I'm taking prisoners."

"Better be on your best behavior, Major." A mischievous glint lit in Laura's eyes. "And for the record, I don't do prisoner. Not even for you."

He grunted. "I knew I should've stayed single." Yet here he was, sitting in his kitchen in the middle of the night, eating Cheerios and peaches—a hell of a combination—wanting to make love with the woman across the table from him, knowing damn well a real marriage was impossible and he'd be begging for disaster. He'd clearly lost his mind.

He took a bite of cereal. An odd mix, but it didn't taste half bad. "Timmy mentioned he'd asked you, now that you're his real mom, if you're going to stay with us or move back into the apartment." Jake bet Timmy had fidgeted, too. Maybe even shrugged as if it didn't matter.

Laura tilted her head. "He said if I wanted to stay, he wouldn't mind."

Jake debated, and then confessed. "Neither would

I.'' That had to be the biggest understatement of the millennium.

Laura squirmed, definitely uncomfortable. "I assured him I'd love him regardless, and that we'd discuss it. It'd be okay, but Madeline's increased antics worry me."

So she wouldn't mind staying, then? His heart thudded hard. "She'll calm down."

"She's drunk and watching soaps, Jake," Laura said, deadly serious. "More likely she'll gear up, fight the adoption, and continue making us miserable."

"She'll do that whether you're here or not. If we have to go back to court, you not being here could jeopardize our chances." That was true, but not the whole truth. He wanted Laura here. He shouldn't, but he did. His stomach muscles clenched. "The biggest problem is she's insanely jealous of you."

Laura frowned and swallowed a crunchy bite of cereal. "No, it's Timmy."

"I don't think so. We had more than a few heated arguments over the jealousy bit." Jake sipped at his milk. "She was convinced we were having an affair."

"Absurd." Laura grunted, stilled her spoon midair, then cocked her head. "Why didn't we, do you think?"

Remembering their wedding kiss for the thousandth time, Jake swallowed hard. Obviously because they hadn't known what they'd been missing. "We were friends."

"We're still friends."

Were they? That definition should be right, and yet it struck him as being too sparse to fit them anymore. "I was married to her then."

"True." Laura tapped the spoon, and faint chinking sounds filled the cozy kitchen. "Did you ever think about it? I mean, about us, that way?"

Gray area. If he told her the truth about his feelings,

she'd run like hell. Had Madeline sensed the truth before he himself realized it? Her accusations had to come from somewhere. Yet he couldn't lie. Not to Laura. "Not then."

"Me, either."

He wanted to ask her about now, but he couldn't do it. He had to get a grip here. They had an ironclad agreement.

"I think she's afraid of you."

Jake snapped his gaze to Laura, surprised she'd picked up on that. "She always has been. I never understood why. But that never stopped her from cutting tricks like with the traffic tickets." He lifted his right hand. "So help me, Laura, I never gave her any reason to fear me."

"I know. Using your size and strength against women isn't your style. You're more apt to protect them to death." Laura stroked his forearm, then realized what she was doing, jerked back and then laced her hands in her lap.

Why? Before they'd married, they'd often touched, hugged, or dropped a kiss on the other's cheek, forehead, or temple. Why did they both feel all that had been normal was now taboo?

"Are you afraid of me?" Jake asked.

She guffawed. "Not unless you're God or Paul Hawkins. I save my fear for the big gun threats." Paul Hawkins had come so close to killing her in survival school that she still had nightmares about him. "Fear would be wasted on a teddy bear like you."

Jake Logan? A teddy bear? The guys on staff would think Laura had lost her mind. They considered him ruthless. And he was, when on missions.

Laura cocked her head. "So what do you think made her afraid of you?"

"I have no idea."

"Maybe your marrying her only because of Timmy?"

"No." He thought about it, then hiked his shoulders. "Hell, I don't know. I doubt if she knows. The woman's twisted. And half-pickled."

"Every rose has its thorns." Poor Jake looked so weary. Actually, Laura frowned, he looked ill. "Are you sick?"

Connor had authorized disclosure to Laura, but Jake had wanted to wait until tomorrow to tell her. She'd had enough—more than enough—to deal with already. But he couldn't lie to her. And she was no fool. If she hadn't been preoccupied by everything else, she'd already have been asking why he was physically drained. "ROFF isn't a religious organization."

She stilled. "What is it?"

"A terrorist group, Laura."

Her hand slid to her chest and covered her heart. "And they killed three operatives."

He nodded.

"Why?"

Here came the hard part. He wanted to hold her hand to lessen the shock, but he didn't dare. "Because they're amassing a biological warfare arsenal."

"Down in the Everglades?" She let out a stunned grunt, paced the kitchen, then returned to the bar. "No. Damn it, no. Not in our own country."

"That's what the CIA believes," Jake countered. "We picked up further evidence to support their preliminary findings when I retrieved the operatives."

Fear streaked through her eyes, and she ran her damp palms down her sides. "Give it to me straight. What happened to you out there?"

Now came the hardest part of all. "I was contaminated."

Laura sucked in a sharp breath. "Are you okay?"

Fear twisted in her and set her to shaking. "Stupid question. Of course you are, or you'd still be in the hospital."

"I was treated and released. I'm fine."

Thank God. Thank God. She studied him like a microscope specimen, afraid she'd miss a minuscule sign, outrage simmering in her that this had happened to him. "Anthrax or botulism?"

"Strong anthrax," he said. "Good thing, too. I was already suffering symptoms when I took the antibiotics."

Laura's anger crumbled. If it'd been botulism, once symptoms appeared it was too late for treatment. Jake would have died.

The blood drained from her face and then gushed through her. She narrowed her eyes. "You knew going in you faced contamination. Damn it, Jake. Why didn't you wear protective gear?"

Her anger had returned with a vengeance; Laura's defense mechanism kicking in, and Jake was glad to see it. "If I'd been intercepted geared up, how long do you suppose they'd have let me live?"

She opened her mouth to object, but instead switched tactics. "You could have pre-medicated."

"Not without authorization. To get it, I'd have had to break communications silence, and before I could do that, I had to get the bodies out so we could figure out what we're working with down there. As soon as I could, I medicated with antibiotics from my survival kit."

"Oh, God. Without authorization? You self-medicated?" Her voice cracked. "Is Connor pulling your clearance?"

"He gave me a waiver due to the circumstances. He knew we had to have those bodies."

"Thank goodness." Irritation replaced worry in her

expression. "You took a hell of a risk. I don't like that."

"I didn't much care for the feeling, either. But I had no choice."

The heat left her voice. "Were the operatives also contaminated?"

"It's highly likely. The autopsies will be done in a couple of hours. Connor's going to call after the docs finish up."

Laura filled a cup with hot water for tea, put it in the microwave to nuke it, then set the timer for a minute. "Why is it taking so long?"

"The bodies required special handling. The docs just got them this morning, and they've got to run a lot of separate toxin screens. That takes time. And the protective gear is cumbersome for them to work in."

Laura looked more fragile than she had the day Madeline had lost Timmy. "It would have been really bitchy of you to die on our anniversary, Jake," she said, obviously aware he'd foregone both protective measures and special handling.

She'd remembered their anniversary, and it had mattered. But how did it matter? He'd bet his eyeteeth Laura hadn't reneged on their agreement. "Yeah, and with my luck, you've have cursed me from now on about it, too."

"You can bet on it." She sounded ticked.

They sat there silently, staring at each other, and pain filled Laura's eyes. "I could have lost you."

His heart wrenched. "I'm fine."

"This time." She paused a beat, fisting her hand atop the table. "I-I don't think I could take losing you, Jake. You've been my best friend too long."

"You know risks go with the job." Worry coursed through his veins and made mincemeat of his stomach. He'd never seen Laura like this. She was rattled by the adoption, Madeline's antics, the Mustang breaking down, Timmy's room being destroyed, and Jake's own contamination, but the lion's share had to stem from having her integrity questioned. Aside from Timmy, nothing could get to Laura like that. Not with her high standards. Not even losing Jake without warning.

Logically she accepted the necessity of her being questioned, but emotionally it hurt her deeply that he doubted her enough to warrant questioning. "What do you need?"

She stiffened and pulled in a shuddery breath. Anguish clouded her eyes, crippled her voice. "I need to know you're over the shock and you don't doubt me about the treason."

She feared being blamed. Feared the photo. Feared being targeted. Normal, that. But Connor had assured her countermeasures would be taken and countercrews were damn good at their jobs. This wasn't professional concern. It was personal. Laura, the woman, needed to know that Jake, the man, didn't doubt her. "I don't doubt you."

He picked up a piece of cereal that had missed the bowl and landed on the placemat. "Is that what's got you up stealing my Cheerios and putting peaches in them when you should be sleeping?"

"No. Mind clutter. And waiting to hear if Madeline's responsible for Timmy's room," Laura said, being deliberately evasive and wishing she'd asked Jake to put on a shirt. The last thing she needed tonight was to have to self-lecture on curbing lust and retaining discipline. Good God, she could've lost him.

"We should hear soon," Jake speculated, grabbing his bowl and moving to the kitchen sink. "Something more is bothering you. Is it Timmy?"

Laura debated lying, but she couldn't. Not after seeing how much just withholding the truth from Jake had upset him. "Not really." She joined him at the sink and swiveled the faucet, leaving him high and dry. The stream of warm water flowed over her hands, and she rinsed her dish. The smell of chlorine burned her nose. She twitched it. "But the timing is lousy for discussing it." True, even if it wasn't the real reason.

"Odds for there being a good time in the foreseeable future look grim." Jake took back control of the faucet. "We're up waiting for the call anyway. You might as well get it out."

She turned and slumped back against the cabinet. A direct hit. She couldn't not discuss it now. He'd think she was holding out on him again, and after last time. . . . "Before you got home, I was sitting in Timmy's empty room and it all just hit me."

"What hit you?" He paused, still not rinsing his bowl.

A sob cracked her voice. "That my whole life is a lie."

That response, he'd never expected. "What do you mean?" Was she confessing to a crime?

"I sat here and took a cold, hard look at my life, and I've discovered it sucks." Her chin quivered. "I've got a car stuck in first gear. A husband, who isn't really a husband and doesn't love me. A son, who wants to be my son but really won't be, because his birth mother is going to take him back or to die trying. And as soon as I move back to the apartment—when he wants me to stay with him—he won't love me, either. He'll never get over feeling abandoned again. And I've got a job— at least, as of yesterday, I was employed—where I've been totally devoted and yet I've been jerked around, activated, and then fully activated, and my boss, who's normally my boss's boss, suspects me of being a traitor. That's what I mean, Jake. I've got nothing that's real. Not one damn thing that isn't a lie or an illusion."

Expecting the charged air to crackle, Jake stilled. He had no idea what to say. When his mind stopped racing and he could grasp simple thoughts, he weighed his words carefully, knowing they'd both live with them a long time. "If Connor still suspected you of treason, you'd be in the brig."

She fisted her hands on the sink ledge. "There was doubt in his eyes, Jake. Don't deny it. We both saw it."

He had seen it. "True, but he believes you're innocent."

"Innocent? You don't refuse to discuss countermeasures with someone you believe is innocent." She affected Connor's dry tone. " 'That information is classified, Mrs. Logan.' " She scowled. "I've got clearance, damn it. The only reason he said that was because he still had doubts."

She had a valid point. But so did Jake. Figuring the issue was a dead horse, however, he moved on. She wanted something real. Something more. What woman wouldn't? Guilt shrouded him. "You forfeited too much, staying married to me."

"Great." She banged a hand against the countertop, grabbed his bowl, and then bumped him with her hip, nudging him away from the sink. "Now you want a divorce, right?"

He seemed to be screwing this up badly. More at a loss than he cared to be, he raked a what-the-hell-do-I-do-now hand through his hair and then tried a novel approach: the simple, unadorned truth. "I want you to be happy."

"You want me *happy*?" She looked at him as if he'd sprouted a spare head. "Well, of course you do. Suggesting a divorce in the middle of mayhem is bound to make me positively ecstatic, Jake."

Muttering, she turned a glare on him he wouldn't

soon forget. The bowl tilted into the stream, and she doused herself with water. It sprayed down the front of her silk robe, soaking the fabric, chilling her skin, and puckering her nipples.

"Damn it." She swatted at her stomach, causing more damage.

Why was she angry? He'd been telling her he understood why *she* wanted a divorce. That had been what she'd been leading up to, hadn't it?

Maybe. But from her reaction, maybe not. Jake spun her around by the shoulders, grabbed a towel from the counter, and then gently blotted at the rivulets of water running down her neck, those soaking her chest, and finally her breasts. She was so beautiful. Irked to the gills, or calm and soothingly serene, she was an enigma that drew him like a two-ton magnet. A bundle of contradictions; competent and confident and tenacious, open yet private, elusive and fragile. Lingering, he stared into her eyes. The air between them grew thick, heavy, charged. He had to kiss her. Just once. Just . . . once.

The phone rang.

Vacillating, he stepped away from her to answer it, his insides shaking. "Logan," he said into the receiver.

Laura watched him, looking stiff and tense and wary. Because he'd nearly kissed her? Or because of the call?

He listened to the brief report, muttered, "Thanks," then tapped the hook button. Frowning, he lowered the receiver to the bar, then looked over at Laura. "They checked Madeline's prints against those in her Intel file, but found no matches anywhere in the house."

"Then they did lift other prints?"

Jake nodded. "A man's. Off the door in Timmy's room."

Fear rippled through Laura. She strained to squelch

it, and then forced herself to ask a question whose answer she feared would incite sheer terror. "Have they formed a supposition?"

Jake nodded. "ROFF."

Twelve

~

Laura shivered. "Oh, God." She crossed her chest with her arms. "Oh, God."

Jake wanted to hold her, but he kept the bar between them to avoid doing something he knew they'd both regret. "We can't do anything about this yet. It's too soon. The pros need time to nail this down, Laura."

"Right." She kneaded her arms, leaving creases in the silk sleeves covering her upper arms. "You're right."

He fingered the twist tie in the bottom of the fruit bowl, wondered where the penny had come from, and stole a sidelong glance at her. She looked calmer, but she definitely needed to rechannel her thoughts. "I didn't mean to upset you."

"What?" She clearly had no idea what he was talking about.

"Earlier." His throat went thick. "No one deserves happiness more than you do. I wasn't asking for a divorce. I thought you wanted one."

"I don't."

"Maybe you should," he countered. "Then you could find a man who'd make your lies and illusions real." It might be right, but just saying it made him sick. No way could he look at her while doing it. No way.

"Find a man?" Anger radiated from her in palpable waves, and her voice went tight. "That's not an option."

She wasn't making a bit of sense. Maybe she just needed to vent some stress and this wasn't supposed to make sense. Yeah, that had to be it. It was a stress valve. He wasn't supposed to get it. "Why not?"

"It just isn't." She refused to look at him.

She had nothing real, but she obviously wanted it and he couldn't give it to her. What the hell was he supposed to do except offer to release her? Having no idea and feeling frustrated to the max, he held off a sigh by the skin of his teeth and then asked, "What do you want, Laura?"

She looked up at him, her eyes wide and luminous. "I want Timmy safe. I want to feel safe again. I want Madeline to leave us alone. And I want to know ROFF isn't setting me up to take their fall for treason."

"I can't give you those things." If he could, he would. Those things, and more.

"I know." Her voice went soft, nostalgic. "Remember back in survival school how the instructor split us up into teams?"

She, Jake, and ten others had been tagged the A-Team. "Yeah. Six feet of snow, sub-freezing temperatures, and he dumps us in the middle of nowhere for five days with a ten-pound bag of potatoes and a live rabbit."

Laura got misty-eyed. "I fell in love with that rabbit."

"Bunny," Jake corrected her, a hint of a smile tugging at his lips. "You called it a bunny."

"And you knew that the person on each team who

got most attached to the bunny would be the one the instructor ordered to kill it.''

Jake shifted uncomfortably. "I'd been warned by a former attendee."

"And you warned me not to get attached to it."

"Which you did anyway."

"Yes, I did." Her gaze turned tender. "And while the other teams ate rabbit stew, our team didn't."

Jake slid her a wry grin. "Your argument was very persuasive."

She blushed. "I really wouldn't have shot my team members, Jake."

"I knew that, but they didn't," he said. "I meant the other argument, though. The one you levied on the instructor. 'The Air Force oath is to protect *and* serve, and that means extending protection to those smaller, weaker, and unable to defend themselves. And, in context, "to serve" means more than "serving" a small, weak, and unable-to-defend-itself rabbit for lunch.' " A chuckle rumbled in Jake's throat. "My God, you were impassioned, and very convincing."

A poignant smile touched her lips and her eyes hazed. "And the team backed me."

"Yes, it did." Hell, who could have resisted backing her? All fired up, she'd been irresistible. She still was.

"Only because you backed me," she said softly. "They respected you, and you insisted they back me."

"You weren't supposed to know that." Feeling his face grow hot, Jake frowned. "But you're wrong. They respected you."

"I wasn't supposed to know you put the fear of God and Jake Logan into the other teams too, and kept them from touching Bunny, either. But I knew." She visually caressed him. "Saving that rabbit meant a lot to me, Jake."

Was she bent on saving him, too? Is that where she

was going with this trip down memory lane?

An insight flashed through his mind. Smaller, weaker, and unable to defend itself, the rabbit had been vulnerable. She'd saved it and set it free. Timmy, a child, was vulnerable. Just as vulnerable as the child Laura had been. No one had saved or set her free, and she was determined not to let that happen to Timmy.

A knot swelled in Jake's throat. Now he understood the reason for her depth of loyalty, her steadfastness. And now he knew just how deeply his doubting her had hurt her. Buying time to get a grip on his emotions, he filled a large glass with ice water.

He couldn't not acknowledge that he'd hurt her any more than he could not acknowledge all she'd done for him and Timmy. "You're an important part of my life, Laura." She and Timmy were his life—them, and the job.

"Yes, I am." She walked around the end of the bar, then stopped beside him. "You asked me what I wanted."

"Laura," he cut in, the words he had to say slicing at his heart and his sense of worth. "I can't give you any of those things. I wish I could, but I—"

"You can give me what I want most right now." She looked up at him, beheld him, her eyes glossy and overly bright. "I want most to be held by the man who saved my rabbit."

Certain he'd never faced a more dangerous adversary, Jake stiffened. She affected him on all levels—physically, emotionally, spiritually. Sexually. And while he had a will to resist her, he also had a need to succumb to her, and little confidence about which would prove stronger.

The heart always wins.

Remembering that, he inwardly grimaced. "I can't do that." Outwardly, he downed the large glass of ice water, fighting the temptation when he wanted nothing more than to just give in to it.

"Then just let me hold you." Hands raised, she hesitated, then slowly circled his waist with her arms and hugged him as if she feared letting go.

He ordered himself to object. Ignored it. And insisted his arms stay at his sides. But when she looked up at him and he saw how upset she was, he couldn't convince himself of one logical reason why he shouldn't hold her. Until they'd married, they'd hugged often. If she'd dated since their marriage, she'd been discreet and he knew nothing of it. She needed to be touched, appreciated as a woman. She needed more. But from him? The last time he'd had physical contact with her had been the kiss they'd shared at the chapel in Lake Tahoe on their wedding day.

Her face against his bare chest, she swallowed a whimper that jerked at his heartstrings. "Please, just put your arms around me, Jake. I won't consider it a break in our agreement or anything, but I . . . I need to be held."

Laura didn't rattle easily, but she was rattled now. He hated it with conviction, and he wanted it to stop. Just hold her, he ordered himself. Just do it. It, and nothing more. His water glass dripping condensation, he set it onto the bar, feeling his resistance melting away as quickly as the ice in his glass, then lifted his arms and coiled them around her back. Oh, God. He squeezed his eyes shut. She felt so good. So warm and perfect, and so good.

Her mouth, sensually soft, and her eyes, dead serious and that stormy blue color that rocked his senses. She held his gaze, her teeth parted, revealing a hint of her tongue. She pressed closer, breasts to chest, thighs to thighs, and he nearly came undone. Untethered, her robe-clad breasts flattened against his chest, warming the thin silk pressed between them, warming him far beneath the skin touched. Every hormone in his body rocketed into overdrive.

"I want to kiss you too, Jake," she whispered, letting her lips trail over his clavicles down to his turgid nipples.

Do it. Do it! His heart knocked against his ribs. "That's, um, a bad idea right now." They were both too raw, too vulnerable. Holding her like this had his emotions churning and those damn fantasies of her being his wife giving him unadulterated hell. He was human, for God's sake. Flesh and blood, muscle and man. And logic, common sense, and good intentions were getting blown out of the water by emotional, erotic longings. They didn't stand a chance against her. Not a chance.

"It's an awful idea. But I'm going to do it anyway." She lifted her chin, aligned their mouths, and her breath warmed his face. "I want to feel close to you, but I won't forget you don't love me—not for a second," she promised, then claimed his lips.

His reaction was instantaneous, electric. The simple meshing of mouths, swirling of tongues, grazing of teeth and lips, aroused, energized, empowered, then turned frantic, frenzied, frenetic, spurring hands that had been tender to grope, to greedily claim pleasures too long denied. Tactile sensations, sweet scents, and moans uttered from deep in her throat bombarded him, drove him wild, and burned to pure heat. He struggled, grasping for reason in a last-ditch effort, demanding that it and logic prevail. But it had been too long since he'd been held by a woman. Too long since he'd dreamed of holding and being held by any other woman. He failed. And conceding defeat, he resigned himself and let go. The heart's time had come.

With possessive hands and lips, she skimmed his

chest, cruised his back, and stroked his neck. His skin seemed to sizzle. Shuddering, sucking in sharp breaths, he forgot everything except how long he'd wanted her in his arms. Nuzzling him, soft and trembling, her body molded to his, she summoned him, and Jake answered, lifting her to him. She buried her fingertips in his hair, cradling his head in her hands, and locked her legs around his hips, murmuring urgently between hot, lusty kisses and rapid, urgent ones, "Make love with me, Jake."

Craving, thick and hot and dense, gushed through his veins. She wanted him as much as he wanted her. The knowing inflamed him, unraveled him, made him ache to see her come apart in his arms, to see her mindless, reckless, desperate, satiated and still wanting more. Always wanting more of him. They couldn't have forever. They had no tomorrows. But they had tonight. Yes. Oh, yes. A night of loving Laura.

The thought stunned him through desire's haze, and he jerked back, severing their mouths and gasping staggered breaths against her cheek.

No. No, Jake. No, please. "Don't say it. Just don't say anything," Laura whispered raggedly against his chin. "I know it all, and I don't care. Right now, I just want you. I really want you." She tangled their tongues in a kiss steeped in passion, feeling intense resentment against the layers of clothing separating them. She wanted him closer. So close she couldn't feel where he stopped and she began. So close there was no stopping and beginning.

His hands at her waist unsteady, and quaking, he set her to her feet on the floor.

Was he refusing her then?

Dread bolted through her, and she forced herself to gaze up to his face. He just stood there, solemn and sober, staring down at her, his eyes reflecting a thousand emotions at once. She'd never needed a man to feel complete, but she wanted this man. Desperately.

Vulnerable, nearly petrified by a fear of rejection, she summoned courage and boldly reached out, letting her hand glide down his chest to the waist of his jeans, pausing where bare skin met denim, then drifting on further, down over button and placket and zipper, feeling him under her hand. Rigid. Engorged. He wanted her, and reassured at knowing it, she cupped him in her hand, then gently squeezed. "I need you, Jake."

A strong shudder racked through his body. The vibrations from it coursed up to her elbow, and he let out a massive sigh that heaved his chest. "I tried, Laura. I tried. But I'm too weak to fight us both."

He embraced her to her silent refrain, giving thanks. "Hurry."

Lips melding, hands hasty and clutching, they stripped off their clothes and made their way down the hall, pausing time upon time to indulge and invest in hungry kisses that just couldn't wait. By the time they reached his bedroom, they were naked and needy, far too eager to satisfy to endure the delay of catering to tender, gentle needs. Those, Laura promised herself, she'd share with him later. Now, she had to stop this heat—feed it, satisfy it, and stop it, before it consumed her.

They fell onto the bed in a full embrace, and he quickly, fluidly filled her. She let out a shuddery moan and rocked against him, legs stretched, knees bent, and back bowed. She lost herself in the lush sensations of sweet heat and driving friction, of long and hard kisses and hungry nipping ones, opening herself to him in ways she'd never opened herself to anyone.

Jake reveled in the feel of Laura loving him, of her clenching her muscles to caress him in a fisted grip, and he fought hard to hold part of himself back from her. They had only tonight, only this once, and he had to persevere to survive whatever tomorrows they had together. But he couldn't refrain or withhold. He wasn't a green kid. He was a twice-married man with a son. And though it'd be easier on him if he could say his reaction to her lovemaking was normal for a man who'd been celibate during the course of their marriage, he couldn't. It'd be a lie. It was her. Her sharing with him, demanding he share with her, letting him see her eager and needy. She was vulnerable and irresistible. And his. He was lost to her.

Heat radiated from his bare skin, warming her, inciting luscious quivers that rippled through him in waves of scorching heat. She trailed burning kisses from his chin to his shoulder; he throbbed in response, groaning and savoring every tremor curling his arms around her back and straining, furiously pounding flesh to flesh, unleashing the explosion of passion taking him by storm.

The force of it stunned Laura and elated her. She let him feel it in her response, lifting to meet him stroke for stroke, clutching the wadded sheets in her hand at her side, and crying out in little moans of sheer pleasure. His gaze blazing the depths of his desire, he murmured her name and withdrew from her, ignoring her protests that he stay. He rolled over and tossed a pillow that had dared to get in his way onto the floor. It clipped the lamp, then landed on the carpet with a thud, and he rolled again, with her, from the spill of light streaking across the bed from the hall into the deep shadows.

The sheets were cool, but her body was on fire. He captured her aching breast in his hand, then claimed it with his mouth. Every nerve in her body felt it; strung tight. She closed her eyes, clenched her hands into fists on his shoulders, and let him do what he would. His muscles shivering, shuddering at her slightest response, he marked every inch of her skin with lips and mouth, adding tinder to the fire raging inside her, sparking a fevered blaze in her core, and, when she swore she'd burn straight to ash, he let out a feral growl and arrowed into her with slamming thrusts that drove her to sanity's door.

"You're mine," he whispered on ragged breaths, sweat sheening on his pale golden skin. "Tonight, you're mine."

Her body and heart at one with the man in her arms, she smoothed her hands down his sides, then curled her fingers into his damp flesh and held tight, cresting, tumbling, then cresting again, watching his sleek muscles ripple and bunch, his buttocks hollow and round. Caught in the grip of the vicious climax claiming him, he rammed into her body, stiffened and stilled, and then shuddered, letting her carry him over the edge.

When rapid gasps calmed to even breaths, and shudders calmed to ripples, she remembered her promise. Longing to give him the gentle, tender caresses that only he had given to her, she raised her hand to his chin, urging him to lift his face from the curve of her neck and look at her.

Agony flooded his eyes.

And memories of their agreement, of their friendship, ripped through her mind. Her heart slammed against her ribs.

What in the name of God had she done?

The phone rang, rousing Jake from a restless sleep. He cranked open an eye, hoping he'd dreamed he made love with Laura and hadn't actually done it, but the smell of sex hung heavy in the room, dispelling that possibility.

How could he have been so stupid? So out of control

and selfish and stupid? Out of habit, he checked the clock. Four A.M. When the phone rang again, he grabbed the receiver, then grumbled, "Logan."

"Major Logan, this is Lieutenant Harvey, Clare Air Force Base Ops Center. You need to report to General Connor's office at 0800, sir."

The autopsies were back. A little fissure of anticipation opened in Jake's stomach. "Fine. Thanks for the call."

"Sir?"

"Yes?"

"The general recommends Mrs. Logan accompany you."

After last night, "Mrs. Logan" would probably file for divorce since they'd now negated the possibility of an annulment. Likely, before noon. "Thanks."

"Yes, sir. Good night, sir."

Hearing the dial tone buzz in his ear, Jake stretched to hang up the phone and pursed his lips, more than a little curious. Now why would Connor want Laura there, too?

A soft knock sounded on his bedroom door. It had to be Laura. Only they were at home. And that she'd come back after leaving him so abruptly surprised Jake. "Come in."

She opened the door far enough to lean against its frame. "Everything okay?"

Everything was shot to hell. But she'd meant the phone call, not their lives in general. "The autopsies are in. We're to report to Connor at eight."

She looked as uncomfortable as Jake felt. "We?"

Glancing across the room at the shadow of the antique oak dresser, he again reeled mentally. He'd actually made love with Laura. He had to have lost his mind. "Mmm-huh."

"Why?"

She shifted on her feet and he caught a whiff of her perfume—subtle undertones of mystery and musky seduction. She'd always worn that scent, and no other had ever set him on fire so quickly. He resented that. In fact, at the moment, he resented everything about her. She scared the hell out of him. He'd lost total control. Never before had he lost total control when making love with a woman. And what the hell was going to happen between them now?

He loved her, and she wanted and deserved more. But that didn't include more heartbreak and, until he nailed ROFF and survived, no matter how much he wanted her, he had no right to encourage her to love him. Encouraging her was heartless. Selfish. Wrong.

Sober, regretting that things had to be this way between them, and mourning what could have been, he sobered. "General's orders."

"Probably a kink in communications." The door opened a little wider, and he glimpsed what she was wearing.

His T-shirt.

Only his T-shirt.

God help him, why? And why did it hit him as being sexier than silk?

Damn it, here he was worried sick, and she was strutting around wearing his T-shirt, talking about communication kinks? "He didn't say. All I know is we have to be there." Jake knew his voice was sharp, but he couldn't seem to help himself. Nothing in his life had prepared him for making love with Laura. But their relationship—their entire lives—had changed drastically, and he didn't know if they could ever go back to what they'd had before. He could take losing a lover. But he couldn't take losing Laura. He thought he might just hate her as much as he hated himself for even risking it.

"Jake?" She tilted her head to look at him, and swept her sleep-tossed hair back from her face. "I'm sorry about last night. I accept full responsibility."

He yanked the covers up over his chest. At least she was uncomfortable about this shift, too. If she hadn't been, he'd have been furious. He shouldn't have to go through this hell alone. "It was my fault, too."

Her eyes that stormy blue, she dropped her voice to a strained whisper, as if she wanted and needed to know, but was afraid to ask. "Do you regret it?"

Regret it? Making love with a woman he loved, even if he knew he wasn't supposed to love her? It had to be the most awesome experience imaginable. But he couldn't have her. And now he'd glimpsed what he'd be missing. His stomach furled. "Yes, I regret it."

"Me, too." Her tone turned adamant. "It was wrong."

It had been. Laura wasn't in love with him. He couldn't—wouldn't—forget that. And he wasn't supposed to love her. They had an agreement, damn it. And no future.

Yet seeing her standing there in his T-shirt, looking so soft and sleep-tumbled and sexy, he knew that with so much as a hint of encouragement, he'd make love with her again. And that lack of discipline and control scared him in ways little else could.

He wouldn't lie to himself about it, and that was the best he could say for himself. He would have sworn it impossible, but he wanted her now even more than he'd wanted her last night. Knowing it was wrong and could only lead to disaster for both of them didn't seem to matter, and yet it did. The man who was human, who understood he wasn't just a warrior who attempted to do what was right, came face to face with the demon in him who was a selfish, self-centered bastard, who would put what he wanted before what was right. He didn't like it, but he couldn't deny it was there. And, God, but its pull was strong.

With the taste of her still on his lips and the feel of her indelibly imprinted on his mind, he'd play hell denying it. He didn't want her in her room. He wanted her with him, in his bed, in his life, loving him. And at that moment, he resented everything and everyone keeping them apart.

Yet knowing how destructive those kinds of thoughts could be and the power negative emotions could wield, he mentally shook some positive sense into himself. "I'll wake you in time to get ready," he said, wanting to end the conversation and get her out of here before he went over and brought her back to his bed.

She closed the door, and he heard her footfalls in the hall fade.

God help him. He didn't want to want her. But there were no guarantees either of them would be there tomorrow, or even five minutes from now, and he wanted whatever time he had left to be spent with her.

Selfish bastard. The costs of that would be steep, and Laura would be the one paying them. Hadn't she said she couldn't take losing him? Hadn't she sacrificed enough?

There was a hell of a lot of difference between losing a best friend and losing a husband. Nothing could hurt more than losing a beloved spouse. If he pulled this selfish stunt, she would lose him, and she would suffer. And he wouldn't be there to help her pick up the pieces.

Was it selfish? To want the right to love someone? To love her and to love the way she touched him? The sensations against his skin felt great, but he loved the underlying messages in her touch even more. *I like the way you feel. I want you to know you're here with me, and I'm glad. You're important to me. . . .*

Hell, what man wouldn't love that? Better than anyone, he knew she could be an angel or a stubborn
cuss—often simultaneously. He loved that about her,
too. And he hated it, because it touched him in places
he didn't want to be touched.

What the hell had happened to them? When had they
started noticing each other romantically? Why hadn't
he stopped them last night by just remembering the
agreement before they'd made love instead of after-
ward?

And why, when he felt it so strongly himself, did
Laura's regret burn him like acid?

Hungry.

No, nothing so mundane as hungry.

Starved.

He'd loved her as if he'd been starved for her. And,
this morning, he'd noticed her wearing his T-shirt.

If he'd asked why, she would have answered with a
"Do you mind? It's, um, comfortable." She was becoming a pro at navigating through these little gray
areas and opting for alternate truths. She'd been fully
prepared to give him a truth, but not *the* truth. The
agony in his eyes had devastated her, and she'd needed
comfort. But he hadn't asked.

Making love with him had been electrifying. Mag-
netic. Magnificent. But it also had been a huge mistake.

Laura stood under the shower, letting the hot water
sluice over her body, hoping to heaven it took some of
her regret down the drain with it.

That regret had been inevitable, she supposed. He
didn't love her, but she did love him. And something
had happened when she'd moved in with him this time.
Something . . . different. Right from the start, this time,
she'd seen him as an attractive man and not as a friend.

"Stupid." She grabbed the bar of soap and rubbed it roughly over her tender body. It had been stupid, considering their bargain. She'd blown it big-time. He'd warned her, too. *I won't ever love you. And I won't forget it—not for a second.*

Yet in his arms, she'd felt loved. Loved and adored. She'd felt far from alone, and definitely not like an outsider. She'd made love before, but never like that. Never like that.

He doesn't love you.

He didn't. He never would. And, from the expression on his face just moments ago, she had no doubt he felt nothing but regret. *Oh, why had she done it? Why did something that felt so beautiful and good hurt so damn much?*

True, she'd had a hellish couple of days, and she really did need to feel close to him, to feel cherished and comforted. And all the crazy fantasies of him she'd been having for the past three weeks hadn't helped. Who could fight a constant barrage of sizzling fantasies? She was flesh and blood, a normal woman, not a machine, and certainly not a nun. Hearing that sexy Celtic music he played every night before going to sleep hadn't helped, either. It only enhanced those damn fantasies to the point where she'd lay awake for hours, thinking of him. Imagining. . . .

She rinsed off, grabbed the shampoo and squirted some on her hair, then worked it into a rich lather. Okay. Okay. So she was human. A hungry woman who had followed her heart and made love with her best friend: a man who also happened to be her husband, even though they'd agreed to remain only friends. Fine.

But now what?

That she hadn't considered beforehand. And it was that frightening question she now wished fervently she had considered thoroughly.

Suddenly cold, she cranked the water hotter. Would he want a divorce? Most likely.

Would he treat her differently? Highly probable.

Would he withdraw? Become cold and indifferent? Most definitely.

And all of that would hurt like hell.

But maybe she deserved that. She had lied to him, and after last night he had to know it. How could he not know she'd crossed the line, taken the chance, and fallen in love with him? She'd melted in his arms.

And, God help her, agreement and honor or no, she'd do it again.

Distance between them was for the best.

Hot tears rolled down her cheeks. She closed her eyes, slumped against the stall, and positioned her head under the shower spray. The water hadn't washed away any regret, but she prayed it would rinse some of the pain from her heart. Feeling as she did about him and knowing he would never love her, made parting really best for them both.

They had no future.

"Judge Barton?" Surprised to see him of all people standing on her doorstep at 5:00 A.M., Laura tightened the belt of a thick robe and opened the door, grateful the security crew had replaced the broken glass last night so she wouldn't have to explain it. "Come in."

"Call me Bear," he said, stepping inside. "I'm sorry for coming at this ungodly hour, but I urgently need to talk with you, Mrs. Logan."

"Laura, please." She motioned him to the living room just as Jake entered it from the hallway wearing khaki slacks and a pale yellow pullover that did wonderful things for his eyes. "This is my husband, Jake," she said. "Jake, this is Judge Bear Barton."

They shook hands. "I'm sorry to intrude," Bear told

Jake, "but this couldn't wait any longer. Grab a cup of coffee, then we can talk."

"I'll get it." Jake headed for the kitchen.

"It's made," Laura called out, hoping Bear would hold off disclosing any bad news until Jake returned. She ushered Bear to the sofa. "Please, sit down."

He looked different in a navy suit than in his judge's robe. Though he still had a commanding presence. What in the name of heaven could he want?

Cups clinking, Jake came back and put one on the table beside Laura's chair, then handed another to Bear. "What's wrong?"

Bear took the cup. "Last night, an attorney came to see me at the office about you, Laura. I tried calling you then, but—"

"We were at the base," Laura said, watching Jake sip from his coffee cup. From the tense squaring of his shoulders, he too realized Bear's visit wasn't to deliver good news. "What did the attorney want?"

"He represents Madeline Drake Logan," Bear said. "I'm afraid she's filing a petition to have the adoption overturned."

Perfect. Laura resisted a powerful urge to toss up her hands and just weep. What else could go wrong? "We were afraid she might."

"I'm sorry to have to say it, but there's more." Bear grimaced, knitting his thick brows. "Laura, Madeline claims you ran her off the road on Manzanita Street."

"I did not," Laura said firmly. "She rammed my car twice on Manzanita, and would have a third time, if I hadn't outwitted her by swinging into a parking lot and taking refuge behind a dumpster. Timmy was there. He'll tell you what happened."

"Timmy was in the car with you?" Bear's eyes turned cold and glittered anger.

"Yes, he was."

"Did Madeline know it?"

"She certainly did," Laura insisted. "She'd already accosted us at Pizza Hut, and she followed us from there."

"Were there witnesses to this incident at Pizza Hut?"

Thinking back, Laura nodded. "The manager, and maybe the waitress. I'm not sure if the waitress saw what happened. But I'm certain the manager did."

"Good. Good." Judge Barton nodded and paused to drink some of his coffee. "But you did leave the scene of an accident."

"Madeline tried to run into my car. I got out of her way and she rammed into the dumpster. Her car was a mess, but she was fine. So I left."

His forehead wrinkled and he hiked a bushy brow. "You checked to see that she was all right?"

"Yes. I'm not heartless, Bear, though the woman's been doing her damnedest to drive me in that direction. And I didn't want her back behind the wheel. She was drunk. She could've killed somebody. But the car wasn't drivable."

"That gives us a little leverage, then. Did you report her?"

"No." Laura swung her hair back from her face. "It sounds trite, but I didn't have time."

Bear looked her straight in the eye. "Did you threaten to kill her?"

"Yes, I did," Laura confessed. "*If* she endangered Timmy again." She let out a sigh. "I meant it, Bear. I won't say I didn't."

"I had a hunch that was the case, which is exactly why I'm here."

"We also think she broke in here last night," Jake said.

"Someone cleaned out Timmy's room and left a bottle of Scotch on the floor," Laura explained. "But please keep that confidential because it could be . . . someone else."

Bear frowned. "Military related?"

"It's possible," Laura said.

"Is Timmy safe?"

Laura gave him an earnest frown. "If he weren't, would I be sitting here?"

"No." Bear smiled. "No, you wouldn't."

He sat still for a long moment, sipping at his coffee, digesting, and then looked at Jake. "May I use your phone?"

Jake got the cordless from the kitchen, then passed it to the judge. As the judge dialed, uneasy glances traversed between Jake and Laura.

"This is Judge Barton," he said into the receiver. "Is Chief Wilson in?"

"The chief of police," Laura whispered to Jake, who stood near the arm of her chair.

After a pause, Bear said, "Frank, Bear Barton here. Yeah, I'm fine. Ready for some fishing. You don't say. Up at Folsom Lake, eh? Well, why don't we go up there this weekend and fill us a stringer or two?"

Bear stared off into space, listening. "Good. Good. I'll look forward to it." He shifted on his seat, propping a hand on his knee. "Listen, Frank, I need to give you a heads-up on something. There's a Madeline Drake Logan filing a custody suit to overturn one of my adoptions."

Bear paused, smiled, and then turned serious again. "I know it's rare, but she's a special case. An alcoholic with an attitude and not much sense. She's also pressing charges against Laura Logan, and possibly Jake Logan. The charges are trumped up. If you could drag your feet a little and give us time to sort it out . . . ?"

"Good." Bear smiled. "Good. Yes, I'll give you a

call when we're ready. And I'll have Emily give you a shout about the fishing trip on Friday. Thanks, Frank.''

Bear hung up the phone. "That'll buy us some time."

Laura swallowed a knot in her throat. In one phone call, a judge she'd seen only twice had done more for her than her own father had done for her in her entire life. "Thank you, Bear."

"Not necessary," he said, sounding grumpy. "I take it kind of personal when someone screws with my decisions—especially when they involve kids. You might not know this, but I'm very persnickety about my children's cases."

How could she not know it? She'd survived one of his grilling inquisitions. Still, he looked as serious as a heart attack, so she bit back a smile and nodded. "I knew you were thorough. An asset, I think, considering your decisions impact children's lives forever."

"Damn right." He stood up, and cleared his throat. "Call your lawyer right away. On the possible military-related incident, if you can, file a complaint. On all the other incidents, file complaints against Madeline as soon as possible."

"We will," Jake said, though Laura knew as well as he did that any proposed complaints would first have to be approved by Connor. "Parts of this situation are . . . delicate."

"I understand." Bear walked to the front door, then paused, his expression grim. "I know this is the last thing you two need to hear after the case just settling, but I have a feeling this could get a lot worse before it gets better. I'm rarely wrong about these things. Keep your guard up. The woman lacks sense and stays drunk, and that combination makes her dangerous. Timmy's counting on you. And I'm counting on you to take care of him.''

Laura nodded. And at her side, so did Jake.

When the door closed behind Bear, Jake swiveled his gaze to Laura.

She sighed, then walked down the hallway toward her room without glancing at him. "Let me know when it's time to leave."

Didn't she want to talk about this? Any of this? All of this?

Her bedroom door swung closed.

Evidently not.

Jake went back to bed. It'd been one hell of a night in a succession of hellish nights. And it appeared they were in for even more of them. He closed his eyes and forced himself to doze off. A few hours later, he awakened abruptly.

To an explosion.

Thirteen

～

Jake's ears popped, then rang.

The walls shook. The bed rocked and, some-where damn close, glass shattered. He sat straight up in bed, looking for the source of the explosion.

Laura ran into his room. "What happened?"

Jake rolled out of bed and onto his feet. "Sounded like a bomb." He grabbed his khakis, jerked them on, then pulled out his Glock from the bedside drawer. "Stay here."

Laura followed him down the hall. "Front of the house?"

"The driveway, I think." He pulled hard, but the front door refused to open. "I told you to stay put."

"I heard you."

And obviously she'd chosen to ignore him. He ran through the house to the back door with Laura hard on his heels. The top half of the door was window. Spreading the lacy white curtains with the barrel tip of the Glock, he looked outside. Nothing seemed out of place. He scanned past the patio table and chairs and swept his gaze down the wooden privacy fence.

"Anything?" Laura asked from behind him.

"Did you plant marigolds near the gazebo?" In the

photo he'd found in the dead operative's hand, she'd been planting flowers near the gazebo.

"Yes. Shortly before going to court. Why?"

The photo had been taken even more recently than he'd suspected. "No reason." Jake reached for the doorknob. "Stay close to the house."

She nodded.

Easing outside, he looked down the walkway to the side gate. It was closed. Laura pushed through the waist-high shrubs between the house and sidewalk, slowly moving from the back to the front yard. Her back to the siding, she inched down, looking for the same signs of intrusion he sought: plastic explosive devices. Multiple plants were extremely common.

On the other side of the gate, he looked over the roof, and saw black smoke billowing up into the sky from the driveway area at the far front of the house. He caught Laura's attention, then pointed.

When she nodded, he went on, making his way past the junipers and flowerbeds to the front corner of the house. "Stay back," he whispered to Laura. "I mean it."

"I'm not an amateur, Jake."

"I know that. You're not armed, damn it."

"Okay." She leaned back against the house and scanned the trees, the neighbor's roof, the little vegetable garden with its six-foot tomato plants in wire cages.

Jake stepped around a huge oleander, paused, and looked toward the driveway. Laura's Mustang was on fire, belching black smoke and paint-curling flames. The windows had blown out, flames engulfed the entire interior, and liquid red paint dripped off the frame and ran down the concrete toward the street.

"My car!" Laura gasped, stricken.

Seeing movement off her right shoulder, Jake

blocked her, leveled the gun, and took aim.

"Don't shoot, Major." A sergeant in an MP uniform walked out from behind the trunk of the old oak that had led Jake to buy the house, his hands raised. "I have a message for you from General Connor. He says for you and Mrs. Logan to get out to the base STAT."

Jake pocketed the gun in his khakis, noted the man's name tag, and then grimaced. "Do you know what happened here, Boudreaux?"

"Yes, sir." Soot streaked a black mark across the young soldier's face. "We were keeping watch, observatory status, posted down the street. A white Lincoln, no tag, sir, pulled up, and two men got out. They planted a bomb in Mrs. Logan's car. From watching them, my partner and I suspected it'd detonate on opening the door. We called the bomb squad right away. They're en route now, sir."

"So what detonated the damn bomb?" Jake asked, not grasping why if they'd watched it being planted, one of them hadn't prevented the door from being opened and it detonating.

"Oh, God." Laura started gulping in deep, deep breaths of air.

Jake pulled her close to his side. "Laura?"

"Bill Green said to put the key under the mat. He'd tow the car." Her eyes reflected terror. "Oh, God, Jake. Bill Green opened the door." She went pale, collapsed back against the house's siding, and covered her face with her hands.

Jake looked to the sergeant for verification. Sympathy filled his eyes and he nodded, then glanced purposefully toward the foot of the drive.

Jake wheeled his gaze past the car and the neighbor's island of palms. Through the fronds, he saw the rear end of the tow truck. There was no need to ask if Bill had survived.

The sergeant cast Laura a worried look, then stepped away, both to give her and Jake privacy and to hustle curious neighbors back into the safety of their homes.

"Laura," Jake said softly. "Honey, we need to get to the base. You go back inside and get dressed now."

"But Bill—"

"We can't help Bill without getting to the base. Connor said STAT," Jake insisted, giving her something else to focus on and turning her around. He led her through the dew-damp grass back to the walkway, then to the rear door. He stopped at the threshold. "Get dressed now. I'll be back in just a minute."

He pulled the door closed, then returned to the sergeant, who now stood out in the middle of the front yard, keeping watch. "Was the man—"

"Killed instantly, sir." Regret flooded the soldier's eyes. "We'd called the bomb squad, and we thought the area was secure. Then this guy barrels up the street in a tow truck. I ran full steam from the cruiser, but before I could get to him to stop him, he opened the door and the bomb exploded."

"Why wasn't someone posted at the end of the drive?"

"Direct orders to hang back, sir." Guilt flooded the soldier's face. "So that's what we did."

"Where's your partner now?"

"He had to, um, take the cruiser back to the base. I was left on foot to give you the general's message and to secure the scene until the squad arrived." Anguish burned in the soldier's brown eyes. "Sir, I tried to get to him in time—ran full-out—but I just . . . couldn't make it."

"I understand, Sergeant." Jake softened his voice. "It wasn't your fault."

He lowered his gaze to the ground. "It, um, doesn't feel that way, sir."

Empathy filled Jake. "I know." He clapped a hand to the young man's shoulder. "I know."

Jake walked toward the driveway, but couldn't get anywhere near the car. Incredible heat poured out of the fire. The red paint on the car had melted, and the bare metal left under it glowed hot and charred. He saw flames, scorching, the smoke and curls of ash swirling up into the sky—everything except the one thing he expected to see.

He looked back over his shoulder at the sergeant. "Where's the body?"

"It's been removed from the scene, sir. Taken to the base in the cruiser. Don't worry, sir. We're trained on the proper handling—"

They removed the body? Anger ripped through Jake's chest. He had to work at it to keep his tone civil. "By whose authority?"

"Direct orders, sir. General Connor."

Now why the hell had Connor interfered in a crime scene that was definitely out of his jurisdiction? This didn't make a damn bit of sense.

"Sir, was your wife expecting the car to be towed?"

"Yes, she was." Jake stared at the molten mess still churning flames and lethal-smelling smoke. "The transmission was stuck in first."

Hearing a vehicle approaching, Jake turned an eye toward the street. A dull green armored vehicle pulled to a stop at the curb, and men began pouring out of it. The bomb squad . . . a little late.

"We'll take care of everything here, sir," the sergeant said, then cocked a brow. "I blocked the front door so no one could get out before I could warn them—just in case. I'll take care of that, too."

A shudder rippled up Jake's spine. What if Laura or Timmy had . . . ? Curbing those thoughts, Jake said, "Thank you. I appreciate your thinking of it."

Boudreaux nodded, looking pleased. "Sir, the general did say STAT."

"Yes, he did." Jake turned away and went back into the house, his insides now starting to shake.

Two steps inside the back door, he heard mewling. "Laura?"

No answer.

He called again, louder. "Laura?"

Still no answer.

His heart in his throat, he rounded the corner into the hallway and nearly stepped on her. Lying on the floor, she'd curled into a ball. Her hands covered her eyes and she sobbed so hard she couldn't have heard him call. She whimpered over and over on choked sobs, "I . . . killed . . . him. I . . . killed . . . him. I . . . killed . . . him."

"Laura." He bent down beside her, then lifted her to her feet. "Laura, no." He closed his arms around her. "Honey, no. Shh. . . . It's not your fault."

"It . . . is." She sagged against him, shaking so hard it jarred him. "He was towing the car . . . for me, Jake. For . . . me."

Deep sobs racked her body and tore at his heart. "You didn't plant the bomb."

She looked up, sheer agony in her eyes, her face tear-streaked and red, her chin quivering, her body shaking. "Oh, Jake. Bill Green is dead. I know he's dead. If I'd driven the car down to the shop, then he'd still be alive."

"It's not your fault." Jake hardened his voice, narrowed his eyes, and put on his professional facade. "Get a grip, Laura. You can fall apart later. Right now, we've got to get to the base."

"But I need to talk to Mrs. Green. To tell her how sorry—"

"Later. No buts." Weak morning light flooded in

from the window and streamed over her pain-ravaged face. "Bury it, Laura." He urged her down the hallway, then into her room, careful to not let even a sliver of sympathy sneak into his voice. "Duty first. You know the drill."

That had the effect he'd hoped it would have. She visibly stiffened, pulled in all the horror and raw emotion, and then buried it deep. Her expression cleared, then turned to a sleek, smooth mask of control. It'd been a while since she'd left Special Ops, but she hadn't forgotten the drills. No one ever forgot the drills. In training, they were branded into your brain for life.

"Give me ten minutes," she said, then slipped into her bedroom.

"You've got five," Jake countered. "Connor said STAT." She knew as well as Jake that the only time the general used that command was when he considered it essential and unavoidable.

In his own room, Jake put the Glock back into the nightstand drawer, then pulled off his khakis and slung on his uniform. Anger churned so deep inside him he couldn't pinpoint exactly where it started or stopped, but it had him shaking. Before the car bomb had exploded he'd wanted ROFF because wanting them was his job.

Now they'd made it personal.

Bill Green had died. On any other morning, Laura or Timmy would have opened that door. They often rode together. Jake could have lost them both in one fell swoop.

Every muscle in his body went into revolt, clenching in spasms from tension created by cold fury. ROFF had made it extremely personal.

And now the sons of bitches were going to pay for it.

* * *

Laura followed Jake into Connor's office, hoping to God it didn't smell like lemon. No way could she stand the smell of lemon right now and not lose her stomach. A dull ache throbbed behind her eyes; a combination from lack of sleep, an overload of stress in the last seventy-two hours, and crying over poor Bill Green. God, how was she going to explain this to his wife? She'd be devastated.

Jake cleared their entry past Gladys, Connor's secretary, who'd been aptly dubbed "the dragon lady" because she guarded his domain as if it were a lair.

"Go right in," Gladys said, not a single brown hair out of place or an unnecessary crease in her brown suit. "He's waiting for you."

She checked her watch, and even though less than thirty minutes had elapsed, Laura had the distinct feeling Gladys's smirk was a visual reprimand for their slow response to a STAT order to report.

Jake opened the door, then ducked his head in through the crack. "General?"

"Come in, Jake, Laura." Connor stood up to greet them. "Thanks for coming so quickly."

He'd summoned them STAT, for God's sake. Had he really expected them to meander in at their leisure? Laura chided herself for that ungracious thought. It seemed ridiculous to condemn the man for being courteous. Especially when he was calling her *Laura*.

"I'm sorry about Bill Green," he said to Laura. "I understand you considered him a friend."

Laura nodded. The smell of lemon overwhelmed her, and her head felt light. She swayed on her feet.

Jake's arm closed around her and he guided her to the first of two visitors' chairs in front of Connor's desk. "She's exhausted, General, and in shock."

Laura looked up at Jake, ready to blister his ears for making excuses for her, but the worry in his eyes stopped her cold and took the sting out of his comment. He was being solicitous and caring, not condemning. "It's the lemon," she corrected him. "I hate it, and it smells so strong."

"So do I," Connor said. "Stinks like hell. Jake, open the window, will you? And let Gladys know." He swiveled his gaze to Laura, then to the coffeepot. "Would you like a cup of coffee?"

She decided then she liked Connor. Opening the window was a security risk, and Gladys would have to notify the security staff to keep them out of here. And few generals would bother taking care of such a trivial task as getting Laura a cup of coffee themselves. They'd fob the courtesy off on their version of Gladys or an assistant. That Connor didn't spoke well of him, and favorably of his views toward his staff and the value of their time. "Please," Laura answered him. "Black."

When he passed her the cup, she looked up into his eyes and saw empathy there. Empathy and regret. It scared her in a way him being suspicious of her hadn't. "Thank you."

"You're welcome."

He went around his desk, then sat down. "It's been a rough couple days for all of us, hasn't it?"

"We've had better." Jake sat down beside her, then reached for the coffee Connor had placed on the edge of his desk.

Looking through the steam rising from her cup at Connor, Laura thought he looked weary, and she expected he was weary. Having one of his staff suspected of heading ROFF had to have him up nights gnashing his teeth.

"Are the autopsies in?" Jake sipped from his cup.

Connor nodded. "Strong anthrax."

Laura knew as well as they did that this was the best possible of the bad news.

Connor rocked back, then glanced up at the portrait of General Patton. Now why would that have Jake grimacing?

"We're ninety percent sure," Connor looked at her, "that your consultant status has been compromised, Laura."

Her heart began a slow, hard beat. Yet today, unlike yesterday, he called her by her Christian name, not *Mrs. Logan* and not *Captain*. He had to believe her innocent of treason. He'd authorized disclosures to her as well. Of course he believed her innocent. She didn't know whether to thank him or to yell at him for doubting her, and decided it wisest to resist temptation and do neither.

"Why?" This from a worried-looking Jake.

"Our team found a listening device planted in Laura's Mustang. We're seventy-five percent sure Bill Green put it there some time ago."

"Bill? No," Laura objected. "He wouldn't bug my car."

"A mechanic from his shop claims he did. We're checking into the backgrounds of both men to see if either of them had formal skills, and we're trying to confirm or disprove the statement."

Bill couldn't do this. He couldn't. Laura felt sick inside and damn close to tears. *Bury it. Bury it, Logan. Duty first. Nothing stays hidden.*

Jake reached over and clasped her hand. "You okay?"

"Fine." She squeezed his fingers in a death grip. If he let go of her, she was going to fall apart. Pure and simple. He would just have to forgive her for it.

He spoke to Connor. "That's why you retrieved

Green's body from the scene and brought it to the base.''

Surprise darted up Laura's backbone. ''You retrieved his body?'' When Connor nodded, she went on. ''But we live in a private residential area off base. You don't have the jurisdiction to retrieve a man's body.''

''Normally, no, I don't. But in this case, I do. Green's body and your car are evidence in an ongoing military investigation.''

An ongoing investigation against her. ''Are you still thinking I might have breached security or committed treason, General?''

''No, Laura. I'm not.''

Thank God. ''Then this ongoing investigation is against Bill?''

Connor nodded.

''You think he's connected to ROFF?'' Seeing that's exactly what he believed, she let out a laugh lacking humor. ''That's absurd.''

''Laura,'' Jake whispered, softly warning her she was going too far.

''No. I'm sorry, but it is absurd. I don't believe it, and I'll say so until I'm proven wrong.'' She let out a little grunt. ''Are you forgetting who Bill is? He's the man who's hassled me as much as you have to replace the heap they think he's bugged. The man patient enough to show Timmy how to replace an air filter on a car, how to check the oil and the tire pressure. It just doesn't fit that he'd plant a listening device in my car, or do anything to hurt us. He was a good man, and I won't believe otherwise until I see it in black and white.''

She swung her gaze to the general. ''I'm sure you have strong evidence or you'd never have said this about Bill, but I'm telling you, General, it's just not possible. He's owned that shop for twenty years. His wife still works the front desk for him. Everyone in town knows he's the only honest mechanic around. He just wouldn't do this.''

"I appreciate your insight, Laura, and I'll note it. If you feel this strongly about the man, I'm sure there's merit." He jotted down some notes on a yellow legal pad. "What can you tell me about the mechanic who works with him?''

"There isn't one. At least there wasn't when I picked up the Mustang a month or so ago." A memory flitted through her mind and she gasped. "Wait. Mrs. Green did say Bill was looking for help in the shop. They wanted to take a trip up to Oregon to see their son and his family.''

"For what it's worth, I agree with Laura," Jake said. "This wouldn't fit in with what I know of Bill Green's character or his habit patterns.''

"I'll note that, too." Connor's pen scratched across the width of the pad. "On the flip side of this, in the last twenty-four hours, our problem with ROFF has grown more complicated." He put the pen down and looked first at Jake, then at Laura. "The folks upstairs estimate a ninety-nine-point-nine percent probability that both of you have been exposed as Special Ops known entities to ROFF. And they're predicting that after this bomb attempt Timmy will be targeted next.''

"No!" Feeling as if she'd been kicked in the stomach and all of the air had been squeezed out of her lungs, Laura clenched Jake's hand even tighter. "No.''

"Don't panic," Connor said. "There's no time for it, or value in it.''

She dug deep and warned herself to calm down. She'd be useless to Timmy otherwise. *But he's just a little boy. My son!*

Connor tapped his pen against the blotter on his desk. "Until we wrap this up, I strongly recommend we fly Timmy to Colonel James for protective custody.''

Laura nearly choked. ''You want to send my son to Colonel James? B-But Madeline worked for him.'' It was a lousy excuse, but hell, he'd stunned her by suggesting James. Good God, of all people, why him?

''We worked for him, too,'' Jake said, sounding totally reasonable.

''Timmy knows him,'' Connor said. ''We've got to get him into protective custody, and I thought he'd be more comfortable with someone he knows.''

''Thank you for considering his comfort. I mean that sincerely, but my son will *not* be going to Colonel James,'' Laura said. Exactly why she'd said it as she had she didn't know. True, she had strong, strong feelings on this matter and against Colonel James, but she didn't want to have to explain them. She should have been more discreet. More subtle. More diplomatic.

Jake rubbed the back of her hand with his thumb. ''We've got to put him someplace safe.''

A snake wouldn't be safe with James, and she knew damn well Timmy wouldn't be. But she couldn't explain why, not here and not now. ''I'll take him to a place I know he'll be safe.''

''Where?'' Jake asked.

''Trust me on this.'' Someone with Special Ops training was heading ROFF, and until Laura knew who, she wasn't taking any chances. Not with Timmy at stake.

''Laura,'' Connor interjected. ''I can appreciate your concerns and your apprehensions. A blind man can see how much you love the boy. But we need to know where he'll be. How else can we protect him?''

''He's my son,'' she said softly. ''I'll see to his protection.''

''Where? With whose help?'' Connor asked. ''No

great-aunt Tilda is up to the job, Laura. You know how ruthless terrorists can be. Don't let your personal feelings against a highly decorated officer get your son killed.''

She clenched her jaw. ''I don't have a great-aunt, nor do I have any intention of going against my instincts on this. My instincts are Special Ops honed, and they're telling me to keep my son out of Colonel James's hands.'' She shrugged. ''I'm listening.''

''At least tell me where he'll be,'' Connor insisted. ''So I can have backup security on alert.''

Laura lifted her chin. ''No.''

Surprise flickered through Connor's eyes, and he perked up. ''No?''

She didn't dare risk looking at Jake. He couldn't look much different than the general. She spoke firmly, but quietly. The last thing she needed or wanted was for either of them to think her emotions were running the show, though in a way, she supposed they were—her woman's were—specifically that of woman's intuition. ''Where and with whom I place Timmy is classified information, General. Mine. If you want absolution from any liability, you have it.''

Laura held her breath, half-expecting Jake to raise hell, but he didn't utter a sound.

''Major?'' Connor looked at Jake, clearly surprised and worried.

''She's his mother, sir, and she's got great instincts,'' Jake said without so much as a glance in her direction. ''If she says she'll handle his protection, she'll handle it.''

Laura could have kissed him.

''Very well. We're here if we can be of service.''

''Thank you, sir,'' Laura said. ''I mean that sincerely.''

The skin knitted between Connor's brows, and he

shoved aside a stack of files. "You know we've had your home under surveillance."

Laura schooled her voice to keep from yelling. "I have *not* compromised my integrity."

"I believe that, Mrs. Logan."

Hell, she'd crossed him and now they were back to formalities again. Unfortunate, but when it came to Timmy and his safety. . . .

Someone knocked on the office door.

Connor rubbed a weary hand over his neck and elevated his voice. "Enter."

Gladys came in and passed the general a large brown envelope. "The photos," she said softly, glancing disapprovingly at the open window. She sniffed, then left the office and tugged the door shut.

Connor opened the clasp. The stiff paper crackled. "Hopefully, these will tell us what we're working against down there." He pulled out a fistful of letter-size photos. "These were taken by the observation team posted in front of your home," he explained, glancing through a couple, then passing a stack to Jake and another to Laura. "Intel is running them through the computer for ID."

Laura took them, her hand not quite steady. Three people were in the first photo. One was obscured by the car. Of the two men getting out of it, one had his face turned ninety degrees away from the camera. The second one didn't. He stared right at the viewer. She'd never seen him in her life.

Jake groaned.

"What?" She snapped her gaze to him.

He started to hand a photo to her, hesitated, and then passed it on. "I'm sorry, Laura."

Dread flooded her. She knew what was coming was bad. Jake's reaction made it impossible not to know it. Her mouth stone dry, she pulled up a reserve stock of courage, then took the photo. Her hand shook hard, and she willed it to stop. Before she looked down, she steeled herself, mentally preparing for the worst. To see anyone's face looking back at her.

"Oh, God." The photo slipped from her hands, and she covered her mouth to hold in a scream. She couldn't breathe. *She couldn't breathe!*

"Jake?" Alarm elevated Connor's voice a full octave.

"Paul Hawkins, sir."

Fear explôded and anger boiled in Laura's veins. "There's your Special Ops trained head of ROFF." When Jake looked at her, she remembered him asking her once if she was afraid of him. *Not unless you're God or Paul Hawkins. I save my fear for the big time gun threats.*

Connor reached for the phone, and Laura let out a sigh of relief. For a moment, she'd doubted what she was seeing, had wondered if only fear had made her see her worst nightmare there.

Connor cut in. "Is this the same Paul Hawkins who once attacked you?"

Laura sat quietly, trying to calm herself down and form a plan, while Jake refreshed the general's memory on the survival school incident. Connor then relayed it to whoever was on the other end of the phone line, adding a personal note that time obviously hadn't healed Hawkins's hatred for Laura.

The shame and humiliation he had brought on himself but blamed on her still ruled the man. Obviously, he continued to blame her. She had suffered, lost, forfeited, but all that wasn't enough. He wanted her to suffer more.

Her nightmares of him returning to her life were coming true. Fear and anger assaulted her. She stiffened and worked hard to squelch those emotions. To do battle with Paul Hawkins, she needed God's help, luck, and logic. Strong, clear thinking. A plan.

She'd have to make sure Timmy and Betsy didn't return to the house. Betsy should be fine at Alice's. But there was only one place in the world Laura considered safe for Timmy. And she wasn't at all sure he'd be welcome there.

"Laura," Connor said, claiming her attention. "Survival school was a long time ago. Are you sure this is Hawkins?"

She looked the general straight in the eye. "When a man's working at choking you to death and he's coming damn close to succeeding, you tend to remember what he looks like." She did. In full color and vivid detail. From the incident itself and the uproar it'd caused to the nightmares she'd had about it ever since.

"Fine." Connor had the grace to look away. "Did Hawkins and Bill Green know each other?"

"Not that I'm aware of." Jake turned to her. "Laura?"

"I have no idea." She stared sightlessly at her hands in her lap. Hawkins had been tried and convicted of "conduct unbecoming" and dishonorably discharged. Except for her nightmares reliving the episodes of his attack, the trial, and his conviction, she'd thought he was out of her life forever. But as much as she hated knowing he had wrangled his way back in, she had no trouble accepting it. He'd proven himself capable of anything. Even murder. What she hated accepting was what his actions represented: hatred that runs deep never diffuses, it only feeds on itself. To get involved with ROFF, he had to hate her ten times more now than after he'd been court-martialed and kicked out of the Air Force. Maybe twenty times more.

A stray thought popped into her mind. Connor had wanted to send Timmy to Colonel James? An uneasy shiver crept up her spine. How had he gotten involved in this? "General?"

"Yes?"

"Did you brief Colonel James on this situation?"

"More or less." He frowned. "Why?"

She lowered her gaze to the desk, avoiding his eyes. "I was just curious," she said, shrouded in guilt. She had suspected James of being corrupt. Knew he and Sean Drake had conspired against her to ruin her career. But she hadn't mentioned it to anyone for fear of not being believed and of being humiliated professionally as well as privately. That professional humiliation would have been inescapable had she stayed active duty. Those two men carried a major amount of clout. But most of all, she hadn't wanted to tell Jake.

Now it was too late. Whatever damage Colonel James had managed to do in this ROFF mission was already done. Her instincts screamed he hadn't just appeared on the scene incidentally. Men like him didn't depend on coincidence. He'd intentionally insinuated himself. She knew it as well as she knew she sat in General Connor's office, still smelling—God help her— lemon. And she was to blame for whatever damage James had done because she'd done nothing back then to stop him.

How in the name of heaven could she live with this, much less explain it to Jake?

Connor eyed Laura warily. "You have strong feelings against Colonel James. I would like to know the nature of them."

"I don't trust him."

"Any particular reason?" he asked.

Oh, God. "Several." She lifted her gaze to the portrait of Patton, then lowered it to the general. It'd take a miracle to get by with this. "None of which I care to discuss." Her gaze turned pleading. "I would ask you to trust me, General."

He worried his inner lip with his teeth. "All right. For now, all right."

"Thank you."

Jake passed a second photo to Connor. "This is a better shot of Hawkins's face."

Laura glimpsed it and caught a flash of something that urged her to look closer. "May I see that?"

Jake glanced at it again, and turned ashen. "Oh, hell. Oh, bloody hell."

"What is it?" Connor leaned over his desk to get a look at the photo.

"Laura," Jake said, passing the picture to her. "Check out his cheek."

Nerves crackling, Laura examined the photo—and saw the scar. Images of the attacker who'd broken into her home and come at her with the knife, images of her taking it from him, then slashing his face through the ski mask clicked through her mind. "That sorry bastard. That sorry, sorry bastard."

Connor dropped his hands to his desk. "Will somebody please tell me what is going on? Why is that scar significant?"

Laura looked up at the general. "I put it there. Two and a half years ago, when he broke into my apartment."

Connor rocked back in his chair, perplexed. "Why the hell would Hawkins break in on you after so many years?"

"Revenge," Jake suggested. "He was publicly humiliated and dishonorably discharged for attacking Laura."

"Maybe," Laura commented. Yet if he and James were working together on this, there could be another reason entirely. "But maybe not."

"A point worth factoring into the equation," Connor said, "is that the attacker could have been someone else. Hawkins isn't the only man in the world running around with a scar on his face."

"That's true," Laura conceded. "But his smell . . ."

"What?" Jake frowned, clearly as perplexed as Connor.

"Since the attack," Laura explained, "whenever I have the nightmare of the masked intruder the nightmare of Hawkins' attack always follows. Always. They smell the same, Jake."

"The nightmares?"

"No, damn it, the men. Hawkins and the masked attacker. They smelled the same. I wondered why one dream always triggered the other one, and I assumed it was because in both of them I was being attacked. But it wasn't. It was the smell. Their smell. . . ."

Fourteen

General Connor stood up. "Why don't you get Timmy settled and then take Laura home and get some rest, Jake? I'll be conferring with the other team members during the day today. By 1800, I should have a clearer picture of the events transpiring in the last ninety-six hours." Connor looked more than tired himself. "Let's meet back here, then."

Jake left the office with Laura. Her shoulders slumped, and agony and an exhaustion she worked hard at trying to suppress twisted her face. It was normal under the circumstances, but he hated seeing her looking as if any second she'd keel over. She'd suffered too many shocks. Too much stress, too many demands, and too many shocks.

He should've killed Hawkins for hurting her back then. Jake had thought about it, with every raspberry she'd consumed, every pound she'd lost, every tear she'd cried, and every damn nightmare she'd awakened from in a cold sweat. What man wouldn't have thought about it? If Jake had done it then, this wouldn't be happening now. The sorry bastard wouldn't be hurting her again.

They left the building and crossed the parking lot,

and still she hadn't said a word or looked Jake directly in the eye. He keyed the Jeep's lock, opened the passenger's door, and she got in, then buckled her safety belt. It snapped into place.

When he'd buckled up and cranked the engine, he glanced over at her. A fat tear rolled down her cheek. "Are you okay?"

"No." Her voice sounded flat, devoid of emotion. "No, I'm not okay, Jake."

She didn't try to hide the tear by wiping it away, but knowing she'd prefer it, he pretended not to notice it. Still, his stomach churned acid, and his chest went tight. Under pressure, Laura always came through. He knew that. But this time, she was struggling. Hard. He understood why. Hawkins was her Achilles' heel, and the lousy bastard had tried to kill her again—twice. Breaking into her apartment, and then planting the explosive device in her car.

Jake blew out a frustrated breath. And he, her husband, asks if she's okay? God, who could be okay? Jake felt like an idiot. A helpless idiot, because he didn't know what to say or do to alleviate her fears. It'd be easy to spew platitudes, but they'd only insult her intelligence, and they'd both know it. That left Jake only one option, and one thing to say. "I'm sorry, honey."

She stared straight ahead, not acknowledging him.

At a loss, he tapped the gearshift, then drove down to the parking lot exit.

A line of five tanks rolled down the street, heading past the water tower toward Hangar Row. They were probably about to be transported in the C-5s he'd seen belly-open on the flight line on the way in. Jake waited for them to clear out, and then entered traffic.

"Stop by Green's Automotive on the way home, Jake."

He braked for a red light, his arm draped over the steering wheel. Some kid with green hair pulled up in the next lane. Even through two sets of closed windows, his radio blared loud enough to set Jake's teeth on edge. "I understand your need to talk with Mrs. Green, but I think she needs a little reaction time."

"If you don't want to stop there, fine. I'll get there on my own." Laura reached for the door handle.

With a restraining hand on her sleeve, Jake stopped her. "Laura, don't. Honey, I'm not the enemy. I'll take you anywhere you want to go, anytime you want to go. I just thought Mrs. Green might need time alone first. That's all."

"I know she does, Jake." Laura looked over at him, her eyes haunted by fear that ran soul-deep. "But I seriously doubt she'll be at the shop."

"Then why—" Jake sighed. "The mechanic."

"Yes. I don't know what he's trying to pull, saying Bill planted a listening device in my car, but he's not going to get away with it. Bill Green didn't have a dishonest bone in his body, Jake. And no one is going to tag him as corrupt without proof."

"At the risk of getting my head bitten off, may I suggest you put a little faith in Connor and the team, and let them do their jobs?"

"Connor?" Laura guffawed. "For God's sake, Jake. The man wanted us to put Timmy in Colonel James's care, and you want me to trust his judgment? I don't think so."

"Connor's a good man. He doesn't deserve—"

"Yes," she interrupted. "I believe he is a good man. Sincere and genuine and deserving of trust. But about James, the general is also uninformed. I won't trust his judgment when I know he's uninformed. Not with Timmy's life. And I can't believe you'd want me to."

Strong words, and very strong feelings. A sinking

feeling lodged in the pit of Jake's stomach. The light turned green. He tapped the gas and checked his rear-view mirror. "What's wrong with Colonel James?"

"You worked for him. Can't you answer that?"

Though in no mood to play twenty questions, Jake buried his temper. She was stressed out. So was he, but one of them had to stay calm. From the looks of it, he'd been elected by default. "Evidently I can't answer it, or I wouldn't have asked the question."

Laura glared his way. "James is just like Sean Drake. A corrupt manipulator. I wouldn't let him within a hundred yards of Timmy."

Sunlight streaked through the side window, heating Jake's arm. He flipped the air conditioner up a notch. "Is that character analysis based on evidence, or instinct?"

Laura wheeled her gaze back to the windshield. "A fair share of both intuition and hard facts." God forgive her. Even now, she couldn't tell Jake the truth. She had no choice but to navigate into another gray area, pull in another alternate truth. "But if you want the evidence, you'll have to talk with Dr. Harrison. What I know was told to me in confidence."

Dr. Harrison was the surgeon who implanted Laura's tracking devices. James was in Intel. He and Harrison crossed paths on a lot of research projects, and it appeared from Laura's reaction that Colonel James had crossed a lot more than just the good doctor's path.

Jake passed the gate guard, then took the normal route home that would have them pass Green's Automotive. Laura didn't want to discuss the basis for her feelings on James further, and that was fine with Jake. He trusted her judgment and greatly respected her instincts, especially regarding Timmy. She seemed attuned to him on an unseen level, and her feelings had proven accurate time after time. Even if these circumstances weren't normal and she was stressed to the max, Jake still trusted her. He'd never doubt her again. Not now that he understood her vulnerability issue. That aside, she didn't fear James but felt angry at something he'd done to an associate. She had a grip on this. Laura was loyal to those she loved and those she respected. She respected Dr. Harrison.

During the fifteen-minute ride, Laura didn't say anything more, nor did she move. She sat like a stone statue in her bucket seat, staring sightlessly through the Jeep's side window. Exhaustion and shattered nerves could account for some of her reactions. Hawkins and ROFF could account for more. James, Green, the adoption, Madeline's antics, and the bomb, more still. But something else lurked in her haunted eyes that hadn't yet come to light; Jake sensed it as strongly as he sensed the sun heating his arm.

What exactly it could be, he didn't know. Habitually, when confronted, Laura didn't withdraw like this. She rebelled, vehemently, kicking like a hellcat, or turning ice cold under fire—whichever the situation demanded. Yet this was Hawkins confronting her, one of her two big-time fears, and Jake couldn't afford to forget that. Connor had made a valid point. Why would Hawkins wait all these years to come back for revenge? That didn't make sense. If that motivated him, wouldn't he have acted long before now?

Seeing an opening in traffic between a white van and a Blazer, Jake pulled across the street, then up the slope into Green's Automotive's parking lot. Space at a premium, Jake edged into a cramped slot between a Chevy truck and a Taurus with its hood up. The little brick building was barely visible behind all the cars that had been dropped off for servicing. The last honest mechanic was dead, and Jake wondered who'd service all those cars now.

Laura reached for her purse. "Before we go home, I need to make a couple phone calls—but not from here."

She'd convinced herself the mechanic who'd pointed the finger at Bill Green was guilty, not Bill. "Sure," Jake told her. "How about the pay phone outside Food World?"

"That'll be fine." She reached for the door handle.

"Laura?" Jake clasped her hand. He'd supported her decision about Timmy in front of Connor. Now he wanted some information, and he didn't much care for feeling doubtful that she'd give it to him. "Where do you plan to hide Timmy?"

Something inside her snapped. The mask slipped off her face, and she reached up to stroke his cheek. "With someone who hates abuse and corruption as much as we do. But let's take care of this first, okay?"

Relieved to see her acting more normal, Jake nodded, only slightly disappointed that she hadn't given him the person's name. The tenderness in her touch made it clear that she would tell him once she had arranged things.

Sun glinted against the shop's wide, front window. Both big bay doors were closed. And no one was around. The office door was locked, and the lights inside were turned off. Jake felt more than a little relieved that Laura's confrontation with the mechanic would be delayed. He also felt more than a little suspicious. The Taurus's hood was up. Someone had left in a hurry.

"Damn it." She turned around and headed back toward the Jeep. "Connor probably has him."

He probably did. And for that too, Jake felt grateful. He looked around a little more, just to be sure, but found no signs of anyone, including Ginger, the Greens' overweight hound. Her little pen behind the shop stood empty. Dry food still filled her dish.

On the way back to the car, Jake stepped over a crack in the concrete that had sprouted knee-high weeds and closed the Taurus's hood. Then he joined Laura in the Jeep.

She held her silence, worrying him. What was going on in her mind?

The short ride to Food World went without incident, and Jake pulled into a yellow-line parking slot right in front of the pay phones, then cut the engine.

Laura fished in her wallet for two quarters, then tossed her purse back onto the floorboard. "I'll be right back."

"I'm coming with you." When she opened her mouth to protest, he insisted. "If ROFF got to your car, they can get to you."

"No one is following us, Jake."

"I've watched the rearview, too, and I haven't noticed anyone following us, but I'm not leaving you standing alone in the open. You'd be an easy target."

Resigned, she waited for him to walk around the front of the car, then surprised him by reaching for his hand. He laced their fingers, and she gave his fingers a squeeze. Some of the rocks in his gut eroded to pebbles. She was rallying. Still, she needed the support of his touch. And despite less-than-two-percent-survival odds, and regret or not, by God, she was going to get it. After some of these things settled down and the pressure on her eased, then they could resolve their problems. Until then, he was there for her however she needed him. She still might feel vulnerable, but she damn sure wasn't going to feel alone.

The storefront walkway was busy. Morning shoppers departed from the store with loaded carts, while others entered it with empty ones. A young mother wearing white shorts and sandals stood smiling and watching her toddler ride a little merry-go-round not far from the phone.

Laura dropped a quarter into the phone slot, then dialed Alice's number. When Betsy got on the phone, Laura dispensed with niceties and inquiries about Timmy and the ball game. As if she flipped a switch, her whole demeanor changed to her professional-and-controlled mode.

Jake slid a hand into his pocket, damned relieved.

"Betsy, you and Timmy need to stay at Alice's for a while. No questions, please. Just watch Timmy closely, and don't leave there until you hear from me. We'll bring you some clothes. No, not for anything."

Laura paused a moment, obviously listening. "Fine," she said. "Just stay there. No. No, not until you hear from me. Tell Timmy we love him." She closed her eyes and her voice went soft. "Yes, with all our hearts."

She depressed the phone hook, and then, without missing a beat, dropped another quarter into the slot and dialed. Jake didn't recognize the number.

"Emily, this is Laura Logan. I need an appointment. Yes, it's an emergency."

Who was Emily? And what kind of appointment did Laura need?

"Twenty minutes will be great. Yes, I'll hold."

The mother lifted her toddler from the merry-go-round, pulled a tissue from her pocket and wiped at the child's nose, then entered the store. Jake scanned the parking lot and the walkway, looking for anything suspicious, but saw nothing out of the ordinary.

"I need your help," Laura said into the phone. "Timmy's in grave danger, a suspected target, and I can't trust anyone else. I need a safe place to—" She halted abruptly, relief washed over her face, and unshed tears filmed her eyes. "Yes, I'll bring him right away.'' She tucked her hair back behind her ear. ''It could be for a few days. Maybe even longer. I just don't know.''

She glanced up at Jake and nodded, looking more relieved than pleased. ''Fine,'' she said into the phone. ''A few hours.'' She licked at her lips. ''Thank you. This means so much—''

Jake had no idea what the person on the other end of the line had said, but it'd touched Laura deeply. She had that look; kind of wistful, kind of awed.

She hung up the phone and turned to face him. ''Let's go get Timmy. Bear's expecting him.''

''Bear?'' Surprise streaked up Jake's back. ''You're taking Timmy to Bad Ass Bear?''

Laura nodded. ''Besides you, right now, he's the only person in the world I trust.''

''Honey, you've met the man twice. In a professional capacity. I agree, he's helping with Madeline, but—''

''Sometimes twice is enough. Sometimes you meet a person and you sense things. You know exactly what I mean about that. I know he's good.''

''Are you sure enough to stake Timmy's life on it?''

''After the hell he put me through in his inquisition? Yes, I'm sure.''

No hesitancy. Full support. ''If you feel that strongly about it, then it's fine with me.'' Not that she'd given him a choice, or any say in the matter. But that too was a good thing. If suddenly Jake weren't in the picture anymore, she'd have to act alone. Seeing how she'd handle a situation like this put Jake's mind at ease. She hadn't hesitated at going toe to toe with Connor, or in seeking Bear's help.

''You know Bear isn't young, Jake. He isn't particularly physical, either. But when it comes to children, he's the most protective man I've ever seen. He'll do everything humanly possible to guard Timmy, and Timmy likes him.''

"That devotion is more important than physical strength." A Glock was a hell of an equalizer on age as well.

"I think so."

"Then let's go get Timmy and get him settled in with Bad Ass Bear."

Laura looked up at Jake, her eyes wide. "Bear's done more to help me than my own father. More than anyone in the world, except you. I want you to know that, Jake."

That admission startled him. "I thought you and your parents were close." They were dead now, but he could almost swear she'd told him that.

"They were close. To each other. Not to me."

Jake understood too well, and he hurt for the lost little girl Laura had been. He thought again of Timmy and Bunny, the survival school rabbit she'd saved and set free. "Bear will keep Timmy safe. Try not to worry," Jake said, knowing he was suggesting the impossible.

"If he can, he will. I know he will."

By two P.M., Laura and Jake had left Betsy armed with fresh clothing and essentials at Alice's and had gotten Timmy settled in at Bear's. Now they were standing at his front door, preparing to depart his home.

Jake hugged Timmy. "You be good, Tiger."

He nodded solemnly, and from the seriousness in his eyes, he understood far too much.

Laura kissed his cheek. "Got your rabbit's foot?"

"Yes, ma'am."

"Good." A knot lodged in her throat. "You take care of Bear and Mrs. Barton, okay?"

"I'll hold down the fort, Mom."

Bear put a protective arm around Timmy's shoulder. "Why don't you go help Mrs. Barton in the kitchen? I think she's got some root beer and ice cream in there. Maybe she'll make you a float."

Bear remembered that was Timmy's favorite. Jake picked up on it, too.

Timmy's eyes lit up from the bottoms. "Bye, Mom and Dad." He took off for the kitchen in a full run.

"We'll be fine, Laura," Bear said. "Try not to worry."

She looked up at him, her gratitude in her eyes. "You haven't asked why I called you."

"I know why." His blue eyes shone. "Bad Ass Bear kind of says it all."

The hint of a smile tugged at her lips. "It says a lot, but that's not the reason."

"Oh?" Bear looked surprised. His white bushy brows hiked up on his forehead.

"She trusts you," Jake said.

"Of course she trusts me." Bear sounded gruff.

He did that, she realized, when he was touched. "I figure if you're as protective of Timmy out of court as you were in it, he'll be safer with you than with anyone else in the world."

Bear nodded. "I can't promise he won't be in danger. He is, or you wouldn't have brought him to me. I can promise Annie and I will do our best to take care of him."

"No one could ask for more." Laura touched his forearm, her eyes stinging. "We're grateful, Bear. For everything."

"Very much so," Jake added.

Timmy came running back to the door. He thrust a package of gum into Laura's hand. "I borrowed it, and I almost forgot."

She smiled at him, then dumped it into her purse.

Timmy went serious. "If you see a leaky dike, Dad'll chew it for you, Mom. Or you can come get me, and I will."

Laura nearly crumbled. "Thanks, honey."

"Laura, we've got to go." Jake urged her with a hand to her upper arm.

She nodded, then walked down the steps from the front porch to the car.

When Jake unlocked her door, Bear stepped up to close it. "Laura," he said, his eyes steady, clear, and more intense than ever before. "With my life."

He'd protect Timmy with his life. A little whimper of sound escaped her throat, and she squeezed his hand hard. "*That's* why I called you, Bear."

With Timmy settled, Laura could switch focus. But what occupied her thoughts now worried her nearly as much as Timmy's safety.

Jake would hate her.

No, worse. He'd pity her.

And maybe he should. Anyone who screwed up so badly that they'd carry the guilt of it with them to their grave needed pity. God knew they had little else left between them that was untainted enough to sustain them. But she didn't want Jake's pity. Compassion, she could accept from him, but never pity.

In the bath adjoining her bedroom at Jake's, Laura cranked the faucet closed, then stepped out of the shower and dried off with a fluffy white towel, wishing the hot water had calmed her down, or at least had helped clear her thoughts.

It hadn't.

Unfortunately, she still had no idea how to explain her keeping her confrontation with Sean Drake a secret from Jake. She should have told him about Drake's threatening to unleash Colonel James, who'd stop funding her research and ruin her career. But if she had, Jake would have been livid, and then Drake and James would have destroyed Jake's career, too. That's as far as she'd thought it through back then.

She slathered lotion on her body. The soft scent usually soothed her, but the only thing that could soothe her now would be to tell Jake the truth: that Drake and James were the reason she'd gotten out of the military and had gone inactive in Intel. He wouldn't take the news well; she could bank on that. She hadn't been open and honest with him, and, after Madeline and her antics, honesty ranked paramount with Jake. Laura knew it, and, God forgive her, but she just didn't think she had the courage to risk losing anymore. Not after risking making love with him and it ending in regret and disaster. She just didn't have an endless supply of courage to draw from, and her reserve balance sat at zero.

Her footsteps as heavy as her heart, she walked into the bedroom.

Jake lay in her bed, looking all the more masculine surrounded by sea green linens and feminine, antique cherry wood furnishings embellished with swirling scrolls and hand-carved leaves. Her breath caught in her throat, and she stopped. "What are you doing here?"

"We're going to take a nap." He rolled onto his side, then pulled back the covers on her side of the bed. "I've already set the alarm clock so we don't oversleep."

Laura was tempted. God, but she was tempted. It'd be so easy to crawl into bed with Jake, to take shelter in his arms. But she'd have to do it with this guilt on her conscience, and she'd already learned the hard way that lies between them carried stiff consequences.

Nothing stays hidden. The truth always finds the light.

She'd known it, seen it proven true time and again, but this business with Hawkins and Colonel James had driven home the point and staked it right through her heart.

Less than twenty-four hours after she and Jake had broken their agreement, she couldn't break it again, not without knowing the consequences. The problem was, how could she be straightforward about Sean and James without alienating Jake? God, she didn't want to alienate him. He'd doubted her over what he perceived as a lack of trust. What in the name of heaven would the penalty be for not telling him about Drake, James, and her career? Jake would hate her.

It's not fair. He doesn't even know I love him yet.

But he can never know that, she reminded herself. Never.

"Come on."

Her throat went thick, then turned dust dry. "I can't."

His expression didn't change. Still passive and quietly insistent. "It wasn't an invitation. Regret aside, you're dead on your feet and you need rest, not sex. So do I. And I know you. You'll lay here afraid to sleep. Afraid you'll dream." His expression softened. "I want to be here for you, Laura."

The thought warmed her heart. "I didn't mean that."

"Oh?" He still held up the corner of the covers. His chest was bare. Was he naked?

She had to tell him. She couldn't look at him while she did it, though. No way could she bear seeing more condemnation and disappointment in his eyes.

"Whatever it is, it can wait until later." Jake patted the mattress. "Right now, I don't want to talk. I want to sleep, and I want to do that knowing you're resting easily, too.''

Her heart wrenched. She had to tell him. Yet how could she refuse him? He knew she stood on the brink of telling him something important, and he'd given her a reprieve. She dropped the towel, and he passed her one of his T-shirts.

Surprised and feeling tender at the thoughtful gesture, she took it, then pulled his shirt on over her head, knowing her cheeks were flushed. She felt the heat. ''I, um, had hoped you hadn't noticed I wore these.'' Had he guessed the reason as well? She got into bed beside him.

He pulled up the covers and tucked them around her shoulder. ''I've been tired, not dead.'' His gaze turned tender. ''But even dead, I'd notice everything about you.'' He opened his arms. ''Now, come here and let's rest.''

She went willingly, longing to feel safe and secure and calm again—longing to feel loved—even knowing that he couldn't give to her. On his back, Jake closed his arms around her, his hold tender and so gentle it had tears stinging her eyes. She lay on her side against him and felt his warmth seep to her, her knee crooked over his thighs, her face and hand against his chest.

''Ah, that's better.'' He rested his chin against the crown of her head, then let out a content sigh that lifted his chest.

The soft hair there cushioned her cheek, and Laura closed her eyes. Visions of Hawkins, of Colonel James, and of her burning car flashed through her mind. The snapshots she could deal with. It was her underlying emotions about the men themselves giving her hell. And her feeling like a traitor for taking comfort in Jake's arms without telling him the truth. The guilt threatened to smother her. She couldn't stand it, or justify it, or forgive herself for withholding the truth from him again.

And those feelings proved, reprieve or no, she couldn't wait to talk about this after all. Jake had said he didn't want to talk now; he wanted to sleep. But he'd only said that to reduce stress and pressure on her. He wanted to know. He deserved to know. And as agonizing as it would be, she had to tell him. She licked at her lips, praying he wouldn't hate her. "I suspected Colonel James of being corrupt, Jake."

"I know. I picked up on it when we were talking with Connor." Jake stroked her back with reassuring wisps of touch. "I did, too."

Tears burned her eyes and stung the back of her nose. "You didn't. You never mentioned you suspected him of professional wrongdoing." Treason sounded like too ugly a word to even say aloud.

"I had no proof. But I did have a gut feeling, Laura. Something way down deep. I'm not sure I even recognized it for what it was until I heard Connor suggest we send Timmy to him. But on hearing that, I felt what I did with Hawkins. When I saw his photograph, my biggest surprise was that I wasn't surprised."

Jake gave her a reassuring little squeeze. "James was too damn interested in your tracking device designs. He never got that involved on other research projects. And he asked me too many questions about you personally. That made me uncomfortable, but I brushed it off as him just being inquisitive. It was easier to accept it as that than to talk to you about it. Especially with no concrete evidence against the man to back it up."

A catch formed in Laura's throat. She swallowed until it went away. "Jake, Sean was working with James. I found out at the Pentagon. I was TDY there, still active duty." Her voice cracked. "I was such a fool, Jake. I should've told you this then. Everything he's done now . . . I'm to blame.''

"We don't know that James has done anything.''

"I know,'' she insisted, looking up into Jake's face. "To me, it's not a matter of *if* James is involved in ROFF, it's *how* he's involved.''

"How does James tie to Sean Drake? The man's dead, for God's sake.''

"He wasn't then. I should've spoken up back then, but I didn't. Sean threatened me, Jake. Madeline was unhappy about our friendship, Sean said. And miserable, she drank more. So Sean paid me a concerned-father type of visit. He said I either stayed away from you and Timmy or else he'd have a talk with his friend, Colonel James, and I wouldn't be able to get funding for my research. He'd dump my career into the toilet.''

"And Colonel James subtly let you know he'd help Drake do it.''

Nothing stays hidden. "Right, when I went TDY to the Pentagon.'' She went on. "But the biggest reason I didn't say anything about this was that I couldn't risk you taking the two of them on and ruining your career.''

"That should have been my decision, Laura.''

"I know that now,'' she said. "But then I thought I was protecting you.''

"So instead you got out of the military and deactivated in Intel.''

A strong urge to hedge assailed her. *No. No gray area refuge. Not on this. Not anymore.* She nodded. "I was determined to remove myself from their reach, and that was an effective way to do it.''

"You did it to protect me.''

"I should have filed complaints against both of them.''

"You knew they'd ruin your career whether you

complied with their demands or not. And you didn't want them ruining mine as well.'' Jake stared hard at her. ''You knew that in jobs as sensitive as ours any inquiry whatsoever would have hung over our professional heads like black clouds forever. We never would have escaped the scandal, or the doubt.''

Jake's conclusions mirroring her own gave her validation of her judgment, if not vindication of her actions. This would be so much easier if she could say that before the Pentagon TDY she had trusted Colonel James. But she hadn't. She'd only ever had faith in Jake. And now Bear. ''I never trusted James or Sean Drake,'' she confessed, absently fingering a curl of black hair teasing Jake's nipple. ''Sean, for the most part, I could avoid. But James held the purse on my research. His questions grated at me from the start. Early on, I became adept at avoiding answering them.''

''Intuition.''

''I guess. But I wasn't really aware of the reason until Sean confronted me and levied his threat. And that TDY to the Pentagon where I encountered Colonel James confirmed it. Before then, it was more a nebulous feeling. But there, the reason I didn't trust him hit me like a sledge.''

''I remember how upset you were when you got home after that trip. What exactly happened?''

''James asked me about you and Timmy, then about the tracking device. When he linked you and my work like that, these warning signs flashed in my head. I felt like a major fool. As if he'd used me, and I'd not only let him—until then, I didn't know he'd done it.''

''I'm not following.''

''I'm not sure myself exactly what I mean. But I'm convinced that him ruining me was a return favor on some bargain he'd made with Sean Drake. You know those guys never do anything for nothing. They network.''

''Manipulate. 'Play the game, or get off the field. Spies always spy on spies.' ''

''What?'' Laura frowned, not understanding.

''Nothing. Just something Drake told me once. He was a manipulative bastard.'' Jake tightened his hold on her, wrapping his arms around her back and holding her firmly against his chest. ''All this happened to you because of me.'' Guilt riddled his voice. ''I'm so sorry, Laura.''

She was sorry, too. So damn sorry. Sean was dead, but because she'd handled that situation as she had, James had probably spread his corruption and done only God knows what to only God knows whom. It was bad; she felt certain of that, and a lot of innocent people would suffer for her selfishness. ''I've got to tell Connor about this. But I had to tell you first.''

Jake's chin bumped against her forehead. ''What exactly are you going to tell him? That you had suspicions but no proof that Colonel James was overly inquisitive about the tracker? That you suspect he cut a deal with a man now dead to keep you away from me so Madeline wouldn't drink so much?''

''Yes.''

''I hate to break it to you, but everyone in Special Ops has friends, family, neighbors, or acquaintances who ask too damn many questions. They don't realize it, of course, but they do it. Sean worrying about his daughter's drinking, and Colonel James—her former boss, who was genuinely fond of her—worrying about her drinking was . . . human. My point is, even if you'd reported this to OSI, without something more substantial than a verbal claim that Sean had threatened to get James to cut your funding, nothing would have changed. And even now, we can't really tie Sean Drake to James.''

· Jake had a point. The Office of Special Investigations couldn't follow up on every lead that lacked evidence of wrongdoing. They didn't have the manpower, and they considered an individual's privacy rights inviolate. Still. . . . "Filing an OSI report might have scared Colonel James into not getting involved with ROFF."

"We don't know that he is involved."

"I know it, Jake."

"We can't prove it," Jake said, rephrasing in the name of peace. "But if he is involved, no one could have stopped him without concrete evidence against him. You didn't have that then, and you don't have it now."

"But—"

"Laura." Jake pulled her back into his arms. "You're not responsible. He is. Let him carry his own burdens."

"Tell Mrs. Green I'm not responsible. Her husband is dead."

"Yes, he is, but you didn't kill him. It wouldn't have mattered. You could have notified CNN, and it wouldn't have changed anything."

"I should have gotten proof, and then gone to the OSI with it. They would have nailed them both. You know they would have."

"Yes, if you'd survived long enough to get the evidence and then to get it to them. But I seriously doubt Sean Drake would have stood still for that. He had the inside track, honey. You would have been searching blind. If you'd tried to nail him, odds are right now you'd be dead."

Knowing Jake was right, she shuddered hard.

"I'm sorry." He rubbed her back with gentle sweeps

of his hand to calm her down. "I didn't mean to be so blunt."

She lay quietly, her mind churning, foggy from exhaustion. And too confused and weary to sort through everything and look for the truth, she pressed her cheek to his chest and closed her eyes. "Jake?"

"Mmm?"

"I'm scared." God, but that'd been hard to admit. So hard.

"I know."

"And I'm tired, Jake. I'm so tired. . . ." Her voice trailed to silence.

Jake held her, aching inside, knowing all she was feeling and the fear she'd felt in telling him. It had cost her plenty to admit the truth, but she had done it, and that set Jake's mind at ease. For a moment, he'd wondered if she'd known more, and he'd hated having even a fleeting doubt about her. It didn't sit well on his shoulders, or in his heart. And that made him intimately aware of how much she'd hated having to keep all this from him.

And yet, she'd carried the burden for him. She'd given up a career for him. She'd given up the possibility of marrying a man who'd make her illusions real. Not just because she owed Jake her life, but because she'd pledged him her loyalty for her saving her life. He knew how deeply Laura took her oaths, and how much she hated being vulnerable.

She had to be the bravest woman he'd ever known.

Tender, his heart contracted, and he looked down into her face, at the sweep of her lashes against her cheeks, at the softness of her face, relaxed in sleep. A fierce surge of protectiveness rippled through him, and he knew he'd do anything to see to it that she could go on sleeping safe.

He stared up at the ceiling, at the bars of light seeping through the window into the darkened room from between the slats of the closed blinds. There was only one way to keep her safe—to nail James and ROFF. And to kill Hawkins . . . before he could kill her.

When Laura and Jake returned to Connor's office at 1800, she sat down in the visitor's chair she'd occupied that morning, feeling a lot calmer and more stable. She opened a portfolio, snagged a pen, and then cranked it open, preparing to take notes.

Reports littered Connor's desk. He shoved aside a stack of them, then rolled his chair deeper into the desk's kneehole. The pages rustled. "I learned this afternoon that Paul Hawkins held a civil service job at the Pentagon, which he left over a year ago."

"With a dishonorable discharge? How did he land a civil service job?" Jake frowned at that statement and jotted down something on the pad in his lap. "And where did he go?"

"Let me clarify," Connor said. "Hawkins isn't physically at the Pentagon, though he's still a government employee. He's officially on stress leave and has been for a year."

Laura jotted that down in her notes, feeling irritation overtake fear. Everyone remotely connected to the system knew stress leave had become a serious problem for the federal government. False claims ran rampant, forcing the OSI to spend an inordinate amount of time policing them. Too many employees claimed job pressures had them stressed out, and they convinced a doctor they were being honest, which resulted in the doctor ordering stress leave for the employee. The employee then collected his or her salary until fit to go back to work. In more cases than not, it was fraud, pure and simple. And picking up the slack created by the missing employee's absence too often caused genuine stress and burnout in coworkers, which led to more cases of stress leave. These were genuine. This situation produced a vicious cycle. The widespread abuse made the genuine cases suspect, and those victims were regarded with suspicion. And the poor OSI, overworked and understaffed just like everyone else, had to sift through and decipher which cases were which. It wasn't an enviable task, or an easy one. The agents had to deal with hot tempers, defensive doctors, irate bosses, and frosty victims—often simultaneously.

Now Hawkins had done it. But why? Just to punish the government for kicking him out of the military? "Planting bombs can be stressful, I suppose," Laura said, knowing her disgust was apparent in her voice. She hoped the OSI hung him from the highest tree in D.C.

Connor rubbed at his neck. "Rest assured, Paul Hawkins will be charged with fraud and everything else the OSI can tag him with, Laura. Jake, you asked about how Hawkins secured a civil service job with a dishonorable discharge on his head. Well, someone forged documents giving him a clear military record and an honorable discharge. We aren't sure yet who is responsible, but the OSI is already working on it."

She looked over at Jake, saw the worry in his eyes, then looked back across the desktop at Connor. "You might suggest the OSI take a look at interactions between Hawkins and Colonel James," she said. "I'm making no accusations here, only saying that the effort might be worthwhile."

"Is there something you want to tell me?" Connor asked.

"No, sir. Only offering a suggestion."

"I see."

He saw, all right. Too much. She swallowed a lump

from her throat. "They might also check connections between Hawkins and Sean Drake."

Connor narrowed his eyes, and the light of understanding flickered in their depths. "It would strike me as logical to extend that cross-check to interactions between Colonel James and Sean Drake."

Laura's palms began to sweat. "That would be a reasonable course of action, in my opinion."

"I appreciate your suggestions, Laura." Connor's tone rang sincere.

She was relieved to hear it. So was Jake. At least he was getting some color back in his face now.

"I wish the rest of the news was good." Connor glanced down at one of the dozen reports near his left elbow. "Is Timmy safe?"

Jake answered. "He's secure."

"Good." The general looked relieved, obviously feeling concern and responsibility for the people assigned to him, and for their families.

Jake crossed a leg over his thigh, then balanced a pad atop it. "I take it the news from the team conference could've been better."

"I'm sorry to have to say it, but it looks grim." Connor leaned back. "For apparent reasons, neither of you has had full access to ROFF intelligence," he said. "We believe Paul Hawkins is the leader of ROFF, and it's obvious he has a personal vendetta against you two as well as one against the United States."

"Even with forged records, being dishonorably discharged can be challenging to live with. You know he had to fear he'd be caught," Jake said.

Laura doubted Hawkins had lost a moment's sleep over that. "It's easier to blame someone else rather than to take your own hits."

"Laura," Connor said, "the team feels strongly you

should be placed in protective custody until Hawkins is arrested.''

"No.'' Resolve hardened like steel in her chest. She rapped the pad with her pen, her grip tight. "I can't hide, General. I won't.''

Jake reached over and clasped her hand in his. "For what it's worth, I think you should agree to this. We don't have full access to all the information the team does. If they're suggesting this, they've—''

"No, Jake.'' She glanced over at him. "I won't hide.''

"I want you safe. Timmy needs you, Laura.''

Tenderness shimmied through her insides, and her voice went soft. "I'm thinking of Timmy. Truly. And your concern touches me, Jake. But I have to assist in capturing Hawkins.'' And Colonel James, too, she thought, if he proved to be the man who'd doctored Hawkins's records. She'd never be able to live with herself, not if she didn't help to nail them both. Surely Jake could see the parallels she'd seen between the men. "I'm trained and qualified. No. No, I won't hide.''

"You're trained only because of a screwup in your orders," Jake said.

They both knew she had been supposed to receive only the communications segment of survival training. Fouled up orders had landed her in the entire program. By the time the administrative error had been rectified, she'd been two-thirds of the way through the course, so she'd finished it. "Regardless of the reasons, I'm trained.''

"What about Timmy?''

"He's probably safer away from me than with me, Jake. I've been targeted.'' She lowered her gaze, then turned in her chair to face him. "Listen, I have to do this. You know I do. It's the husband in you talking now, not the soldier.''

''Damn right, it is. I *am* your husband. Don't expect me to not act like one because it's inconvenient.''

She stroked his arm. ''It isn't inconvenient, and, yes, you are my husband. Which is why you should understand this is something I have to do.'' Fingers of fear clasped her throat. ''Don't you see, Jake? I·can't run from Hawkins. I can't. If I do, I'll never stop running.''

Jake stared at her for a long moment, then glanced over at the general. ''Could we have a moment, sir?''

Connor nodded, his lips pursed, and then left his office.

When he closed the door, Jake stood up and tugged at her, urging her to stand. When she did, he cupped her face in his hands, letting her see the worry in his eyes. ''Laura, I really do understand why you feel you have to do this, but I'm asking you not to. I'm asking you to trust me and to let me handle it.''

''You're my husband, not my guardian.''

''I want to protect you. I have to protect you.'' His clouded eyes turned turbulent. ''I can't lose you, honey. Not now. You're my best friend, Laura. The mother of my son.''

His arrows had been aimed accurately, and, boy, were they sharp.

Though the agony of regret still burned in his eyes, he kissed her hard; a furious mating of lips and tongues tasting of desperation, and he wrapped her in an embrace that both sustained her and bordered on pain. Too tight! When he separated their mouths, he hugged her fiercely and breathed into the curve where her shoulder met her neck. ''Please, Laura. For Timmy. For me.''

Amazed that he'd included himself, she caressed his tense face, his beloved jaw, torn between doing what he asked of her and what she felt she must do. Timmy was the deciding factor. Formidable enemies had to be faced. But if both she and Jake faced them and they failed, Timmy would be vulnerable. He'd be returned to Madeline and placed in her inept care. That made the decision easier to stomach, which Laura felt sure had been Jake's intention in mentioning it. "For now, okay, Jake."

"Good." Relief sluiced over his face. "Good."

"But I reserve the right to change my mind if I feel I must."

"That's reasonable." He released her. "Thank you, Laura."

Only Jake would take the dangers and responsibilities upon himself, placing her squarely in the safety of the sidelines, and then thank her for it. How could she not love him?

Jake walked toward the door, finally able to breathe again. As he reached for the knob, he heard Laura call him and looked back at her.

"Don't make me a widow," she said. "I'll be extremely ticked if you make me a widow."

She was rallying. Thank God. Despite the odds, a smirk teased the corner of his mouth. "I'll hold that thought." Jake opened the door and then nodded at the general.

Connor walked back in with two guards. He'd known, of course, that Jake would convince her, though by his expression, he hadn't expected it'd happen quite so quickly. And it wouldn't have, Jake knew, if he hadn't pulled out the secret weapon: Timmy.

Laura gathered her purse and closed the portfolio she'd dropped open on the chair.

"These men will escort you, Laura," Connor said. "We'll move you from the building to a safe house as soon as possible."

She nodded at the general, then offered the men a shallow smile.

"You're making the right decision," Connor said, his eyes kind, his expression solemn. "The hardest one for you, I would say, but the right one."

"I hope so." She looked over at Jake. "Take care of you."

"I'll be in touch," Jake said, then watched her leave with the guards.

When they'd left the office, the general sat down at his desk. "I'm glad to see you've gotten your marriage on the right track, Jake."

It wasn't on track. "It's an illusion," Jake said, hating the resentment he heard in his own voice.

Connor leaned forward over his desk. "I don't mean to pry but, if I can, I'd like to help. What exactly is the problem?"

Jake stripped off the veneer and let his misery shine in his eyes. "I love her."

"Uh-huh." Connor frowned, clearly stumped. "In my experience, love comes in handy in a marriage."

"But I can't have her."

"So she doesn't love you, then?"

He didn't get it. Jake walked to the window, stared out sightlessly to the street, and tried to explain. "No, I think she loves me too—more or less."

"More or less?"

Jake nodded.

"I see." Connor kept his face passive.

Jake paced from the coffeepot to the desk, then back again, stuffing one hand deep into his pocket and rubbing his neck with the other one. "Until recently we were just friends."

"That much, I'd surmised." Connor took a drink from a can of soda at his elbow, then set it back down. "So let me see if I've got this. I have the feeling I'm missing a puzzle piece. You were friends, and then you got married. Then you fell in love—more or less—with each other.''

"Exactly." Jake lifted a hand, feeling like the bastard he was.

"These things shouldn't have you looking like you've just been sentenced to a lethal injection, Jake."

"They don't. The not being able to have her does."

"Why can't you have her?"

"I run missions with less than two percent survival odds. Do I really need to explain?"

"Ah, I see." And for the first time, Connor appeared to understand perfectly. "She doesn't want to risk you being killed and leaving her."

"Not exactly." Unable to stand still, Jake paced some more and raked a frustrated hand through his hair. "It's complicated, General. I don't want her to risk losing me. She'd be devastated."

"Of course she'd be devastated. She'd intended to spend the rest of her life with you."

"Exactly."

"Ah, the rest of her life." Dawning lit in Connor's eyes. "So if you have a real marriage, and you die, then she's devastated."

Jake nodded, letting his gaze slide to the gray carpet. "I can't put her through that."

"I'm confused," Connor said, rubbing at his temple. "Be patient. I'm trying to muddle my way through all this and get up to speed. Until today, I thought yours was a marriage between friends and no more, though it's always been as clear to me as the nose on your face that you two love each other. Yet you say love only came into this recently."

"No, love's been there. I'm not sure how long."

"But until recently, you only loved each other as friends."

"Right."

"And now it's different."

"Yes. I love her, and I'm in love with her. I don't know if she loves me—as a woman loves her husband, I mean—but I'm sure the possibility's there and she could. She does want more than illusions."

"And you want more for her?"

"I do. But, selfish bastard that I am, I want more for her *with me*." He frowned. "I tell myself I don't want to die and leave her bitter, and I don't, but—"

"Wait," Connor interrupted, holding up a hand.

"Sir?"

"What do *you* want, Jake?" Connor asked simply.

Jake's answer felt anything but simple. "I want her. Happy."

"And not a grieving widow." Connor sighed, then sat back and looked up at Jake. "I'd never claim to understand women, Jake. Any man who claims to is, in my humble opinion, a fool. But the way I see it, if you two love each other and you died, then either way she'd be devastated. And I'll give you something else to mull over that I think is important. There's something a widow has that a woman who loves but doesn't have a real marriage with her husband lacks."

Puzzled, Jake hiked a brow.

The general's gaze went soft. "Memories."

He was right. If Jake died, Laura would have no memories of their marriage to support her except one night of lovemaking and regret because of it. Good memories would soften the pain of loss and make enduring it more bearable. He only hoped they had the opportunity to make some good memories. That he hadn't waited too long. That she'd be willing. Did he have the right to ask her? To even suggest it?

"In your shoes, I'd be thinking about killing Hawkins." Connor's eyes narrowed knowingly. "I'd check your pulse if you weren't considering it. But it wouldn't be a smart move, Jake.''

"Why not?"

"Because there were two other people in that Lincoln who haven't yet been identified. Hawkins might be our only link to them.''

Kill him, and Jake and Laura would be looking over their shoulders for some faceless stalker the rest of their lives. The truth trickled through to Jake, not from what had been said, but from what hadn't. "You think there's someone higher up in ROFF than Hawkins.''

"The team thinks so, yes. And we've got to tread carefully until we identify who.''

Jake agreed. He didn't want to agree, but facts didn't bend to convenience. Not even when they presented themselves at cross-purposes with a man's desires.

"I didn't mention this to Laura because she seemed genuinely fond of Bill Green, and, frankly, she's suffered a lot of shocks in a short span of time. But we've got evidence, Jake. He's guilty of planting the bug in Laura's car.''

Jake forced himself not to grimace, to bury any reaction. "What kind of evidence?"

"The part-time mechanic who hired on there was a CIA operative. He observed Green and Hawkins talking. Green was upset, refusing to do something Hawkins wanted done. The operative couldn't hear Hawkins's comments, but on hearing them, Green turned physically ill. He was definitely shaken by the meeting, and the next morning he put the device in Laura's car. This morning, the operative learned from Mrs. Green that Hawkins had demanded Bill bug the car. He'd threatened her life, and those of their son and his children.''

So Bill had acted against Laura out of fear, which explained why he had harangued her to get rid of the

Mustang. He felt he had no choice but to do what Hawkins said, but it preyed on his mind. So he'd done what he could by strongly and repeatedly suggesting Laura get rid of the car. "Why weren't we told?"

Connor sent him a level look. "Because at the time, Hawkins hadn't been identified. All we knew was that the head of ROFF was Special Ops-trained, and that your wife had that training."

"Laura is still a suspect?" Jake fisted his hand around the chair arm. "You put her into protective custody to immobilize her?"

"Yes and no. The team considers her a suspect. I personally don't. So far as I'm concerned, she's in protective custody."

"But the team views it as her being detained."

"I'm afraid so."

Fifteen

The Ops Center hummed.

Letting the door swing closed behind him, Jake automatically looked up to the electronic wall map of the world. Three areas were flashing, denoting active hot spots. None were in Florida. The sweep of ROFF headquarters had to be over.

The dozen men and three women were busy on the phone, pounding computer keyboards, or both, and from the crowding, extra personnel had been called in. At the far corner of a long line of desks, Captain David Perry stood up. The phone at his ear, he waved Jake over.

Jake had worked with Perry before; he was a good soldier. A little on the fanatic side about being a soldier, but that only sounded like a liability until you needed a man to cover your back.

As Jake walked up, David hung up the phone and swiped a hand through his close-cropped blond hair. His round face was even more ruddy than usual.

Jake nodded.

"Have a seat." David pointed toward a chair beside his desk, then yelled over to the man at the next desk. "Director of Safety reported yet?"

"Ten minutes ago," the guy said, grabbing an incoming fax out of the machine. "They're pulling together the investigative board now. We'll have the members' list ASAP."

David looked back at Jake. "We've got a Class-A in Guam. Convening the board. Twelve men down."

"I hate to hear it."

"Don't we all?" David grunted.

"What's going on in Saudi?" Jake asked, recalling the map.

"A breach in the No-Fly Zone." David pulled out a package of gum and offered Jake a piece. When he refused, David tossed the gum back into the drawer. "We're working a search and rescue out in the Pacific, too. Shipping accident with possible survivors."

The Ops Center hadn't just been busy; it'd been a zoo. And suddenly a morning of team conferences, reviewing CIA preliminary reports, and OSI briefings seemed a lot less frantic to Jake than it had at the time.

"When it rains, it pours, eh?" David took a healthy swig of orange juice from a carton on his desk. "General Connor asked me to update you," he said, then dropped his voice. "He's tied up with the team and totally pissed. Hawkins eluded arrest on the sweep. ROFF had set up a secondary headquarters, a tent city. Someone got word to them because by the time we were in position and ready to move, they'd bugged out. Intel picked up on it, so our guys didn't go in. They're on observatory status. All the factions in the coordinated effort have activated but so far no signs of Hawkins have surfaced."

Jake nodded. He could curse, stomp, and raise hell, but that wouldn't put Hawkins in custody. Jake decided to reserve his energy for something that might help.

"The white Lincoln used to bomb your wife's car has been located," David went on. "Three miles east of your house. Gassed and torched. No hope for any evidence that will help identify the other two persons in the car. We traced the Lincoln to an airport rental agency. Bogus credit card, reservation for automatic pickup, so the clerk never saw who actually took the car. That's about it, Jake. Other than a personal commentary.''

Jake lifted a brow.

''Everyone in the loop is taking this personally. Most of us have wives and kids, and we all know this could be happening to any one of us, or to our families. We're doing all we can. I just wanted you to know that.'' David's blue eyes glittered. ''And to tell you, if you need any help nailing the sons of bitches, you can count on me.''

''Thanks. I appreciate it, David,'' Jake said, then left the Ops Center.

He went to check on Laura. Until dark, she was being held in a basement security vault. With nothing to look at but walls, Jake didn't have to wonder how she was. He knew she was fit to be tied. If she suspected everyone on the team except for Connor still had doubts about her integrity and considered her detained, she'd be even worse. Connor had made Jake's dilemma of whether or not to tell her about that easy. For Laura's peace of mind, and Jake's, Connor had issued Jake a rare direct order not to tell her any of it.

Obviously Connor had meant that sincerely—about her peace of mind—or he'd have pulled Jake off the mission. When push came to shove, Laura was his wife. And yet neither Connor nor anyone from the team had suggested replacing Jake. Unless some team member had suggested it and Connor had interceded.

Actually, odds favored that having taken place. The team would have been obligated to claim conflict of interest. There could be only one reason Jake hadn't been pulled and replaced: Connor had to have accepted personal responsibility for Jake's actions. And he'd chosen not to mention it to Jake.

Watching the floor-level lights descend above the elevator door, Jake's respect for Connor doubled. He genuinely backed his men. No lip service, no bull, and no glory. He just backed them all the way.

Jake stepped off the elevator and passed a guard, then turned the corner leading to the vault and passed two more. At the mouth of the vault, he nodded to the security guard who sat at a small desk reading Grisham's latest paperback novel. He set the book down, then passed Jake a pen and a clipboard to sign in.

Scraping the pen across the appointed line, Jake gave the clipboard back. "Is she giving you any trouble?"

"No, sir," he said with a strong Mississippi accent. "Just raising a little hell, sir."

Jake had to work at it not to smile. He waited for the buzz, for the steel door to open, and then walked through. It slammed shut behind him, halting the draft of fresh air flowing into the stark white ten-by-twelve room.

Laura stood in the middle of the vault pacing the white linoleum. The walls were as bare as the room. The only furnishings were a small black table and a folding chair. Three cans of soda sat on the table. And a pint of raspberries.

Jake's stomach furled. Damn, but he hated seeing her again upset to the point of eating raspberries. The only time she ever ate them was when she was falling apart inside. Yet seeing them here proved Connor knew her habits well and that he was trying to make her comfortable. Maybe he just had assumed she'd want them and Laura hadn't requested them. That was possible. So far, she hadn't eaten any. The cellophane wrapper covering the green basket was still intact. Jake could only hope that what he had to tell her about Bill

Green wouldn't have her shredding it to get fistsful of the berries.

Her face flushed, and fury burned in her eyes. "I should break your nose again, Jake Logan."

"I see you're doing fine." Remembering the blow she'd accidentally landed on him—a blow intended for Hawkins during their confrontation—Jake rubbed at the bridge of his nose, tempted to kiss the outrage out of her. He strolled over and stuffed his hands into his pockets. "You've really got to quit all this fawning over me, Laura. It's going to go to my head."

She glared up at him. "Kiss my—"

"Is that an invitation?" He dragged a fingertip over her lower lip. What Connor had said about memories had replayed in Jake's mind off and on all morning. Laura would probably think he'd lost it, considering the regret, but nothing ventured, nothing gained. He damn well intended she have some good memories of their marriage to ease her through the mourning process. "I've missed you."

"Don't you even think about getting gentle on me." Her chest heaved. "I agreed to protective custody. I did not agree to be locked up in a windowless vault like a—whatever!"

His wife needed soothing. A lot of it, from the looks of her. "It's only until dark. Then they'll move you someplace safe."

"With windows?"

"Yes. With windows." Jake nearly smiled. She wasn't claustrophobic, but being locked inside a windowless vault with concrete walls six feet thick repelled her; made her feel helpless and out of control. Vulnerable. Being closed in had affected her that way back in survival school, too. When they'd been crammed into coffin-like boxes and left there for hours as part of their training, she'd come out steaming. Jake remembered those feelings. They'd been ten times worse than a caged animal sensation. The total sensory deprivation left the person feeling disoriented and totally helpless, like a victim to whatever the captor wanted. He'd hated it, too. Immensely.

She slumped back against the wall. "Have you talked with Timmy?"

The halogen lights were harsh and unforgiving, yet still she looked beautiful. Cream slacks and an emerald green blouse that made her skin look like sweet cream. She was beautiful, but worried.

"No, I haven't. I've been in meetings."

She looked down to the toes of her shoes. Her hair swung forward like a curtain, blocking her face. She tucked it back behind her ear. "It's probably not a good idea to call, anyway. If there's any trouble, Bear will let us know."

"Yes, he will. He has the Ops Center emergency phone number."

"Right." She looked up at him, tense and uneasy. "No news to share?"

He hated to tell her this. But Laura, being Laura, would still be feeling responsible and chewing herself up over Bill Green's death. She needed to know the truth about that, if not the whole truth about her detention. Jake hated it, but it appeared he had no choice but to step into one of those gray areas he'd griped about her treading in on occasion.

"Jake?" Laura crossed her arms over her chest. "You're scaring me."

He glanced at the box of berries, clasped her arms, and let his hands glide up to her shoulders, then down to her elbows. "It's about Bill Green."

Her eyes widened, silently pleading with him not to tell her Bill had betrayed her. But she stiffened, bracing herself, as if already surmising he had.

"He did it, Laura. He planted the listening device in your car."

She swallowed hard. "Are you, um, sure?" Hope lingered in her eyes.

He doused it, nodding. *Please, don't let her reach for the raspberries. I can't take that. Please.*

She blinked, then blinked again. "Jake," she said, just above a whisper, her eyes misting. "I think I need for you to hold me. Would that be okay, or would it make you feel regret, too?"

The uncertainty in her voice cut through him like a knife. "It'd be okay." He looped his arms around her, greatly relieved. Weighty resignation etched her face and she was pale, but she cried no tears and ate no berries. Considering she'd had total faith in the man, her disappointment had to be crushing, but she was coping.

They stood there for long minutes. Him with his arms circling her back, her with her hands at her sides. Then she took in a deep breath that had her breasts flattened against his chest, stepped back, and slumped against the wall.

"He was a good man," she said, knocking the toe of her shoe against the floor. "They backed him up against a wall, and he had nowhere safe to go."

"I know."

"How is Mrs. Green?"

Devastated certainly. "About as well as you would expect."

Laura looked up at him, and her eyes clouded. "I'm sorry for her."

So was Jake. If they'd used another automotive center, Bill Green would still be alive and well and fixing cars. But they hadn't, and neither of them would forget that for the rest of their lives.

Laura let her gaze fall to his chest. "I've been doing

a lot of thinking while I've been in here. About everything . . ."

He could imagine. There wasn't a hell of a lot else to do in here.

"About Hawkins and Colonel James, and even about Madeline and Sean. But mostly about Madeline." Laura risked glancing into Jake's eyes, then dropped her gaze back to his chest.

"Bear won't let her pull anything, honey. While you and Mrs. Barton were settling Timmy into their guest room, I talked with him about the adoption and the hate message she'd left on the answering machine. If she tries to pull anything, he'll let us and Chief Wilson know immediately."

"Did you talk with Connor about filing the complaints?"

"Yes. He suggested we hold off until we have a fix on this ROFF situation. It could antagonize it, and make things worse for Timmy."

"I agree. I should have known you'd think to take care of it." Laura caressed him with her gaze.

He smiled. "Glad to hear I have my moments."

Her gaze warmed more. "You do, though you could benefit from a little more practice."

"I kind of like the sounds of that."

"Me, too." She closed her eyes and looked down. "Jake, I know we discussed this and we both felt regrets about us making love, but I've thought about that a lot too, and I want you to know that all I regret is that I broke my word to you."

What exactly did she mean by that? "Is that all you regret? Really?"

She nodded, unwilling to risk his gaze.

"It'll be a good memory, then."

That thought seemed to please him, and she was

grateful she could answer honestly. "Yes. It'll be a good memory."

She swept back her hair with a careless hand. "This is unrelated, but I want you to know something else, too. Connor wanting to send Timmy to Colonel James got my antenna up." Her gaze warned she wouldn't be flexible on this and she wouldn't change her mind. "After what happened with him before, I'll never again ignore my antenna."

"What are you saying, honey?"

She looked up at him, her eyes wary and her expression tense. "I don't know exactly. I guess I'm just warning you to be careful. Don't trust anyone, Jake. Promise me that you won't."

Not even the team? Connor? "Anyone?"

"Anyone." She stepped closer, hesitated, and then touched her hand to his face, her eyes solemn and earnest. "You said you didn't want to lose me. Well, I don't want to lose you, either. At this point, I don't trust anyone, and I don't want you to trust anyone. It's important, Jake."

Feeling her slight tremble, he caressed her upturned face. "I trust you."

"Of course," she said, affecting Bear's matter-of-fact tone.

She believed in his complete faith in her, and pleased at knowing it, Jake smiled. "You trust me, too."

"Has there ever been a doubt?"

He thought back, sifted through the thirteen years they'd been friends. "Only once. About your reactivation."

Sadness flickered through her eyes. "I've never doubted you."

"No, but I thought you had. I thought I'd somehow failed you and that's why you didn't trust me. But I only felt that way until the shock of seeing your photo wore off and you explained the reactivation. My mistake. I want you to know that. I've always considered you steadfast and loyal, Laura. Always.''

Clearly uncomfortable, she changed the subject. ''Any ideas floating around on the identity of the other two people in the Lincoln?''

''Not yet.''

She sighed and backed away. ''Then you'd better get out of here and get busy.''

''Okay.'' His smile in his eyes, he kissed her once . . . twice . . . then a third time before he could stand to turn her loose. He'd surprised her and, when she kissed him back, she surprised him. ''I'll be back.''

''You'd better,'' she replied, soft and husky.

When he got to the vault door, she called out. ''Jake?''

He looked back at her.

''Hurry, will you? It's kind of cramped in here.''

He winked at her. ''I'll do my best,'' he promised, then signaled to the security guard he was ready to leave.

It wasn't until Jake was back in the Ops Center that it occurred to him Laura hadn't mentioned getting out of custody until after Jake resolved this issue of ROFF.

She knew she was being detained.

Connor stormed into the Ops Center. ''Jake,'' he called out, lifting a hand and motioning Jake over to him.

''Yes, sir.''

''Read this on the way back to my office.'' Connor thrust a report into Jake's hand. ''CIA preliminary.''

Jake scanned the pages. ROFF intended to contaminate Jacksonville, Florida's water supply system with botulism bacteria? Good God, didn't Hawkins have even a fragment of a conscience?

When Connor closed the office door, Jake stopped

beside the coffee bar and turned to him. "Hawkins will contaminate it himself."

"Why would he take those kinds of risks?" The general sat down at his desk, then scanned through a ream of reports that had gathered there since Jake last had been in his office.

"Arrogance is his Achilles' heel. Check his undoctored personnel records or his court-martial file. He'll contaminate the water himself just to prove that he can."

"Prepare to stop him." Connor glanced down at his watch. "The team's convening in the briefing room in twenty minutes. You'll need to be there. Right now, they're alerting local authorities and their field agents. You'll have assistance, Jake, including Captain Perry's."

Connor finished scanning through the loose pages on his desk. "You all have blanket authorization to self-medicate. The flight surgeon will be at the briefing with appropriate antibiotics."

That got Jake's adrenaline pumping. "Yes, sir."

Connor didn't meet Jake's eyes. "You can't tell Laura you're leaving headquarters. That's a team decision, not mine."

Them and their damn doubt. "She's innocent."

"I know that, and you know it. But her photo being found in the dead operative's hand puts her in a gray area, Jake. It has the others nervous."

"Nothing is black and white." Jake reiterated a phrase from Madeline's answering machine message.

Connor let out a sigh reeking of frustration. "Look, I agree with you. Doubt is a bitch, but the team's weighed the possibilities, and the scales don't balance. If they're wrong, Laura's no worse off for being detained. Hell, she's probably better off. If they're right, they've neutralized her."

"They're not right," Jake said. "Just answer one question for me. She's my wife. I love her, and you know it. So why have you kept me assigned to this mission?"

"You're the best man for the job."

"And?" There was more; Jake sensed it.

Connor looked away. His gaze slid to the portrait of Patton. "Because I asked your wife why she married you."

"And she said to help me keep custody of Timmy."

"Yes." Connor slid a hand into his pocket and turned back to Jake. "But she also told me . . . other things. She admires you greatly, Jake, as a human being. And her respect for Special Ops . . . Well, that's why I've kept you on this assignment."

"Because of Laura's admiration for what we do?" This didn't make sense.

"Because she admires. You get to be a pretty good judge of character in this job, and you develop a nose for when someone's paying you lip service. Laura wasn't. She was speaking from her heart. There's no way she could be guilty, Jake, and I know there's no man alive who'll work harder to prove her innocent than you. That's why you haven't been replaced."

Whatever she'd told Connor, it had to have been powerful to inspire him to put his stars on the line. That was the bottom line here. The team *had* claimed conflict of interest, and Connor had personally accepted responsibility for Jake. If Jake screwed up, and the team felt it was intentional, Connor would forfeit his stars, possibly his command, and perhaps even his pension. All because of what Laura had said to him.

And Jake couldn't even tell her he was leaving. Knowing he might never see her again, he could say nothing, not even good-bye.

Connor cleared his throat. "Gear up and meet the

team in the briefing room in fifteen minutes.''

"Yes, sir.'' Jake turned for the office door.

"Jake?'' Connor called out.

Looking back at him, Jake paused.

Connor's expression tensed and grew even more serious, tightening the corners of his mouth. "I don't want to have to tell your wife you didn't make it. Put me in that position, and I'm going to be pissed.''

"No, sir,'' Jake said, then left the office.

He gathered his gear and changed into his combat uniform. Timmy often had said the camouflage BDUs looked like pajamas. Jake had told him the battle dress uniforms were fatigues—fighting clothes—and Timmy had warned Jake that fighting upset Laura. She would *strongly* suggest he not fight to settle his differences, and if he did it anyway and got caught, she'd put him on restriction. She might even cry.

Remembering that jewel of an interchange with his son had Jake smiling all the way to the briefing room.

Just before he entered the door, one of the vault guards approached him. "Major?'' he said. "Mrs. Logan's very upset, sir. She kept at me until I promised I'd come tell you something.''

Very upset? How upset? Downing-raspberries-by-the-box upset or yelling upset? "Yes, Lieutenant?''

"She says to tell you Timmy's in trouble, sir. She . . . um. . . .'' His face flushed.

"What?'' Jake frowned, restraining himself from pulling the words out of the man's throat.

"She feels it, sir,'' he said, definitely uncomfortable with reporting intuitive feelings.

"She feels it, but there've been no messages, right?''

"That's correct, sir. She said to tell you and made me swear on my rank I'd tell you right away, no matter what you were doing.''

"Did she say 'mother's intuition'?'' Jake asked,

praying she hadn't and dreading that the man would answer she had.

"Yes, sir. That's exactly what she said."

A shiver shot up Jake's spine. She'd been right too often for him not to pay attention to this warning, or for him to hope that this time she was wrong. When it came to Timmy, Laura had always had a built-in radar that signaled when he was in trouble. And she'd rarely, if ever, been wrong. "Thank you. Tell her I'll take care of it."

Maybe it was stress and not intuition, Jake thought, watching the vault guard head back toward the bank of elevators. Timmy was safe with Bear. If there was trouble, he would've called, and he hadn't.

"Jake," Captain Perry said. "The team's waiting. Better get your backside in there."

Jake walked into the briefing room.

Ten men and three women sat at the conference table. Some wore uniforms; some, street clothes. Some Jake knew—like Colonel Jim Mather, the Judge Advocate General, commonly referred to as the JAG, and Agent 27, the CIA representative—but the others he didn't recognize. None of them wore BDUs, including Perry, and that absence gave Jake a sinking feeling that there'd already been an alteration in plans, and he'd be going it alone.

Perry whispered something to Connor, who sat at the head of the table, then left the room.

"Jake," Connor said, pointing to a chair at his right. "Sit over here."

When Jake sat down, Connor addressed him.

"I understand Laura's got an intuitive feeling that something is wrong with Timmy."

Perry. "Yes, sir," Jake said. "She's done that numerous times over the years with him."

"Has she been accurate?"

"Yes, sir." A sliver of uneasiness widened inside Jake. "Often."

A lean-faced team member frowned. "Jake, do you think Laura could have claimed having this feeling to prepare the foundation, so to speak, in an attempt to get herself released?"

"Maybe." Jake looked at the man. "If she knew she was being detained and she thought Timmy needed her, she'd move heaven and earth to get to him."

"But would helping him be her only motive?" a woman asked. Sitting at the end of the table, she looked a lot like a blonde Connie Selleca. "In your opinion."

"In my opinion, yes. Laura only agreed to protective custody for him. That'd be the only reason she'd attempt to break it."

Connor passed over a fax. Worry flooded his face, and seeing it had Jake's skin crawling. "What's this?"

"A message, we presume, from ROFF," Connor said. "It was sent directly to my office."

Jake looked down at the single sheet of paper. The words on it had been composed from letters cut out of the newspaper.

LOGAN
EXCHANGE
WIFE FOR SON
EVERGLADE RENDEZVOUS
TONIGHT
OR
SON DIES

Sixteen

They had Timmy?
      Jake couldn't breathe.

Connor softened his voice. "You'd better check this out."

Jake was nearly to the briefing room door when someone knocked. He yanked it open. Captain David Perry stood there, and Jake shoved past him.

"Jake," Perry yelled out. "I've got an emergency message for you from a Mrs. Barton."

Halfway down the hallway, running for a secure phone line, Jake stopped and then turned back.

From inside the room, Connor called. "Bring it in here, Perry."

Ruddy-faced and frowning, he entered the briefing room.

Jake followed him. "What is it?"

"A team of six broke into the Barton residence. Heavily armed. Mr. Barton was shot twice in the chest. He's alive, but in critical condition. Mrs. Barton's given a fairly decent description of the men who weren't masked. They took Timmy, Jake."

"Oh, God."

"Mrs. Barton says a woman was with them." Perry's grimace deepened. "Timmy called her Madeline."

Seventeen

~

$\mathcal{M}$adeline had kidnapped Timmy? She worked with ROFF? The fax wasn't a hoax. Laura's intuition wasn't wrong. They had his son. Madeline had helped them kidnap his son. "Perry," Jake said softly, feeling a storm of emotions; so many he couldn't slot them all: anger, outrage, resentment, disbelief, and fear. So damn much fear. "Bring my wife up here. STAT."

Connor swept at the yellow pad with his pen. "What the hell would Madeline be doing with ROFF?"

Stiff shouldered and tense, Jake stood with his hand stuffed fisted in his slacks' pocket, afraid to so much as blink or he'd lose control. Chin dipped, he slid Connor a level look, his voice bitter-edged. "She's Sean Drake's daughter. Because of her drinking, I let myself forget that." Now Timmy was paying the costs of Jake's lapse in judgment.

Connor blinked, frowned, and then blinked again, clearly seeing where Jake's thoughts were going on this. "We all forgot that."

The blonde Connie Selleca lifted a finger. "Wasn't Madeline connected to Intel at one time?"

"Yes," the CIA representative, Agent 27, said,

kneading at the muscles in his neck with an impatient hand. "She was on staff, working for Colonel James, but only because of her father."

"Excuse me?" The blonde lifted her brows.

"Sean Drake held one of the most powerful positions in the CIA. He worked closely with Colonel James, and James hired Madeline. We all know that type thing goes on. But even then she was an alcoholic. We couldn't risk using her for anything. When the woman was sober, she was still incompetent."

Connor interceded. "What Agent 27 is trying to be diplomatic about saying is, Madeline Drake has no common sense. Even sober, she was an indiscreet liability with an attitude."

"Hell, why play with words? The woman is an airhead." Jake paced a short path alongside the table, then suddenly stopped. "Or she wanted to convince everyone she was an airhead." A cold chill crept up his backbone. Was she really? Unsure anymore, Jake raked an impatient hand through his hair. "The only thing about her I'm sure of is that she appeared to want one thing in life: Sean Drake's approval. She pursued it diligently, and she never got it. Recently, she's physically and verbally attacked my wife and son, threatened to fight to overturn Laura's adoption of Timmy, and now she's kidnapped my son with a group of terrorists. There is a connection between Madeline, Hawkins, and ROFF, but I'm not sure of its purpose. I'm not even sure who the hell she is."

"I'm not tracking, Jake," the JAG, Colonel Jim Mather, said.

"Is she an airhead? Or is she very clever and following in Sean Drake's footsteps, still trying to win his approval? Is she a drunk? Or is she using an alcoholic facade to operate under deeper cover than we ever fathomed her capable?"

Connor expelled a grunt. "Colonel James."

Jake had drawn the same conclusion. "Funny how his name keeps turning up, isn't it?"

"What are you saying, Jake?" an unidentified male team member asked.

Catching Connor's silent message to withhold the information for the moment, Jake sighed. James was Air Force, and Connor wanted to clean house in-house. "I don't know—not yet. But my instincts are telling me I shouldn't have let myself forget she's Sean Drake's daughter." Jake stopped pacing and looked back to Connor. "I'm wondering how she knew Timmy was with Bear Barton."

Connor grimaced. "*He's* the Barton we're discussing? Laura chose to take Timmy to *Bad Ass Bear*?"

Jake nodded, not trusting himself to speak. It had to be James. Connor would have told him Timmy wouldn't be coming to him for safekeeping. So James would have alerted Madeline, who most likely had someone tag Jake and Laura to find Timmy. Jake should have kept the boy with Laura. But at the time, they hadn't known she'd be in protective custody, and they'd felt Timmy would be in greater danger with her than away from them both.

"He was a good choice," the JAG said, the line of notepads on the table reflecting in his glasses. "Don't second-guess that decision. If it were my own son, I'd have chosen Bear Barton. No one on earth is more protective of children."

But because they had chosen him and he'd agreed to help, Bear now lay in critical condition in the hospital, suffering from multiple gunshot wounds. He'd fought to protect Timmy. Now he was fighting to save his own life.

Connor claimed Jake's attention. "What are your feelings regarding the exchange?"

Charles, who was about thirty and fair-skinned with a thin face and a broad nose, interceded. "FBI policy is not to negotiate with terrorists, General."

"This is an atypical situation, Charles," Connor said, then looked at Jake. "What are you thinking?"

Jake's heart hurt; it felt as twisted as the lump of molten metal that once had been Laura's Mustang. Looking from person to person around the table, he saw in their eyes that some felt Laura had planned this, that she'd arranged Timmy's abduction to secure her own release, and anger boiled inside him. "Laura did *not* do this. She hasn't been told that any of you doubt her, or that you consider her detained. She's only been told she's in protective custody."

Charles studied Jake. "Detained or in protective custody, the result is the same. Effect an exchange, and she's no longer out of commission."

"Pardon me for saying so," Jake said from between his teeth, "but you're talking through your ass. Laura would die before jeopardizing Timmy. If you had read her damn file instead of condemned her on speculation and appearances you'd know that."

"I read her file, Jake, and I agree with you," Connor said. He then addressed the team. "Only an ass or an idiot would believe she'd set up Timmy's abduction *or* Bear Barton. He granted her the adoption. If he'd refused it, then there'd be room for doubt, but he supported her—without Jake even being at the hearing. She took Timmy to Bear for protection. Dr. Laura Taylor Logan isn't a suspect, people. She's a victim."

Charles turned to Connor. "Are you willing to put your stars on that, General?"

"I already have." Connor turned a gaze on the man that had sent troops running for cover. "And unless I lose them, I expect the full support of everyone at this table on the issue."

No one refused him.

Jake appreciated the general's support, but held off saying so. If he voiced his gratitude, the team could interpret it as an in-house political maneuver that Connor's support was a gift and not based on merit Laura had earned. Still, Jake felt grateful. Deeply grateful.

"These developments, especially as they bring Madeline into the situation, leave you with a dilemma, Jake," Connor said. "Hawkins *will* kill Timmy. He's a cold bastard, and we all know it. Laura is skilled. A trained intelligence professional. Her odds of survival would be better."

Charles frowned. "You're suggesting the exchange?"

"Perhaps," Connor replied. "I see merit in considering it as an option."

Jake sat back down and rubbed a weary hand over his eyes. "I don't need the bean counters to tell me the survival odds are zero for either one of them," Jake said. Just speaking those words had his whole body rebelling. "I love them both. I can't choose. What husband or father could choose?"

"Only one person has the right to make this choice, Jake, and it isn't you." Connor sent him a look laced with empathy and resolve. "It's Laura."

"I can't ask her to do this. For Timmy, she would. She's always been willing to do anything for Timmy. Don't you see? I can't put her in that position."

Connor dropped his voice, and in it, Jake heard echoes of his own pain. "I don't think you have a choice, son."

Jake's throat turned dust dry, his chest went tight, and he recalled her sitting in the kitchen under the light from the stove, eating Cheerios and peaches and hassling him about Traffic Safety School. *For the record, I don't do prisoner. Not even for you.*

And he didn't know whether to rejoice or mourn.

*   *   *

Laura entered the briefing room wary. These people doubted her integrity, and deep down inside she knew it. Regardless of what Connor had said about protective custody, only a moron couldn't deduce she was being detained. They could tag it by whatever name they chose, but the result was the same. They'd taken her out of commission. Neutralized her. And she had a gut full of resentment because they had.

Jake walked over to her, his face as white as death. "Sit down, honey."

Honey. Fear was pounding off Jake in waves. *Oh, God. Oh, dear God.* "It is Timmy." Fear shot through her. "What's wrong with him, Jake?"

The chair seat bumped against the back of her knees. Sensing Connor sliding it under her, she let her knees fold and slid down on to it. He looked as worried as Jake, and that escalated her fear to sheer terror. No one else in the room said a word, but their sympathy was palpable; she sensed it, tasted its bitterness on her tongue. It had her fighting the urge to scream because she knew—*she knew*—whatever had happened was horrible.

Please, God. Please. I'll do anything. Anything at all. Just please don't let my baby be hurt. Please don't let me lose him. Please!

Jake briefed her on the abduction, omitting Madeline's participation in it, keeping his voice as succinct and steady and normal as possible. Then he showed her the fax.

Laura read it, the page crackling in her hand from her shaking. Her heart thudded so hard it threatened to beat through her chest wall. She blinked hard and pulled in three deep gasps. *Bury it, Logan. Don't panic. There's no value in panic. Responsibility isn't a coat.*

Connor started to say something, but Jake held up a

hand. "Give her a minute, sir. Just a minute."

Jake would give anything not to have to make this worse. Laura looked ash white, but she was holding it together. The drills were kicking in; he could see it in the shifting of her expression. When it turned attentive but passive, he squatted down before her chair and then looked up into her eyes. "A woman was with them. Mrs. Barton said Timmy called her Madeline."

"Madeline?" Laura's jaw gaped. "But . . . But she's—"

"We know, honey. None of us dreamed her capable, but she's Sean Drake's daughter. We let ourselves forget that, and we know what kind of man he was."

"Manipulative. Powerful. Very powerful," Laura said. "But *Madeline*?"

Jake understood her shock, her lack of being able to grasp the fact that Madeline could be involved in this. It seemed unbelievable that she had the skills, the savvy, and the discipline. But the evidence was unfolding right before their eyes, and they had little choice but to accept it, just as they had little choice but to accept that she'd kidnapped Timmy.

"She said she'd get back at me and Bear. That we'd regret ever having met her. But to do this to Timmy? How dare she do this to Timmy?" Laura's eyes blazed. "I should've killed her," she said more to herself than to him. "When she ran me off the road with Timmy in the car, I should've killed her."

That statement aroused murmurs among the team members. Connor filled the team members in on the antics Madeline had been putting Laura and Jake and Timmy through. "Calm down, Laura," Jake said.

"Calm down? She's got our son. Her and a group of terrorists." Laura swung her gaze to Connor. "Are the preparations in progress for making the exchange?"

"Laura," Jake cut in and put a hand on her knee. "You'll be killed."

She flinched, her every muscle spasming in revolt. *Bury it, Logan. Bury it. Responsibility isn't a coat.* "I know, Jake."

Torment riddled his eyes. He started to reach out and touch her but stopped, lowering his hand to his side.

"He's my son, too," she said. "I promised to love and protect him. I won't just sit here and watch my son die. You can't ask me to do that. You . . . can't."

"You don't understand. There are . . . circumstances." She had to know about the detention—about the team's doubts.

Connor interrupted, his face grim. "There are *no* extenuating circumstances, Jake."

Laura glanced around the table. In the eyes of the team members, she sensed pity and empathy, but she no longer sensed doubt. "I have to do this. If I don't, Timmy will die. Surely you all realize that." She turned her gaze to Jake. "I don't want to die. But if I don't go and they murder Timmy, then I'll have to live with knowing I might have been able to save him and I didn't do it. I'd rather be dead than have to live with that, Jake. Everything good inside me would be dead."

Jake looked inconsolable. And when he broke protocol and hugged her, she tried to soothe him, to soothe herself. She was doing the right thing. There was nothing else she could do. But the idea of never seeing Jake or Timmy again was almost more than she could bear. "You'll get Timmy to safety, and he'll be okay. He'll be okay."

And Madeline's message replayed in Laura's mind. *Nothing is black and white. Only shades of gray.*

One couldn't know joy without suffering sorrow. Couldn't understand the full capacity of love until feeling the full force of hate. Couldn't know the depth of a mother's love until its bounds had been tested and challenged.

Laura feared the challenge, but she had to face it honestly. She couldn't lie and tell Jake she would be fine. She wouldn't be. Hawkins had hated her for thirteen years, and that was a lot of time for hatred to fester into pure evil.

And she saw her feelings echoed in the eyes of every person at the briefing room conference table, including General Connor's. They all knew the truth.

Knew they were looking at a woman who soon would be dead.

Eighteen

Time was tight.

According to the latest Intel reports, the contamination of Jacksonville's water supply was imminent. Terrorists, foreign or domestic, perpetrated these acts with one thought paramount: getting the body count up as high as possible. Maximum impact. Connor knew what ROFF was after: the exchange for Timmy had been set to keep Jake and Laura, both of whom had been identified by ROFF as Special Ops officers, out of the way. The general scrambled forces to Jacksonville and then issued a waiver so that Jake and Laura could act as a team on the exchange leg of the mission.

Husband and wife teams working together on a single mission were expressly prohibited by regulations and strongly discouraged in practice. Waivers were rare. The policy was a logical one. With less than two percent odds for survival, children of husband and wife teams could become instant orphans, losing both parents within a split second. Spouses tended to be overprotective of their partners as well, increasing jeopardy to both team members. But the needs of the country always supersede the needs of individuals sworn to protect and serve it, and this was no ordinary mission.

Jake and Laura made the flight to Hurlburt Field. Homestead Air Force Base would have been the preferred site, but, having been nearly destroyed by Hurricane Andrew, it had only just returned to operative status. At present, Hurlburt Field stood better prepared to best serve the mission's requirements.

The plan set gave Laura a hope of surviving. It was slim, but hope nonetheless. No matter who insisted, or how strenuously, she steadfastly had refused to have reinforcements interfere until after Jake had Timmy out of harm's way. She'd gained Connor's support, and nothing Jake said had managed to sway her decision.

That all the people in the briefing room had spouses and most had children, Laura felt sure, had persuaded them into going along with her. It didn't take much imagination for them to picture themselves in her and Jake's situation. At the Christmas party where they'd recognized the men and women who'd died performing a myriad of Special Ops missions worldwide and Connor had honored them as heroes with the emotional toast and then had shattered the glass, everyone in the room had mourned the dead. But they'd also felt grateful it hadn't been them or their spouses who'd been killed, and they'd felt guilty for feeling that gratitude. It was a human reaction, of course, and one Laura had banked on to successfully assist her in this situation. It had.

Connor had been her most staunch supporter and when Laura had asked that the lab at Hurlburt be ready and available for her, he'd agreed first and then had asked, "Ready for what?"

"Microscopic implant surgery," she'd said. "On me and Jake."

When their plane landed, a police car awaited them on the flight line. Local contacts whisked them to the lab, where everything Laura needed and had requested stood waiting, including the top-notch surgeon, her former associate, Dr. Harrison. Laura had worked closely with him on previous incarnations of the communications device she intended to have implanted in both her and Jake's arms.

"It's a minor procedure, Jake," she said as they walked down the quiet corridor.

"Shouldn't we be in a hospital?"

"No." She smiled. "Everything we need is in the lab."

About sixty, graying, and distinguished-looking, if slightly round-shouldered from all his years of bending over operating tables, Dr. Harrison stood waiting at a stainless steel surgical table.

"Thanks for coming." Laura extended her hand and clasped his warmly. "I don't believe you've met my husband, Jake."

The men shook hands, and then Laura got down to business. "Here are the units." She passed two small cylinders to the doctor. "Go ahead and get started on mine, while I explain how this works to Jake."

Dr. Harrison smiled. "Are you going to stop long enough to sit down?" He nodded to the stool on the opposite side of the table. "Or do you want me to just implant this as you pass through?"

"Sorry." Laura had the grace to blush. "We've been rushed." She dropped onto the stool, propping her foot on the raised rung and extending her left arm. "This is a new design," she told Jake. "It's not field-tested, I'm afraid, but we're going to have to risk it." Feeling one of Harrison's assistants restrain her arm, Laura went on. "It's a tricolor system, Jake. A tiny speck under the skin changes color. It shouldn't be evident to anyone except you, so don't worry about that. It's subtle, so you really have to be looking for it to see it.

And since it can be implanted essentially anywhere in the body, anyone else spotting it carries a low probability rating.''

"How do you activate it?" Jake asked, deliberately not watching Dr. Harrison or his assistants.

"Simply depress the skin directly above it lightly three times, pause, then depress it twice, pause again, then depress it once. That sequence prevents accidental activations. You must depress the exact spot, or it won't activate. Safeguards for unfavorable conditions.''

Jake understood her meaning. If taken captive, during torture or questioning the tracker could be accidentally activated. The sequencing substantially lowered the probability of that happening. "You said it was a tricolor system.''

"Here we go, Laura," Dr. Harrison said. "A little sting to numb the area, and then we'll be in and out in a flash.''

"Okay." She looked back at Jake. "Red means I'm alive and being tracked by satellite. Blue, I'm dead and being tracked by satellite. This way, home base stays apprised and we also know what's going on with each other after we're, um, separated.''

Something akin to pain flickered through Jake's eyes. "What's the third color?"

"White," Laura said. "It's a send code that can mean whatever you want it to mean.''

"What does it mean on this mission?" His voice went from soft to softer.

She looked up at him. "When you send it to me, it'll mean Timmy is safe.''

"And when you send it to me?" Jake asked.

"If you can, bring in reinforcements and get me out of there." She swallowed hard. "If you can't, it's me saying good-bye.''

The look in his eyes told her he rebelled against that as a possibility. Just knowing he'd turn every stone for her made her feel better. If a way existed or could be created to spare her life, Jake would find it. Laura took solace in that.

"You're done, Laura," Dr. Harrison said. "The numbness should wear off in half an hour."

"Thank you." She stood up.

The assistants sterilized the work space and instruments and, within fifteen minutes, had implanted Jake. While Dr. Harrison ditched his gloves and cleaned up, Laura and Jake tested the signals. Home base verified via a secure phone line that they were satellite-linked and the trackers were working accurately.

"So far, so good." Laura smiled, infinitely pleased her design was performing well.

"You're brilliant." Jake stared at the dim red light emitting from his arm. He'd been concerned about the visibility of it until he'd seen the size. Laura hadn't been joking about noticeability. The light was about the size of a pin head, and the incision looked like a scratch.

"Dr. Logan?" Dr. Harrison returned.

Laura didn't look his way. Jake nudged her. "I think he means you, honey."

She gave him her best you're-being-testy look. No one ever called her "Doctor" except Dr. Harrison. She despised titles, probably because Sean Drake and Colonel James had used theirs to put her into the position of having to give up the one that had meant most to her: Captain. "Yes?"

"Good luck."

"Thank you." She'd admired the doctor for a long time, and afraid she might not again have the opportunity to tell him, she decided not to let this one pass. "I appreciate everything you've done, working with me on this project. You're very talented.''

"It's been a pleasure," he said, his voice low and husky. "I hope one day we can entice you to return to your research full-time. It's where you belong, Laura.''

In his eyes, she saw the same look she'd seen in the briefing room. Jake must have noticed it, too, because he curled an arm around her waist and pulled her close to his side.

"Major?" A male nurse addressed Jake. "The chopper is waiting, sir."

"Thank you." Jake turned, nodded to the doctor and his staff, and then left with Laura. They headed back to the flight line, hoping to hell they were all wrong. She'd said she had to do this to live with herself. Jake understood that. Just as he understood that he couldn't fail to get her and Timmy both safely out of there. Not and live with himself.

The chopper ride went swiftly. Though never publicly demonstrative, Jake couldn't sit beside Laura and not touch her. He held her hand the entire way.

"I haven't given you a wedding ring." Why had he said that now? It sounded fatalistic.

She smiled softly. "I haven't given you one, either."

The tenderness in her eyes had his every nerve screaming. Seeing his ring on her finger suddenly seemed vitally important to Jake. "When you get home, we'll fix that.''

Her eyes went wide, and he heard her swallow. "Either way?''

She meant dead or alive. His eyes burned and his throat muscles constricted. Unable to speak, he nodded.

"ETA ten minutes, Major," the pilot said, giving them the estimated time of arrival. "Ground transport is ready.''

"Thank you," Jake said.

Connor and the team at headquarters had scrambled

forces and dispatched three specialist teams to Jacksonville to intercept ROFF and work with local authorities in securing the water system. The problem was that the main supply couldn't easily be secured. According to the statisticians, that portion of the mission carried a risk factor which had everyone involved edgy. Too edgy, thank God, to just storm ROFF, which would surely result in Timmy's being killed. Another factor was that storming ROFF's headquarters in no way guaranteed they'd stop the contamination attempt.

Was Hawkins still at ROFF headquarters? Had he departed for Jacksonville? He could be holed up anywhere, as could Madeline. Until the team had a firm fix on their locations, their hands were all but tied. Jake still had a hard time accepting that Madeline was neck-deep in this. He knew he should, but she'd seemed so ill-equipped. He'd forgotten how conniving Sean Drake could be. And how powerful he'd been. She was neck-deep, all right, still trying to win Drake's approval, though the man had long since dead and buried. The one thing Jake couldn't figure out was how she and Hawkins had connected. In any case, the team's hands being tied just might save Timmy's life. And, with luck, it would also give Jake a little more time to assist Laura.

By the time they departed the chopper and hauled their gear to the airboat, twilight had fallen. Laura had three bags of communication equipment and survival gear.

Jake put on his night vision goggles and got into position to drive the boat while Laura stowed her bags. "There's no way you can drag all that through the swamp."

"I know. I'll stash it along the way. It'll enable us to communicate with home base." Laura sat down, then nodded that she was ready.

Jake gunned the engine. The boat gathered speed and sliced through the reedy water. Darkness fell and the night wind felt good on his skin, but with every inch forward they moved, his heart rebelled more.

A mile out from the drop-off area, Laura tugged at the hem of his BDUs. He looked down, and she motioned for him to stop the boat. When he knocked the gear shift into Idle with the heel of his hand, she reached up to him. He tugged off the night vision gear and helped her to stand up.

"Jake." She hugged him hard. "I have to tell you something."

He could barely see her. Clouds scudding across the sky all but obscured the moonlight. He closed an arm around her back. "What is it?"

"Whatever happens, I want you to know that it's okay. As long as we get Timmy out, that's all that matters."

"Not to me."

"I know you'll do all you can for me, Jake. If you succeed, I'll be thrilled." Her voice dropped a notch and she forced him to look into her eyes. "But if you don't, it's all right. Don't blame yourself. Ever. Understand?"

He looked away.

"Jake, you're not going to pull this on me. I can't do what I have to do, not knowing going in that if I don't come out you'll feel guilty. I want your promise."

He looked down and let her see his agony in his eyes. "I can't give it to you, honey. I would if I could, but I . . . can't." He touched his forehead to hers.

She glared at him. "Don't be a testy pig about this, Jake Logan. We've been friends for thirteen years, and until seventy-two hours ago, I've never asked you for a damn thing."

She'd asked him to hold her. He had, and they'd made love and felt regret.

"Now I'm asking you for your promise, and I expect you to come through for me." She licked at her lips, forcing her voice strong and insistent. "If something happens to me, Timmy's going to need you more than ever. If you're eaten alive with misplaced guilt, you can't take care of my son. I've waited so long to have a son, Jake. I can't face death afraid that you won't be here giving him what he needs. Please. Please, promise me."

"Honey, I—"

"Damn it, Jake, *please*!" A tear rolled down her cheek. "I've got to know you'll both be okay. In my heart, I've got to know it."

Be okay? Without her? Jake's insides cramped and then crumpled. How could he be okay without her? She and Timmy . . . they meant everything to him. Everything.

How can you deny her?

Jake damned his conscience to hell. It asked too much. He was a man—just a flawed human being who loved her and was terrified he might lose her. The truth was as simple and as awful as that.

Odds were strong that they'd all three be killed. He hadn't asked Connor their survival odds. He hadn't had to ask. Less than two percent seemed too great a chance to expect. If one of them were spared, it'd probably be Timmy. And unless Connor broke Madeline's deep cover and proved her involvement with ROFF was not one of Colonel James's Intel assignments, Timmy would be returned to her. And what if Connor succeeded? What would happen to Timmy then?

He'd be raised by strangers who neither knew nor loved him. How could Jake stand it?

How could Laura?

She couldn't, Jake realized. Which is why she'd asked for his promise. She was counting on him getting out, on him being there for Timmy so he wouldn't be vulnerable. So he wouldn't be an outsider. And that belief was giving her the strength to do this.

She needed the lie.

Though it ripped him to shreds inside, Jake gave her what she needed. "I promise."

Her lips curved into a watery smile. "Thank you, Jake."

He kissed her hard, terrified he might never kiss her again, letting out his frustration and anger and outrage. And Laura soothed him, gentling her mouth, her hands on his back and chest until he calmed down.

When their fused lips parted, she looked up at him, her eyes wide and shining. She cupped his jaw with her hand and beheld him as if she were memorizing every nuance of his face. "I love you, Jake Logan."

His heart wrenched. They'd both broken their agreement. "I love you too, Laura."

She smiled. "Of course."

He didn't want to, but he couldn't help smiling back. "Of course."

She sat back down. "We'd better go."

Jake gunned the throttle, swearing to God, man, and himself that he would do whatever it took to keep both her and Timmy alive and with him.

An hour later, they left the boat and set out on foot in the thick swamp grass. Fifteen minutes in, Laura set the communication gear down between two oaks. "I'll leave this here. Should be easy to relocate."

The oaks were rooted on a little island of swamp grass, surrounded by marshy wetland. "Looks like a good spot."

While she stacked the gear, Jake gathered a couple fallen limbs to cover the cases. When they had them in place, they hiked on, heading for the clearing where Jake had found the operatives' bodies, both fearing that, when they arrived, they'd find Timmy in that same position.

"It's about twenty meters, straight ahead," Jake whispered to Laura. He motioned for them to start circling.

Laura went south; and Jake turned north. They crossed paths midway, then met again at the point of beginning. Neither had anything to report.

The clearing stood empty.

"A diversion?" Jake suggested the obvious. "To occupy us while they contaminated the water supply?"

Laura couldn't disagree. She wanted to; Timmy was still with them, but it appeared Jake was right. "Too obvious. We underestimated Madeline once. Let's not do it again. She's far more devious than we gave her credit for being. Let's get back to the equipment and notify the base."

They made their way back to the two oaks. Laura reached to remove the branch concealing the cases and heard Jake thud to the ground. *An ambush!*

Her heart in her throat, she spun around. Something hard collided with her skull. Her knees gave way, and she fell to the marshy ground.

"She's dead," a man said. "Get Logan."

Laura struggled to stay conscious, to move, but couldn't seem to manage it.

And then she felt . . . nothing.

Nineteen

Laura awakened face down in the mud.

Groggy, her head throbbing, she lifted a hand and felt a lump the size of an egg on the back of her skull. What had happened?

She opened her eyes. Faint moonlight shone on the uneven ground. Looking through spindly branches, she felt something prick at her hand. Leaves. Soggy, pointed leaves. Pungent. Pine. And something jabbed into her hipbone. She eased her fingers to it, felt the outline of a package of gum, and remembered tucking it in there for good luck because Timmy had mentioned it when she and Jake had left him with Bear. Why was she lying face down in the mud?

Go back. Remember the last thing that happened.

She'd been moving a branch away from her stacked communications equipment, and—*Jake!*

Her heart sped up, pounded through her chest and her temples. "Jake?"

No answer.

She sat up, woozy, feeling as if an all-base band was holding a jam session inside her head. The smell of pine and wet earth had her stomach threatening to heave. She blinked to clear her focus, to force her eyes to adjust to the dim lighting and saw Jake's small black tool bag on the ground not far from the oaks. All of her communications equipment and survival gear were gone.

So was Jake.

She remembered the man's voice. *She's dead. Get Logan.*

Fighting panic, Laura swiped at the mud on her arm, depressed the skin over the tracker in sequence, and then waited. There'd be a slight delay in relaying the signal from her to the satellite, then to Jake. Two seconds elapsed . . . five . . . ten. . . . It seemed like ten hours. Finally, she saw the tiny red light. *Jake was alive.* Wherever he was, he was alive.

She touched the skin again to stop the transmission, hoping home base was picking up the signals as well. With a little luck, she pulled herself to her feet and retrieved Jake's tool bag. The team would give her time to search for him before converging. That act surely would result in Jake's death. And maybe Timmy's.

But where should she start to look for them? Without her equipment, she couldn't pinpoint Jake's location, and ROFF wouldn't be stupid enough, or brazen enough, to take him to their official headquarters. They knew they were under surveillance.

Afraid using her flashlight would alert ROFF that she wasn't dead, she strained to see in the faint moonlight. Jake had been behind her when she'd heard him fall. She had heard two men, though there well might have been more of them. They had to have been buried in the mud and hidden under leaves. Otherwise she and Jake would have seen them. As soft as the ground was here, they could have stepped on the men and never known it.

Unable to determine much in the dimness, she dropped to her knees and worked her way out from the oaks to the last point she remembered hearing Jake. The ground there was packed and dense. That was where he'd fallen, she surmised. She began checking the ground for further signs, ones of their departure. Skimming her hands over the damp ground, her left palm dipped into a valley, came up onto a ridge, and then dipped again into a second dense valley. Two indentations about the widths of boot heels. They'd dragged him.

Hope flamed in her chest. If she knew Jake Logan, he would let them go on dragging him until they'd dragged him right into their camp.

If Timmy hadn't been involved, Jake only would have let himself be dragged until he'd pinpointed the camp, then he'd have wrestled the advantage from them. But Timmy was involved, and that changed everything. For both of them.

Laura followed the ruts, deeper into the dank-smelling swamp. Wildlife was abundant here, but the only thing bothering her thus far were mosquitoes and humid heat. She could handle snakes, but not alligators. Unless God was napping, he'd know she was taxed enough and spare her from that.

Something shiny glinted just under the bottom leaves of a spiny bush she didn't recognize. Hoping it wasn't poisonous, she shoved back the leaves and then reached for the object. Jake's watch.

Her muscles tightened and she nearly wept with relief. He was conscious, and letting her know it; leaving a trail for her to follow. The flame of hope inside her grew a little stronger.

Progress came slowly. Frequent puddles crossed the trail, and seven times she lost it altogether and had to backtrack and search in semicircles outward from the water's edge to find it.

An hour later, the throb in her head had diminished

to a dull ache. The oppressive heat and humidity had her sweating profusely, and the sounds of crickets had ceased to be a calming serenade and now grated at her raw nerves. She spotted a rut coming out of a four-foot-wide pool of ankle-deep water. South. They now headed south, deep into the federal reservation.

Another hour passed, and she came to a break in the dense melucca trees. Undergrowth grew thick here. Dangerous due to snakes, but helpful for cover. Ground lights from somewhere not too far ahead hazed through the trees. It had to be the ROFF camp.

She paused, again checked the tracker, and again saw the red light. All total, she'd found three items belonging to Jake: his watch, his flashlight, and his pocketknife.

The men believed him still unconscious. They hadn't bothered to search Jake for weapons.

Laura moved with even greater caution toward the light. The undergrowth was rooted in a thin film of water, and she had to tread lightly—not an easy task in combat boots—to avoid making splashing noises. Sounds carried great distances in the swamp. The light grew stronger, and she came to a clearing. Hanging back at the perimeter, she stopped in a thicket of short squat bushes and dropped down to lay on her belly. Her clothes were wet and soggy with mud. Considering that camouflage an asset that could save her life, she stilled and then slid on her stomach until she had a good view of the compound.

A high fence had been erected about ten feet straight ahead of her. Hastily constructed. Metal, chain link, with razor wire stretched across its top. She'd bet her backside it was electric. Beyond it stood an estimated twenty tents. No wonder the team had a hard time pinning down ROFF's satellite headquarters from the operatives' reports. It was as mobile as a damn MASH unit. Three small buildings, made out of rough-hewn wood and not much larger than field unit outhouses, stood at the center of the tent city. An armed guard was posted in front of each of the three doors, and Laura felt certain Timmy and Jake were in one, or two, of them.

Men ambled all over the place. All dressed in camouflage BDUs and all armed to the teeth. A fleet of airboats stood parked on the northeast end of the camp. Three flat-bottom boats and two canoes also were lined up there. A guard carrying a rifle patrolled the camp's perimeter, walking along just inside the fence, not thirty feet from Laura. She ducked her face down, didn't so much as twitch a muscle or draw a breath until he'd had time to pass her and walk a good twenty meters further down the fence. How the hell could she successfully infiltrate this place armed only with a pack of gum and Jake's little tool bag?

She watched and waited, timing the lapse between the guard's passes. When he next passed her and went down the fence line about forty meters, she moved. Creeping out of the cover of the bushes, she crawled on all fours toward the fence, her knees making sucking sounds in the mushy earth. And she wished Jake hadn't given her the geographical briefing, after all, telling her how many different species of snakes called the reservation home.

Her skin crawling, elbows down, she lifted, then pushed herself closer and closer to the fence, the little tool bag's strap clamped between her teeth.

She pushed, scooted forward, and felt a different kind of wet soak through her blouse. A faint scent cut through those of pine and wet earth, and it tortured her nose. A scent that was both familiar and frightening. Blood.

The adrenaline pouring through her veins tripled and

she paused and studied the ground. A lot of blood.

And the dragged ruts had ceased.

Panic consumed her. Had Jake been found out? Hurt?

Bury it, Logan.

She heard his voice as clearly as if he was standing next to her. *You know the drill. Duty first. Bury it, Logan. Bury it. Bury it. . . .*

Getting a grip on her fears, she checked the fence. It was wired, unfortunately with a device she'd seen in training, but had never attempted to circumvent. She cursed at not having her equipment. With it, she had excellent success odds. Without it, her odds were iffy at best. But she had to work with what she had. A couple of tools and a package of gum.

The camp was too busy. Men still milled around, talking, looking tense. The air seemed charged; she sensed their anticipation. Probably awaiting word that the Jacksonville water supply had been contaminated. Her heart urged her to rush in and find Timmy and Jake. But she couldn't heed it. She'd have one chance to get them out. One. And she couldn't let a lack of patience rob her of it.

As she lay there, Madeline's hate message replayed through her mind. Laura tried to shut it out, tried not to remember Madeline's threat, but it wouldn't go away. *Can't say I didn't warn you. I told you nothing is black and white. It's all shades of gray. You'll wish you'd never met me. . . .*

It had been a threat levied against her and Bear. Had he survived the gunshot wounds? Had he survived surgery?

As hard as it was to believe, Madeline was up to her earlobes in this ROFF organization. But how in the name of God could she put Timmy in the middle of this kind of danger? Subject him to this kind of environment? How dare she do that to him? How dare she do any of the things she'd done to him over the years?

Sean Drake's approval.

It *had* mattered that much to Madeline. So much that she'd sacrifice anyone and anything for it. And realizing that included sacrificing Timmy—a grandchild Sean Drake had insisted Madeline abort—Laura felt a deep rage stir, and she wished Sean Drake were still alive so she could kill him herself for the damage he'd done.

The camp finally quieted down.

Laura crept to the fence, examined it again, and deduced it too dangerous to simply shut down the system. She'd have to rig a continuous circuit, bypass a break, and then crawl through. She pulled out the large package of gum, chewed five slices at once, saving the inside foil wrappers, then chewed five more, and five more, and then five more. Shaping the foil wrappers like horseshoes, she affixed them to the fence in a large circle, then retrieved a pair of cutters from the tool bag, praying this would work, that she wouldn't trip the alarm and electrocute herself in the process. Sweat streaming down her face, her heart stuck somewhere between her breastbone and throat, she made the first cut.

Though braced for it, she suffered no shock—and she heard no sound.

Encouraged, she quickly cut the rest of the wires, and then checked her watch. Four minutes had elapsed.

She had fourteen minutes max to get in and get out before the fence guard noticed the breach.

Hugging the ground, she worked her way toward the tents, taking cover behind a fifty-gallon drum of what smelled like gasoline. A low hum of voices sounded inside the tent to her right, but the two men were talking normally; nothing had alerted them that she was there. The doors to the little shacks were lined up like a row of ducks but no longer guarded. Most likely the guards were now inside the huts.

Working her way tent to tent, she reached the rear of the three wooden buildings. Directly behind the center shack, she saw something odd on the ground. Seeing no one in the immediate area, she eased to it and then picked up the object. Timmy's rabbit's foot.

Her baby was here!

Her eyes stung and her heart swelled, feeling too big for her chest. She moved closer to the back of the shack, listened, and heard a man's light snore. "Timmy?" she whispered.

Low to the ground, a ventilation trap door cracked open. Little fingertips appeared, then stuck out. Timmy's fingertips.

Laura's throat clenched tight. She touched her fingers to his, choking back a sob, debating between telling him to come out and going in to get him. The snoring had to be from his guard. If he awakened, he'd sound an alarm. She'd never get Timmy safely out of here. She had to kill the man.

Oh, God. She knew how to kill. She had the ability. But she didn't *want* to kill anyone. All she wanted was her son and her husband home safe, and the people behind this caught and punished.

Her mind darted between life and death, between murder and alternatives to murder, and finally she decided on her tactic.

On Timmy's palm, she wrote a message with her fingertip. *Come out.*

Tensing, preparing for anything, she waited.

Timmy stepped through the door opening, then made the turn to round the corner to the side of the building.

The man inside stopped snoring, and groggily asked, "Hey, where you going, kid?"

Timmy looked back at him. "I gotta pee."

"Wait for me."

The decision had been made for her.

Laura pulled Timmy behind her and motioned for him to get to the back of the building. She then positioned herself and waited for the man to walk out. When he did, she grabbed him from behind, snaked her arms around his neck in a choke hold, and twisted until she heard bone snap. He crumpled to the ground in a heap at her feet.

Her eyes stinging, her heart rocketing, her blood gushing through her veins, pounding in her temples and toes, she dragged him back into the shack, and then tossed a blanket over him.

Sweeping her hand down his face, she closed his eyes. If anyone looked inside, they'd think him simply asleep.

She stole his pistol, and then returned to Timmy.

He grinned up at her. "Did you find my rabbit's foot?"

She pressed a shushing fingertip over her lip and nodded that she had, giving him the best smile she could muster. "Later, Tiger," she whispered. "Have you seen your dad?"

"No."

Torn between getting Timmy out to safety and looking for Jake, she touched the implant.

The light snuffed out.

Twenty

It's a system glitch. Has to be a system glitch. A fault in the design.

The thought of leaving without Jake made her sick inside, but she had to do it. Jake would expect her to, and she expected it of herself. She'd get Timmy to safety with the convergence crew, and then come back for Jake. That's the only way she could play this out.

She had no choice.

Working her way toward the fence, her hand linked with Timmy's, she paused to check her watch. Fourteen minutes had elapsed. It would be close, she thought. The guard would be within spotting distance.

Near the fence, she stopped, scanned, but saw no sign of the guard, so she urged Timmy through the hole in the chain link, then crawled through herself motioning for him to drop low onto his stomach. "Get to that clump of weeds, Tiger. Fast as you can on all fours."

Timmy scurried, a lot more agile than her, and waited there. She dropped down beside him and pulled him half under her, shielding his head with her arm.

"Now I know how come you carry gum," Timmy whispered.

She winked at him. "It's a different kind of dike."

"Yeah." The smile faded from his mouth. "Mom, I'm glad you came after me. I knew you and Dad would come."

"Always," she promised.

"Madeline shot Bear two times. He was bleeding a lot."

"He's in the hospital, honey."

"She made me go with her. I fought her, but she's bigger. Her and Hawk are here."

Vulnerable. "I know, baby." Laura stroked his hair, wondering how long it would take Timmy to get over this experience. Would there be long-term effects? Her rage at Madeline doubled. "Are they the ones who tell everyone what to do?"

"Uh-uh. There's another man. He's their boss." Timmy shuddered. "I didn't like him."

James. "Do you remember Colonel James?"

"Uh-huh. But it wasn't him. It's a different man."

Someone other than James was running ROFF? But who? "Did that man hurt you?"

Timmy shook his head. "I didn't see him. But he sounded mean, like Grandfather."

To Timmy, sounding like Sean Drake was the ultimate insult. He'd never liked Madeline's father, though he'd tried to downplay that truth with Laura because of her feelings about them having compassion for Madeline. Still, they'd seeped through.

"I told Madeline I didn't want to go with her. But she made me. I hate her, Mom."

"It's wrong to hate, Tiger." God, but those were hard words to say to him when Laura was hating the woman herself. No. No, she hated Madeline's actions. And the fault for them fell largely on the shoulders of Sean Drake for making his daughter an emotional cripple.

"I hate what she does, then."

"Me, too." Hearing the guard's footsteps, Laura clamped a hand over Timmy's mouth and whispered, "Shh. Get ready to run, okay?"

He nodded.

The guard swept his flashlight's beam along the fence. He passed the break, then swung back. He'd spotted it.

"Let's go." She jerked Timmy by the arm, darted with him through the swamp. "Hurry, Tiger," she whispered urgently. "Fast. Fast."

They were making enough noise to wake the dead, but the guard was still there, examining the fence.

A fallen twig snapped under her foot, snagging his attention. "Run, Timmy. Full out, son."

The guard fired his gun, sounding the alarm. Near her right shoulder, bark flew off a melucca tree. Laura fired the stolen pistol, and the man fell.

She caught up with Timmy and they kept running, burrowing deeper and deeper into the swamp. Minutes passed; how many she wasn't sure. When under siege, time seemed to move a lot slower.

"Mom, my side hurts," Timmy said, grabbing himself.

She slowed down, listening for sounds of them being followed, and heard none. "Can you walk, honey?" They had to keep moving.

"Yeah." He reached for her hand.

Holding the gun in her right hand, she gave him her left hand and kept going, heading toward the rendezvous point where the convergence team should be waiting.

There were still no sounds of anyone following. Feeling the immediate threat of danger had passed, Laura slowed their pace, but only slightly. There'd be a few minutes lead time, but not much, and the men would have greater physical stamina than her and

Timmy. They couldn't linger or they'd be caught.

"Timmy, how long have you known Hawk?"

"Ever since I can remember."

Laura's blood ran cold. Madeline had been working with Hawkins all along. The queen of soaps and Scotch had lived her entire adult life pretending to be something she wasn't. But why in the name of God would she jeopardize the life of her own flesh and blood? Why would she do this to Timmy?

She hated Laura. And because Jake didn't hate Laura, Madeline hated Jake. What didn't make sense was Timmy. Why would she hate Timmy?

Because Jake had divorced her and taken Timmy? Because, remembering her neglect, Timmy had shunned her? Or maybe she didn't see kidnapping Timmy as dangerous?

No. No one could be that deluded. There had to be more.

And there was.

Sean had wanted her to abort, and she had refused.

She hated Timmy because she could twist the truth, tell herself that no matter what she did she'd never win Sean's approval, and then blame it on Timmy. If only she hadn't had him, then Sean would have loved her. Then he would have accepted her.

She was sick. Twisted and deluded, rationalizing and sick.

Laura checked her implant. Still no signal. She should contact home base and let them know she was out with Timmy. But if she did, they'd converge and trap Jake inside. If he was still alive, he wouldn't be for long. No. No, she couldn't do it. She couldn't do it!

God, please. Please, let home base be picking up Jake's signal. Please, let Jake be alive.

They passed the two oaks and continued on. Two-thirds of the way back to the rendezvous point, Laura's trained senses picked up on someone following them. She looked for cover and found no suitable place. She couldn't outrun pursuers, not with Timmy. She had to dig in.

Dropping to her knees between two roots of an ancient oak, she shoved mud, prepared a bed for Timmy, and then urged him to lie down in it on his back, his head turned aside. Knowing roots protruded from the ground near oaks, the pursuers would steer clear of them to avoid tripping, especially if they were moving with any speed. She worked quickly, efficiently, frantically, covering Timmy with mud and leaves and grass, then shook loose leaves on him. "Don't move. For God's sake, whatever you do, don't move. Not until I come for you."

He didn't utter a sound. Grateful for that, Laura rounded the oak, bent low to the ground, bracing the flat of her arm against a distant tree trunk, and aimed toward the approaching sounds. *God, Jake. I need you. I'm scared. I'm so scared I won't be able to protect him.*

The sounds stopped. Laura stayed still, pouring sweat, smelling her own fear.

A crackling noise sounded—sixty degrees south. A twig on dry leaves. She arched her trigger finger, prepared to fire, and felt the hold-heated metal gain pressure from her finger.

The man stepped into the open.

Fire. Fire.

Laura tried to squeeze, but something stayed her finger. She couldn't pull the trigger. *Why in the name of God couldn't she pull the trigger?*

Twenty-one

The silhouetted man came closer, and she realized why she couldn't shoot. She recognized him. A whine crawled up her throat. "Jake."

"Laura," he whispered on a rush of sound, then ran toward her.

She jumped to her feet and flew into his arms. Her chin collided with his chest. "Oh, Jake. Jake, I thought you were dead. The signal—"

"I know, baby. I know." He moved the flat of the gun jabbing into his side. "Are you okay? I found the guard's body. Where's Timmy?"

"He's right here." She turned toward the tree. "Timmy, come out."

He sat straight up, and Jake jerked. When the mud and leaves started falling away, he smiled and grabbed his son in a hug that lifted him off the ground.

Timmy wrapped his legs around Jake's waist, and over his shoulder, Laura met Jake's gaze. His relief and gratitude shone in his eyes.

"Are you all right, Tiger?" He swiped mud from Timmy's face, his big hand shaking, his voice emotional, low and husky.

"I'm okay." He swallowed hard. "Madeline shot

Bear, Dad. I saw her do it. She said they kidnapped her, but they didn't. She shot Bear two times.''

"We know about Bear," Jake said softly, stroking mud from Timmy's face.

Jake refrained from commenting on whether or not Madeline had been kidnapped. Laura wasn't sure how she felt about that. It would be easier for Timmy to think Madeline had been kidnapped than for him to know she'd played a part in kidnapping him. Yet playing ostrich was dangerous, especially for Timmy. Now, however, wasn't the time to discuss it. And while Laura hated to spoil the tender reunion between Jake and Timmy, she knew standing still wasn't wise. "Jake, we've got to get out of here."

"Right." He set Timmy down on the ground, but held tight to his hand, leading the way.

Laura understood that need to hold. She felt it herself, for both of them, but she was determined to bury the urge until she could do it safely. They rushed through the brush and tall swamp grass, hurrying toward the rendezvous point.

About ten minutes out, a forward team met and escorted them back to an airboat. There were half a dozen others on-site now, and several crews. Connor, bless him, had pulled out all the stops.

Laura sat down on the floor of the boat and bent her knees. Timmy scooted back against her, and she hugged him, looping her arms around his middle. Jake got behind Laura, sat down, and fitted her hips between his bent knees, then held them both. With Timmy in front of her and Jake behind her, Laura knew her time to hug and be hugged had arrived.

They sat that way all during the ride back to the chopper. And long before they got there, Laura swore to herself that life would never again feel this good. This sweet, or this good.

She'd expected death, and instead, she was alive and unharmed, and with Jake and Timmy. A tear leaked from her eye.

Timmy, his hair slicked from the headwind, looked back at Jake. "It's okay, Dad. She's not really crying. She's touched." He nodded to add weight to his claim. "Bear said."

Jake winked at Timmy and then gave Laura a tender smile, one that said how much her being touched by him and Timmy meant to him. "Yeah."

Leaning her head against Jake's chest, she smiled back. "Yeah."

The chopper ride to the base gave Jake time to get his heart out of his throat and back into his chest where it belonged. If he lived to be a thousand, he didn't think he'd ever forget the look on Laura's face in the airboat. She loved him. She'd given him the words, though she'd been careful not to reveal that she meant them as more than friends. But she felt them. He'd seen it on her face in his bed, in the swamp when she'd recognized him, and again on the airboat. And he knew exactly what he wanted to do, first chance, to show her that he loved her too. To hell with their agreement. To hell with them having no future. They'd make one. They'd make memories. He'd show her that they could.

Fifteen minutes before their California ETA, the pilot relayed a message from the general. Judge Barton was doing fine. His condition had been upgraded to stable.

"All right." Timmy offered his dad a high five, then one to Laura.

She clapped their hands, laughing. Jake laughed too, and so did the crew.

Then Timmy went on to tell them how Bear had hidden him and Mrs. Barton. Bear had faced the men who'd broken into the house alone. Even after he'd been shot, Bear wouldn't tell where he'd hidden Timmy.

Laura, with my life. She recalled Bear's parting words to her. "How can we ever repay him, Jake?"

"We can't. Some things you just can't repay. You're grateful for them, and you never forget, but you can't repay them."

And looking into Laura's eyes, Jake knew the reunion with Bear would be a tearful one.

When the plane landed, a car stood waiting for them on the flight line. They rode to base headquarters, then hit the showers. Connor and the team were waiting for a briefing, and to debrief Jake and Laura on developments. Someone scrounged around and got some clothes for Laura and Timmy—surgical greens. Connor's secretary, Gladys, Jake guessed.

When they were ready for the briefing, Laura held out a hand. "Come on, Timmy."

Jake started to object. "I don't think he should—"

Laura interrupted, looking as opinionated as a heart attack. "I'm not letting him out of my sight again until Hawkins and Madeline are in the brig, Jake. Be testy if you want to, but Timmy's coming with me, and that's final."

Jake couldn't blame Laura. Hell, he loved her for being so protective. He felt the same way, though he doubted the team would give two figs about either of their feelings on the topic. The information being discussed in the briefing room was extremely sensitive.

Not wanting to rile her, Jake held his tongue. Connor could have the pleasure of trying to convince her. Jake already knew that when Laura tagged an "and that's final" on something, that's exactly what she meant. Nothing, short of laying her out cold, could sway her.

They walked in, and Connor smiled. So did the rest

of the team. "It's good to see you all," Connor said. "Timmy, are you okay?"

"Yes, sir." He clung to Laura's hand.

"I, er, suppose you'll be joining us here."

"My mom said." He nodded, then shrugged. "She's really nice, but I don't mess with her when she gets like this."

Connor bit his lips to keep from laughing, and around the table, hands clapped to mouths to hide smiles, and fake coughs muffled chuckles.

Jake tensed, waiting for the surefire objections.

They never came.

"Sit down," Connor said. "Perry, grab Timmy a chair."

Captain Perry slid a chair to Connor's right, next to the two empty ones waiting for Jake and Laura. They all sat down.

Ten minutes into the briefing, Jake stopped being stunned.

Laura finished narrating events from her perspective. "Timmy left his lucky rabbit's foot where I'd find it. There was an armed guard sleeping in the tent. I elected to try to get Timmy out without killing the guard. But he awakened and followed Timmy outside." She couldn't make herself look at her son, not during this disclosure, and she prayed that he'd never look at her with hatred in his eyes for her killing a man. "It was a clean kill," she said, her voice low but even. "I broke his neck, dragged him back into the shack, and then got Timmy out of the compound. I had to shoot a fence guard. I don't know if he's dead. I didn't slow down long enough to check."

"He was killed," Jake interjected. "I saw him when I left the compound."

Feeling something touch her hand and forearm, she looked down. Jake held her fingertips. Timmy, her forearm. A wad of emotion gushed through her, and her chest went tight, her eyes stung. She glanced down at him.

"They would've shot us, Mom."

She gave him a shaky nod. "Yes, they would have, Timmy. But I didn't have to like killing them."

"You hated it," he said solemnly.

"Yes, I did."

"But you had to do it."

Absolution. Choked up, she couldn't answer, so she nodded.

Jake cleared his throat and then began sketching out the layout of the tent city, giving descriptions of weaponry and resources he'd noted. Laura added her findings, giving the team a clear picture.

When they had finished, Connor began debriefing them. "ROFF headquarters is now under our command. The biological lab has been locked down. Last count, forty-three members had been apprehended, but neither Hawkins nor Madeline was among them."

Jake didn't like hearing that. From her expression, neither did Laura.

"The convergence crew reported a lot of movement in ROFF's tent city. Obviously, the intent was to bug out. Team crews overtook it and seized their weapons. Normal ordinance, with a few exceptions that are typically found only in Intel circles."

That had happened along about the time, Jake figured, they'd been flying over the Gulf of Mexico.

"It appears from a communications intercept," Connor said, "that the terrorist attack on Jacksonville's water supply is still operational and imminent."

"Dad," Timmy whispered, tugging at his sleeve. When Jake looked his way, Timmy went on. "It ain't Jacksonville."

Laura snapped her gaze to Timmy. So did half of

the people at the table, including Connor.

"It isn't Jacksonville?" Jake asked.

Timmy gave Jake a negative nod, clearly uncomfortable at being the center of attention. "I heard the man who sounds like Grandfather tell them to say Jacksonville so nobody would know where they're going to poison the water."

Puzzled, Jake asked for clarification. "The man who sounds like Grandfather?"

Laura interceded. "Madeline and Hawkins have a boss, Jake. Timmy didn't see the man, but he heard him, and the man sounded like Sean Drake."

That disclosure set off a buzz of speculation around the conference table. Jake frowned, not sure what to make of this. "Did you hear anything about this man from anyone else?"

"He's mean." Timmy looked up at Jake, his eyes as wide as saucers. "The man guarding me told me he was a mean sonofabitch."

"Timmy." Laura chided him for cursing.

"Sorry, Mom." He glanced over at her. "But that's what he said." Timmy's expression shifted, as if he wanted to add something, yet he hesitated.

"What is it, Tiger?" Laura clasped his hand in hers.

Timmy shrugged and fidgeted. "Madeline really wasn't kidnapped like she said. She lied to me, Mom." He looked up at her, his pain in his eyes. "She lied to Bear, too. But he knew who she was 'cuz he saw her picture in my wallet when we went to court, and he told her so. That's when she shot him. I saw her shoot Bear two times. Here." He pointed to his chest, and then to his right shoulder. "And here." Timmy lowered his hand to the armrest. "She didn't know I saw her, but I did. And I think the mean man really was him, too."

"Who do you think he was, son?" Jake asked.

"Their boss."

"Who do you think their boss was?" Laura tried again for clarification.

"Grandfather."

"He can't be, Timmy," Jake said. "You know your grandfather is dead."

A tingle started at the base of Laura's spine. It worked its way up her back to the roof of her mouth, and suddenly so much made sense. So many pieces fell into place. "Jake, wait a minute."

He looked over at her.

"Maybe Timmy's right. Maybe Sean's not dead."

"Honey, we went to the man's funeral."

"But Madeline didn't."

She hadn't. And they'd always thought that didn't make sense.

"Maybe she didn't go because she knew he wasn't dead."

"Maybe," Jake agreed.

"That's a big jump, Laura," Connor said.

"I know it is," she said. "But we never saw the body. It was a closed-casket service. Why would there be a closed-casket service for a heart attack victim? An accident victim, yes. But a heart attack victim?"

"Can we check out his personnel records?" Jake asked.

"No," Connor said. "CIA files are sealed."

"Not from me." Agent 27, the CIA team member, looked at Connor over the top of his glasses. "I have access."

"Get on it, then. Maybe we'll find something that explains why Sean Drake would stage his own death."

The JAG, Colonel Jim Mather, spoke up. "All we need is a court order to exhume the body."

Connor nodded. "Get it going, Jim. Shove it through."

"Will do." He slid back his chair and then left the conference room.

Agent 27 left on Jim's heels.

"Him staging his death fits, General," Jake said to Connor. "Drake had a jaded philosophy toward interpreting the Constitution and its rights. If he isn't dead, he's got the connections and the money to finance ROFF."

"Timmy." Jake returned his attention to his son. "You said it wasn't Jacksonville they were going to contaminate. Did you hear where it was?"

Timmy nodded. "Hawk told Madeline."

"Where is it, son?"

"Miami."

Jake looked at Connor. "Miami." That too fit. More densely populated, greater damage, higher body count: all the elements terrorists looked for in an ideal target.

Connor stared at Timmy, then let his gaze drift around the table. Jake sensed the other team members' skepticism, and he suspected Connor did too. It was easy enough to guess what the general was thinking. *Did he dare to put his trust and the lives of everyone in Miami and Jacksonville in the word of a nine-year-old?*

Twenty-two

Connor returned his gaze to Timmy. "Son, are you sure that's what you heard?"

He didn't hesitate. "Yes, sir. I don't know if it's true—Hawk could have been lying—but that's what he told Madeline."

Hands against the edge of the table, Connor paused for a tense moment, then shoved back and walked over to a credenza behind him. A gray phone sat atop it. He reached for the receiver. When he pressed a single button, Jake knew exactly whom he was calling. The Ops Center.

Looking at Jake, Connor spoke into the receiver. "Scramble forces to Miami. Same orders as Jacksonville. STAT."

When Connor returned to the table, Jake said, "Sir, I need to get down there."

Connor nodded.

Laura stood up. "I'm coming with you."

"No, you're not," Jake insisted.

"Don't get tes—"

"No, Laura." He clasped her upper arms. "Until we catch them, Timmy's not safe. Madeline has used him once. If she can, she will again. He needs you."

Laura again felt torn. Madeline had to be an operative. She had to be. But not one of theirs, not with the OSI. Maybe CIA, like her father, though Laura doubted it. Most likely, she worked only for her father. Regardless, Madeline now had become a traitor. One who always had cited stress as her reason for drinking. Was that real, or part of her cover? And what tied her to Hawkins? He had to have something on her to have some kind of leverage. Of course if Sean was running ROFF, no further explanation was needed. Madeline would do anything he told her to do. Even kidnap her own son.

"I have to go with you, Jake," Laura said softly. "I have to do it."

"What about Timmy?"

"I'll keep him with me," Connor said. "I agree with Laura on this, Jake."

Jake's heart rebelled. She'd been in enough danger. He didn't want her in any more.

"I know how Hawkins thinks, Jake," Laura reminded him. "Let me help you."

Jake looked at Timmy, who nodded. "Mom's gotta do it, Dad. Responsibility isn't a coat."

Timmy was right. She did have to do it. She couldn't back away from a confrontation with Paul Hawkins. Not and ever stop looking over her shoulder again. "Okay."

In flight, Laura reached over and clasped Jake's hand.

He looked over at her, and his chest went tight. "Some marriage I've gotten you into, isn't it?"

She gave him the ghost of a smile. "I'm not complaining."

"You never have." Jake rubbed the tips of their fingers. "But I somehow don't think this is quite what you had in mind."

"It wasn't." She looked at him, love shining in her eyes. "But I'll take this with you, rather than anything without you."

A knot lodged in his throat. "Me, too."

She blinked, then blinked again. "Connor's going to take a lot of heat for letting me come with you."

"Yes, he will."

"He's a good man. He scared me at first on Colonel James, but Connor is a good man."

"Yes, he is." Jake looked over at her. "Connor's ordered Colonel James detained for questioning. If our hunches about him pan out, the man is going to have a hell of a lot of explaining to do."

"Explaining?" Laura grunted. "He won't be able to justify any of this."

Thirty minutes outside of Miami, the pilot turned to Jake. "General Connor is on the horn, Major." He passed Jake a set of headphones.

Jake fitted them over his ears, then spoke into the mouthpiece. "Yes, sir."

"Timmy was right. It was Miami. We stopped them in time, Jake. I'm putting the boy in for a Special Ops Special Commendation."

Jake smiled. "He'll like that."

"He's earned it. When I think of what could have happened. . . ." The general's voice trailed to a sigh. "We apprehended Madeline. She swears she was kidnapped just prior to Timmy's abduction. Timmy swears she wasn't. I believe him, of course. We're using Bear Barton to break her story."

"I'd think Bear would be effective at that."

"No doubt," Connor said. "Hawkins is still at large. James—I refuse to call that lowlife bastard 'Colonel'— is singing like a canary. He'll do serious time for this."

"So our hunches were on target." Jake stared at Laura. She looked tired. Bone-weary, actually.

"I'm sorry to have to say it, but they were. It makes me sick that one of ours would turn traitor."

"Me, too."

"I've ordered Madeline and James brought here, and, since Miami and Jacksonville are secure, your plane to return to base."

"What about Sean?"

"Some backwoods bastard judge blocked the court order to exhume his body. Agent 27, the CIA rep, called in. His people have done some digging and they've found something solid that's just as effective. We'll discuss it when you get back to the base."

Did that mean Sean was alive and heading ROFF? Jake wanted to know, but for the sake of security, he didn't ask. "Yes, sir."

Jake removed the headset, then returned it to the pilot and turned to Laura. "We've got Madeline and James," he whispered. "Miami and Jacksonville are safe. It was Miami. Connor's putting Timmy in for a Special Commendation. And Agent 27 has found something on Sean Drake."

She stared into his eyes. "He's alive, Jake. I feel it in my bones."

God, he hoped she was wrong. But his own bones warned him she was right.

Just after 1600, Laura and Jake walked into the twelve-by-twelve detention room where Madeline was being held. Like the vault, furnishings here were sparse. A squat table that could seat six and some chairs. She sat across from Connor, her blouse mud-splattered, her jeans dirt-crusted, and her black hair matted.

Timmy wasn't there.

"Where's my son?" Laura asked Connor, fighting a flicker of panic she knew was unreasonable.

Madeline glared at her. Laura glared back, daring the

woman to give her an excuse, any excuse, to punish her for using Timmy and putting him in danger.

She must have sensed that Laura was teetering on the edge of control, because Madeline lowered her gaze and then looked away.

"Timmy's in my office with Gladys," Connor said. "I didn't want him in here."

Knowing he meant around Madeline, and that the dragon lady, Gladys, wouldn't let anyone within a mile of Timmy, some of Laura's tension ebbed. She sat down, all but collapsing from exhaustion onto a chair at the far side of Jake, grateful the windowless room didn't reek of lemon or of pine. Either one would have had her retching.

Thirty minutes into the interview with Madeline, they hadn't learned anything, except that she was definitely not an airhead. Then Agent 27 reported in by phone, and asked to speak to Laura.

She went into a cramped but neat office across the hall to answer the secure-line call. "Logan."

"Agent 27," he said. "I asked to speak with you because I wanted you to know firsthand that your son might just be right about Sean Drake."

Laura's pulse leapt.

"His file netted nothing. But one of our people had an interesting talk with a Michael Cass who worked under Drake. Cass said he'd gathered hard evidence that Drake had broken numerous laws in gathering intelligence. Cass discreetly reported it to a friend of his, Senator Wade. Wade was in the process of calling for a congressional hearing to investigate Drake when Drake died."

"And because he was dead, they dropped it," Laura speculated, twisting the phone cord around her fingertip.

"Right."

"Convenient, wasn't it?"

"It appears so. Though the stress of him knowing a congressional inquiry was on the near horizon could have incited a heart attack."

"I suppose so." She seriously doubted it. The arrogant bastard would have sworn he could beat it.

"It's not conclusive," Agent 27 said. "We'll know more after the body's exhumed. We've, er, come to terms with the judge, who happens to be a distant relative of Colonel James."

Now why didn't that surprise her? "I appreciate the update." Laura said good-bye, then hung up the phone and returned to the room where Madeline was being interviewed.

A few minutes later, it became glaringly apparent that Madeline had no intention of cracking. But why should she? She'd been trained by the best: her father.

Watching for an opportunity to induce a bluff, Laura saw one, then took it. "Enough." She stood up and leaned across the table. "Here's my take on things, Madeline. You weren't kidnapped. You're a willing member of ROFF, and kidnapping Timmy was just fine with you. You and Paul Hawkins have worked together for years."

Madeline stared at her, her eyes gleaming, but held her silence.

That was exactly the way it had been, Laura realized. Exactly. "You wanted Jake to marry you and he wouldn't, so you did the one thing you knew to do that would change his mind: a pregnancy. And it did. Only your father vehemently opposed. He wanted you to abort—a child would just get in the way of your career in Intel—but you wanted Jake, and without the child, you wouldn't get him. So for the first time in your life, you defied your father and married Jake—or so I thought, until I took that phone call. Now I know better.''

Laura stopped and let her gaze drift to the ceiling. "You opposing Sean never made sense. You *always* did what he wanted. Sean changed his mind. He wanted you married to Jake. He sold you out for his career because he wanted access, an opportunity to manipulate Jake like he manipulated you. Only Jake wouldn't cooperate. So you got pressure from both sides—from Jake and from your father, who reminded you with monotonous regularity that you were blowing his deal with Colonel James. You were a plant there, in James's office, gathering OSI intelligence data to pass on to your father. Only you weren't coming through for him, were you, Madeline?'' Laura shrugged. "Everyone knows spies spy on spies, right? Isn't that what Sean always said?''

Laura leaned forward. "He's still saying it too, isn't he, Madeline? Sean didn't die. He faked his death to avoid a congressional inquiry. He'd been caught with his hand in the proverbial cookie jar and was about to get it cut off. So he faked his death to avoid prosecution for blatant intelligence-gathering illegalities, and you helped him.''

In Laura's mind, more and more of the puzzle pieces fell into place. "Only now Sean was working against this country, and you had no choice but to work with him. You had to continue to do what you'd always done: exactly what he said. The stress got to you. And so you drank. And drank. And drank.

"When you'd sober up, you'd feel guilty and agree to Timmy's adoption. But then Sean would yank your chain, and remind you that if you let go of Timmy you'd be cutting off your access to Jake, and so you'd pull the papers. Sean started ROFF. You and Hawkins worked with him. And when Hawkins and I had the run-in at survival school, you recruited him to work with you because, like you, he hated me."

Yet another piece of the puzzle slotted into perfect place in Laura's mind. "Back then, Hawkins wanted my bicolor tracking design. He figured he'd kill me and get it. He knew I had the plans for it with me. And for that same reason, he broke into my apartment—to get the design for my tricolor tracker."

It made perfect sense. Perfect sense. "In the interim years, all of you thought I'd stopped my research. But then Colonel James heard through channels it was complete." Possibly from an unsuspecting Dr. Harrison. "And James passed that information along to Sean, who thought such a communications device could be helpful to ROFF." Laura shrugged. "Of course, killing me was fine with Sean, too. He hated me as much as you did, because he couldn't manipulate me. I screwed up his plans to do that by getting out of the Air Force. And God knows Paul Hawkins was just chomping at the bit to execute Sean's kill order on me."

Laura paused a moment, then went on. "The only thing I haven't figured out is what Hawkins has on you. Why is he manipulating you, Madeline? Why are you letting him manipulate you?"

"He isn't. Hawk loves me," Madeline said, defiance etching her voice. Her face paled to white and tensed with anger. "He's the only one who's ever loved me."

I hate it when people walk away from me!

Remembering Madeline's shouted words the night she'd nearly driven into Jake's kitchen, Laura pegged the woman's motivations. Sean emotionally had walked away. So had Jake, who also physically walked away from her. Madeline was ripe for a man like Hawkins. Ripe. So he came along professing love and acceptance: exactly what Madeline always wanted from the men in her life and never received.

Laura stared down at Madeline. "And because Hawkins loves you, you'll do anything for him." Just like with Sean. "You'll put your own flesh and blood in danger? You'll bomb my car and kidnap Timmy? Poison innocent people with contaminated water? What kind of love is that? What kind of man would ask those things from you?"

"The same kind who'd ask a woman to marry him for his son." Her eyes glittered black. "Don't you dare get on your sanctimonious high horse with me, bitch. I'd do for Hawk about as much as you'd do for Jake." Madeline's anger drained and a dead calm that sent shivers up Laura's spine returned to her eyes.

"Sean's alive and we know it," Laura said. "He'll blame you, of course, for the ROFF mission's failure. And even after all you've done for him, he'll still refuse to love or accept you." Laura straightened up. "I'm sorry for you for that."

"I don't want your damn pity."

"I know you don't," Laura said softly. "But you do need it, Madeline."

Laura had accomplished all she could. Hopefully she'd stirred up enough dust so that Madeline's temper and sense of worth and self-righteousness would choke on it, and then Jake or Connor could get her to talk. Laura sensed that now the woman wanted to talk. She wanted to tell them how clever she'd been, and all she'd managed to do to the unsuspecting. She wanted to disclose all the reasons she was lovable, and why Sean should love and accept her.

It was pitiful. Tragic.

As for Laura, she'd had a gut full. She turned to Connor and Jake. "Timmy and I are going home." She pressed a kiss to Jake's temple, then whispered so only he could hear. "I bluffed. It's speculation, not fact. See you when you get home."

"You can't just walk out of here, bitch."

Laura stopped and looked back over her shoulder at Madeline. "Yes, I can. We chose different paths, and mine gives me the right to walk out of this room." Laura dug deep for compassion and had a hard time finding it. Finally, she managed an alternate truth and was damn grateful for it. "I hope you receive more mercy than you've shown," she said, then walked out without a backward glance.

Heading down the hallway toward Connor's office, Laura's eyes began to burn. She was tired, she thought, and sick of intrigue and lies. Sick of seeing shades of gray.

She wanted simplicity. Straight lines, where right was right and what was wrong was changed. She wanted people to be exactly who they portrayed themselves to be, including herself. No secret lives. No lies. No alternate truths.

She wanted to hug her son. To hear him laugh, and to laugh with him. To go home and towel-surf across the kitchen floor. To make double-fudge chocolate brownies for Jake, root beer floats for Timmy, and cherry cheesecake for herself, and then to gorge on all three and gripe because she'd overeaten. She wanted to take a hot bubble bath and soak, to sleep eight hours uninterrupted, and to make love to Jake. She wanted to tell him she loved him with all her heart, over and over until he believed her, and to keep on telling him how much she loved him for the rest of their lives.

She wanted to get past the shades of gray and see colors again.

Jake watched Connor and Agent 27 question Madeline through a two-way mirror. How could she seem so cool and controlled? So unaffected by all this?

Laura's bluff had worked. Madeline was talking

freely now, saying Hawkins had discovered the truth about her Intelligence assignments while she was employed by Colonel James and had threatened to expose her unless she did as he asked. She'd fought against coming into the ROFF fold, and Hawkins had blackmailed her into it. He headed ROFF.

The only thing she adamantly refused to discuss was her father. She wouldn't so much as speak his name.

And now it was no longer necessary.

The court order had been obtained to exhume Sean Drake's body. But all that was found in his grave was an empty coffin. Sean Drake was indeed alive. And Jake would bet anything that he and not Hawkins headed ROFF.

Jake walked back into the room. Madeline glared at him. "None of this ever would have happened if you'd just loved me. I was your wife. Me, Jake. But with you it was always Laura. Always, only Laura."

From somewhere inside, he dredged up pity. "We were just friends. Laura isn't to blame. You made your choices, and you're responsible for them."

"You won't have her. I swear it," Madeline vowed in a near whisper. "Regardless of what happens now, or whatever else you do, Laura is going to die."

She was telling the truth. Fighting panic, Jake fisted his hands at his sides. "What have you done?"

Madeline gave him a vindictive, Cheshire cat smile.

"Timmy is with Laura." Panic churned in Jake's stomach. "Will you kill him, too?"

Plucking at the seam of her dirt-crusted jeans, she licked at her lips and then let her gaze drift to the ceiling. "Nothing is black and white."

"You'll murder your own son?" he bellowed.

She glared at him. "That boy stopped being my son the day he first called your bitch 'Mom.' "

Trembling with a rage so deep it took every ounce

of his control to suppress it, Jake scowled at her. "Either of them get hurt—either of them—and I'll kill you myself."

"I'm prepared to die." She lifted her chin, looking so calm it chilled Jake's blood to ice. "But me being dead won't bring them back, will it, Jake? Nothing will bring them back. You're going to know how it feels to be alone. You're going to know how it feels to be me."

Connor was already on the phone. Jake ran past him, praying Madeline had been bluffing and fearing deep in his soul she had been dead serious.

This couldn't happen now. Not now. They'd come so far. Jake couldn't lose them now!

Twenty-three

~~~

The house was dark.

Laura and Timmy went inside. "I'm going to take a bath, Tiger."

"Can I have some ice-cream?"

"Sure. There's root beer in the fridge. Have a float." She walked straight through the kitchen, then down the hall toward her bedroom. Some sixth sense kicked in, slowed her steps, and had the tiny hairs on the back of her neck lifting. She made a U-turn, then headed straight back to the kitchen.

The door to the freezer stood open. Cold air poured out like fog. Timmy wasn't there—anywhere—and her heart started a low, hard beat. "Timmy?"

No answer.

She shut the freezer door. Felt some kind of grime stuck to her fingertips, and flipped on the overhead light.

A thin film of dust blanketed the countertops, the table and chairs, the floor—everything.

And she remembered Jake telling her about the film of dust on the photograph, on the operatives. *Biological. . . .*

"Oh, God." She screamed, "Timmy?"

He came stumbling out of the bath off the laundry room. "What?"

He was okay. Right here, and okay. "Why didn't you answer me?"

"I had to pee."

Bury it, Logan. Bury it, and think. "Don't touch anything." She used her blouse to wipe off the phone receiver, then dialed the Ops Center. "This is Laura Logan. Who is this?"

"Captain David Perry," the man said.

"I need help, David." She reeled off the address. "Bring antibiotics and a biological decontamination crew. Hurry. My son and I have been exposed. Etiology unknown."

"They're on their way, Laura. General Connor already called in. Do you have any antibiotics in the house?"

"I-I don't know. We can't go to the hospital." They couldn't even go outside. "We'll contaminate everyone."

"Yes, you would. Just stay put. We'll be there before you could get to the base, anyway."

"I hate staying inside in this. Timmy is so young." The effects on him would manifest quickly, if this proved to be botulism. ROFF had attempted to use it to contaminate the water supply, so she knew they had access to the technology and experience with the application. In truth, anyone with a jar of mayo and a source of heat as simple as a match could grow a botulism culture. But professionals grew a stronger strain, and, professionally applied in this density, the germs wouldn't take long to kill. The elderly and children were most susceptible to a particularly quick death. Half an hour, ten minutes, or perhaps less, and antibiotics would be worthless counteracting the effects. Clearly, whoever had infested their home knew what they were doing. And Laura would bet her backside that the typical "prime time" in which the germs were most active—and most lethal—had been extended from hours to days with the use of a retardant. *God, please let it be strong anthrax.*

"We don't know what we're working with yet," David said. "The more confined you keep the contaminated area, the better."

"I have reason to suspect botulism. Professionally applied." Laura felt sweat trickle down her back and bead above her upper lip. "Will the crew be prepared for that?"

"Yes, ma'am. Just sit tight. They'll be there momentarily."

She wanted the crew. But even more so she wanted Jake. "Will my husband be with them?"

"He's ahead of them by about five minutes, ma'am."

"Mom." Timmy held a hand to his stomach. "I don't feel so good."

"Hurry, David. Hurry." Laura dropped the receiver. "Hang on, Tiger. I'm going to look for some medicine."

She ran to the bathroom, tore through the medicine cabinet, knocking out bottles of aspirin and Tylenol, and found nothing of use. She checked the other baths. Again nothing. Where else? *Where else could she look?*

Jake's gear.

She tore down the hall, burst into Jake's room, into his closet and dragged out his survival gear bag. Frustrated by trying to rifle through it, she dumped its contents onto the carpet and then saw the blister pack. One blister pack. Enough medication for only one of them.

She snatched it up and ran down the hall back to the kitchen, her fingers fumbling with trying to break open the seal. Finally, she freed the capsule and gave it to

Timmy. "Swallow this, honey. You can't have any water. They've poisoned it."

Timmy looked up at her, his eyes wide. "They poisoned everything, Mom."

She hugged him to her. "It'll be okay. Dad's on his way home and he's bringing some people who know how to get rid of the poison. We just have to stay put and not touch anything until they get here." Air carried the germs as well. *Oh, God, make them hurry.* "Don't talk and don't breathe deep, Tiger. Just little puffs, as few as you can manage, okay?" She pulled up his shirt front, covering his mouth and nose. "Keep this up like this, okay?"

He nodded.

As she pulled up her own blouse, she remembered Jake's mask. The gear she'd dumped on the floor. A mask had been in it. It wouldn't filter out everything, but something was better than nothing. It could only help.

She retrieved the mask and poured a bottle of alcohol on it, then fitted it over Timmy's face.

Her stomach pitched and rolled, and she began to sweat. She had to throw up. "Stay right here," she said near the living room window. "Watch for Dad, okay?"

"Are you leaving me here?"

"No. No, baby. I've got to go to the bathroom."

"Okay." He stood post, watching out the front window for Jake.

By the time Laura got to the bathroom, her head was spinning. Bent over the toilet, heaving, she sensed movement by the hallway door and covertly looked over. Paul Hawkins stood there watching her, a gun in his hand, looking every bit as dark and huge and menacing as he always had.

Oh, God. Oh, God. What now? What did she do now?

He stood between her and Timmy. *Bury it. Bury it. Keep retching. Keep retching, and think.*

Hawkins wasn't wearing protective gear. That was good news—a positive sign that they had in fact used strong anthrax and not botulism. He'd never risk exposure. Whatever they'd used, antibiotics would handle it—provided the crew got their backsides to the house with some before too much more time elapsed. And provided Hawkins didn't shoot her first.

She looked for a weapon. Gagged. A toilet brush and a can of Glade air freshener. Terrific.

And a plunger.

A wooden-handled plunger against a gun? Lousy odds, at best, but if she could stall, it would give the crew time to get here, and—*please, God*—Jake.

"You can quit stalling, Laura. I know you're aware that I'm here."

She lifted her head slowly out of necessity, then looked over at him, her stomach still in revolt. Black pants and shirt and eyes. Sharp bones. Dominant scar on his cheek where she'd slashed him through the ski mask with his own knife. He looked like the devil: menacing, unforgiving, merciless. And, God help her, she had to confront him without a weapon.

"Let's go." He waved her to him with the nose of the gun.

"I'm sick."

"I know." He smiled that oh-so-charming smile, and she resented not being strong enough to knock it off of his face. "Come on, now. Timmy's waiting."

Timmy hadn't made a sound. Hawkins couldn't have done anything to him. No, *Sean!* God help her, Sean was here, too.

"Where are we going?"

"I'm going to kill you, Laura."

He said it so simply, without any emotion whatsoever, which made the threat all the more chilling. What kind of monster could threaten murder and not feel anything? "Why?"

"Why?" He looked at her as if he couldn't believe the question. "You cost me my career. My honor. My damn country. And you ask me *why*?"

She grabbed the plunger, rammed it into him, knocking him off-balance. Before he could get his bearings, she jammed the plunger's wooden handle into his abdomen, elbowed his chin. Dazed, he rocked back on his feet, and she kicked him in the groin.

He crumpled to the ground and curled into a ball.

She snatched up his gun, took aim at him, and then screamed, *"Timmy!"*

He appeared at the foot of the hallway. She nearly cried with relief. "Are you okay?"

He nodded and looked down at Hawkins lying on the floor. "That's Hawk, Mom. Madeline's friend. I saw him in the swamp with her."

"I know."

"If he moves, are you going to shoot him?"

"Yes, honey, I am." Laura looked back at Hawkins. "That's a promise."

Timmy looked down at Hawk, a frown creasing the tender skin between his fine brows. "Don't move, Hawk. Mom isn't like Madeline. She doesn't break her promises. Not ever."

Hawk flinched.

"Timmy, is anyone else here?" she said. "Do you know?"

"Grandfather was, but he left when Hawk yelled."

Hawkins's face blanched white. Laura knew it was cruel, but she took pleasure in seeing it, until she realized Sean had taken the contamination out of the house with him. "Lock the door, Tiger. And then get me some rope from the garage and your ball bat."

"My bat?"

Laura nodded. "I'm going to tie up Mr. Hawkins and you're going to guard him while I go after your grandfather." Hopefully she'd find him before he contaminated the entire city of Fairhope.

"You want me to guard him?" Timmy sounded incredulous.

"Yes, I do. And if he moves more than just to blink, I want you to hit a homer on his kneecaps."

Hawk winced.

Timmy shrugged. "Okay, Mom. If you say so."

"I say so."

In short order, Timmy returned with the rope and his bat and Laura tied Hawkins up to where she doubted he could do more than blink. She reiterated Timmy's orders, then left the hall and retrieved the Glock from her purse. She checked it, double-checked the safety, and then nodded at Timmy, who was standing over the trussed up Hawkins with his bat at the ready. There was no doubt in Laura's mind that if the man flinched, Timmy would crack him. More importantly, Hawkins's expression proved he took Timmy seriously. His expression was tense and sweat rolled down from his temples. He was a believer, all right. Just to reinforce her instructions, she told Timmy, "If he makes a move, do your best to hit a grand slam."

"I will, Mom. That's a promise," Timmy said without looking at her, then warned Hawkins, "I'm not like Madeline, either."

Laura made her way to the front door, then peeked out through the slender window beside it. Sean Drake stood there, not three steps beyond the landing. Wearing a black turtleneck, slacks, and jacket, he blended in with the night. Jake didn't. He stood beyond Drake, his hands up, as if Drake held a gun on him. Drake was holding something in his hand, and Laura strained, but couldn't see what.

Feeling weak, though her blood gushed through her veins, she debated strategies. Should she slip out the back door, come around the side of the house, and try to get behind Drake? Or should she depend on surprise and rush out through the front door?

The deadbolt was on, and she recalled telling Timmy to lock the door. If she opened it, Drake would hear the click. She had no choice but to opt for the quieter approach and go around the back.

By the time she got out of the back door and rounded the front corner of the house, she was in a cold sweat. Pausing by the big oak, looking at the damn ruts Madeline had left in the lawn, she heard their voices. From the sound of it, the men were in a debate. They'd picked a hell of a time for a heated discussion, in her humble opinion, but them being occupied would give her a little cover in maneuvering around and behind Drake.

She inched between the first two in the row of oleanders and then dropped to a squat. The pointed leaves jabbed into her skin, pricked at her face. Peering out from between the leaves, she grimaced and her heart lodged in her throat. Drake held something, all right. She couldn't make out what, but it didn't look like a gun.

"Just keep your distance," Drake said. "Don't come any closer."

Jake didn't move. "What is that?"

Drake held up a small black canister. "Nerve gas. Enough to take out everyone within a mile radius."

Laura's heart skipped a beat, then another, ricocheting off her ribs. Connor had said ROFF had some ordinance typically found only in Intel circles. Drake would discharge it, too. The son of a bitch would wipe out the entire state of California without batting an eye. What was she going to do? How could she stop him?

Drake talked on, clearly unaware she was there. "Years ago, I tried to tell you how things worked in the big league, Jake. You should have listened to me."

"I listened. I just didn't agree."

"Now you know I was right." Drake grunted. "Everyone does spy on everyone. It's always been a matter of power. Control. Even within your hallowed Air Force, spying is a way of life. Corruption is everywhere. The wise man is aware of it, and he manipulates it to his advantage."

"Not everyone is corrupt, and not everyone manipulates. It's still not my way."

Drake glared at Jake. "Why do you do what you do? Eh? Why?"

Jake held his ex-father-in-law's bold gaze, and spoke softly. "Because it matters."

"Because it matters?" Drake harrumphed, and a glint lit in his eye Laura didn't recognize but instinctively hated. "God, spare us from the dangers of an idealistic man." He snorted. "Because it matters. And that it matters makes your system perfect."

Jake frowned and shifted his weight from foot to foot. "With imperfect human beings enacting it, what system can be perfect? At least mine works most of the time."

"For you."

"For me."

"You're still naive, son. You'll never be effective in the big league unless you learn to play hardball. You'd have been better off if you'd gotten off the field before you got hurt."

Laura cringed. Jake had been hurt, but he was effective. And when missions required it, ruthless. But temperance and judicious ruthlessness were obviously not in Drake's repertoire. When Jake shifted on his feet again, she moved to the next bush in the row. He knew she was here, and he was giving her noise to cover the sounds of her moving closer.

"I believe in what I'm doing," Jake said. "I can't think of a better reason for doing anything."

"I can think of two," Drake countered. "Power and money."

Laura inched forward. Two more bushes and she'd be in position to take Drake out. Would Timmy forgive her for killing his grandfather? Could she kill him before he discharged the nerve gas and killed half the people in the subdivision?

Jake shifted again and frowned. "There's one thing I don't understand. Why did you put Laura's photograph in the dead operative's hand?"

"To prove my point." Drake's tone turned bitter. "She ignored my orders, thinking she could get out of my reach by deactivating in Intel and getting out of the military. I warned her to stay away from you. For a smart lady, she made a stupid move. I had no choice but to retaliate and show her that she couldn't escape me." He shrugged. "Having her convicted of treason is a worthy retaliation, I think."

"So you recruited Paul Hawkins to do your dirty work."

Drake smiled, pulling his teeth back from his lips. "Aside from Madeline, no one hates Laura more. Though I have to say I'm a bit disappointed in Hawkins. When he broke into her apartment, Laura disarmed him before he could get her tracker design. He foolishly underestimated her."

"So that's what you were after? Her tracker?"

"Of course. It could be useful to me." The lilt in his voice turned chilling. "Hawkins is a competent operative, but Laura's fear of him gives her an edge. A damn shame, that.''

The demon bastard seemed genuinely regretful that Hawkins hadn't killed her. Laura's resolve doubled. *Keep him busy, Jake. Just a minute more. Just a minute more.*

Woozy from the contamination, nauseous, and sweating profusely, she prayed for the stamina to stay upright, then stepped past the last oleander and pointed the gun at the back of Drake's skull.

"I wouldn't do that, if I were you, Mrs. Logan," he said without looking back at her. "I get a little testy when thwarted, as you well know. I could accidentally discharge this." He held up the canister.

Laura's heart sank to her knees. "You'll discharge it anyway. Knowing you, you've done something to save yourself. You look pretty damn healthy for a corpse, Drake. But at least if I shoot you, you'll die with the rest of us." There was solace in that.

"Yes, I will. So will Timmy," he said softly. "Is that what you want?"

Laura's resolve wavered. Not her baby. Not him, too. The mask wouldn't protect him, not from nerve gas. And his bastard grandfather knew it. Her hand holding the gun trembled with frustration and fear— the effects of the contamination and sheer rage.

"Behave yourself and put down the gun," Drake said. "Now."

"Do it, Laura," Jake added, his voice deceptively soft, his gaze veering to the front door.

Her stomach churning acid, her head light, she stooped down to put the gun on the sidewalk and heard a definite click behind her. Skirting around Drake to stand near Jake, she didn't dare to glance at the slender window beside the door. The noise had been the deadbolt; of that she felt certain. But who had turned it? Timmy, or Hawkins?

The door flew open. Timmy charged through, swinging the bat. It collided with Drake's left kneecap. Howling, he dropped the canister, and before he crumpled in a heap on the grass, Jake and Laura dove for it. Jake caught the canister, and Laura snatched up her gun, then aimed it at Drake.

"Don't you move." Timmy stood over his grandfather, his chest heaving, his eyes stretched wide, the look in them wild. "Don't you move. Don't make me hit you again." His voice pitched high, anxious. "Don't make me hit you again."

Laura and Jake flanked Timmy, and Laura passed the gun to Jake, then smoothed a hand over Timmy's shoulder. "He won't move, Tiger. It's okay. Dad and I are fine now. Timmy, look at me, honey. Look into my eyes."

He finally overcame the shock enough to swivel his gaze.

"It's okay now." She dredged up a smile and softened her voice. "Let's go back inside now and make sure Hawkins is still tied up."

"He is," Timmy said. "I put a chair over him so I could hear if he moved."

"Great. That's great. So let's go back inside now. We don't want to spread any more germs out here, okay?"

"Huh?"

Jake gently squeezed Timmy's shoulder. "Go with Mom now, Tiger. I've got control."

Timmy glanced from Jake to Sean Drake, lying on his side across the tire ruts Madeline had left in the lawn and clutching at his knee. "Dad?"

"Yes, son."

Swinging his gaze up to Jake's, Timmy frowned. "If he moves, shoot him, okay?"

"I will, Timmy."

Laura nearly wept at the sadness of the situation. A child feeling forced to ask that his grandfather be shot. She could have killed Sean Drake then and there for that alone. Instead, she looped an arm around Timmy's shoulder and led him back into the house.

"I should have made Madeline abort that little bastard."

Laura heard the crunch of Jake's fist hitting Drake, of bone snapping. Timmy tried to look back, but she slammed the door shut, hoping Sean had a broken jaw and a broken kneecap.

When the MPs arrived, Jake's knuckles were still stinging like fire. He heard running, looked behind him, and saw the Military Police coming up the sidewalk and cutting across the lawn. "Watch out for the tire ruts," he shouted in warning.

The decontamination sweepers arrived as well, pulling up to the curb in muted green vans. Men poured out, then streamed past him and into the house.

Within a matter of minutes, Sean Drake had been handcuffed, read his rights, and tossed into the back of a cruiser. Jake glared at him through the window. "Of all the miserable things you've done, what you did to Madeline and just tried to do to Timmy is the worst. You're an abusive bastard, Drake, and I'm glad you've been dead and Timmy has been spared from seeing you. Kids and grandkids are a gift, not tools. If you learn nothing else before you really die, I pray to God you learn that." Jake lifted a finger. "You contaminated my home. My family better be all right, or I'll be back for you. You can't hide, Drake. Not anymore. Not ever again."

Drake looked away, slumped and defeated. His empire had crumbled.

Jake turned over Drake's canister of nerve gas to an officer, then ran to the door. The house was crawling with people wearing contamination gear. Laura was in the kitchen, sitting on the floor with Timmy and surrounded by a medical team. "He's been medicated," she said, motioning to Timmy. "I haven't. And I feel like hell."

Jake's heart constricted. She had had medication. But only enough for one person. And she'd given it to Timmy. But if Jake mentioned it, she'd give him that you're-being-testy look and say, *Of course.*

A medic with a stethoscope looped around his neck gave her an injection and then passed her two pills. "Take these, Mrs. Logan. You'll start to feel better in about fifteen, maybe twenty, minutes."

"Thank you." She swallowed the pills.

"Laura."

Tilting back her head, she saw him and scrambled to her feet. "Jake."

He hugged her hard, lifted an arm to motion Timmy to come to him, and then pulled him into their circle. *They were all okay. Everything was going to be okay.*

Jake let the litany replay in his mind, giving it time to sink in and settle—giving himself time to believe it.

After decontaminating the three of them, the medic turned to Jake. "You can take them out of here, sir. We'll finish up the sweep. While there isn't a field test to prove it, we've taken samples and they match the others ROFF has used. We're ninety-nine percent sure it's strong anthrax. Same specifics as with the operatives. Timmy's reacting well to antibiotics, and Hawkins isn't wearing protective gear."

"What about outside?" Both Laura and Timmy had been out there.

"The air samples are within the safe range. It's not a problem."

"When can we come home?" Laura asked.

"Within a few days. The house will be ready within a week, max. Even with retardants, applied like this, strong anthrax is harmless beyond that time frame."

"Thank you." Arms around their shoulders, Jake led Laura and Timmy out through the front door. The crew would vacuum, disinfect, sanitize, and sterilize every single thing in the house, and the house itself.

Laura didn't want to let go of Jake. She couldn't force herself to let go of him. When she saw that they were heading to his Jeep, she stepped off the damp lawn and onto the concrete driveway. The streetlight cast a shadow over Jake's jaw. "Where are we going?"

"Alice's." He unlocked her door, then Timmy's. "Betsy won't sleep a wink until she sees for herself that you two are okay."

Timmy grinned. "She's a little protective of us, huh, Mom?"

"Yes, I guess she is," Laura said, sliding into the bucket seat.

Timmy settled in the backseat, then clicked his seatbelt closed. "Can me and Betsy stay at Alice's until the house is okay again?"

Jake cranked the engine, turned on the headlights, and then answered, "Sounds like a good plan." He closed his door, and the overhead light snuffed out.

Recalling the moment of panic she had felt when the tracker light had gone out and she hadn't known if Jake was dead or alive, Laura started to shake. She couldn't fasten her seatbelt. "Where are we going to stay?"

Jake leaned over and clicked it into place. Noting that he wasn't exactly steady-handed himself, for some reason, comforted her.

The light from the streetlamp streamed in through

the window, fell across his face, and the look in his eyes warmed. "I thought we'd stay at your apartment."

Her heart turned over in her chest. Maybe Madeline had been wrong. Maybe Jake could love her as more than just a friend. Laura courted disaster by risking to hope it, but hope flamed inside her anyway, and she wanted it badly enough to go for it.

Considering what they'd just gone through because of his ex-wife, he would probably think Laura had lost her mind for thinking he'd even contemplate another relationship with a wife. And maybe she had lost her mind. Or maybe she just loved the man so much nothing else mattered, including their agreement.

Just after midnight, it started raining.

Laura couldn't have cared less. Bear was well on the road to recovery, Betsy and Timmy were snug and safe at Alice's, and Laura and Jake had showered and now lay in her clean, warm bed. She was curled up next to him, talking over all that had happened. The darkness was soothing, not chilling, and it gave them both the freedom to say things they might be hesitant to say in the light of day. Slowly, they were working through it all, and making the transition back to a normal life.

"When I heard you took down Hawkins, I nearly died." On his side, his leg tossed over hers, Jake lifted a strand of her hair, then rubbed it between his forefinger and thumb, his free arm folded under his pillow.

"I was terrified, and I seriously considered killing him," she confessed, glancing up to a ceiling she couldn't see. "But you know what, Jake?" She fondled the hair on his forearm. Rough and smooth, and hard and soft—all at once. "I *chose* not to kill him, and it felt really good to be that tempted and stay in control. And to get rid of the fear."

"I'm glad." He pecked a kiss to her forehead.

"Me, too." She let her eyes drift closed, wondering how he'd react to her coming disclosure. "I'm going back into research full-time. I think I can do it now and not feel it's tainted." Laura opened her eyes, and let her hand skim up his arm to his chest. "Jake?"

"Mmm?"

She scooted over, shoving the sheets out from between them so she could touch him skin to skin. So what if he thought she'd lost her mind? She needed comfort and to feel close to him. Needed reassurance that this time they'd both survived. "Madeline was wrong about a lot of things, but she was right about some of them, too."

"What do you mean?" He wedged a knee between her thighs and let his hand slide down her side from ribs to waist, as if he too needed life-affirming reassurance.

"Just that there are always extenuating circumstances, and different perspectives, and special considerations in things." She paused, then shrugged. "I guess that things just aren't simple."

"Life isn't simple. It's messy," he said, adding his thoughts. "Sometimes, so are the fears and doubts and decisions that despite our logic our hearts make for us. But we have to deal with them, Laura. And just because they start out messy, that doesn't mean they can't end up being good."

Exactly what did that mean? "I suppose it doesn't," she said, following her instincts. Wanting to see his face, to gauge his mood and reaction, she reached over and turned on the lamp beside the bed. Light pooled on the nightstand, spilled across the flowered sheets, and he opened his eyes.

She worried her lip with her teeth, then took the plunge. "I know we've had a lot going on since the adoption and everything, but I want to tell you something.''

He stroked her chin with the back of his hand, the line of her jaw, and his eyes went solemn. ''You look worried.''

Dragonflies swarmed in her stomach. She pressed a hand to it to still them. ''I am worried.''

''Why?''

Tender and gentle. God, but he did choose the most lousy times to get gentle on her. ''Because you might not want to hear what I have to say.'' If ever she needed courage, that time was now. ''I know I promised I wouldn't, but I broke our agree—''

He interrupted, pressing a fingertip over her lips. ''I love you, Laura.''

Truth burned in his eyes, and she caressed his face. ''I know you do, but that doesn't mean you'll want to hear this.'' After Madeline, how could he want to hear this? Laura must be crazy to even think of telling him now. Maybe later would be better. Maybe when Timmy graduated from high school, or college. Yes, surely by the time Timmy finished college, Jake would be over the shock of it.

No, she swore to herself. No, no, no. No more evasive tactics. No more alternate truths. No more taking shelter in those gray areas. Only the truth. The glaring, unadorned, simple truth.

''No, honey, you don't understand.'' Jake grabbed something from the nightstand, rolled over and braced himself above her, and then cupped her face in his big hand.

God, but she loved the feel of his hands on her. Strong. Capable. Gentle. And, when the need arose, ruthless. His knuckles were swollen from the blow he'd landed on Sean Drake. Fortunately, he hadn't killed the man, or he'd still be at headquarters filling out the reports.

"I bought you a gift," Jake whispered against her ear. "Until we were on the chopper, I didn't think you'd want it."

Until that moment, she would have sworn only losing Timmy could arouse fear in Jake Logan. But he was afraid now. And she hated it.

He opened a white velvet box and tilted it so she could see its contents. A sparkling white solitaire diamond winked at her. And a slim gold wedding band.

His eyes went sober and his voice shook. "Will you wear them?"

"Oh, Jake." What it must have cost him to ask her this. Her eyes filled with tears. "They're beautiful."

"I don't mean for them to be part of a lie or an illusion, Laura. I mean for them to be part of something real."

"You want me to be your real wife?" So much joy bubbled up inside her she feared she couldn't hold it all. "But what about our agreement?"

"To hell with it. We'll make a future of whatever time we've got together." He nuzzled, whispered close to her ear. "We'll make memories."

She got suspicious. "When exactly did you buy these rings?"

He arched a brow. "Does it matter?"

"No, I'm just curious." She affected one of Timmy's shrugs. It mattered a lot.

Crushing his pillow under his arm, Jake dragged a fingertip down the slope of her nose. "Now look who's being testy."

She glared at him. "There's nothing wrong with curiosity, Jake. It nets us trackers—and truths."

"Okay, I bought them a while back," he confessed, staring at her T-shirt.

The truth dawned. "Ohhh, I get it now."

"What?"

"You bought them right before you got assigned to the ROFF mission, but your survival odds kept you from giving them to me. That's why you asked me how I'd handle it if something happened to you. Am I right?"

Jake grimaced. "Evidently your intuition is working on me *and* Timmy these days."

She gave him a wicked smile. "Better remember it, Major."

He fisted his hand near her head on her pillow. "So will you wear them?"

Too moved to speak, she nodded.

He slipped the slim gold band onto her finger, and then the diamond. They fit, and he kissed her fingers where the rings circled them.

A reverent moment. One Laura thought she'd never live to see.

"I love you, Laura." The twinkle faded from his eyes and they turned serious. "Not just as a friend, but in every way a man can love a woman."

Stunned that he'd recognized and admitted it, Laura couldn't breathe. Couldn't get her mouth to form the words she wanted to say.

"Honey?" Worry flickered through his eyes, and his voice turned apologetic. "I guess my timing is lousy, but I had to tell you. I couldn't stand the idea of not telling you any longer. We've already wasted so much time."

Finally, she found her voice. "I love you too, Jake."

He stilled, cocked his head, and eyed her warily, as if he wanted to believe her but was afraid to hope. "As a friend?"

"Yes." She nodded. "And in every other way a woman can love a man."

The tension fell from his face, and he smiled. "Of course."

"Of course." She smiled back, happy and at peace.

"Thank God." Jake closed his arms around her and kissed her.

And Laura kissed him back, exploring what would be for a time her last cohesive thoughts. There would always be another mission, another Sean Drake. Jake would always tackle them, and Laura would always worry about his safety. And if he survived, there would be frequent moves to contend with, and vacations that had to be canceled because duty called, and missed anniversaries and birthdays. There would be times when he'd be gone and socks would get stuck in the washer hose and the laundry room would flood. Times when Timmy would get the flu and she'd have to pace the floor and worry alone. And there would be times when she needed her husband and he couldn't be there.

But during those times she'd know that, because Jake had the courage to do what he had to do, and she had the courage to support him and to carry the load at home while he did what he had to do, others could rest easy. They could sleep safe. And she'd have the comfort of memories of other times. Good memories of them being together, sharing a life with Timmy, with love. There was solace in that.

And in wearing his T-shirts.

Nothing is black and white.

No, she thought. Nothing is black and white. But, so what?

Fulfillment of the deepest desires just patiently waits for any brave enough to seek it . . . in those shades of gray.

DON'T MISS VICKI HINZE'S
EXCITING NEW NOVEL

Duplicity

COMING SOON FROM
ST. MARTIN'S PAPERBACKS

Turn the page for a sneak preview . . .

This couldn't be happening to her. It couldn't. It just . . . *couldn't!*

How could they expect her to defend Captain Adam Burke? Defend the man officially assigned to Personnel and unofficially assigned to Intel under the command of the ambitious Colonel Robert D. Hackett? Defend the coward accused of treason, of deserting his men and abandoning them to die?

Again, the edict reverberated in her ears. *Keener, I've assigned you to defend Captain Adam Burke.*

This couldn't be happening to her . . . and yet it was.

Captain Tracy Keener, a Staff Judge Advocate relatively new to Laurel Air Force Base, Mississippi, swallowed a knot of dread from her throat. "Is that a direct order, sir?"

"If necessary, yes, it is, Captain."

Cringing inwardly, Tracy tensed her muscles to keep her boss, Colonel Vic Jackson, from seeing how appalling she found the notion. Only a sadist would be elated at hearing they'd been assigned to defend Adam Burke. What attorney in their right mind could feel anything other than appalled at being ordered to defend him? He'd *deserted* his men. *Abandoned* them to die.

Refusal burned in her throat, turned her tongue bitter. This had to be a bad dream—a nightmare. It couldn't be real.

But from the look on Jackson's face, it was real, and there was no escaping it.

Resisting an urge to squirm in his leather visitor's chair, she clenched her jaw, choking back an audible groan, and fixed her gaze on an eagle paperweight perched on a neat stack of files at the corner of his desk. Sunlight slanted in through the blinds at his coveted office window. Washed in its stripes of light and shadows, the bird looked arrogant. Mocking. Sinister. . . .

Suffering a shiver, she insisted she react logically to this edict, not emotionally. She should have seen this coming. Burke's was the last case *any* staff JAG officer would want to take on. It was a guaranteed career-breaker. One the guys called a ball-buster—which is why, as low man on Laurel's Judge Advocate General's office totem pole, she'd gotten stuck with the unholy honor.

Visions filled her mind. The eagle devouring the captain's bars tacked to the collar of her pale blue uniform. Her standing at a podium before the press, trying to justify Adam Burke's actions while strenuously opposing them herself.

She cursed silently, struggled to suppress a gutful of panic without reaching under her blouse to rub her gold locket, and studied Colonel Jackson, desperately seeking a chink in his armor. There had to be a way out of this assignment.

Jackson was a big, imposing man, pushing fifty and graying gracefully at the temples. In the months she'd been at Laurel, he had earned her respect. Lanky and trim, he had a lean, intelligent face, and more than once during case discussions at the morning staff meetings, compassion had burned in his eyes. That compassion came through in his recommendations.

According to Tracy's overqualified assistant, Janet Cray, the only thing that sent Jackson through the ceiling was clutter. He was a freak about tidiness in the work place. So much so that when Janet had been giving Tracy the lay-of-the-land orientation briefing, she'd commented smilingly that Jackson had adopted "cleanliness is next to godliness" as his personal motto.

That melded into an odd combination of human characteristics, to Tracy's way of thinking. How could he show a murderer compassion, but lack so much as the scent of it for any staff member who tolerated a staple on the carpet near his or her desk?

Yet Tracy had worked for worse. Gutless wonders who'd rather fold than fight were a dime a dozen in the military. Fortunately, so were the dedicated, the proud, the sincere. Men and women who took their oaths to serve and protect into their hearts, and did their best to live by them.

Jackson fell into the ranks of the latter. But no compassion shone in his eyes now, nor any latitude. There was no chink; his armor unfortunately appeared intact, though he did look . . . guilty.

Smoothing her uniform's dark blue skirt, Tracy set out to find out why. "You do realize that in taking on this case I'd be begging for career disaster, right?"

Jackson snapped his lower jaw shut, and the veiled empathy flickering in his eyes snuffed out. Pressing his forearm flat on his desk blotter, he darted his gaze to his office door, as if assuring himself of privacy, and then nodded. "Frankly, yes, I realize the risks. The potential for disaster is remarkable."

He meant worthy of comment, not awesome, but his tone removed any doubt about his damage-assessment expectations. Enormous risks. Enormous.

Should Tracy feel relieved that he had acknowledged the risks, or despondent that he had realized them and had put her in the direct line of fire anyway?

Before she could decide, Jackson rocked back in his chair. The springs groaned under his weight, and his stern expression turned grave. ''I'm not going to sugar-coat this situation, Captain,'' he said. ''The Burke case has tempers running hot and hard up the chain of command, and the local media are nearly out of control. Between the two of them, they're nailing our asses to the proverbial wall.''

Hope flared in Tracy. If he could see that, then surely he would see reason and assign someone else to the case. ''I'm up for major, sir,'' Tracy interjected. ''My promotion board meets in about a month.''

''I know.'' Jackson nodded and a frown formed on his lined forehead. He doodled with a black pen on the edge of his blotter; a frequent habit, judging by the density of his previous scrawls. ''And I know that you're up for Career Status selection.''

Bloody hell. Tracy hadn't yet even considered Career Status selection. This was her fifth year in the Air Force. Her first—and, by new policy adopted three weeks ago, her last—shot at selection. If not selected, she'd promptly be issued an invitation to practice law elsewhere, outside of the military.

This was not a pleasing prospect to an officer bent on making the military a career.

Colonel Jackson cleared his throat, decidedly uneasy and fidgeting with his gold watch. It caught the sunlight, winked at Tracy from under the cuff of his shirt sleeve. ''I understand the personal risks to you, and the potential sacrifices you may be called upon to make. But I also understand that there's more at stake here than your personal career. The Air Force Corrections

System is on trial, Captain, and all eyes are watching to see if it's up to the test.''

He paused and let the weight of that comment settle in, then went on. ''Burke is a sorry bastard who deserves to die for his crimes—you yourself have said so openly—and I have no doubt but that he will die. Yet he is entitled to a defense, and—''

''I agree, Colonel,'' she interceded, doing her best to keep her voice calm. ''Burke does deserve a defense. But can't someone in this office who would have time to recover from the political impact of defending him *prior* to being personally destroyed for the privilege give it to him?''

Jackson lowered his gaze to his desk blotter. ''I'm afraid not.''

The regret in his tone set her teeth on edge. This was another slick political maneuver; she sensed it down to her toenails. Some jerk with more clout, rank, or backing from his superior officers didn't want his butt stuck in a sling, so they were planting her backside in it first. The unfairness of it set a muscle in her cheek to ticking. ''May I ask why not?''

''I'd prefer that you didn't.''

She just bet he did prefer it. Tracy stiffened and a stern edge crept into her voice. ''I don't mean to be disrespectful, sir, but if I'm going to risk sacrificing my career then I think I'm entitled to know why it can't be avoided.''

Unaccustomed to being challenged, even respectfully, Jackson clearly took exception. Red slashes swept across his raw-boned cheeks and his tone chilled, nearly frosting the air between them. ''Officially, you've developed a reputation as a strong litigator.''

An uneasy feeling that she had indeed been slated for sacrifice crept up Tracy's backbone and filled her mouth with a bitter taste. ''And unofficially?''

Jackson pursed his lips and held his silence for a long beat, as if deciding what to tell her and what to keep to himself. Tension crackled in the morning air, threatening to snap the one nerve Tracy had left.

As if sensing it, Colonel Jackson opted to disclose the truth. "General Nestler specifically requested that you be assigned to defend Burke, and Higher Headquarters agreed."

A by-name request? From Nestler? Oh, hell. Oh, bloody hell. No one refused Nestler anything. Within two days at Laurel, while assisting a fellow attorney on a contract case, Tracy had learned that. Now she'd learned his clout extended straight up the chain of command.

She was screwed. Screwed. Pure and simple. "I wasn't aware General Nestler even knew my name."

Jackson's resigned look faded and the corner of his wide mouth twitched. "Don't be fooled by the actions of some generals, Captain. General Nestler knows everything that goes on with his staff, on the base, and in the community—within and outside of the military."

No conflict there with what Tracy had heard and observed. At last month's First Friday gathering at the Officer's Club, Janet had referred to Nestler privately as Laurel's god. *Sees all, knows all.* Since then, Tracy had heard others use the same analogy. But innately she knew she wasn't going to like his rationale for choosing her to defend Burke. "So why me?"

"Why *not* you?" Jackson issued a challenge of his own.

She could think of a dozen reasons. But they all rated personal. Not a single one could even remotely be dubbed professional.

Jackson stood up and turned his back to her, then stared out the window at the red-brick building next door. Two airmen were washing its windows.

A long minute passed in taut silence. Then he stiffened his shoulders, braced a hand in his slacks pocket, and faced her. "Frankly, Captain, the general feels your professional acumen, poise, and appearance will be an asset in dealing with the media."

"What?" That response she hadn't expected. She forced her gaped jaw shut.

"I'm sorry, Tracy," Jackson said, for the first time calling her by her Christian name. "But it's vital we keep this incident as low-key as possible. That's why we're trying the case here at the local level."

He plopped down in his chair. Air hissed out from the leather cushion, and he leaned forward, lacing his thin hands atop the blotter. "The truth is, the local media are chewing us up and spitting us out on this case. We don't want CNN crawling up our backsides and blowing this out of proportion. The last thing the military needs is another fiasco of the magnitude of Tailhook."

How could she disagree? That scandal had caused a lot of people sleepless nights, agony, embarrassment. Careers and lives had been ruined. And innocents had suffered the shame as much as the guilty.

"We need every possible advantage," Jackson said. "You're bright and beautiful—that surely comes as no surprise to you. You're an asset, and as unfair as you might deem it, we've chosen to exploit our assets."

Frustration knitted his brow. "Look, we're fighting budget cuts at every turn, base closures that could include Laurel—we escaped the latest short list by the skin of our teeth—and the end of the fiscal year is breathing down our throats. Hell, we have to exploit our assets. This case has every military member's reputation on the line."

He let his gaze veer to a bronze statue of Lady Justice sitting on the credenza below the window, and then to the flag beside it. His voice softened. "We're an all-volunteer force, Tracy. I don't have to tell you that a nation of people depend on us to protect them."

"No, sir. I'm aware of it." Who in the military could be unaware of it?

"Then you understand that Burke has complicated our mission. He's tarnished the image of the entire military, and it's up to us to salvage all we can, any way we can."

She was a means to an end. *It could destroy your career and your life, but, hey, it's nothing personal, Tracy.*

Her stomach churned acid. She forced herself to stay seated, commanded her temper to stay buried. Staring at the eagle paperweight, at the glints of light reflecting off of it and at the dark shadows between the glints, she mulled over the matter. As much as she hated admitting it, Jackson and Nestler's rationale made sense. The local media *were* chewing them up and spitting them out. Burke *had* tarnished the image of the entire military, and the image of every single man and woman in uniform. As a senior officer in the same situation, she'd be strongly inclined to use whatever assets she found available to diffuse the situation. Could she fault them for doing what in their position she would do herself?

Not honestly.

Still, she couldn't stop visualizing her shot at promotion and selection sprouting wings. Burke was guilty. Everyone knew it. And while she might diminish his impact in the public's eye, she wouldn't get him off. She didn't want to get him off. But even F. Lee Bailey couldn't get Burke off, or come out of this case unscathed.

Yet the man was entitled to a defense. The best defense possible. Would any other JAG officer make a genuine attempt to give it to him? Knowing the costs? Knowing personal disaster was damn near inevitable?

Probably not. And Tracy couldn't condemn them for it. Not with a clean conscience. Given the sliver of a chance, she too would have avoided this case as if it carried plague.

But she couldn't avoid it. And that made only one attitude tenable. She had to handle the case and give Burke her best. Not so much for him, but because it was right. When this was over, she had to be able to look in the mirror and feel comfortable with what she'd done and the way she'd handled the case, and herself.

Since she'd lost her husband and daughter five years ago, she often had imaged herself as an eighty-year-old woman, wearing the same gold locket she wore under her uniform now, looking in the mirror and asking herself where she'd screwed up, what she'd done or left undone that she wished she hadn't.

In grief counseling, she'd learned that losing loved ones to death changes a person's perspective, sharpens it, and forces them to focus on what most matters to them. She had been no exception. And she had long since determined that the one thing she would *not* face that eighty-year-old with was more regret.

Hard choices seldom resolve easily, but feeling the locket against her breast, its gold metal warm from contact with her skin, she reconciled herself to doing the right thing.

Resigned, she lifted her gaze to Colonel Jackson and accepted responsibility. "I understand, sir. I'll get started on it."

Jackson blinked, then blinked again, clearly expecting her to body-slam him with a sharp-tongued comment.

When it occurred to him none would be forthcoming, he gave her a curt nod. "Fine, Captain." He lifted a pen and turned his attention to an open file on his desk. "Dismissed."

Tracy unfolded her legs, hoping her knees had enough substance left in them to get her the hell out of his office before she crumpled. *Dismissed*. And how. From his office and, she feared, from her chosen way of life.